Movers and Shirkers

Russell Campbell

For Iain, Jean, Anne, Fraser and Struan.

Prologue

Why on earth would anyone carry a nail gun to a Halloween party?

It wasn't as if he'd created an adroit, ingenious portrayal of contemporary life, guising as some kind of lazy, DIY-obsessed Don Quixote, or even if he'd ventured out as a Hollywood-style fixer, and simply didn't possess the necessary hardware or a decent replica. His outfit was just a messy synthesis of different garments and a builder's helmet, combined with this concealed threat. Not creative, not astute and not cool.

The gig was taking place at the Underground—a dark and dingy club within the oldest purpose-built student union in the world. The combined volume, heat and human swell of the place mugged the senses, numbing the inebriated into believing in special prowess or perhaps simply revealing their underlying vulnerability. Yet this guy was neither special nor vulnerable.

A tall, dark-haired student had observed the nail gun while on the edge of the dance floor, recognising the owner's green eyes which tracked his own, followed by a slight smirk accompanying the visual response. The tall one attempted to ignore this mind game, though he momentarily considered if the nail gun was actually loaded, and how it had been transferred past the renowned bouncers at the door of the club. Nail gun man had been watching a cute blonde girl in a platinum mini-dress on the opposite side of the dance floor, despite the fact she'd already rejected him for a dance. The tall guy, despite the mocking response from his friends, had been contemplating a night of sexual success, sporting a fake beard and long hair in the persona of what he considered the ultimate Scottish

1

aphrodisiac for the opposite sex: Billy Connolly. The grey woollen strands with which he'd manufactured the beard and wig had engendered light-hearted ribbing from a couple of girls beforehand in the flat he shared with fellow students at Fountainbridge, particularly as he could play the five string banjo in keeping with the famous comedian.

As the evening progressed, the predictable alcohol and hormone-induced mood accelerated. Akin to Custer at the Little Big Horn, some students began to circle others, principally the males of the species circumnavigating the females. As with all such fraternities, degrees of protocol existed. Upsetting pre-existing relationships was usually taboo, for example, but other considerations also applied. Who'd chatted up whom first? Who dared to intercept someone else's imminent conquest while they'd nipped to the loo? These were grey areas, yet they constituted unwritten rules that most observed, if some ignored.

The tall student's own heuristic in such circumstances was that it mattered not if another male had shown interest in someone of the fair sex first, providing the said individual had been rebuffed. They'd had their chance, so to speak, and careful observation from the edge of the dance floor often confirmed what was *not* happening, as much as what was. Some guys liked to mark their territory like dogs in a musical pack, but he felt that such expectations were absurd. For the second time he saw the nail gun guy harass the blonde, and this time the guy had attempted to lift her dress while she was dancing, displaying the behaviour of a naughty five-year-old—or a dirty old man—depending on your perspective. This time the girl retreated rapidly from the dance floor, leaving her friends to chastise Mr DIY. The tall student immediately deduced that the girl was single, for no self-respecting boyfriend would have endured such audacity. What it also confirmed, however, was that the nail gun guy was a menace, one they'd been aware of for some time. He was one of these individuals incapable of impressing either males or females, yet still able to hover around the pack, a parasite of the social vibe.

The blonde girl was named Lucy. Funny, she looked like a Lucy, the tall guy intoned, when he found her near the bar. What did that mean, she enquired, suspicious of another potential predator. The tall one, though, had devised some interesting lines in his tenure in Edinburgh, and he explained that Lucy meant she was 'born of light, signifying a new dawn', which had classical overtones from the great civilisations of the past, and that as someone cultured, the name mirrored her obvious physical aura.

'Absolute bollocks', she replied, yet with a spark to which he warmed.

After they'd danced to a Guns N' Roses number, he bought her a Jack Daniels and lemonade and they retreated to a booth. With the pulse of the music and inhibitions disappearing they locked eyes, but just as that magical moment materialised she suddenly frowned, looking beyond him to the edge of the booth. He swivelled round.

The nail gun pointed directly at him, approximately two feet from his forehead.

The dense volume of the music may have drowned out the expletives employed in response, but the sentiment remained obvious. One or two of the tall student's friends had spotted the imminent confrontation, and had backed off a few feet, concerned as to where the action was leading. The nail gun and staring green eyes remained in place, so the tall one brushed the gun aside, turning back to Lucy, who had by now grabbed her handbag. Then, as she stood up to make an exit, the menace issued a direct challenge to the tall guy, gesturing to the door behind.

Outside!

Perhaps it was due to the sheer volume of people in the club, or a shortage of stewards on that particular night, or even the fact that fancy dress events can blur the boundaries between gravity and bluster, but for some reason the incident remained unnoticed by other groups. No one called for management intervention, and no one took direct action to avert further conflict. Instead, a small group marched upstairs and outside, anger levels matched only by testosterone. As they spilled out to the freezing air of Bristo Square, nail gun man screamed. 'Round the back!' The small band then stomped into Charles Street Lane behind the student union, out of sight. Four of the tall student's friends followed. One shouted at the nail gun holder to forget it, but was ignored.

Then, as they backed into the dimly-lit alley, the tall student suddenly shot forward, lunging for the gun, but he slipped on the concrete surface, which was covered in ice. As he screamed in pain, the nail gun was thrust violently against his forehead, and he was locked on the ground as the green eyes willed him to move. His home-made woollen wig and beard now looked ridiculous, hanging from his face.

'*Back off!*' one of students screamed. But as they all moved forward in unison, the nail gun holder also slipped on the ice onto his side at the corner of the alley and the street.

Then, almost in slow motion, his hand titled backwards behind him and the nail gun pressed against something firm. Something human. Perhaps it was panic, perhaps just evil, but as the solid contact continued the trigger of the gun became engaged several times in quick succession.

The sound that emanated from immediately behind him was certainly no scream, but rather, more of a gurgle. A nauseating, almost inhuman gurgle. Even in the poor light, the unmistakable crimson hue of blood spurted from the mouth of an old man, who must have been sitting on the ground right behind them.

A vagrant, it seemed, who had gone unnoticed as they entered the alley, had just taken four nails directly in the face. One had obliterated his left eye, leaving a multicoloured ménage of tissue and blood, and two others had lodged in his mouth and nose. A further nail had punctured his Adam's apple.

Green-eyes knelt beside the old guy, desperately trying to hold his head upwards. 'Help me!' he screamed, as he turned to the wider group.

But as he looked round, the other students all suddenly retreated in unison, as if a magnetic, external force was hauling them from behind. Green-eyes suddenly raised his voice, holding his hands up in a desperate appeal. 'You can't leave me here! He's…he needs an ambulance!'

But they backed off further, except for the tall student, who stood, transfixed.

'*Help me.* Call an ambulance! It was an *accident.* Please!'

But then the tall student turned too, and his pace quickened as he thrust himself around the corner onto the main street, away from the scene. He threw up on the cobbled street, the bitter taste of adrenalin scorching the back of his throat. Despite his efforts, he could barely see ahead, the street a freezing, muffled haze merging with the night and the newly gathering crowd. Was that an ambulance siren he could now hear? Or was it a police car? In an emergency you can never tell the difference.

Chapter 1

When Calum Mack first regained consciousness, the initial catalyst of the striking morning sunlight was soon replaced by recognition of a familiar secondary factor: dehydration. The inner conflict between remaining in bed and making the short journey into the bathroom for that elusive hangover cure softened as he realised that his headache would not disembark without chemical intervention.

He mixed a soluble painkiller and peered into the bathroom mirror, where he monitored the tiny wrinkles that had gathered some friends since his thirty-fifth birthday. Being off work officially on Monday mornings was purely a function of the fact that for him, as with his colleagues, Sunday night was Saturday night. The predictable pattern of money talk with the guys, followed by spending the said commodity in pursuit of the opposite sex often concluded in the worst hangovers, where the toxic synthesis of lager, whisky, and champagne destroyed future recall. What the hell had he said to that little red-head? London was a vast city, and he'd never see her again.

He wandered out onto the balcony, one of the benefits of this residence at the West Riverside apartments. The faint odour of burning oil permeated his nostrils in the light spring breeze. A small commercial tug then passed on the Thames below, the deck bearing three or four men in blue overalls. The cogs of commerce. Or *real* work, as his father had often retorted: the underlying graft that ultimately dictated the intangible millions upon which he deliberated and staked his reputation.

Monday was often a bastard, though. This was the day where his predictions began to transmute, and it was often the day on which he was subject to early judgement. His Sunday share-tipping column for the *Sentinel* aimed to provide exclusive, powerful analysis that predicted share price movements. When the markets opened on Monday mornings, early indications of any market reaction could make the difference between a good or bad week. Officially, Monday was a day off, but in parallel with most financial journalists who primarily wrote for Sunday publications, the pursuit of online content by the media world dictated that blog copy and online updates were placed whenever appropriate, including on Mondays when the markets opened. And sometimes that was a bastard, especially if he had tipped a bummer.

His phone buzzed.

'Calum, have you seen the news?'

Calum checked his watch: 10:05 a.m. 'What's up, Ben?' Ben was his closest colleague at the *Sentinel*.

'Dartmouth Petroleum's up. Big announcement this afternoon apparently. I noticed a rise this morning, and then there was a news feed half an hour ago followed by a fifteen percent leap in the stock…and it's still going. Looks like you were on the money, even if you were in your kip, mate. And not with that red-head, eh? She was a babe.'

Calum had tipped Dartmouth Petroleum in the *Sentinel* the previous day after a great deal of soul searching. The company had been involved in a bitter legal battle over exploration licences with both the Canadian Government in Ottawa and provincial officials in Alberta. The shares had halved in recent weeks over concerns about planning approval and the subsequent provision of the licences in land owned by First Nation people. Calum had contacted an old colleague based in Canada who covered oil as part of his investment analysis role, and he'd indicated strongly that the legal case was about to collapse. Calum had followed the stock for some time, and despite reservations, had followed his old friend's advice. As a multinational, the firm's shares were traded in both London and New York. There had been various nebulous claims about Dartmouth in recent times by analysts but the general conclusion had been negative, hence the fall in value.

But this was good news.

It contradicted what his editor had argued, that he should leave Dartmouth alone until more data became available. But Calum had insisted on rating the stock as a strong buy. Readers who had bought the stock immediately after trading opened would be enjoying a pleasant profit before ten o'clock.

'That's a relief, Ben. Might keep Powell off my back for while.'

'I doubt that. Wish you'd bought the stock yourself on Friday, mate?'

'Always tempting but you know the rules. In any case, I'd have been bankrupt in recent weeks if I'd taken my own advice. Powell said I couldn't so much as tip a waitress in the last month, but maybe this will show him.'

'He's a post hoc rationaliser, that clown, expert after the event, every time. And he's totally forgotten about that run you had last year.'

'Yip. Need to go, Ben. I might as well watch this one go. Hell, I think I'll come into the office.' Calum signed off and wandered back inside, using his phone to access the market news. Dartmouth's share price had risen again. Wall Street didn't open until 9:30 a.m. Eastern Standard Time in the US, which was hours away, and analysts reported that although the company was also quoted on both exchanges, an announcement was going to coincide with the US market opening. Calum felt a warm sensation; that sense of minor elation that humans experience when things are going right.

Hell, he *would* head into the office.

The man already knew that there were two points of exit from the West Riverside apartment block. The rear exit backed onto a controlled residents' parking area, but that exit could be excluded. He was aware that when Calum Mack commuted to the office he normally took the tube, but he also knew from the phone call that Mack was shortly going to leave the apartment by the front exit. Breaking and entering was simple, particularly when you had gleaned the secrets of this type of subterfuge from seasoned experts at a juncture where you had endless time to absorb detail. He positioned himself in the shadow, adjacent to a bus stop where three other people were awaiting transport. About ten minutes later Mack appeared at the front entrance, and turned left in the direction of the underground station. The man waited until the next person was exiting the building before simultaneously entering through the front entrance.

A polo shirt boasting an *it-solutions* logo, a small tool case, and an air of superiority proved invaluable; indeed, they were the sorts of tools with which he was comfortable. The security guard at reception—an elderly man—looked up from his copy of *The Sun* as he approached.

'Morning. I need entry to Mr Mack's apartment on the fifth floor. Apartment 502.' He nonchalantly thumbed his smart phone, as if entry to the apartment was a formality. The security guard, whose badge bore the name 'Victor', scratched his head.

'Mr Mack just left a few minutes ago. He didn't say anything about someone else gaining entry.'

'I'm aware of that. I'm just off the phone to him,' the man replied. 'He's had to go into the office on his day off, but I'm supposed to check his broadband connection right now or there will be hell to pay.'

'I don't know.' Victor looked around him, as if searching for some kind of note that would validate lawful entry. 'I'd need Mr Mack's permission.'

'He'll not be happy, but please give him a call. Got his mobile number?' The man showed his phone with the correct number displayed. Victor tapped on his keyboard to confirm the number before making the call.

The man's contact at BT had temporarily routed Mack's number to another number where someone bearing a Scottish accent not dissimilar to Mack's gave instant, slightly dismissive permission, giving the impression that Victor shouldn't have bothered to call. Just let the guy in and not bother him again later. And all it had cost was fifty pounds. The security guard grunted in response before putting down the phone and taking the man to the apartment, enquiring as to how long he would need. The alarm and CCTV system was controlled centrally, one of the apparent advantages of having security personnel present in the building at all times and the primary deterrent for preventing the type of crime that was about to take place. However, as far as the man was concerned, this factor had proved a benefit. It had been important for the security guard to be present when he appeared at the apartment, so that no suspicious entry would be spotted on camera. The man needed five minutes only, after which Victor said he would return to recover the master key.

Inside he was surprised just how pathetic Mack's attempts at personal security were. The passport—his main target—was actually lying in the top drawer of a bedside cabinet, inside a plastic wallet. How ironic. Here was an individual who could calculate moving averages, interpret momentum charts and compare Fibonacci ratios, yet when it came to basic security, he placed his faith in the illusion of safety proffered by people such as Victor. He quickly took note of some financial information, including Mack's current account details, just in case. He took nothing else, and when he exited the apartment he left everything exactly as he found it. However, he indicated at the front desk that he'd agreed with Mr Mack he'd return in an hour or two to check if the system had booted up properly. Victor nodded vaguely in agreement, before the man left the building.

An hour and a half later, he appeared again and was given entry to the apartment as agreed, where he replaced the original documentation in the same place within the bedside table. He was aware of more than one forger from his time served at Her Majesty's pleasure, but the one he trusted most required originals for the most efficient results. He was quietly impressed by what could be achieved in just over an hour in this city. On exit from the apartment block, he mentioned to the guard that Mack was a serial complainer, and that the last thing he should do is remind him about the call or the job. He noted that the guard did not really employ his full sensory capabilities. *He* on the other hand, noticed *everything*. In another life years previously, he'd been nicknamed *Hawk*, which in many ways summed him up. A lethal loner, who missed nothing.

After the ride to Tower Hill tube station, Calum grabbed a coffee and a tuna baguette from a small coffee shop three hundred yards from the *Sentinel* offices. His hangover had ebbed, the recovery encouraged by the good news emanating from Canada. Sometimes the little things in life held sway over his mood for the day—considerations such as bright sunlight or a corker of a share tip that would keep his editor, Rod Powell, at bay.

Powell had proved to be a frustration. Two years previously, he'd given Calum his journalistic break after he'd departed from investment banking in Edinburgh. In the initial interview, Powell had seemed engaging—genuinely encouraging—in respect of Calum's proposal, which was to speak with the voice of a professional investment manager, whilst employing the instincts of a hack with something to prove. The aim was to transfer Calum's investment experience into a communicational show piece, and help galvanise readership for the *Sunday Sentinel's* business section. Powell, a tall, capricious character of fifty who sported salt and pepper hair, had initially argued with the managing editor for the need for a more encouraging salary for Calum, coupled with something of a roving remit when it came to reporting the dirt or cream at any interesting listed company. This was to be the perfect safety net for a former investment banker.

And yet, just a few weeks into the role, Calum had discovered that Powell was a serial interferer, an editor who nitpicked with detail in the most inconsistent manner. Calum had been aware that professional journalists required thick skins when it came to the editing process, but he'd redrafted numerous items six or seven times before Powell had been satisfied, often concluding with copy barely differentiated from the piece he'd originally submitted.

Two years in the job and he was more experienced as a hack, yet no more able to return to his former furrow due to the shakeout within investment banking. Perhaps Powell had simply expected more of him, but as he sipped his coffee, Calum felt a sense of relief that this Dartmouth Petroleum development had deviated in the correct direction before his next conversation with Powell. A quick check on his phone indicated that Dartmouth had risen another five percent. Time to cross the road.

The *Sentinel* building was known to both insiders and outsiders as the *Hub*. The quasi beehive shape stood testament to its 21st century architecture, contrasting subtly with some of the historic edifices which graced this part of the city. Located a short distance from Tower Bridge, the Hub glistened in the morning sun, providing a hint of the bustling media nerve centre housed within.

At his desk, Calum quickly confirmed the Dartmouth share price, which had edged up again. He figured that on this occasion an early blog update would be more appropriate than awaiting the additional clarity which would accompany the announcement from the States in the afternoon. He was aware from reader panels that many of the small investors who followed his column on Sunday really valued updated online advice as early as possible in the week. Such investors were not solely reliant upon him for information, but if he broke a story through tipping a stock, people would naturally look to the same source for further interpretation as events progressed. In the case of Dartmouth, some would aim to take early profits, but many of the more savvy investors would want to know if it would be worth undertaking the opposite investment strategy: buying *further* into a rising market. In the column, Calum had often relayed an old truism in stock picking, that many lost opportunities—and profits—were created by selling too *early*. The salient question then, was how far did this thing have to run?

He began his blog update in the usual manner, cogently summarising the early, known facts and subsequent market reaction, before moving to the more subjective components. He decided to go for it. His recommendation as of 11:30 a.m. on Monday morning was to 'accumulate'. The rationale was that many of the large institutional investors such as the insurers would wait until the US update at 2:30 p.m., by which time the market would have already reacted. As Jimmy Goldsmith had famously said, *if you see a bandwagon, you're already too late.*

Just as he confirmed the submission of the blog content, Rod Powell appeared in his line of sight. Powell furrowed his brow slightly, perhaps surprised to see Calum at the office on a Monday morning, as he usually made any Monday blog updates from home.

'Finished that Radiant story yet?' Powell's opening gambit hit Calum abruptly. He'd sidelined the story on Radiant Insurance some weeks back due to the lack of reliability of a source he'd cultivated inside the firm. A whistleblower had been about to blow the company apart on the ethics of selling 'new for old products', or *churning* as it was known in the trade. Calum had talked the story up to Powell, before being forced to retreat as his source had acquired cold feet.

'Still pursuing that one, Rod, but I don't want to jump the gun on the story unless I can get access to those key documents that we were promised.'

'But you didn't have any key documents on Dartmouth Petroleum, yet you insisted on a buy recommendation yesterday. Tell me the difference?' Powell held out his arms before scratching the salt and pepper hair.

Calum smiled, his dark eyes staring at Powell. 'That must be down to gut instinct, then.'

'Or pure luck?'

'The luckier I get, the more readers we shall have.' Calum mirrored Powell's body language.

'We'll see.' Powell marched off to his office, allowing Calum to continue his blog. If Calum had mentioned his intention to Powell, there would have been further conflict, followed by micro-management, and instructions to back off the recommendation until the announcement in the afternoon. He uploaded his copy and watched the share price. Within two minutes, there was further upward movement. Calum wasn't naive or egotistical enough to believe that he alone could move the stock significantly via a blog comment, but the implication was that his recommendation was proving to be in tune with the market, and therefore credible. Perhaps some of the more cautious investors were now beginning to accumulate the stock in anticipation.

He viewed the cityscape outside. Having been raised in the Scottish Highlands, and then subsequently having worked in Edinburgh, Calum still marvelled at the sheer scale of the city of London; the diversity and complexity of its rhythms, the pulse of people, of ideas, and of course, money. He still felt like an outsider, but then most people in offices such as this one, and more than half of the people in the financial nerve centre, originated from elsewhere. Some even joked that London rhyming slang was now better understood outside of London, certainly outside of its centre. Calum grabbed his jacket and headed out to the *Frontier*, a pub frequented by hacks and suits. The bar retained one of its large screens for business news.

He ordered a double espresso, though his preferred choice would have been a pint or single malt, perhaps a Glenlivet. He was technically on a day off, after all, but he wanted to keep a clear head. A suit who worked as a senior analyst for one of the banks, and who Calum had once interviewed, entered the bar and ordered a pint. The man, an overweight, ruddy-cheeked type, spotted Calum sitting in a corner seat and headed over.

'I read your column yesterday. Went out on a bit of limb with that Dartmouth tip.'

'Market seems to think differently.' Calum motioned to the screen to his right, where the stock was currently listed. The price had fallen slightly since he had left the office.

'I'm not so sure,' the man continued. 'I read a note on the FT online about fifteen minutes ago that it might go pear shaped, legally. You should be telling your readers to *sell*.' The man, whose name escaped Calum, gulped his pint, before Calum responded.

'I'll give you a tip. *Never* take a tip from a banker,' Calum said.

'Weren't you a banker?' Ruddy cheeks frowned.

'Ex.'

'Poacher turned gamekeeper? Well, oil is one of the hardest sectors to predict, you know. It might be a finite commodity, but no one actually knows how much of the bloody stuff is left. You can only store so much processed oil at a time, and its use is weather dependent and at the mercy of the economy, which humans have also failed miserably to predict accurately. Oil's controlled by irrational people, one half of whom are nomads made good, and the other half are crazed dictators with no conscience. The industry's subject to the obsessions of cheating cartel members and environmental planet-saving bloody hippies. And that's not to mention you Jocks shouting about the North Sea. But you think you can outwit them all? If I were daft enough to own that stock—even if I'd bought it at the high two years ago—I'd sell the lot right now.' He returned to the bar to order another beer, and Calum glanced at the screen again.

The news feed along the bottom of the screen said: *breaking news…Dartmouth Petroleum announcement imminent.* The volume had been turned down, but Calum could see a reporter standing outside the Canadian Parliament in Ottawa. He stood up immediately, fetching the remote control from an adjacent table. A Canadian Government spokesman then appeared, reading a prepared statement.

Due to pressure from the media and because of intense speculation about the nature of the issues involved, the Canadian Government has decided to bring forward today's planned announcement regarding the legal position with respect to Dartmouth Petroleum's drilling licences. Contrary to reports that the national and provincial authorities were due to drop legal action in the existing case against Dartmouth Petroleum, the two legislatures can jointly announce that our special investigators have uncovered both serious fraud and attempted bribery by executives of the company in relation to licences in Alberta, together with substantial evidence of fabrication of environmental reports regarding the dangers of drilling in some existing fields…

Calum closed his eyes, the remnants of his hangover suddenly re-emerging. He stared at the screen, running his fingers through his dark hair. *Shit.* This wasn't supposed to have happened. He immediately texted his contact in Canada. *What's the score here? You assured me that…*

The news report switched back to the studio, where a presenter and an expert were discussing the news. Another oil blunder, they opined. These guys just can't shoot straight. The *courts* will no doubt decide the stock price. The screen indicated that the stock was in freefall, instantly marked down. Within two minutes the price had nosedived to substantially below where it had finished on Friday. Calum considered the analogy of the Old West, and the phrase 'the quick and the dead'. Any small investor who'd bought this morning on the strength of his tip or blog would be screwed unless they'd sold right away. A few minutes away from the data streams—a trip to boil the kettle—and they'd be stuffed. Even standing instructions to sell at key trading levels simply didn't apply when a stock had no buyers.

His phone buzzed: Powell.

'I've just read your blog update, Calum. Nice of you to pass things by me this morning, given current events. You left the office just in time.' Calum could almost taste the sarcasm.

'Those who bought and sold early this morning turned a quick buck,' Calum replied defensively.

'But you just told readers to accumulate less than an hour ago! How stupid does that make us look?' Powell had a point, though Calum felt he needed to respond.

'Okay, okay, Rod. Look, I admit that I got this one wrong. My source in Canada *assured* me of the opposite position. He's been accurate in the past. Anyone who reads the column and knows anything about investment understands implicitly that prices in stocks such as oils are volatile. I don't have a crystal ball.' Calum turned to see the pudgy analyst who'd just given him the spiel on oil stocks smugly pointing up at the screen. He ignored the man as Powell continued.

'If you're going to out on a limb, you need to show the *downside* within the column and the blog. Given the manner in which you argued the case online, you'd think that it was a racing certainty.'

'So you want me to sit on the fence with bland, hedgy copy that no one will read?'

'Absolutely not!' Powell raised his voice. 'But when I hired you two years ago, you assured me that you'd do your *research*. Produce original analysis. Get in behind the bluster and set the heather on fire with *exciting* advice that will make readers money. Find gold mines. We can't afford to let readers down by talking shit.'

Calum felt his temperature rise. 'So the columns on Edgeways and Gifted were *shit*, were they?' The prices of both of these stocks had more than trebled after Calum's initial, ground-breaking research.

'That was *six months* ago. This is a *weekly* column within a 24/7 operation, in case I have to remind you. You are employed to bring readers *in*, not to generate critical emails from pissed-off investors, who happen to be the backbone of our readership. Do you know how many emails I've had complaining about your column?'

'Every journalist gets complaints about what they write.'

'I've had a lot about you lately. I want results *now*. You'd better pick up your game, mate.'

As Powell cut him off, the fat analyst across the bar raised his glass, smiling at the screen. Schadenfreude, Calum figured. Stuff it, he'd have a drink after all, consolatory rather than celebratory, but not with that conceited bastard at the bar. He ordered a large Glenlivet and moved into a corner seat on the far side of the bar, overlooking the street outside. Throngs of passersby flowed by the window, a river of human movement, each with his or her own stories, emotions, aspirations and personal disasters. Life could indeed be shit for everyone, but right now he personally felt like throwing in the towel. After leaving investment banking as a career, he'd experienced that most undervalued emotion—relief—when he'd landed the job at the *Sentinel*. His limited journalistic experience had been compensated by natural charisma and a genuine knowledge of how the market operated. He'd needed a change and the role had offered a completely new dimension to his career. He'd split from his girlfriend just before the move from Edinburgh, and although he missed Scotland a lot, a stint somewhere else had proved to be the shakeup he'd needed. The job paid less—considerably less than what he'd earned before, and less than what most of his contemporaries from university now earned—but it had been an interesting diversion.

Until now.

With Powell on his back, the pressure had escalated and market volatility had rendered stock picking more irrational. Reliable contacts were no longer as consistent, but the expectations of readers were no less onerous. His phone rang once more. He didn't recognise the number, but at least it wasn't Powell.

'Bit of a bummer, that Dartmouth development.' He didn't recognise the voice. Middle England somewhere, strange modulation.

'Yes. Who's this?'

'Let's say I'm a friendly ship in an ocean of predators.'

'What? Look, I'm not having the best of days. If this is some kind of crank call, I could do without it.' Calum sipped his whisky as he spoke.

'I'm certainly not a crank, but I am making a call. A *judgement* call, by getting in touch with you.'

Calum frowned. 'I don't follow you.'

'You're damaged goods, by the look of it…but I can repair the damage and really help you,' the caller said flatly.

Calum hesitated. He'd experienced time wasters on previous occasions due to the exposure he got through the *Sentinel* but normally such types used email as their preferred modus operandi.

'What is it you want? Let me guess…you have a unique insight into the share tip of the year; precious information that is unknown to others?' Calum employed a little bluster to encourage a response. If there was nothing positive on offer, he'd end the call and place a bar on incoming calls from this number.

'Well actually, yes. Now, listen carefully, Calum. Within the hour, the Food and Drug Administration in the United States will give their approval for a drug called Limderon. Limderon is a revolutionary treatment for bowel cancer, which as you may know is one of the most prevalent forms of the disease. This decision has been a very closely guarded secret, as the trial data on the effectiveness of the treatment has not been published. The life sciences firm that makes Limderon is based in Cambridge—Cambridge England, that is.'

'Walltex? Small firm quoted on AIM?'

'Yes…I'm glad you're keeping up with the markets.'

'So how do you know this information?'

'I have my sources, which I cannot reveal. However, I want you to monitor events today. Have a think about the validity of what I am telling you, versus, for example, the farce that you have just had with Dartmouth

Petroleum. Consider how cool it would have been if yesterday you'd tipped this stock instead. I'll be in touch.'

The man hung up, precipitating a brief headshake from Calum. Probably another idiot trying to muck up his day. He headed back to the bar, deliberately standing at the left hand side so as to be served by an appealing brunette barmaid whom he tipped a fiver. He sat on a bar stool, engaging in sporadic small talk with the girl as he mellowed, influenced by the effects of the whisky. About an hour and twenty minutes later, after his fourth, he checked his watch, before putting on his jacket to leave. But as he headed towards the door the business channel screen once more captured his gaze. This time the news feed read: *Stock price doubles as FDA unexpectedly approves cancer drug for Cambridge minnow.*

Chapter 2

Aurelia Harley inadvertently spilled her coffee on the glass table that adorned the centre of the breakout room. She attempted to mop up the spillage, but when her colleague Adam shouted sarcastically for her to rejoin them next door, she hesitated. When she'd begun working in the Financial Conduct Authority, she would have completed the clean up in earnest, a conscientious streak having impregnated her personality during her formative years. But several years of service with an unrelenting caseload coupled with increasingly partisan competition from some of her colleagues had left their mark. The coffee break had lasted all of three minutes. Would Adam waste two seconds with a sponge or a mop? Stuff it, she'd let the cleaner clean. A tinge of guilt crossed her mind as she suddenly recalled a ticking off her mother had given her as a child in Dublin, where she'd left a real mess in the kitchen one day. But this was different, she'd moved on, hadn't she?

She returned next door to the main conference room where the team were in the midst of a gruelling five-hour meeting, straightening her pin stripe navy business jacket and skirt as she entered the room. Adam awarded her a fake smile, before giving her the once over. A large element of his attitude towards her was that she'd shown absolutely no interest in him despite his advances. Subconsciously, she flipped back her dark shoulder length hair before taking her seat, the azure eyes avoiding Adam completely. Her boss, Max Telford, appeared oblivious to the whole charade. The director of enforcement and financial crime was something of a financial zealot, obsessed with protocol and endeavour, yet somewhat limited in interpreting the emotional quotient or work-life balance issues that were also essential for any organisation to function. His mantra was simply to *get the job done.*

The department dealt with one of the FCA's key objectives: fighting financial crime, which linked directly to one of its other objectives, which was to maintain market confidence. Max Telford had a team of financial specialists in his section, drawn from various backgrounds, each charged with investigating individuals who breached the standards set out in the FCA guidelines on financial crime. Times had changed. The scope for insider dealing was in some senses more limited than in times past, especially where large trading deals were concerned. The software now available to identify unusual trades was also more sophisticated, as was the multilateral cooperation between various international financial jurisdictions. What remained the challenge, however, was proof of connectivity. As with unusual bets prior to high-odds football results, correlating the source of an original tip with the apparent beneficiaries required resources and tough investigative skill.

In Aurelia's case, she had been a robust performer. She was one of only three females in the team, and experience had told her that she was expected to surmount substantially higher obstacles than most of her male counterparts. She invested the hours, and had been instrumental in some high profile convictions. The FCA had only recently helped secure the conviction of Daniel Fleeting, who, as a former market maker with a large London stock broker, had been party to the takeover of Chistec Electronics by a Chinese rival. Fleeting had tipped his father-in-law about the deal one day beforehand, and Aurelia had been the executive investigator who'd uncovered the trade and the marital connection. It turned out that Fleeting's father-in-law had netted just over £48,000 in profits, and had returned a cheque to Fleeting two months after the trade for exactly half the amount. Honour and equity among familial thieves, apparently. Fleeting had subsequently been jailed for 21 months, and the FCA had issued a statement to the effect that the gloves were off, and that they would use every weapon in the armoury to combat market abuse. Aurelia had been allowed to draft the key concluding statement; yet just within a couple of weeks life had simply returned to normal, her caseload rising further.

Telford, a short, bald man of sixty who sported bifocal glasses and a strange taste in floral ties, literally thumped the table. In many respects, he had been an ideal appointment for the role, as he seemed to genuinely care about the law, the integrity of the markets, and convictions, if not the hours worked by his staff. He'd been divorced for around a decade and had since devoted himself to public service. When he banged tables, the chatter ceased, and his team paid attention.

'We're behind on our target for convictions,' he said directly. 'Both the French and the Germans have a much higher conviction to investigation ratio than we have here. We can argue the toss about the burden of proof, or whether the light touch that was so maligned in the City of London still manifests itself. But that is not the point. We must play the game as it stands. And the bottom line is that it is of no value to this organisation to pursue cases where we cannot secure big convictions.' No one dared interrupt, and almost everyone avoided eye contact.

'Well?' Telford outstretched his hands.

'You're absolutely right, if you ask me, Max.' Adam Smart spoke first, consistent in his acquiescence to whatever critique Telford currently purveyed. 'The way I see it is that we should add further strategic focus to the cases that will net the biggest offenders, and then secure convictions in these cases.'

'Exactly,' Max said, surveying everyone around the table. Aurelia sighed, just audibly enough to catch his attention. 'You disagree, Aurelia?'

Adam interjected. 'I think that Aurelia is probably defensive as the Fleeting case didn't net that much in the scope of things.' Aurelia's eyes focused directly on Adam.

'Adam, I worked my butt off on that case.'

'Aurelia, stop. No one is questioning your commitment,' Max said. 'I'm sure that Adam didn't mean to be critical. And he put in the hours on that case too, remember.' Aurelia raised her eyes to the ceiling, and attempted to inhale slowly. In reality, Adam had piggybacked onto a winner at the very last juncture.

She turned sideways to make dedicated eye contact with Max. 'I do not disagree with your sentiments, Max. I do, however, disagree with Adam putting words in my mouth. The Fleeting case was not the biggest fish, I accept, but it *was* our most recent success. How does Adam propose to gain *strategic focus?*' Aurelia emphasised the term by miming imaginary inverted commas.

Adam raised his chin, apparently perplexed with Aurelia. 'It's *very* simple, Aurelia. The data *is* there. The big fish spend time trying to conceal their activities, so what *you* need to do is work harder, longer hours to analyse the patterns more deeply. It's as simple as that.'

'Me, specifically? *I've* to work harder. Is that it?' Aurelia felt her skin redden, her teeth gritted behind tight lips.

'Aurelia…don't take this so personally,' Max said. 'Adam makes a good point. Perhaps if everyone put in ten percent more hours, we'd gain twenty or thirty percent more convictions, particularly in some of those cases that are most difficult to prove.'

For the remainder of the meeting Aurelia disengaged with the discussion, letting others hold court with the minutiae. Some people just talked shit, and she wished she'd played one of those games of lingo bingo, just to satisfy herself as to how much tosh was generated. Adam had achieved exactly what he'd intended. The obsequious pandering to Max had proved beneficial to his cause, and had created the simultaneous advantage of placing her on the defensive despite her recent track record. Adam was the sort who would ultimately do well. He was an ambitious egotist. He'd no doubt ascend the berry tree, a proud exponent of the *Peter Principle* where confidence, ambition and sycophancy dwarfed endeavour or indeed an objective track record.

As the meeting came to a conclusion, Max banged the table once more. 'All I ask is that everyone becomes more alert. What happened to the investigative part of this job? Let's leave no stone unturned. Redouble your efforts. There are online announcements every hour. Remember, the media is our friend and can provide impetus, these little gems of stories that hint of hidden lies and deception.'

They left the meeting, and Max pulled Aurelia aside, handing her a note. 'Have a look at this website, Aurelia. It's a new site, but one that might help illuminate the sorts of things we want to look into. You did well in the Fleeting case, and you're good at sniffing out financial crime.' Aurelia smiled briefly, pleased that Telford had made some kind of acknowledgement of her contribution.

Back at her desk she briefly shuddered at the volume of work she faced, before grabbing a quick coffee. As she sipped the coffee, almost absentmindedly she accessed the website that Telford had suggested. The most notable story concerned an Alternative Investment Market listed company called Walltex, which had gained unexpected approval by the American Food and Drug Administration for a cancer drug called Limderon. The stock price had risen substantially. Aurelia jotted down the company name on a pink post-it pad.

Hawk handled the phone cautiously. It was crucial that the phone was used for this specific call. When the number rang, a gatekeeper answered in a polished accent. Even the receptionists in these companies were blue blooded. As expected, his request to speak to Nigel Tomlinson was initially rejected, until he explained that the call was an absolute emergency. He then passed on a subtle password that only Tomlinson would recognise. Hawk specifically wanted to call Tomlinson at his place of work. Not for the first time recently, he employed an app that altered his voice pattern. This clever little piece of software had been discussed in sections of the media after being utilised by radio stations to instigate fake celebrity wind-ups of unsuspecting members of the public. It had been designed for entertainment purposes, but now seemed the perfect device for concealing Hawk's tracks. As he was placed on hold, he briefly considered Nigel Tomlinson, the CEO of the Pan-Euro Investment Bank. Hawk had always considered him to be a fake, an accidental success born of wealth and privilege. Tomlinson, as his antecedents would have assumed, had risen effortlessly through the corporate ranks despite his mediocre academic calibre. Daddy's old boy network had guaranteed an otherwise elusive post-university placement at the Bank of England, which had opened doors to exciting corporate ventures and ultimately led to his position in command of a successful private bank.

'Tomlinson.' The voice hadn't altered in years.

'The albatross has landed, then?' Hawk smiled as he relayed the concluding element of the password in this modified accent, to all intents unrecognisable due to the electronic alteration. The truth was that Tomlinson had always reminded him of an albatross.

'You know what? I know who you are. This is ridiculous, all this cloak and dagger. I should call the police.' Tomlinson's frustration was borne out of an attitude of entitlement: how *dare* anyone force him to behave in any way differently to how he wished?

'You will not call the police, call anyone else, nor use Facebook or any of the rest of the social networking sites…and you will follow my instructions to the letter, or suffer the consequences. I hold all the cards.'

Hawk detected an audible sigh from the other end. Tomlinson momentarily hesitated, perhaps considering a further line of defence before resigning himself to the futility of further argument. The confidential package that he had received some time previously in the regular mail, sent to his home address, had provided shocking photographic evidence of his complicity in an unfortunate event, the exposure of which could result in the destruction of his career and marriage. He knew that the photographic evidence was not entirely doctored, for the event had indeed taken place, if not exactly the way it appeared in the pictures. The reality was, however, that he'd had absolutely no knowledge that the event had been recorded. He was forbidden to discuss anything whatsoever on any calls or with any of the other parties involved in the incident. He was under surveillance, apparently, and any attempt to circumvent that surveillance would have the same ultimate result. His life would be ruined. He'd been forced to liaise with the caller when the time was right, and now a call had materialised.

And the demand? Confidential information. Tomlinson himself was not above cheating or manipulating things. His lack of ability to read markets had caused him to veer off the straight and narrow on occasion, but he'd been in *control* of these events and had trusted those who'd supplied the information. He'd certainly not been subject to the demands of a dangerous blackmailer.

'Do you have the information I requested?' Hawk asked bluntly.

'Do you know how dangerous this is for me to divulge this information?'

'Yes.'

'And you have no concern for me? If you're who I think you are…just because your career—'

'Enough! This is your very last warning. Now, do you have the information requested?'

Again, hesitation. 'Yes.'

'Continue.'

Tomlinson sighed. 'Oh…in two week's time—that's Tuesday the 24th—a special share issue will be announced for the online betting and casino firm X4D4.' Tomlinson sighed again. 'It's in the FTSE 250. They operate casinos in more than twenty countries.'

'And?'

'And the Chinese Government will confirm…that they will take a…a thirty three percent stake in the new, expanded X4D4.'

'Go on.'

Tomlinson grunted. 'They will open up the provinces to unique systems, allowing special access to operate special casinos, and run state of the art online betting in China.'

'Very interesting indeed. All funded by the Chinese investment? No new borrowing?'

'No.'

'So this is costless to X4D4?'

'Some loss of control, seats on the board by proxy, but essentially costless.'

'And what is your estimation of the impact on the share price?'

'Oh for God's sake, how much do you want here? Is there anything else I can do for you? Wipe your arse?' Tomlinson barked.

'Just *answer the question*. Give me an estimate, and you should never hear from me again.'

'There's no guarantee of that, is there?' Tomlinson's frustration was palpable.

'No there isn't, but you have no choice.'

'Well, internally, we estimate that the share price could…double, and that's conservative. This is a shift in Chinese policy, another move into the capitalist realm. But *please*, whatever you do with this, don't spill specific details in the press. If there is a leak, it could scupper the deal.'

'I'm not stupid.'

'And I have your guarantee that—'

Hawk cut the line. He'd acquired the information that he needed. Tomlinson was pathetic because under the thin veneer of respectability he was just as vulnerable to the problems of greed and fear as everyone else. Just as Calum Mack would fear all those emails his editor had received about the quality of his column.

Inevitably, Tuesday also held frustrations for those principally writing for a Sunday publication. Many journalists writing online could write within a continuum, developing stories as they broke while saving an addendum for Sunday. However, those working primarily for Sunday publication faced the dilemma of timing. Should they jealously conceal knowledge of a story from colleagues writing daily or should they share the news? If they chose the former route, and a competitor publication grabbed the story before Sunday, editorial staff would become infuriated if it became apparent that the story had been parked without benefit. If the latter route prevailed, especially where newsrooms were encouraged to employ collegiate endeavours, trust and reciprocity became crucial. Hacks compete with hacks in other publications, but in truth, they also compete with colleagues in the same stable. Every journalist deliberately stores snippets, some for short periods, others for longer term potential benefit. The question is whether anyone else finds out.

Calum shuffled around in his chair, chewing on a pencil. Whilst merely a subtle sign of a pensive moment, the action nonetheless caught Ben's attention across the floor at the far side of the newsroom. Calum nodded across, before Ben casually strode over. Ben, either by accident or design, looked like someone from a boy band, if a tad older. He had a clean-cut, angular bone structure and sported shoulder length blond hair, often complemented by designer labels aimed at impressing seventeen-year-old girls. He was a genuine East Ender made good in his own city.

'What brings you over to the sunny Sunday side?' Calum posed this question as Ben contributed mainly to the daily grind online.

'I try to give some of my time to you poor, bedraggled ones over here. Needing some help, Calum?' This was a restrained reference to the Dartmouth Petroleum incident the previous day. Most colleagues had teased Calum, though he'd avoided Powell who'd been out at a business seminar all morning.

'Bit of a bastard.'

'The way it went?' Ben threw back his hair, frowning.

'I mean that old ex-banking colleague I have in Canada who gave me assurances. I'd string him up if I got close enough. He's not returning calls or emails of course, especially the way,' Calum squinted at his screen, 'the stock's gone now. Bombed out is a polite description.'

Ben scratched his chin. 'You'll be all right once you weather the usual complaint onslaught. Personally, I never listen to a word readers say. Bunch of bastards, the lot of them.'

Calum smiled. 'Today, Ben, I deliberately haven't opened any such communications. But unfortunately, Powell actually listens to them.'

'Yeah, thank Christ he's only fractionally my boss. No luck for you, Calum. So what's up? Any new tips I should know about?'

Calum swivelled about in his chair again. 'There are a few bits and pieces in the pipeline. I'll see what the week brings. Some oddball called me when I was in the *Frontier* yesterday, tipping a firm an hour before it leapt in value. Now, why can't that happen on a Friday for an announcement the following week?'

'What was the firm?' As Ben enquired, Calum grinned and held his index finger to the side of his nose. Ben shook his head forlornly, aware that although they were pals the principle of 'need to know' still applied as far as Calum's morals were concerned.

As Ben wandered back to his desk, Calum accessed a stock analyst's website, and logged in before undertaking a quick search for Walltex and its new wonder drug, Limderon. Sure enough, there was an update about the stock.

The galling thing was that it would have been an ideal tip had the timing been more apt, as the news had obviously been guarded carefully. Walltex, it turned out, had actually experienced three previous high profile trial failures which had decimated its share price, so the triumph that Limderon now presented was a real money spinner for those that had invested at the low.

Why would someone provide him with a tip too late to benefit, though? People sometimes called or emailed with apparent inside information so that he would write up the story in his Sunday column in advance of something happening. Much of this information was useless, however. In many cases suggestions came from individuals attempting to lift a stock price as they'd already lost money on the company and were trying to recoup losses, or where punters were attempting just to make a quick buck. So, when he tipped a stock he normally relied on either an expert or his own analysis, or preferably both.

He spotted Rod Powell entering the news room. Powell made instant direct eye contact with Calum, making a circular pointing motion for Calum to come into his office. Social niceties were regularly omitted from Powell's repertoire.

Calum entered the glass-walled room, taking a pew as Powell made some cryptic comments in a phone call before pointing at Calum.

'You're occupying wafer-thin ice.'

'I thought we'd been through all this, Rod.' Calum folded his arms instinctively.

'Management wants to cut costs here. Readership is a big issue. Your everyday copy is okay, but I can get that sort of stuff free from wannabe students eager to make their mark. So what do you have to offer? Stock tips that leave small investors with half of what they had before you spilled the beans?'

'That's a bit unfair, Rod.'

'Is it? Yesterday, you came in here to soak up what you thought would be reflected kudos, but you ended up looking like an idiot by doing sloppy research on Dartmouth. Do you know how many emails I had complaining about this tip?'

'I delete them.'

Powell struck the desk. 'See, that's the difference between you and me. These people are our customers. They pay *your* wages, so I'm going to be blunt. You have three more weeks to make a difference. I've told you that I'm getting complaints. If you don't have a winner by then, you're out.'

Calum took a deep breath, pursing his lips. 'Three weeks? Stocks don't necessarily move that quickly—it's far too tight. And I have six months left on my current contract.'

'We'll pay the six months,' Powell said, folding his arms. 'You won't have much of a reputation to take with you, but you can have the money. The way it's going, it would save us money letting you go.'

'But Rod, readers read for a number of reasons. My column isn't going to be a deal buster.'

'*Exactly.* See my point? In that case, letting you go would make no difference,' Powell said, smiling. He'd won the argument.

'Surely a couple of months would be realistic? I relocated from Edinburgh for this job, as you know.'

'*Three weeks.*'

Over the following days Calum submerged himself in data, employing his contacts to acquire snippets, working into the small hours to undertake analysis and compare advice generated by specialists. He recalled one economics lecturer from university who said that information was like holding sand in your palm: a compendium of such tiny fragments might be useful when combined, but the grains were manifestly useless on an individual basis.

To placate Powell for his next column, Calum identified two firms that might have made a decent Sunday splash but the news broke online for both stories almost immediately after Calum had been tipped, just like sand inevitably falling from his palm. On Friday he then produced a piece for Powell on a busted bank, and the column was published on the Sunday, but with no immediate market reaction on the Monday morning.

Then, the following Tuesday, when buried in another analyst's report, his phone buzzed.

'Mack? Busy at work are we?' Calum recognised the voice. It seemed somewhat distorted, but was still clearly recognisable as the individual who'd called him in the *Frontier* with the Walltex tip.

'As always. Walltex man?'

'The very same. Impressed?' A brief silence ensued before Calum replied. He looked around and checked that no one could overhear him on the news floor. Given that nothing special had elapsed over the past week, he'd hear the guy out.

Calum spoke quietly. 'Who was your source for Walltex? You had to have inside information on that one.'

'Not your concern. But I'm sure that tipping winning stocks would be good for you. Your readership would grow. If you were able to obtain regular information you'd get the heads up on real movers...before the market moved.'

'Mmm. What's your name?'

'No need for names.'

'Okay. So are you a one hit wonder? What, your uncle or brother works at Walltex and gave you the nod?'

'Actually, no. You'd be surprised what I know. I have access to information others don't.'

'Really? So why are you telling me this? Your Walltex tip was too late for my benefit, as you know.' Calum detected that the man was considering his reply as the gap in conversation was too long.

'I needed to demonstrate my ability to predict stock changes. If you're not interested, I'll take my business elsewhere.'

'Business? I'm sorry, but we've no budget to pay for information here. This industry has changed.'

'I'm speaking in metaphorical terms.'

Calum pondered what this might mean. 'So what exactly is it you're offering?'

'To provide you with special market insights. Unique pieces of information that you can publicise in your column. I will remain anonymous, but will provide you with some information in good time. You would have sole rights to this information, but you would have to remain silent as to the source. No discussions with others, or my offer will be withdrawn.' The strange modulation in the voice disguised the underlying motivations, whatever they were, so Calum asked the obvious question.

'Why me? If you have special information as you say, why not wait until corporate announcements are made officially? If making money is your objective, why not contact a number of analysts or tipsters? Why do you need to have tips publicised solely by me?' Calum hesitated, briefly considering that he might be repelling a perfectly good source.

'Because I like your column, and it would be mutually beneficial. *Trust me.* There will be a package arriving by courier at about two o'clock on Thursday afternoon to your office. Be around and use what's inside accordingly. It will keep things anonymous.'

'Okay.' Calum reflected momentarily on Powell's threat.

Hawk could tell that Calum was motivated. Those negative emails to Rod Powell must have been making an impact. Excellent. 'You'll gain more readers.' The voice remained flat. 'But you could also have the opportunity to make an absolute packet.'

Chapter 3

Max Telford's drum-beating rhetoric about convictions had now been affirmed through strict new targets. This was his style; like the discharge from a double-barrelled shotgun, direct reports always awaited the second blast. At her desk, Aurelia rubbed her temple, feeling an almost physical weight pressing down on her as she read through the detail. She lifted her coffee cup, which had been placed on a post-it pad she'd previously stuck on the desk, and noticed that a semi-circular stain neatly framed the words 'Limderon/Walltex'. This was the story she'd seen on the website that Max Telford had recommended. She scrunched up the post-it and aimed it at the waste paper bin, but missed. As she sighed and retrieved the paper, she hesitated, before recalling the names that she'd written down. What was it—some kind of pharmaceutical product that had hit the news?

Nosiness prevailed, and a quick online search revealed the details. The shares had gone through the roof after an announcement of the approval of the Limderon cancer drug by the American FDA, the Holy Grail for the pharmaceutical industry. Aurelia's interest was kindled as she intuitively began to access recent share price charts for the stock. Various software tools offered such immediate charting, where users could quickly assess the pattern of trading for a stock, or an index, in durations stretching from a few minutes to several years.

She was trained to analyse stock price movements in the run up to major announcements—statements about business dealings that were legally confidential until publicised. The FCA software employed complex algorithms to identify odd trading movements and related price spikes, but this was only half the story. The difficult thing was to separate lawful speculation from insider trading. Where firms were under scrutiny due to ongoing analysis pertaining to well known issues, speculators legitimately invested funds before major decisions. However, where well kept secrets were concerned, Aurelia's role was to ascertain if there were any suspicious price spikes prior to related announcements. The trading volume data for Walltex for early on the day of the announcement contained nothing suspicious. Volume had been low, suggesting that investors, close to the point, were indeed ignorant of the imminent news from the FDA. The company itself had not made any prior comment on the FDA's imminent approval. However, when she viewed a chart for one week prior to the announcement, and itemised the number of trades and the related prices, something unusual caught her attention. She found that several investments of exactly thirteen thousand shares—equating to around twenty thousand pounds in value each—had been made in each of the five days prior to the FDA approval. All the trades had been made first thing in the morning.

Often investors liked to spread risk—using price averaging—over a period of time. Where 'accumulate' recommendations were posted by analysts this tended to happen. However, a quick check of the timeline suggested that there had been no such recommendation from the main analysts or tipsters. Indeed, had such advice been published, the share price would almost certainly have risen before the FDA announcement as this was a company with a relatively small market capitalisation. She checked again over a longer time span, and ran a simple statistical regression, looking for a correlation between news items about the firm, and price movements. The software that the FCA employed allowed such analysis. However, no correlation was evident. Although at this stage she did not know the identity of the buyer, it seemed logical that the same individual or firm would be responsible for trades of exactly the same value at the same time over five days—a *pattern*. However, where insider traders were attempting to conceal such trading, they tended *not* to transact in such a manner, for fear of drawing undesired scrutiny.

Aurelia also verified that there had been no major share purchases by Walltex directors in the preceding period. By law, directorial purchases were announced publically, and again, tended to impact on the share price of a stock, especially if sizeable. Therefore, someone else had made this series of investments, and Aurelia's nose for dirty dealing was duly aroused. The financial values, at around twenty thousand each, were not huge, but then she considered that the conviction in which she'd been instrumental— Daniel Fleeting's insider trading case with Chistec Electronics—was for a lower total value. Aurelia then accessed the trading data providing details of buyers' identities. This was obtained by the FCA under licence, and she had to login separately due to the privacy laws protecting confidentiality. Within a couple of minutes she ascertained that the five investments had been made through an online broker based in London, on behalf of an investment firm called Black Isle, which was registered in the Cayman Islands.

Footsteps then alerted her to the presence of Adam Smart, who approached her desk, momentarily diverting his eyes to scan her computer screen. Aurelia swivelled swiftly in her chair to make direct eye contact with him, almost daring him to avoid her stare. The Walltex issue might come to nothing but she was damned if she'd let Adam snoop on a lead, however tenuous.

'Busy?' he enquired, rubbing his sideburns, which were unfashionably long, almost reminiscent of the Victorian era. Adam rarely made small talk without an ulterior motive, so Aurelia folded her arms, deliberately attempting to repel him.

'Is there any other mode?' She continued the eye contact.

'You know Aurelia, we really are very similar. Industrious, incredibly focused on meeting targets. What say we *combine* our strengths? Just think of the results we could obtain if we joined forces? We could share the rewards.' Adam ventured one of those smarmy smiles, almost perspiring deceit.

'You know, Adam, that's a *super* idea. If you drum up some data for a major conviction, or use your brilliant detective skills to sniff out some interesting leads, I'd *love* to be the first to know. *Please* don't hesitate.' She tilted her head, awaiting a response.

'Yeah…and likewise,' he said flatly, trying to view her screen. 'Just you let me know of anything similar in *your* case load.' His words tailed off as he retreated, Aurelia returning to her screen to peruse the Walltex trades in a little more detail.

Just after 2:00 p.m. on Thursday afternoon Calum received a call from security personnel about a special delivery. The courier insisted that he sign for it personally, so he duly obliged. Instinctively, he knew that the package was from the unidentified tipster. Inside was a single phone. The arrival of the phone was puzzling; yes, he'd been told to expect a package, but why was he being sent a phone? The caller had had his contact number after all. He put the phone in his jacket pocket and went back upstairs to the newsroom to grab a coffee before finishing off a piece on an advertising agency merger on which he'd been working.

As he pondered a piece of prose—legalese that would satisfy the in-house lawyers on a specific point—he switched on the phone, noticing that a text had appeared. Apparently, a call would be received imminently. Within a couple of minutes the phone buzzed.

'It's good to see that you're following instructions.' The now familiar, odd voice, spoke steadily.

Calum shot straight back. 'Why all the subterfuge? I do have a phone, as you know.'

'This is for your own safety. The phone's unconnected to you, so you can receive calls from me and be assured of your own metaphorical distance.'

'Okay…I guess I can live with that,' Calum said, lowering his voice. 'So, do you have some perceptive tip for me, or what?'

'I do as a matter of fact. X4D4.'

'X4D4. Gambling?' Calum asked, grabbing a notepad.

'Yes, online in China. Got a pen? This firm is about hit the jackpot. Next Tuesday—the 24th—they'll announce a special share issue. The

Chinese Government is going to take a third of a new expanded firm. It's got to be passed by shareholders, of course, but that will be a formality as the stock will rocket.'

'Not heard any rumours about this one, I have to say.'

'I promised you new, insightful information. But you must not speak to anyone about this until you place your copy. No digging with the company itself, okay? It could harm the deal, and if you do you will get nothing else from me. You must give a strong recommendation but not mention any source specifically. Say something like the firm is ripe for expansion, and undervalued given its contacts with the Asian regulatory authorities. Sell it up without being too explicit.'

'And what's the Chinese Government going to do? Give X4D4 access to the provinces or something? Are they looking for increased tax?'

'No specifics. You can work it out for yourself. Online stuff is expanding like mad in China, despite what some people here think.'

'Well...I guess that I should say thanks.'

'You should. I may be in touch again. I will call you on this phone. And *do not* make any calls to anyone at the firm to ask about this information under any circumstances. Got that?'

'Okay, I promise I won't call anyone.' The caller signed off and Calum bit his index finger nail. X4D4? He vaguely recalled the firm because he remembered someone who headed up an investment bank that had raised capital for them, and he'd seen a piece in the FT about the guy afterwards. Nigel Tomlinson, who worked at Pan-Euro Investment Bank. The guy had been an acquaintance of sorts at university. Calum hadn't been that keen on him however, as Tomlinson exuded something beyond confidence, a disdain of others simply for being different. Perhaps the connection to Tomlinson wasn't that much of a coincidence as the alumni from certain universities were in positions of power in a number of large institutions in London, and internationally. Tomlinson had come from a privileged upbringing, and been primed for a high flying career through his family connections. Calum had felt that Tomlinson had merely tolerated him in university through a very thin veneer of public etiquette, and as such, he'd not seen him for some time.

As with all stock tips, he firstly accessed the analysts' ratings for X4D4. A couple had recommended the stock as a hold, yet others suggested that competition from firms based in more benign jurisdictions could threaten the company's longer term viability. There were no current 'buy' recommendations, and no recent news stories that suggested the company was in line for a windfall from the Chinese Government, or anything else of that nature. Then Calum considered the Walltex story. If he'd been given the thumbs up by this mysterious caller in enough time, perhaps he could have used it as a winning piece of stock advice and Powell would have been off his case. Today, there had been nothing concrete that he could write up for the main column.

Powell had been emphatic: he had just three weeks.

Stuff it, he'd write up the story as a single, focused tip for Sunday. A brief slice of research revealed that the firm had enjoyed a lacklustre year. Calum amalgamated the salient facts, explaining that X4D4 was likely to hit an imminent oriental jackpot. The tenor of the article included old clichés such as the need to speculate to accumulate, though he also explained that gambling was an addiction that hadn't been fully targeted by certain governments in a similar manner to tobacco or alcohol. In effect, it offered a licence to print money. Calum alluded to the uninspiring performance of the stock over the past twelve months as some kind of paradoxical rationale for its advancement. He rubbished recent analysts' reports suggesting that the firm was poorly managed, and suggested that the current price-to-earnings ratio could be interpreted in this sector as a signal for spectacular growth.

Such prophecies were rarely accurate, but where the exception proved the rule the invariable source had to be inside information. Calum was fully aware of this fact, as would be some readers, so he framed the piece with no source. He'd no intention of buying the stock personally or recommending it to friends before publication. Such would have been unethical. That way he could forge ahead with a clear conscience because the means by which the anonymous tipster had acquired the information was not his concern. If the tip proved to be a bummer, he would lose his job. Yet, he could lose his job anyway.

Calum approached Powell in his office so he could clear the story at this juncture while he felt confident. Powell raised his eyebrows as Calum relayed the gist of the X4D4 case, minus the crucial part relating to the anonymous caller.

'That's it?' Powell folded his arms. 'You know, normally I'd bomb something like this out. You want to use your entire column to recommend one single stock that has been going nowhere? After all that I said to you last week, this is your response? There has to be a genuine reason for a recommendation. Do you know someone at the company?'

'Actually, I know someone loosely connected, but I haven't spoken to him. This is based on independent research and gut instinct.'

Powell swivelled in his chair before holding up his finger in a pistol shape. There were the beginnings of a smile on his lips, which was never a beneficial sign.

'Okay, suits me. You've said that the news is imminent, so I will await the said news. If you want to hang yourself, fine.'

'Rod—to keep you happy, if you want I'll drop in a paragraph about another stock.' But Powell had already turned round again, indicating that the conversation was over.

As he returned to his desk, Calum experienced sudden anxiety, akin to the post purchase cognitive dissonance that people feel after buying an expensive product. That sensation of having taken an unnecessary risk in the absence of solid facts or experience, thereby courting potential disaster.

Should he really stake his career on the advice of some weirdo who he'd never actually encountered in the flesh, and who refused to be identified? The man had given one solid tip which had been insightful, yet he might lose his job on the basis of a second leap of faith. Shit, Powell had seemed pleased, almost willing the stock to bomb in order that he could justify Calum's sacking. Had Powell himself arranged the call?

Calum ran his fingers through his dark hair, before looking up the number for Nigel Tomlinson at Pan-Euro. Then he paused before dialling. The mysterious tipster had explicitly barred calls to anyone, and he'd promised to keep his counsel. He'd not spoken to Tomlinson for some time, and if he were honest, he didn't particularly wish to converse with the man. Tomlinson had been a snob as a student, stuffy to the point of condescension. The only virtue he'd possessed had been his circle of friends, many of them generally decent individuals, and in social networks Calum knew that there were always individuals at the edges who didn't gel yet still retained group membership because of the wider communal advantages that such networks offered.

Calum hesitated once again, but then popped out into the corridor to make the call. He didn't have Tomlinson's personal number so he called the bank's number and mentioned to Tomlinson's secretary that he was an old friend from university and as he was placed on hold he considered the warning not to make any calls about X4D4. What difference would it make? His need to judge the validity of the information outweighed any potential embarrassment in asking Tomlinson for a comment.

'Nigel Tomlinson speaking.'

'Hi Nigel. It's Calum Mack here. It's a while since we've spoken.'

'What's going on here?' Tomlinson asked.

Calum frowned before replying. 'Eh…just thought I'd give you a ring, that's all. I'm a columnist now. For the *Sentinel*.'

'I bloody well know that! What is it you want?' Tomlinson's voice became raised.

'No need to become angry, Nigel. Just wondered if you could confirm anything about one of the firms your bank advises, X4D4? Is the firm due for expansion in Asia?'

'What? I'm saying nothing more.'

The call ended abruptly.

Calum scratched his head, pondering Tomlinson's attitude. It appeared that he was harbouring some kind of grudge. Calum hadn't previously written anything in the column about Pan-Euro, X4D4, or any other company connected to the man, so either he'd retained some kind of loathing for Calum from their days at university, or else he was cracking up. In his relatively short period as a journalist, Calum had taken some heated calls, but these were usually as a consequence of something he'd *already* written rather than an item which he was researching. Tomlinson had said he knew of Calum's role at the *Sentinel*, so he'd obviously not mistaken him for someone else.

Calum bit his upper lip as he returned to his desk, pensive. Perhaps Tomlinson would only have reacted the way he did if he *did* have something to hide. What had the anonymous tipster said? That the deal might collapse if too much was revealed? Maybe Tomlinson was under pressure, losing the plot because of the need to keep a major deal under wraps until an announcement was officially made? Appeasing capricious, powerful and perhaps unfathomable Chinese officials? Yes, this made sense. The man might have been fielding calls from other people about the same issue, and could have been ready to snap.

He checked the share price for X4D4 once more. It had slipped a few pence within the past few minutes, and he reminded himself that the stock was down 25 percent over twelve months. On that basis, he modified the story, focusing on how well the company was managed and the opportunities that Asia offered. For the sake of placating Powell, he also added an addendum about Walltex. Although the Walltex tip had been too late to publish or generate any credit, he mentioned the firm's success and hinted he'd been aware of the imminent FDA announcement. Slightly cheeky perhaps, but what the hell?

'I don't how you pulled it off, but one lucky strike doesn't constitute a gold rush,' Powell chirped at Calum, before walking back to his office. Calum felt damned by the faint, mixed metaphors. The X4D4 story had assaulted the headlines first thing on Tuesday morning, causing a deal of merriment in the newsroom. Everyone, it seemed, knew of Calum's impending dismissal and the subsequent nature of the reprieve appeared to have engendered a bizarre explosion of mirth. Suddenly, it was safe to make jokes as he'd earned another week of employment. Ben had congratulated him personally, again having enquired as to the source of the recommendation. Calum had remained silent as he had pretty much done since taking the role. Colleagues often wanted the nod, aware that a winning tip from Calum ahead of publication could be farmed out to some apparently unconnected acquaintance or long lost aunt in order to generate a little supplementary income. Yet Calum had retained a sense of propriety over the privileged information that he'd acquired.

Amazingly, the X4D4 share price had more than doubled. The company had successfully brokered a deal to facilitate and radically develop online gambling in China, an event that no one on the outside world had predicted. Calum considered Tomlinson, the ultimate lucky bastard. The man would make a substantial sum from this deal through his bank's advisory fees, his charmed existence emblematic of the notion that money often does indeed 'go to money'. Calum still couldn't entirely explain Tomlinson's discourtesy on the phone, but put it down to potential fear of affecting the deal. The column he'd submitted had been resolute in its recommendation of X4D4, but unspecific about the details, and there had been no contact from Tomlinson on Monday after publication, so the guy couldn't have been too bothered. A couple of hacks from competitive publishers had called to enquire about his source, but again he remained silent, savouring his stay of execution.

Hawk had enjoyed himself over the weekend. He'd relished the concept of treating himself to a professional girl on Saturday night, funded by a tiny percentage of his recent gains. The girl was just eighteen, a nervous blonde of eastern European extraction, perhaps coerced into the game through addiction, people trafficking or violence. But Hawk didn't care. He'd paid six hundred pounds for her company, so how could she complain? He'd never enjoyed successful relationships with women, his awkward, introverted nature clothing him like a leper's skin. He was aware that women were attracted to warmth, humour, trust or money, only one of which he could now offer, and even that commodity had been in short supply until recently. But that was going to change, thanks to his plan. And in any case, he didn't want ties. When this project was through, he'd escape to better climes, able to afford all the hookers he wanted.

He was also keen to leave his current apartment— a tiny, one bedroom rented flat in Hammersmith—which was well below what he had anticipated for himself in his optimistic youth. He sometimes reminded himself of the comparison between where he'd grown up, this flat, and the hell of the prison cell in which he'd spent time; the difference being that the flat afforded a springboard to better things, and the opportunity to fund his plan.

His next call required a degree of subtlety. The target, a junior energy minister at Westminster, was not only difficult to get hold of, but subject to a level of scrutiny and legal governance that would require Hawk to choose his words very carefully. Blackmail was far from a novel concept within politics, but the checks and balances today were greater than had been the case previously, as politicians had lost the confidence of the public, the civil service and perhaps most of all, each other. The bastards deserved greater scrutiny, Hawk thought, though at this juncture he wished to tread cautiously as the balance of power between him and the target was less than transparent. They'd spoken once recently, without commitment on the part of the politician. Hawk had been told of the problem of timing, and this individual had the power to destroy his scheme, Hawk knew, so he needed to emphasise once again the reverse; how he, Hawk, had the power to destroy the politician.

'I wish to speak to Anthony Rowland.' Hawk spoke slowly, his voice modification app once again adding a distinctly different accent.

'Mr Rowland is unavailable,' a male voice responded, probably Rowland's private secretary. Hawk already knew that Rowland was in Whitehall at his office because his schedule was a matter of public record.

'This is extremely urgent. It is imperative that Mr Rowland calls me back immediately. Let him know that it's about the *investment*.' Hawk had already explained to Rowland that he would use this code word in the next communication. He left the number of the phone he was currently using, and made himself a coffee, awaiting a response.

He waited around half an hour before Rowland called.

'You're treading on very dangerous ground. I'm not even going to mention your name, as I do not wish to be associated with you or say anything that could be recorded. And I have not contacted anyone via social networking anyway as it would also leave an imprint. What you are doing is strictly illegal, and I could have you arrested. Have you considered that?' Hawk imagined Rowland in some austere musty office, with leather chairs and embossed wallpaper.

'What *you did* was strictly illegal. A tad more illegal than a touch of blackmail, wouldn't you say? You have substantially more to lose than I have.'

'Really? You sound odd, different. Has the city changed your accent as well as your sense of moral fibre?'

'I am aware that I sound different, and it is deliberate.'

'I am not sure that I understand that. But what I do comprehend is that you are playing a perilous game. I have the power to have your life turned upside down.' However, Rowland's voice partly communicated a sense of uncertainty, so Hawk attacked.

'Do you think I'm stupid enough not to have copies of the evidence? Should anything happen to me, you will come toppling down. It doesn't take much these days, public perception and all, not to mention the costs of employing divorce lawyers.'

A momentary silence ensued before Rowland replied. 'You know, I considered what you requested after our first conversation. I don't like corruption or blackmail. It may surprise you, but not all politicians are bent. Some of us have scruples.'

'You should have thought about that before the night in question. But in this case you're going to make an exception, aren't you?' Hawk could hear a change in tone that indicated Rowland was going to acquiesce.

'Once and *once only*. You are extremely lucky that I can offer you something at this point in time. Come back at me again though, and I'll blow you out of the water.'

'Cut the counter threats. What have you got for me?'

Hawk listened intently, jotting down the details. Rowland occupied a position of trust in the government, which was ideal for Hawk's purposes. It meant that Rowland could glean crucial information without raising suspicion of duplicity. Senior ministers needed to confide in junior ministers as a matter of efficacy in making policy, and junior ministers were usually selected on the prime criterion of loyalty and trust before any other attributes. Thus, Hawk had set Rowland the task of acquiring pieces of highly confidential information from senior sources, in the expectation that something could be used for financial gain. The man was scared, thus motivated.

The first piece of information concerned what was due to happen in relation to the stake the state owned in a renewable energy consortium, Unreal Power, in which it had invested for strategic reasons. The consortium produced products for domestic generation of electricity. There had been significant speculation that the Government would sell its stake. However, Rowland happened to know what decisions had been made on the future of renewable energy, including the level of subsidy being offered to homeowners for micro-generation. It turned out that the public purse would invest additional substantial sums in the firm imminently, meaning that those who currently held stock privately in the venture, or who bought at current prices, stood to make a killing.

The second sliver of inside knowledge concerned macro-economic management. Rowland had a close friend, an academic from Cambridge, who sat on the Bank of England's monetary policy committee. The committee was supposed to be free from political manipulation, yet the decisions they made were ultimately influenced at least indirectly by political policy. Thus, politicians had an extremely close interest in the committee's proceedings. Although the minutes of each quarterly meeting were published before the next meeting, meaning that the recent interpretations and views of the various members were public knowledge, what could not be readily predicted was a change of heart, for example, when a hawk suddenly morphed into a dove. Intriguingly, Rowland's friend on the committee intended to change his voting pattern, together with another two colleagues. As the committee was currently polarised, Rowland explained that his friend was now due to argue, along with two others for a reduction of half of one percent in interest rates. As Hawk listened intently to Rowland, he considered the value of this information: a fall in interest rates, and thus a fall in the value of sterling, would mean that selling the currency short could net a tidy sum. Speculatively buying a foreign currency such as the dollar before a rate change could also provide short term profit, all things being even. Even if interest rates did not move, if the minutes of the MPC meeting reflected unexpected sentiment to this effect by three committee members, it could still induce a fall in the currency as the markets interpreted that such a move would come the following month.

When the call ended Hawk smiled to himself, content that he could manipulate others so easily. How could they be so inept, these so called champions of industry? Those pillars of commerce and politics. They were failures; they just didn't know it yet.

Hawk accessed the account he had set up in the Cayman Islands. He admitted to himself that the favourable timing of stock movements so far had worked well for him, but then he had spent a lot of time getting fearful people motivated. His recent sale of shares in Walltex and X4D4 had netted a six figure sum in profits, which meant that he had the resources to make some real money this time. Using the same mobile phone he had used to contact Rowland, he invested around a third of his funds to take out three positions against sterling. The odds were good. Next he purchased shares in the alternative energy firm that Rowland had tipped, using the remaining available funds in the account. When the transactions were complete he made himself a coffee and contemplated the fun he was going to have. Previously, he'd toyed over whether the account could believably be established in the name of the individual he'd had in mind, and in the end the emotional need for revenge had conquered the minor irrationality of the plan.

Chapter 4

The Citadel overlooked the Thames on the South Bank near Blackfriars, the river being one of the primary attractions for its eclectic clientele. The menu boasted a number of dishes largely unknown outside the owner's native Tuscany. Max Telford scrutinised its contents as if interpreting a complex financial document, briefly removing his bifocals to peer at the detail.

'Just how many of these dishes are presented on a bed of bullshit?' he asked rhetorically. 'It's as bad as annual accounts these days. Flowery language aimed at disguising the truth. Those bloody marketing people should stay out of finance.'

'And restaurant menus,' Aurelia replied, sipping a glass of perfectly chilled Pouilly Fume. Although business lunches weren't high on her list of priorities, the invitation from Telford offered a welcome break from the grind of the office; an opportunity to put her case in the absence of Adam or any of the other career wolves. And Telford rarely blew the expense account—a puritan streak usually outgunning the need to eat—so any diversion was refreshing. They both ordered Caesar salads.

Telford replaced his glasses, refocusing on his direct report. 'The politicians are pushing for more convictions. Got a call again this morning. You know, Aurelia, I've got a lot of faith in you, especially after the Fleeting case. You've proved you can deliver. What's new—anything in the pipeline? Did you check out that website I told you about?'

Aurelia paused briefly. She could choose to moan about her current workload, or take an optimistic stance about new possibilities. What would Adam do?

'Yes, I did actually. And there are some interesting new possibilities, Max.'

'Go on.'

'Well…there's something else I'd like to say first.'

'Okay,' he replied, arching his eyebrows.

'I'd like the opportunity to pursue something myself. Can I speak in confidence?'

'Of course.'

'It's just that I'd like to really prove myself—to see if I can work a whole case on my own from inception to conclusion.'

Telford pursed his lips. 'We take a team approach to big cases, you know that. What's on your mind? Got a sniff of a big fish?'

'Possibly. And I'll be straight, Max. You got where you are today through hard work and personal reward. Is it so bad for me to desire the same thing?'

Telford grinned, sipping his wine. 'You know, I do see something of my younger self in you. But as the director, I've got to wear a different hat. Yes, I've got to motivate and nurture, but that applies to everyone. I've got to assess team cohesion, employ people by utilising their greatest strengths. Everyone deserves to be included in big projects. And some people have skills that are more subtle. Take Adam, for example.'

She looked away, frustrated. 'Yes, Adam. I wondered how long you'd take to bring him up.'

'Look, I realise that you two don't get on that well. It's not unusual, given that you probably see each other as rivals. Maybe for my job?'

Aurelia held her hands out in protest. 'Max…'

'I'm joking, at least for now. I'm not retiring just yet.'

'So what about my request?'

'Look, I do need stars. Every organisation does. Run your lead past me and we can make a decision on it right now. Fair?'

'Fair. This is just a hunch, but I spotted something on that site that might be part of a bigger sting. Walltex, heard of it?'

'Walltex? Vague recollection. Is it a drug firm?' She could tell from his reaction that she had his attention.

'Yes. They just made a breakthrough with a new cancer drug called Limderon. It recently got FDA approval in the States, so the shares rocketed. It appears that the firm kept quiet about the possibility of the announcement. They appear to have played straight, officially. However, I ran a check of recent trades for the week before and there was…well, an unusual set of purchases. Five purchases of around 20K, spread out evenly, bought via an online broker and registered to a company in Grand Cayman called Black Isle.'

'Interesting,' Telford said, seemingly pleased with the endeavour Aurelia had displayed—there was an almost imperceptible look of pride in her work as he watched her. 'So you think that someone wasn't so surprised by the announcement?'

'Exactly.'

'It could just be speculation, though I must say it looks curious. Any buy or accumulate recommendations by brokers or analysts?'

'Nope. Did the usual cross-checks. I wondered, given the geography, if someone in the FDA in the States might have tipped a pal, who traded via the Caribbean. We could alert the Yanks, of course, but we're not paid to do their research, so I delved a little further.'

Telford's expression indicated that his curiosity had indeed been tickled. 'Good work, Aurelia. Go on.'

'Well, this is the interesting part. I'm going to contact an old friend who works in Grand Cayman, and he might be able to ascertain the owner of this Black Isle company. He's got contacts in all the banks, but also with the authorities over there. Their confidentiality laws are tight as you know, but there are ways. It may take a little time, but I'm owed a favour.'

'That's excellent.'

Aurelia smiled. 'The hunch I referred to is that I think the buyer has links right here in London.'

Telford scratched his chin. 'How would you know that?'

'I ran another check on trades through the same firm, and it offloaded the Walltex stock, generating a tidy profit, but also bought and sold stock in a firm quoted on the London Stock Exchange. Similar pattern, five trades spread out before a big announcement, and then a quick sale, post hoc. I take it that you read the business media on Sunday?'

'*Sunday Times* and *Sunday Telegraph*. Why?'

'Well, the second set of trades was in X4D4, the casino and gambling firm.'

Telford looked upwards. 'I seem to remember reading something— about China, was it?'

'Correct. I did a quick online search of news articles before the announcement and it turns out that this stock was tipped by the *Sunday Sentinel* just beforehand, against the run of play. The company was going nowhere until this piece of news. And again, there was virtually no speculation about the deal anywhere else, so how did the columnist know?'

'This is very interesting indeed. Who writes the column?'

'A bloke called Calum Mack. Used to work in investment banking.'

Telford hesitated briefly. 'Haven't heard of him. I wonder where he got his information. You know what hacks are like; these guys cultivate sources all over the place.'

'That's true. But in the same column, he mentioned that he'd known of the *Walltex* deal before it happened. What's the chances of that?' Aurelia sat back in her chair, letting Telford soak up this information.

'Really? That's a hell of a coincidence. You think that Mack is a player? Inside info, buying, tipping publically, then selling? He'd be crazy to do a thing like that. And why would he announce knowledge of something like the Walltex thing after the event? Even if it's through a Caribbean holding company, if he's in a prominent media position he'd be taking a risk. We should wait to see if there's more to come.'

Aurelia smiled. 'My thoughts exactly. Why alert him that we might be onto him if there *is* more to come? You were on about catching bigger fish, after all. I hope to know more when I speak to my friend. Or if there's another set of trades through this Black Isle lot, we can see if there's a trail.'

'Yes, as they say, two's a coincidence, and three, well…'

'I'll email my contact in the Cayman Islands later today—make some enquiries. So I can go for it?'

'Absolutely, Aurelia. Definitely go for it.'

Calum had received a second phone at the office, accompanied by the same set of instructions: the phone was again only to be used for receiving calls from the unknown party. The first phone was to be kept securely at his home, as it might be used again later depending on instructions. Although he felt confused as to why the mystery tipster would go to the bother of such subterfuge, he conceded the point, accepting that future tips were dependent upon agreement for this specific point of 'security'. Despite the ribbing he'd received at the office about his job being only temporary, he experienced a strange feeling—perhaps unwarranted—of his luck having changed.

On Friday, when the expected call came on the new phone bearing the next tip—this time regarding government policy—Calum's initial scepticism began to subside as he felt a small degree of power, having acquired what could be very influential information. Interest rate changes? Hell, would Powell allow him to drift onto macro-economic policy in his column? He'd asked the caller if he could include the information in a separate column, but the instruction had been very specific—keep it in the usual column, and justify it any way he liked. He wanted readers, didn't he? And a reputation? Calum enquired how the caller could possibly know about monetary policy decisions in advance, being fully aware of the sensitivities of voting intentions in the Monetary Policy Committee. His curiosity had, naturally, been aroused, though he was again rebuffed on the 'need to know' basis.

Momentarily, Calum considered the upside…how prior knowledge about an unexpected rate reduction of half of one percent, if accurate, could be utilised to tip a number of shares in addition to the obvious issue of currency speculation itself. There was also a counter argument in that the consequences of rate changes could be difficult to interpret if other central banks acted in concert—competitor currencies might also be planning parallel rate reductions. However, he checked the latest analysis for both sterling and other major currencies, and there were no specific recommendations about imminent rate changes. Thus, the anonymous caller was either extremely well connected, or a master of invention.

What was even more peculiar was that a second tip was forthcoming: also in relation to official policy. This news was not to be employed until the following week, but Calum was told that it was a sure thing: the Government would increase its investment in Unreal Power, the consortium in which it had previously invested in order to keep the green lobby content. The initial decision to invest had been taken for strategic reasons but the shares would now produce an excellent future yield as the subsidy for micro generation was also going to rise. In essence, the Government was going to benefit directly from its own policies. It also meant that other existing shareholders would make a packet; and potentially those who acted promptly on a tip he might make in his column. Again, Calum fielded a number of questions about how the tipster ascertained the information but he was rebuffed with the now familiar warning that no more advice would be forthcoming unless he cut the questions and followed instructions.

The MPC meeting didn't take place until the following Thursday, so Calum began digging into firms that would benefit more immediately from a fall in the value of the pound. He made an initial draft of his Sunday column, suggesting two companies specialising in exporting, and one engineering firm that was subject to foreign acquisition. He decided that the column should be framed as if a rate fall was a given, despite the fact that there was little objective evidence to support the view. Powell would probably complain that he was drifting away, using supposition rather than solid intelligence, but what the hell? Calum was knowledgeable enough to comprehend that there was always a downside to such unexpected interest rate announcements—sometimes they spooked the markets, creating fears—but in this case half of one percent would probably be tolerated.

When Ben approached his desk, he jumped in fright as he had been so engrossed in his work. 'Jesus, Ben, don't creep up on me like that.'

'It's a fucking open plan office, you dough ball! How can anyone *creep* up?' Ben grinned, chewing gum and resting his arm on Calum's screen. 'What's so important anyway?' He squinted at the screen, so Calum adjusted his position.

'It's an email from my great, great, great, great-grandmother. She's ascending Everest as we speak.'

'Wow! That sounds…*great*, so she's probably got more fucking life in her than you have these days. Hey, fancy a blow-out after work? A few shooters, then a night out on the town? Get rid of those cobwebs in your boxers? I know we're in here tomorrow, but fuck it, let's chase some of these office girls who want screwed after a hard week running after some tosser of a boss.' He looked around, and then thumbed in the direction of Powell's office. 'Except not any of those girls in here because I've bedded all the decent ones already.'

'And they all love you dearly for it, as I've discovered during those staffroom coffee chats.'

'I never kiss and tell, mate,' Ben said as he ran a finger across his lips. 'Blowjobs, however, I tell everyone about.'

'So you actually haven't a clue as to who this guy is? Honestly?' Ben sat with his legs resting on a low oak table, Peroni bottle in hand.

'No, I don't,' said Calum.

Ben shook his head, berating Calum's deficient investigative skills. It had taken a mere beer and a half for Ben to erode Calum's attempts at concealment. They were lodged in the corner of a busy bar three blocks from the office, top buttons undone, and tongues loosened.

'I'd have identified the source within a day. See, the difference between you and me is that you're an investment banker who is masquerading as a hack. I'm a hack, pretending to know a bit about business. Plain and simple. The only reason that I write for the business section is that it pays more. I don't give a toss about business, and I certainly don't give a toss about smoke and mirrors or threats from sources. And what's all this shit about phones?' Ben put on a goofy look and held imaginary phones to both his ears.

'I haven't worked out why the phones are needed,' Calum said, folding his arms. Ben roared with laughter, eventually forcing a smile out of Calum. When it was highlighted, it did seem a little over the top.

'Right Sherlock, you should let *me* speak to this guy. I'll sort the fucker out, figure out why he's so benevolent. Why he's keeping Vodafone in business—hey, that could be his next tip! Or maybe he'll give *me* new some tips if I speak to him. I could just buy the bloody stocks and forget the column. What's to stop *that* happening if the tips are so good? They're talking about another famous *Sentinel* wage freeze this year anyway, and the price of booze in places like this just keeps rising.'

'Ben, I need my job, remember? This is the only thing that has kept Powell off my back. He's expecting something of me now, so I'm going to exploit this thing as long as I can.'

'There are no free lunches, mate,' Ben said, sipping his Peroni.

'He's not asked for anything and I'm not buying any stock. All we're doing is a bit of mutual back scratching.'

'So what's Sunday's tip, then?'

'I can't say. It's a bit different this time, to do with policy more that a direct tip.'

'Some pal you are. What is it?' Ben raised an eyebrow.

'Can't say,' Calum blurted, a little too quickly.

Ben shuffled on his seat. 'You'd be a useless poker player, you know that? If he knows about the *Government's* policy and stuff like that he's very well connected. Or an ace hacker.'

'I think he's just got some contacts, that's all.'

'I dunno, mate. Seems a bit odd to me.'

'No, but there's something odd right there,' Calum said surreptitiously. Ben stretched round to see to what Calum referred.

'Aha! She's all yours, mate,' Ben said, eyeing a huge woman in a flowery dress who stood by the bar, holding a glass of Champagne.

'Hey, I'm not leaving until you give us a song, darling!' Ben shouted loudly, drawing scowls from the woman herself and a few other customers.

Calum intervened, shouting over the group. 'Sorry guys, we'll be leaving shortly.'

'Oh, screw her Calum…though only if you want to be crushed. Come on, you should *live* a bit.' Ben slapped him on the back and got up.

They moved onto an upmarket club at Victoria Embankment called *Viva*, with Ben determined to have a blow-out. The place was tastefully designed, bedecked with an amalgam of marble and glass, and complemented by prices reflecting the decor. Ben had ventured there previously, boasting that he'd never failed to pick up. Calum didn't disbelieve him; Ben had that kind of easy charm to which women related— his persona just secure enough to appear reliable, yet cheeky enough to entertain and push the boundaries. On occasion he'd told a string of lies about being a professional footballer or city millionaire, though he'd admitted to Calum that this strategy could only work when the girls he was interested in were too drunk to check on their phones. Essentially, Ben was a metro-sexual man of the moment, and journalism and chasing women suited him as he had the drive to secure the next conquest but less interest in the longer term. Calum reflected that this was probably why they got on, in the sense they were not competing at all, Calum being a little more conservative and Ben being a bit of a chancer.

The two Dutch exchange students were in some respects easy prey. Ben had a theory that female students were particularly open to chat up by professional guys as they were unable to balance the books due to having acquired now unaffordable shopping addictions as teenagers, particularly in relation to shoes. International students were no exception, he argued, as the universal need to show off any form of heels in a paid-for, expensive environment outweighed any reservations that such single professional men only wanted one thing. As an added bonus, Ben knew just enough about fashion to sound sympathetic, understanding how to interpret the nuances of the Jimmy Choo shoe or the Prada handbag, whilst quoting from the pages of *City Gal*.

Ben had an extra bedroom at his place so after three bottles of Mumm the girls—Amber and Adele—agreed to a euphemistic coffee back at his pad. When Ben and Adele disappeared, Calum joked with Amber that this signalled a 'green' light for them. For some reason this kick-started the giggles for Amber, though this quickly expanded into a more amorous embrace before they entered the shower attached to the spare room. Amber proved to be more adventurous than her nineteen years would have implied, and their mutual desire exploded into powerful sex before they crashed out in bed.

All the guys had discussed was the prospect of sexual conquest. Everything appeared surreal, yet very real, but wasn't that what parties were all about? Before he knew it, he was strutting bravely across the dance floor with this tantalising blonde, and boy, was she into him! Was she Dutch or Scottish? He asked if she was called Amber, but she shouted something indistinguishable over that fabulous guitar solo in Sweet Child of Mine.

Then, from the ranks of the inebriated at the edge of the dance floor an enemy appeared, carrying some sort of weapon. What a prick. Despite how focused this all appeared, he was sure he'd experienced something identical before. The same guy, in the same place. Could that be possible? But when the girl led him away to the safety of a sofa, the idiot with the gun followed and demanded a fight. 'Outside! Outside!'

A misty haze enveloped the lane, and he tried desperately to see, as if his eyes were permanently glued shut. But then, suddenly, he witnessed colour, as vivid waves of crimson flooded down the street like an Atlantic breaker in winter. The enemy with the gun was desperately surging towards him in the tide with his arm around an old man, crying for help.

And then the police car floated from nowhere, powering amphibiously through the blood. Had it been anchored close by all the time? Siren. Lights. And in an almost choreographed response, a group of people recoiled back as they stood high above on a rooftop close by. 'Go…just go!' He heard the words in what could only be described as a shouted whisper. An insistent, clear instruction appealing to that base emotion called fear. A command.

And that's when he swam through the blood, before reaching dry ground, and they all ran, dispersing into the night. His legs were hammering, and he was open-mouthed, desperate to scream, but unable to utter a sound, arms thrashing out…

'Calum! What's wrong? Are you okay?' A girl's voice cut through the night like an axe.

'*Christ*…eh…yes…Julie…Amber? *Yes, Amber*…sorry.' Reality flooded back, his head pounding as the bedroom light suddenly dazzled him.

Amber peered directly at him. 'You hit me on the head! Was it a bad dream?' She stared, suddenly unsure whether to feel sympathetic or threatened.

'Yeah, sorry. Shit. I haven't had that, well, dream…for a while.' He sat up, running his fingers through his hair, feeling the warm sweat on his brow.

'I'd better go,' Amber said, quickly rising to put on her scattered clothes. 'You look like you could use a bed to yourself.'

'Amber…I'm sorry. Give me your phone number… maybe we can…go out sometime?' Calum rubbed his eyes.

'Yeah, sure… I'm sure that you can pick up a replacement to scare the shit out of tomorrow night.'

'Amber…'

'Forget it!'

And with that she quickly changed, gathered up her few belongings and left the bedroom. Less than two minutes later he heard the front door close.

He made the decision to call a cab himself and head home. The dream had jolted him, his recent confidence in life having suddenly been conflicted, the emotions now exacerbated by the dawning of a hangover in the dead of the night. Always in the dead of night.

Chapter 5

Calum began finalising the piece on the effects of a half-point interest rate change on Friday morning, pleased that he had begun the article the previous day. He hinted that a 'little bird' had told him of the impending change of heart by MPC members, and the likely subsequent influence on the following Thursday's interest rate vote. It hadn't been the first occasion he'd nursed a hangover at the office, and he pretended to have a heavy cold when someone commented on his rough exterior. Ben had called the office saying he'd an emergency visit to the dentist, prompting Calum to text Ben and ask if his dentist happened to be called Adele and come from Rotterdam. There had been no response. Ben had presumably fared better with Adele than he'd done with Amber. He'd almost knocked Amber out. How could you be accountable for your actions whilst asleep? He recalled the court case of a man who had stabbed his wife to death while apparently dreaming; at least that's what the judge and jury had believed.

He'd been instructed to wait until the following week before utilising the story about Unreal Power, though the journalist in him wanted to pre-empt any other snooping hack or analyst making a connection. This story had obviously originated from official sources, perhaps from the civil service or a politician, and politicians were notorious for leaking information to the media when it suited them.

Further public investment in Unreal Power contradicted the previous statements made by notable politicians. Not that hypocrisy was a surprising facet of political life. The energy market and related policy was something of a moveable feast in these times, difficult to predict due to the immense geopolitical factors that weighed upon the sector. The Government probably needed to put its money where its mouth was on alternative power, but there were related benefits for other shareholders so he would make this known in his column. As he sipped a coffee, he briefly pondered if a guy called Anthony Rowland might be able to confirm the story. It was a long shot. Rowland was another old acquaintance from university, one who'd chosen a political career and had done quite well, now occupying a junior ministerial role in the energy department.

Then Calum froze at his desk, the hair on the back of his neck instinctively rising.

How odd.

Anthony Rowland had actually been briefly cast in the nightmare of the previous evening. As he sat at his desk, he momentarily considered the normal dissipation of dream content during waking time, how it was often impossible for the conscious mind to retain the bizarre stories the subconscious invents during sleep. Yet this dream was different in two ways—not only had it been repeated so often in the past that his conscious mind had retained virtually all the pieces of an intangible jigsaw, but the cold, horrible reality was that the dream was based on an inconvenient truth. A truth that he had made significant efforts to eliminate from his conscious thoughts. It had been a while since the previous nocturnal episode, which was but minor consolation.

Should he phone Rowland? The strange caller had told him not to make contact with anyone about these tips. He tended to use his phone and blog to contact others rather than things like social media, but either way his writer's instinct and previous experience usually suggested that he double check any detail with knowledgeable sources wherever possible. However, after the angry reaction he'd experienced with Nigel Tomlinson in respect of the X4D4 story, he hesitated. But then his jaw suddenly tightened. Bizarrely, there was actually a connection between two of the tips he'd received—he actually knew of two people who were connected to these stories, Rowland and Tomlinson. These men also knew each other, and had *both* been in the dream, albeit vaguely. There was no apparent relationship between the stories themselves though—an online gambling development in China differed entirely from a public stake in a green energy company, but there was indeed a human connection.

Calum shook his head, and thought on reflection that he'd avoid Rowland for the time being. It would probably be impossible to get hold of him anyway, and no doubt he'd be told by some gatekeeper that such information was strictly confidential. Government officials and elected members were more wary of the media where absolute trust was an issue, and in any case Calum hadn't spoken to Rowland since before he'd been promoted to his ministerial role.

From the corner of his eye, he then spied Powell, who was making his way over. Powell sported a navy pinstripe suit and a red tie, which probably meant he'd been in a managerial meeting and would be on the warpath. Calum swallowed, and rubbed his eyes, keen to disguise the effects of the previous evening's alcoholic adventures.

'What have you got in mind for this Sunday's column?' No "hello", or any attempt at social niceties.

'Just about to forward it to you, Rod.'

'You look rough. I hope that your social life isn't obscuring the need to write well-researched work.' Powell folded his arms, staring. Calum stood up to make direct eye contact on the level.

'Actually, quite the reverse. I've a heavy cold, but I came in, in earnest, as I wanted to pursue a couple of really decent leads that I thought would fit the bill. I can send you the copy as soon as you get back to your office,' Calum said, attempting to deflect Powell's demand by return.

'Nice try. What is it you have?'

'Can we do this in your office?'

'Oh, if you must,' Powell said as Calum followed him back to his lair.

'Different angle this week, which I think readers will like.' Calum framed the line in the affirmative, as if the column would necessarily go ahead as planned. 'I'd rather keep this tacit at the moment, if possible. I can send it electronically.'

'Spit it out, for God's sake,' Powell said.

Calum lowered his voice. 'Okay…I have it on fairly good authority that there could be a half-point fall in rates.'

'What? How would you know that? That's pure speculation. And it's a long shot. The minutes of the last meeting were neutral on a rate change.'

'Well Rod, as you know the last column contained another tip that, if employed by readers, would have proved profitable very quickly. All I'm trying to do is keep up the momentum. I have cultured a couple of sources much closer to the action than I am, and I'm confident that the information on which the column is based is, well, prophetic.'

'Really? Who, exactly have you spoken to?' Powell frowned. 'Tell me that you're not bugging politicians or making bribes to officials? We've seen enough of that from the media in the past.'

Calum smiled to himself. One thing the mystery tipster had not requested, actually, was money. 'I can assure you that I am doing nothing of the sort, and my sources, as you know, are *my* business. And you, as a…*successful journalist*…will of course be aware of that aspect of our work.' Calum smiled, though there was no humour in the expression.

'Don't patronise me.' Powell played with his tie, checking it for nonexistent stains. 'So that's it? A hocus-pocus piece on the Bank of England? You're hanging by a thread, in case you've forgotten. But write it up—you've not much to lose'

'The BoE piece is not hocus-pocus, Rod, and I can tie in a couple of firms that might benefit from a rate cut. In any case, I have something else too.'

Powell's eyes briefly darted downward, partnered by a brief shake of the head. He offered his hands in a flippant, open gesture, unable to signify that he could possibly be impressed. 'Go on.'

'Okay. This is also kind of sensitive.'

'Look, cut the drama. I'm going to be late for another meeting. What's the story?' Powell folded his arms.

'The story is that the Government is going to invest further in Unreal Power, the alternative energy firm. The rationale is that it's got to be seen supporting this venture, and any future subsidies can be directed back into the national coffers if it aligns those subsidies the way I hear is going to happen. The shares have underperformed since the flotation, so there is an opportunity here. Same considerations apply—I can't say where I acquired the information—but it's solid. I could do this story this week too.'

Powell stood up abruptly, brushing down his jacket. 'Wait until next week to cover this Unreal Power story—get some more background. And this interest rate story better be correct. No more embarrassments as per Dartmouth Petroleum. Get Sunday's copy filed,' he said flatly, before ushering Calum from his office.

A light breeze flirted with Aurelia's dark hair as she strolled through Hyde Park, having enjoyed a lazy lunch at the *Serpentine Kitchen*. Free Sundays were a luxury that she once again appreciated, given that the majority of Sundays from the previous two years had been consigned to the attainment of her MBA. She briefly considered that particular paper chase, wondering if it had been worth the effort. The economist part of her had attempted to weigh up the 'opportunity cost'—the value of *alternative* actions. But how could people possibly re-run their lives to experience the benefits or drawbacks of taking a different course of action? All we have is hindsight, she figured, and even that's rarely accurate, especially given the lunchtime conversation in which she'd participated.

Her lunch partner—an old friend from school in Dublin who also now lived in London—had abruptly announced that she was pregnant when Aurelia had joked that she was virtually consuming the bottle of Pinot Noir on her own. Aurelia provided the obligatory girlie congratulations, though beneath a fragile exterior she experienced more than a hint of envy. Her attempts to conceal her inner emotions consisted of a series of gushing comments culminating in a crescendo of praise for her friend: how *brave* she was, what an *exciting* time, how *profound* child birth must be. Unfortunately for Aurelia, her friend's response proved to be frustratingly framed with equally dramatic emphasis. Maybe the right bloke for *you* is *just round the corner*, I bet *you'd* make a *fabulous mother too*. Hey! You should give it a try—*a one night stand is all you need!*

After lunch she walked to Hyde Park Corner tube station, flustered at what amounted to unintended condescension. She wondered how life appeared so seamless for certain people. The friend she'd lunched with had previously stated with conviction that she'd absolutely no interest in becoming a mother. What had been the phrase? Motherhood was for 'those without ambition'. What interested observers suggested was accurate: Aurelia was already married, the only problem being that it was to her job. Others advised her that the solution for the professional woman was to meet someone through work. Yet, how could you meet "Mr Right" at the FCA? Most of the single men she knew there were either pathetic dweebs or ambitious plonkers. Characters like Adam made her puke; in fact she would pity any girl who landed with him, and God bless any offspring who might one day know him as "Dad".

On her train to Piccadilly, she grabbed a corner seat and accessed her phone, checking the *Sunday Sentinel*. On the site, she was initially drawn to a story about a Euro Millions lottery winner who'd netted over a hundred million pounds, but now considered his windfall to be 'a problem'. She shook her head subconsciously, confused as to why someone in that position would utter such a comment. Secret wealth, or at least the ability to keep one's counsel regarding money, was surely a much more prudent approach. A grossly overweight man entered the train at the next stop and sat to her left hand side, accidentally nudging her and causing her phone to fall onto the floor. When Aurelia picked it up, she noticed a by-line about an imminent fall in interest rates. Instinctively, she spotted that this was the column by Calum Mack, the journalist she'd suspected of having some kind of inside line with stock movements.

Scrolling down the story, she realised that he'd chosen a different approach from pure stock tips this week, pushing the theory that some members of the Monetary Policy Committee might drive ideological policy changes on interest rates, almost out of the blue. How would he know about that? This was outside of her remit. However, she made a mental note to run a check on Mack's background though, as Max Telford would be asking such questions as she pursued her other suspicions.

At Piccadilly she walked north toward her diminutive, if expensive, apartment in Broadwick Street. She was pleased to be home, appreciating the flat. She'd only been able to afford the expense of a home in this location owing to the funds her late father had left her in his will, though she would readily have given up the lot for another day in his company. She ran a bath, and then checked the water in the bath, almost scalding her fingers. Rather than re-filling, she opted to make a call to George Town in Grand Cayman, where it would now be just after 7:00 a.m.

'Hello?' A slightly strained Irish accent responded after around ten rings.

'Vinnie? Don't tell me you were asleep at this late hour in the day?' Aurelia tried to stifle a snigger as she spoke.

'Aurelia? You're still a daft bitch...even if I do still love you. You do realise that the time is different over here from over there? That the world's round you know, and it spins around and around, making it night and day in different places. Well, technically it's a compressed sphere I think, something to do with a bulge in the middle because of the poles, or some shit like that.'

'Gosh Vinnie, is that what's been going on? No wonder I'm confused. Well, if you'd prefer me to call back once the world spins round a bit more...or maybe you've got company?'

'Aye, right. Not for the want of trying, my girl, and now you've got me up your word is my command.'

'Vinnie, it was about that email I sent you? You were going to enquire about the owners of a Cayman firm that was making some equity purchases in London? I'm under a bit of pressure here, and wondered if you'd managed to make any progress?'

'Ah, yes,' Vinnie said, before pausing to cough. 'In fact, I made some discreet enquiries on Friday. Out at sea, actually. Been out sailing both days. Booze and boats really don't mix, but it's a cultural necessity here.'

'Sounds like real hard work compared to my office,' Aurelia replied, before permitting Vinnie to continue.

'Indeed. A senior guy in the regulatory authority over here—if you can actually call it that—owes me one. I owe *you* one too, so when I met him on Friday I asked for some help. He insisted that I text him the details on the boat, so he'd remember to check for me afterwards. We were all pissed, you know. Hang on a minute, and I'll see if he's gotten back.'

Vinnie put Aurelia on hold. She smiled pleasantly, recalling how although now a successful international banker, Vinnie was once a cash-strapped student like many others. Though Vinnie might technically owe her a favour—as she'd once loaned him money while studying at Trinity—she sensed that he'd also had a soft spot for her and would probably oblige if she'd asked for half a dozen favours. Sometimes she felt saddened that so many Irish graduates left the country to pursue their careers, but at least they tended to maintain contact, and in Vinnie's case she could always buy him a liquid lunch the next time he came over on business.

'Aurelia,' Vinnie said, after a couple of minutes. 'I suspect this isn't a big help.'

'Okay. How so?'

'The names of the directors of Black Isle are A Smith and A Jones.'

'Contrived?'

'Exactly. I've seen this type of thing before. As you know, adherence to the normal sorts of regulations can be a joke in the Caribbean,' Vinnie said.

Aurelia sighed. 'I wonder if I could investigate the money trail, see if anything is leaving Black Isle's account leading back to London. Criminals always take their profits at some stage. The greedy ones usually can't wait.'

'As you'll know the banks here in the Caymans are notoriously tight-lipped about account ownership details. They figure that if they divulge identities it will destroy their business—especially if there's a big case in the media—and potential customers will bugger off somewhere else like Lichtenstein or Antigua. But look, give me a couple of weeks, Aurelia. I'll see if I can do some further digging.'

'I appreciate that, Vinnie.'

'And Aurelia, one other thing that occurred to me.'

'Yes?'

'It's just a thought. It's the name, Black Isle. I know that there could be several places with this name round the world. But the only one I know of is in the north of Scotland. Ironically, it's not an isle at all, more of a peninsula where I visited once upon a time, playing hurly. That's another story, probably mainly about sheep and beer, actually. I don't know if that helps or not, but good luck.'

Aurelia thanked Vinnie again before signing off and promising him that next time he visited London the Guinness was on her. She slipped out of her clothes and sunk into the herbal bath, which was now the ideal temperature. Immersing herself in water had always been her preference to showers, the herbal soak having a therapeutic effect, almost a meeting of mind and body. As she pushed her toes against the far end of the bath she considered the trades by Black Isle, alias Smith and Jones. The pattern so far had been to buy shares in advance of a tip in the *Sentinel*. The tips could probably generate interest from analysts who could in turn recommend the stock, raising the stock price in advance of the actual announcement of whatever news had been forecast. However, the stocks in question had been *sold* by Black Isle before any official media announcements by the firms concerned, meaning that the interest generated by the tips had been sufficient to make a decent profit at that stage.

She considered that this was possibly an attempt to cover the tracks, as investigators usually looked at pre and post announcement trades, rather than shares which were actually sold *prior* to news announcements. In most insider trading cases, equities were usually sold after positive news had been publically announced, which in theory would maximise any profit.

She dried herself using one of her M&S extra fluffy towels before sinking into her most comfy arm chair and switching on her iPad. She figured she'd try to get inside Calum Mack's head. Part of her remit at the FCA was to look beyond the figures, to build background evidence that in isolation might appear as useless conjecture, but when spliced with other complementary data, might prove incriminating and lead to potential prosecution. As her father had been a detective in the Irish police for many years, she often recalled his obsession with painstaking research when she had been in her formative years. She enjoyed the creation of constructs, those more complex theories based on a compendium of more simple initial concepts, and this type of research also allowed the human motivations behind financial crime to be unearthed. It was also the component of the job she enjoyed best, as they could ultimately pass results to the prosecuting authorities, essentially doing the police's job for them, or, as Max Telford liked to say, ensuring that the police did not 'eff' up the job.

The first search was again via the *Sentinel's* own website under 'people'. She was initially struck by Mack's photo—not the typical arty-farty pose you sometimes find in the media. Aurelia paused, thinking momentarily that Mack was actually rather handsome, his 'head and shoulders' style mug shot revealing black hair and very dark eyes, bordered by a navy jacket but no tie. A synthesis of banker and journalist, then, in terms of his projected public persona. She searched further, and retrieved archived articles and a piece by the business editor introducing Mack as a new columnist when he'd joined two years previously.

Briefly, she reviewed some of Mack's columns over the past six months. Already aware of the past two or three columns, she concentrated on previous articles. She then accessed subsequent share prices movements of the tips he'd given, viewing price changes over one week and longer. This proved a little disappointing. While she was aware that share tips often suggested that equities should be bought for longer term gain, in many cases potential investors were looking for quick returns. However, when she compared the performance of some of the recent shares he'd tipped, there was indeed consistency. In a number of them, the stocks had actually *fallen* after Mack had tipped them.

Aurelia laughed out loud, despite having no audience. Bloody hell, you wouldn't want to take this guy's advice if you'd won the lottery. Three weeks previously, he'd even pushed Dartmouth Petroleum, the oil company that had plummeted after the Canadian authorities had begun legal action for a number of irregularities. It was almost as if Mack had had an anti-Midas touch, at least for the time period in question. Who would listen to a columnist that produced poor tips? Failure to generate profits for small investors, or worse, advice that caused people serious potential losses was hardly an advert for listening to advice the following week. So, if in recent weeks Mack was using his column to drive up share prices in firms from which he'd acquired inside information, he'd done so out of the blue. Therefore, there had to be some sort of catalyst.

Aurelia progressed onto Facebook, entering the name Calum Mack. A few were present, but strangely, not the one in question. Other social networking sites provided similar dead-ends. When she added other search information for cross referencing purposes, she noted that this specific Calum Mack appeared to be elusive. She changed the search criteria, using Cal instead of Calum, and then just Mack on its own, aware that he might be using a middle name for some reason, but Mack didn't appear. This was very unusual for a journalist. In fact, as far as she could understand, such individuals usually courted publicity and the media for whom they worked often made compulsory use of social media tools for employees. Wasn't everyone of any note an online social networker? Perhaps Mack used an alias for social networking, but again, this probably defeated the point, as it wouldn't generate publicity for his column.

Flipping back to the *Sentinel's* own site, she then spotted Mack's blog, which was probably used as the sole substitute for the social networking alternative that she'd expected. Perhaps he received so much flack for some of his share tips that the blog helped reduce some the more detractive interactive dialogue of tools such as Facebook. Scanning through his posts, there were various updates on tips he'd suggested over the piece, including some guarded apologies for investment advice that had gone sour. When she perused more than six months previously, Mack seemed more upbeat, able to reflect on successful investment advice, including some more prophetic tips. However, when she logged into the specialist software at the FCA site and cross referenced these share tips against odd share price movements akin to those she'd uncovered for X4D4, she found no such similar trades.

This was one of the most frustrating parts of her role: when a hot lead appeared to fizzle out. Perhaps the Black Isle investments were an uncomplicated coincidence. Maybe Mack had simply read another tipster's copy—some obscure analyst or online blogger who was connected to Black

Isle—and plagiarised their work. His record of recent had been poor, and suggested no subterfuge over the past few months, so perhaps the guy was totally innocent. She made herself a strong coffee, and massaged her scalp, closing her eyes. Then, as various thoughts passed through her mind, something suddenly jumped out at her. She checked again on Mack's blog. Checking through the various posts, she knew the clue was from a couple of months previously. Then she spotted it—a reference to Edinburgh University.

Mack had made an off the cuff comment about an educational software supplier that he'd tipped for growth, noting that his own alma mater was one of its more prestigious clients. Of course, Aurelia knew that Mack had worked in Edinburgh, though she hadn't considered the university angle. Logging on to the university's website, she navigated around, searching for information on former students. She was aware that most universities, including Trinity, where she'd studied, maintained links with and between alumni—in part for posterity—but also to utilise high profile graduates for publicity purposes and to extract donations for research funding.

She was able to access the archives from the year Mack had graduated, noting his degree title. She then amended her search of the university's site to include the degree title and year along with his name. Nothing. Frustrated, she then returned to Google and used the same three pieces of information, and this time a separate set of reference points emerged, one of which proved interesting—an unofficial website dedicated to alumni of the University of Edinburgh's "piss artists club", no doubt one of these societies that seem hilarious at the time, but all too corny a few years after graduation. Two or three clicks later, she was looking at a photo of a much younger Calum Mack on a beach, apparently enjoying a few drinks with some friends. Each of the drunken characters was tagged, but the caption at the bottom was what really struck Aurelia.

It read: *who could forget that totally intoxicated time when we all squashed into Calum Mack's parents' place? We didn't wash all weekend. No wonder it's called the Black Isle.*

Chapter 6

On Thursday, during one of the most energy-zapping meetings Aurelia had ever experienced at work, a colleague mentioned that the MPC had just voted for an unexpected cut in interest rates. Her thoughts suddenly raced to Calum Mack. The tone of that article had alluded to the fact that he *knew* of an imminent fall in rates, as it if were a given. She checked two of the stocks he'd said might benefit from a cut, and noted that they had both risen. Unfortunately, Telford was tied up with EU regulatory matters in Paris until late on Friday, so she decided to await Mack's next column before acting further.

On Sunday evening she then read Mack's latest column, noticing that there was an extended section tipping a rise in the price of the alternative energy company, Unreal Power. She vaguely remembered some previous speculation about how the Government was due to sell its stake in this firm a few months before, but yet again, Mack was making a counter-intuitive suggestion of the opposite, and recommending the stock as a buy.

At 5:45 a.m. on Monday morning Aurelia was already at her desk, the adrenalin flowing. Max Telford usually arrived at about 7:30 a.m. and she wanted to produce a draft report outlining the collection of jigsaw pieces concerning Calum Mack and Black Isle. Having made a strong black coffee to stimulate the senses she settled at her desk, the calm atmosphere in the deserted office contrasting with the pace of her thoughts. She required proof of human connectivity between Mack and Black Isle, but also the monetary connection, and she would have to demonstrate how Mack was benefiting personally from any proceeds. Vinnie might come good in that line of investigation; though an alternative approach was to begin enquiries within the firms themselves, attempting to make links between Mack and employees at these companies.

The interest rate story was a bit of an outlier, as it didn't concern direct inside information on equities, but it had also aroused her suspicions. She'd park it for the time being. However, she wanted to identify if Black Isle had purchased shares in Unreal Power prior to Mack's story, essentially identifying if a similar pattern would again apply.

She logged on, this time entering search criteria including the terms Black Isle and Unreal Power. For some reason, the software took a minute or two to process her request, so she left her desk to make some more coffee. As the kettle boiled in the kitchen, she heard the main door to the office opening, and assumed that Telford, or perhaps his matronly secretary, had arrived earlier than normal. But when she returned through the kitchenette door she momentarily froze, spotting Adam hovering over her desk.

Hawk sipped a mug of coffee, his eyes simultaneously scanning the current stock price for Unreal Power. He smirked inwardly. Mack was hooked and was doing his job blindly, no doubt wallowing in the reflected kudos at the *Sentinel*. As with all deception, all you had to do was create a motive for the patsy, and then devise a plausible diversion. Although the timing of his plan had certainly favoured Hawk, Mack had nonetheless been as eager as he'd predicted, so gullible that he'd failed to see the obvious signs. And Mack had absolutely no idea that Hawk had, using various aliases, authored a number of emails to Ron Powell critical of Mack's columns in the weeks beforehand, precipitating fear, with perfect timing.

And the advantage for Hawk of having communicated the detail about Unreal Power to Mack early was that by Tuesday the market had already moved significantly due to the cascading effect of the rumours. The shares were up over thirty percent as analysts had begun to delve into the story, haranguing politicians and officials about the potential investment from the public purse. As politicians lined up to officially say 'no comment', the market interpreted such obfuscation accurately, aware that for the elected representatives to deny the validity of the story and shortly afterwards be revealed as liars—perhaps having lost constituents money in the process— was not how politics worked. As Hawk had invested more than half a million pounds in this stock, there was a tidy six-figure sum in profits waiting, so he sold.

He'd also sold sterling short the previous week, and though Mack's column had wandered around a little with his explanation of the change of heart on rate movements by two MPC members, this story too had gained a little momentum at the time, with one *Financial Times* journalist running a virtually identical story on Tuesday morning. The Governor of the Bank of England had been asked questions by the media about this story and had been tight-lipped, as regulations dictated, but privately he must have been irritated. Hawk laughed, almost cruelly. Clearly, some people were starting to notice Mack's work, and as it stood, Hawk had made some real money.

After pouring more coffee and soliciting a chocolate donut from his fridge, Hawk made a conscious decision to begin the concluding arrangements for his plan. Key pieces of inside information were required, this time from an IT specialist at an investment bank. This element of the exercise he deemed complementary to the inside information he'd forced from the others, as it was requisitioned from someone spying rather than participants more directly involved. Hawk had considered using this source first, but the timing of other events had dictated the sequence. By this afternoon, he would have accrued a sizeable sum to invest directly, assuming the last contact came good.

Using a new phone purchased specially for the call, Hawk dialled the number. After several rings a man with a broad Glasgow accent answered. When Hawk gave his code word using the same voice altering technology as before, a short silence ensued at the end of the line before the man spoke.

'You know,' the man said. 'I was about to say how disappointed I was. When you made that call to me explaining your little blackmail scheme, followed by these photos, I paused, reflecting why that should happen. The whole fiasco was pathetic. A set up. I even stuck to your rule about no contact with the others via social media. But something's not right here.'

'I'm recording this call, as I advised. No names,' Hawk said sharply.

'You say no names. But you know what? You're not who you'd like me to think you are. In fact, you're almost certainly using voice modification technology as we speak, so you haven't fooled me.'

This time Hawk hesitated before replying. 'What does matter is that your life, as you know it, will collapse if you don't follow my orders.'

'I could contact one of the others.'

'I *expressly forbade* you to speak to anyone else!' The anger cut across the line sharply. 'I could destroy you for that.'

'But you're not going to, are you? You need me. It beats me why I bothered to go to that bloody re—'

'Enough! I need you to follow the plan, or you can say goodbye to your career. The others won't speak to you anyway because they understand the consequences. But I will have no compunction shopping you if you don't comply. As you know I want at least three good tips from you or you're finished. You know plenty because of where you work. So just spit it out.'

The man with the Glaswegian accent cleared his throat. 'So, what's to stop you shopping me anyway, after you've gleaned the information you need? It's the classic dilemma for a blackmailer's victim. Why play your trump card if you still stand a good chance of losing the game?'

'Because it's not in my interest to get involved further if you comply. I don't need loose ends. So be smart, give me what I need.'

A further silence arose. This time, Hawk could sense the hesitation on the other end of the phone   perhaps a subtle shift in the breathing—but nonetheless a detectable nuance. He waited, with a predictable outcome.

'I'm going to do as you ask, against my better judgement. But I warn you, should you ever threaten me again, I will track you down.'

'So what information do you have, tough guy?'

'I need to call you back, asshole. Two items need to be confirmed, and the other is a bit more difficult, but I can get the information. Give me an hour.'

Calum received another phone by courier from the covert caller. The instructions had been clear—he was to keep the phone with him over the next two days, whilst still making sure not to discard the previous phones in case the caller needed to use them again, with the added instruction that he was to store the phones at home for security purposes, and keep them charged. Calum acquiesced. He briefly considered once more how strange this clandestine behaviour was, but what the hell? The phones were unconnected to him so in some respects he could only accrue advantages by being able to follow a few odd instructions to benefit from genuine share tips. As he placed the new phone in his suit pocket Ben suddenly whacked Calum over the head from behind with a card folder. The initial jolt was replaced by a feeling of minor gratification as Ben unfolded a copy of Calum's column, now embossed with pink highlighter. Calum awaited the forthcoming interrogation with pleasure.

'If you're not making some dough out of this you're as daft a bastard as I thought you were when we first met.' Ben sat on the vacant chair opposite, chewing gum and swinging around as he spoke.

'I wondered when you'd appear,' Calum said, biting his bottom lip. 'And now you're advising me to take a cavalier attitude towards ethics?' he asked, grinning broadly.

Ben shook his head. 'The crime is in getting *caught*, buddy. I told you to be careful not to ignore a fucking gift horse! This Unreal Power thing now looks a cert. Jesus, the politicians were all saying 'no comment' and shit like that, which can only mean one thing. I've a dozen pretty unconnected pals that could have bought these shares on the QT and we could both have made a *packet*. Considering the bloody pay in here.' He held his hands up in the air. 'You know, I've calculated that since your mystery guy appeared you could have made a six figure sum with an initial ten-to-twenty grand investment if you'd done what anyone else with the slightest modicum of nous would have done, and placed your profits on the next deal. I mean, this guy's giving it to you on a *plate*.'

'You forget that any one of the deals could go sour,' Calum replied.

'Oh, right. It's all going to go belly up now. Well, I'd take the risk. Remember Jerry Maguire? *Help me help you.* Has the guy given you anything this week?'

'No.'

Ben studied Calum carefully. 'I don't believe you. Come on, let's go out in the corridor and work something up.' As Ben grinned at Calum, the new phone that he'd been secreting suddenly buzzed. Calum held up an arm to Ben, mimicking a traffic policeman.

'Hi, Calum Mack speaking,' he said quietly, pretending that he was unaware of where this call was originating. Ben sat on the desk across from Calum, observing the phone wryly.

'Listen carefully. Have you got a pen?' Hawk spoke softly.

Calum grabbed a pen from his desk as Ben followed his movements. Calum then turned to partially obscure what he was about to write.

'Fire ahead.' Calum listened intently.

'Two tips. Firstly, a company called Simtrex. It makes miniature components for nanotechnology applications. It's about to hit pay dirt as one of the big players—I won't say whom—is going to buy all of its patents, the offer being twice the current market capitalisation. The rationale is that a knockout bid will repel alternative buyers, but as you know, if a battle commences it can only drive the stock further up, so investing here is a no brainer.'

'When's this happening?' As Calum replied, Ben, who had been texting someone, suddenly peered at Calum.

'By the middle of next week, so Sunday's good.'

'Good stuff…and you said that you had something else?'

'Yes,' Hawk said. 'Have you heard of Virtual Bank? The firm that allows you to have a chat with a virtual bank manager?'

'I heard that it was a bummer. Journalist from the *Sunday Times* said it would run out of cash before it ever delivered anything of note.'

'Well, he's an idiot. This company is a takeover target too. It has one piece of incredible software that can used be for applications in virtual shopping. Much more advanced than Amazon's software, apparently, which is amazing, given the size of Amazon. Anyway, the banking bit might be a bit ahead of its time, but the shares are still going to rocket.'

'Thanks very much. I know not to ask any more questions.'

'You're welcome, and something else. I think that you've earned a little holiday. You've done well with your column...and you can't profit *directly* from our little ploy of course...but you could have some indirect benefits.'

'What do you mean?' Calum glanced at Ben, who was still watching carefully and not budging.

'I've taken the liberty to book you on a trip to the Caribbean.'

Calum hesitated, trying not to smile. 'Right...that sounds...interesting. When would that be? I've commitments here of course.'

'A week on Thursday, Mr Mack. How about that? You can't say I'm not good to you.'

Calum's curiosity was aroused. The Caribbean? He'd been there just once with a former girlfriend. This was very short notice, but then he didn't want to upset the caller. Perhaps this was simply an altruistic gesture.

'I've a ticket for the Arsenal game a week on Saturday, but hell, that doesn't matter, I guess. So where in the...' Calum paused, glancing at Ben, whose lips were pursed.

'Grand Cayman. Lovely beaches, a luxurious five star pad. Three nights. You'll be treated like an emperor.'

'I'm not sure about this.'

'Everyone needs a break.'

'Right, it's just a little short on notice.'

'It's a condition of me giving you further tips, okay? No time like the present. Live a little, eh? Now, take a note,' Hawk said flatly, 'as I won't be sending anything that can be traced, for your own security. You're on British Airways flight 2860, leaving at 10:30 a.m. next Friday, business class, of course. Staying at the Caribbean Club on Seven Mile Beach, returning on the five o'clock flight on Sunday afternoon. Pick up the tickets at the BA desk. Here's your booking number.' He gave the reference number. 'Everything is paid apart from your transfers. I take it that you can afford that?' Calum scribbled down the instructions.

'Yes, of course. That's not a problem. And your reason for all this? Assuming I can clear it in here?'

'Because I want you to be motivated, and not attempt to profit from this yourself. It must have been tempting for you…to dabble in these equities.'

'Eh, not at all,' Calum said, without conviction. The irony of the conversation he'd just had with Ben wasn't lost on Calum.

'Good,' Hawk replied. 'So, I suppose I should say bon voyage.' And with that, the phone went dead. What a strange guy, Calum thought.

As Calum disconnected, Ben scratched his head, trying to conceal a smirk, before pointing at Calum with a straight index finger.

'That was *him*, wasn't it?'

'I can't reveal my sources.' Calum replied, mirroring Ben's expression.

'So, you're going out on a date with him, what, a week on Saturday is it? I didn't realise that this tip fetish had a gay element to it.'

'Ben, you're a nosey bastard, you know that?' Calum grinned, aware that Ben was attempting to piece together what he'd heard, so he held the notebook on which he'd jotted details towards his chest.

Then, Ben suddenly grabbed the notepad, twisting it away from Calum to see what had been written. 'Ben, give me that notepad back right now!' Calum stood up and tried to snatch the pad back, but Ben stepped away in a theatrical motion, before staring at the paper, and then roaring out loud, drawing the attention of other colleagues at adjacent desks.

'For fuck's sake, look at these hieroglyphics. I didn't know that you were an ancient Egyptian reincarnated. What kind of shorthand is this? My ninety-year old granny's got better handwriting, and she's got Parkinson's.'

'No one has ever deciphered my shorthand.' Calum smiled confidently, knowing that there was an element of truth to his statement. He'd invented a quirky form of shorthand as a student, having been motivated by the laziness of a friend who'd refused to attend any classes but usually tried to steal his lecture notes afterwards.

'Aha! BA? You're tipping the company that owns British Airways. That company's a dog, mate.' As Ben squinted at the notepad, Calum realised that the only part he'd written normally was the 'BA' part of the flight details that he'd been given.

'Great, go join the FBI,' Calum replied, before snatching the notepad back, in case any further incriminating details were revealed.

'So what's juicy enough to entice you to miss a big footy match?'

'I'll send you a postcard,' Calum said, before sitting down at his desk again, turning to face Ben directly. 'And before you ask, I *can* give you one top tip before Sunday.' Calum motioned in a covert gesture for Ben to come in close.

Ben leaned in, searching Calum's eyes before Calum spoke.

'Listening?' Calum asked, whispering.

'Yes,' Ben whispered back. 'On you go.'

'Use some mouth wash in the morning before invading the personal space of others.'

Max Telford's secretary, Janet, was old-school, in terms of fashion, demeanour, and her expectations of others. She simply didn't expect more junior colleagues to enter her airspace without at least visual approval, or, worse, for them to burst past her into the director's domain in the absence of an invitation. Therefore, her furrowed brow relayed irritation as Aurelia did exactly that, causing Max to spill some of his coffee as the door flew open.

'Aurelia…what can I do for you?'

'Give Adam a talk about basic manners and confidentiality.' Aurelia stood firmly with her arms folded, her bright red suit echoing the colour that had risen in her cheeks.

Max sighed. 'What's he done?'

'You know how hard I've been working? Well, when I came in early again, he suddenly appeared. This is rare for Adam, I can assure you, as I'm always here before him in the morning. Anyway, all I do is make a coffee, and when I come back in he's suddenly standing there, hovering over my computer screen and taking notes using one of *my* post-it pads. You couldn't make it up.'

'Aurelia, please sit down.' Aurelia sat down as requested, but avoided eye contact with Max, who spoke softly. 'Look, this is probably not as big a deal as you might think. We are supposed to be working as a team after all. Are you sure that there isn't something that you've both been working on that he could have been looking for?'

'Yes, there are two or three open projects, but what was on my screen was totally unconnected. I've been developing leads on this Calum Mack thing, which you agreed I could keep completely confidential. I feel I'm making headway with this investigation, and I really don't need someone like Adam to interfere. This has all happened before.' Aurelia looked towards the ceiling, teeth gritted.

Max nodded before buzzing his secretary. 'Janice, would you please ask Adam to come in here right away, unless he's on an urgent call or something.'

In less than a minute Adam knocked on the door, before entering the office. He glanced briefly at Aurelia before smiling at Max. 'What's up, Max?'

Max interlocked his fingers, elbows resting on his desk. 'Adam, this is slightly awkward. Aurelia feels that you were…what's the right word?'

'Snooping,' Aurelia said.

'Well, that's perhaps a bit strong Aurelia. Taking notes at your desk is what you described, Aurelia. I take it that this was for some sort of joint project Adam?'

'Of course, Max. I'm surprised that Aurelia could come to any other conclusion.'

'That's a pile of crap Adam, and you know it. You must take me for a complete fool. You were distinctly standing over my screen taking notes.'

'Yes, I was.' Adam said. Aurelia shook her head, looking away before Adam continued. 'I was looking for a mobile number for John Jones at the Bank of England and I recalled that I'd seen it written down somewhere. Sure enough, it's on a post-it note stuck to the side of your desk. If you don't believe me Max, please feel free to have a look.' Adam held his arms out wide to Max, his facial features displaying the appearance of a victim of a serious miscarriage of justice.

'And you saw nothing else? Nothing on the screen? Because a phone number takes about three seconds to write down, and shit, I bet you have that number anyway.' Aurelia faced Adam directly.

'Aurelia, please calm down,' Max interjected.

'It's okay Max,' Adam said. 'I want to clear this up in a professional manner. As a matter of fact, Aurelia, I do not have that number. If I had the number I would have had no reason to approach your desk in the first place. I would never pry into a colleague's work without permission, and frankly, I resent the accusation,' Adam said, folding his arms.

'I think that you two should shake hands, and that'll be the end of the matter." Adam held out a hand, but Aurelia simply stood and then left the office without a further word.

Calum experienced a whirlwind weekend, enthused by the prospect of a free trip to the Caribbean. He'd considered cashing in some Krugerrands he'd bought and placed in a bank safety deposit box some time previously. The coins were trading at a decent price, and Calum figured he could contribute some buck free spending money to the trip. Then, however, he took cold feet, considering how he'd failed to make a dime out of these share tips—why throw his own money away, when the caller, who presumably was making something out of all this, could pay for it?

He'd also produced some background on both Simtrex and Virtual Bank, crafting his column in a positive manner that reflected a new found sense of belief that had permeated his life within the past month. When he'd submitted the column to Powell, this time the man had barely uttered a word, which was normal—ready to threaten and harass in periods of turmoil, yet less willing to offer reward or praise in the good times. Such idiosyncrasies suited Calum, however, as his job now appeared safer, so he hit the town with Ben, making a dent in his bank account with good grace.

On Monday morning Simtrex shares rose, instilling in Calum a peculiar sense of pride. When the stock exchange opened, had he actually managed to instantaneously move the market? Even a little? There had been an online reaction to the column during Sunday which had almost certainly heightened anticipation before the markets opened on Monday. On a more prosaic note, he was aware of a substantially increased volume of inbound phone calls, particularly from analysts enquiring as to his sources. These guys had become aware that his market intelligence had improved, and wanted some of the action themselves, chipping away at him in the hope that he would reveal secrets. In the columns themselves, he had referred to "market sources", thus revealing nothing. Among colleagues in the office, there was also some curious banter, with one senior hack suggesting that he must be a crook, so why wasn't he investing in his own right instead of telling the world? Calum brushed off such comments in the knowledge that he was totally clean; at least as honest as any *ex-banker* could possibly be. No one argued the point.

The shares in Virtual Bank also enjoyed a rise, though nothing substantial. The firm had been heavily criticised in the recent past and had been rated a sell by many analysts. Then, on Wednesday morning, confirmation of the value of the pivotal software owned by Virtual Bank hit the headlines. Amazon itself had apparently been considering a bid, but another player had jumped first and the shares jumped just as the secret tipster had professed. A further news item concerning Simtrex also appeared on Bloomberg. The AIM listed firm had now been subject to a bid substantially higher than the price to which the stock had risen on two days of market speculation.

Hawk smiled wryly, enjoying the irony of the Simtrex and Virtual Bank stories combusting on the same day. On this occasion he had waited a little longer before deciding to sell either stock. In the case of Virtual Bank, this was partly as the shares had barely budged on Monday or Tuesday. Every hour could bring good news, so he waited patiently, and this strategy had been rewarded. He'd held onto the Simtrex stock because this was his final play and fear of losing early gains had been eclipsed by the possibility of big profits. And what a gamble that had proven to be. As he'd invested the entire proceeds from the sale of the previous equities and currency investment, he had managed to more than double his money. He calculated that after expenses over two million US dollars would be credited to the offshore account.

And the icing on the cake was that he, like Calum Mack, was shortly about to enjoy a trip to Grand Cayman.

Chapter 7

Max Telford seemed genuinely pleased with Aurelia's progress with the investigation into potential insider dealing by Calum Mack. Cases were usually coded in order of priority, and this case had now acquired 'A1' status. The momentary pleasure that Aurelia had experienced when Max informed her that her case notes justified the reclassification of the case had also been tempered by the realisation that details of the case would now be shared at group meetings. Logically, that meant that Adam could legitimately comment on the case and ask to be included, and given Max's track record on such issues, she feared that he would acquiesce should Adam act in character. She hadn't believed one morsel of Adam's explanation about searching for phone numbers on her desk, meaning that he was probably now at least partly versed in the background of Black Isle, and although he could hardly claim instant knowledge when the subject came up at the meeting today, he might have been able to figure a way of muscling in should the opportunity arise.

Aurelia had once again tracked Calum Mack's share tips on Sunday against the trades made by Black Isle before and after the column had been published. Perhaps it was simply in the genes passed on by her father, but she felt a real adrenalin surge when the pieces of a financial jigsaw interlocked. The riskiness of the crime astonished her, particularly this time, as Mack seemed to have become more transparently greedy. The sums were now much larger—in fact the proceeds of each piece of insider trading appeared to directly provide the investment for the next deal. Mack, if acting alone, was behaving like a high roller playing roulette, escalating from small, initial investments to gambles with the potential to provide huge rewards. The latest trades, in Simtrex and Virtual Bank, were different in another way, as the sale of shares had only occurred *after* the official news announcements for the reasons for the rises had taken place, not simply after Mack's column had been published. In the initial stories that Mack had covered in his column, Black Isle had sold the holdings quickly, suggesting that initial attempts to conceal the actions by selling *prior* to any announcements were being replaced by much bolder gambles, almost bordering on recklessness.

One element of her investigation was to probe into the nature of the companies themselves, and the individuals either inside these firms or connected to them who had tipped Mack. She was aware that, although unlikely, it was possible that a single individual was responsible. On this basis, she'd already run a similarity check of X4D4 against Walltex to ascertain if these firms used the same auditors, brokers or solicitors. This had proved negative. Similarly, Unreal Power appeared to use different advisors in terms of commercial services. The latest firms involved, Simtrex and Virtual Bank, did use the same investment bank, but utilised different mainstream professional advisors, which left Aurelia puzzled. Professionals such as lawyers and auditors were the most likely weak links in terms of confidentiality. Most of these people were of course honest, as breaches of confidentiality, if proven, could end up in professional suicide or a custodial sentence. She had however been involved in a number of cases where solicitors or accountants had turned rogue, with the allure of easy money proving just too tantalising. However, this appeared not to be the case here, at least on the first reading of events.

Another thing still bothered her about this case. If Mack was the recipient of genuine insider trading advice, and if she could confirm his specific connection to Black Isle, why hadn't he simply avoided the obvious danger of publicising the information through his column? If he had invested in these shares without the publicity of the newspaper column, he might have made less money, but the authorities would also probably not have identified him. He appeared to have become more reckless as the latest stocks were only sold after the underlying news had broken, not simply after the column had been published. Sure, it was Mack's job to tips stocks, but the nature of public proclamation didn't entirely fit with the methodical nature of the trades, even if the transactions were undertaken via the Caribbean. Thousands of insider trades were tacitly undertaken every year, and Aurelia knew that most avoided investigation as the guilty parties concealed their actions and didn't become too greedy, so why had Mack acted in the manner he had?

Had avarice simply played its hand?

She ran an online personal credit check on Mack to ascertain if the journalist had debts, and also made a phone call to the Inland Revenue to verify if he owed unpaid tax. Neither proved to be the case. A further call to a friend in the criminal justice system confirmed that Mack appeared to be a model citizen. No arrests or warnings, nothing. Nonetheless, the trail was hot. Aurelia, in tune with Max Telford, did not believe in coincidences; such was for the superstitious. She had witnessed too much greed and deception in her tenure at the FCA to have become anything other than a cynic who could smell a financial crime at some distance.

She had also, however, experienced the taut frustration of knowing of a trader's guilt, yet not being in the position to prove such guilt in the eyes of the law. Even the recent convictions they had secured in the Fleeting case had partially been due to good luck, as Daniel Fleeting's father-in-law, who had been the initial recipient of the proceeds, had proved to be both a bumbling fool and a demonstrable liar in court. Aurelia was also aware that they were on the brink of bringing in the police and the Crown Prosecution Service. In her experience, the police, who had been known to blow financial cases through procedural errors, were best alerted only once solid intelligence had been ascertained, but Aurelia could infringe the rules if they engaged with the police and CPS too late. There was always a fine margin in terms of the clichéd "need to know" principle and the possibility of letting a criminal off the hook.

At the group meeting on Thursday afternoon, Aurelia poured herself a coffee and, acting out of character, munched on one of the chocolate brownies on offer. Taxpayer funded fuel for a fight, she briefly contemplated. She avoided eye contact with Adam by sitting two places along from him on the same side of the large oak table. Max droned on about standards and targets once more, before he suddenly appeared to brighten up, announcing that Aurelia had a new A1 case on which he wanted her to provide a short briefing. She'd quietly anticipated such a request, and had decided if the opportunity arose to take a bold, positive approach in order to ensure that everyone else fully understood who had ownership over the case. As she outlined the principal events concerning the journalist Calum Mack and the pattern of trades by Black Isle a few colleagues nodded here and there, and she could detect an air of minor professional envy that sometimes occurs when one member of staff pulls out in front of the pack.

Adam broke the silence. 'That's good work Aurelia, well done.' He compressed his lips slightly, as Aurelia computed the compliment, briefly unsure as to how to reply.

'Yes, I agree, Adam,' Max said. 'It's good of you to say so.'

'Oh, not at all, Max. Aurelia and I have not always agreed on everything, but credit where it's due. Ultimately, we work as a team here, and if one member of the team gets a…lucky break…we should all be delighted, and frankly, we should do everything in our power to ensure that the case proceeds properly.'

Aurelia took a deep breath. 'I intend to ensure that everything proceeds in a *proper* manner, Adam,' she said, miming inverted commas. 'And maybe you're correct. Perhaps I've just had a very *lucky* break. But I'm sure that you will know that the harder one investigates, the *luckier* one becomes.' She blew air up towards her fringe, before Max interjected.

'Aurelia…I'm sure that's not what Adam meant. And he's right, in this office it *is* all about team work. Actually, we are all interdependent. Now, if any colleagues here have some spare capacity, I'm sure that Aurelia would value some input, particularly as the net closes.'

'I'm happy to help with background analysis if you need it, Aurelia,' said Jen Hoffman, a recent young recruit to whom Aurelia had taken a liking. 'And I don't want any credit. It's clear that you have pursued this case and you deserve any plaudits going, but if the need arises I'd be happy to assist.'

'Thanks,' Aurelia replied. Jen smiled back, and had clearly interpreted the semantics between Adam and her, and help from a non-competing source would be welcome.

'Okay, that's the spirit, Jen,' Max said. 'But we may also need experience here, Aurelia, so don't shut Adam out. Remember, Adam also put in the hours with the Daniel Fleeting case, so we'll play it by ear.'

Max held up his hands in an attempt to put a lid on the issue, and for once, Aurelia decided to yield. She wasn't going to entirely win this argument, so she would leave the battle for another day. The important thing was to be thorough, ensuring that her case was airtight. That would put Adam in his place.

From across the circular bar the auburn-haired girl with the stunning hazel eyes proffered a smile that revealed something more than a polite gesture. He'd already spotted her sitting in the lobby when he'd checked in, subconsciously approving of the leopard print short skirt and the red high heels, which made him fleetingly forget the five-hour time difference. When she smiled he recognised that look—a momentary exchange which sometimes occurs in the second or two when erstwhile strangers lock eyes. Chemistry, it was often called, though Calum considered that it might be more aptly named "biology" given where it sometimes led. He returned the smile, content to savour the second malt whisky that he'd enjoyed since he'd planted himself down at the Caribbean Club's beach bar on Seven Mile Beach. This had been his first long haul trip since he'd split with Ailsa, the accountant whom he'd dated for about a year before the move south, and he was enjoying every minute so far. Dotted with white-sailed yachts bearing happy people, the clear waters of the Caribbean glistened and the scene deflected Calum's attention for a brief moment before the girl across the bar spoke.

'How long are you staying on the island?' she shouted, sipping rum punch from a decorated coconut. The accent was American.

'Oh, just three days,' Calum replied.

'That's handy.'

'Handy for what?' Calum grinned.

'Oh, handy for whatever,' she said, moving round to the free bar stool next to Calum. 'I'm only here for the weekend too, and it's a luxury to count Thursday as a weekend day. I'm Lisa,' she said, holding out a slender, manicured hand. Calum introduced himself.

'Let me guess…*Scottish*?' she asked.

'As the Loch Ness Monster.'

'Really? Except you exist in the flesh, so to speak,' she said softly, touching his arm. 'I've always wondered why people visit Scotland to see something that's not actually there.'

Calum laughed. 'Is it not? I'm not actually there myself these days, but based in England right now. London.'

'What brings you here?'

'Work, in a way.'

'Banker?' she asked.

'Used to be. Is it that obvious?'

'Well, you look self assured, groomed…successful.'

'Hey Lisa, just there I thought you were going to say *sexy*,' Calum beamed, again locking eyes. Lisa flicked her hair back, returning the smile

'You know, any man who's confident enough…' Lisa looked down this time, as if embarrassed by the sudden mutual attraction that had manifested itself. 'And you're probably married. Or is your girlfriend upstairs getting ready, maybe talking a nap to counter the jetlag?' She glanced at his hand, a less than subtle sign of social enquiry.

'No, I'm afraid I'm single,' he sighed. 'It's a terrible affliction.'

'Ah…it is indeed. Is this your first time on the island?'

Calum nodded, and Lisa seemed to liven up, apparently enthused that she had a new, single, acquaintance she could enlighten. She explained that Seven Mile Beach was effectively five and a half miles long, and although it harboured some chic hotels and fabulous white sands, her favourite night spots and restaurants were actually in George Town. Lisa mentioned that she'd first come to the island from her native New York for a modelling shoot, and had loved it so much that she returned whenever the opportunity arose. In this case, she said that American Airlines had included a free flight with the last modelling job she'd done a fortnight previously, so suddenly the Caribbean beckoned.

As they ordered two exotic cocktails, Calum listened intently, absorbing the company. A few weeks previously he'd been on the brink of being sacked, a series of poor judgements and cruel luck having almost precipitated a personal crisis. Nothing had appeared to present anything positive in his life. After his initial run-in with Rod Powell, he'd considered chucking the job and returning to Edinburgh. He'd figured the only solution was to retrace his steps and rekindle his bank balance, and credibility. Yet, look how serendipity could strike? Not only had his standing at the *Sentinel* and in the wider industry been resurrected, he presently occupied a free ringside seat in paradise, the only distraction being a twenty-something model from New York whose single crime appeared to be that she was an outrageous flirt. Wow, perhaps the planter's punch had assisted, but she really did possess the most alluring eyes.

Calum suddenly raised his glass to his new acquaintance, toasting 'mystery callers'. She responded, slightly confused but enthusiastically joining in by adding some off-beat toasts of her own—to 'world peace and hedonism'. By the time they'd ordered some snacks and a further drink, Calum had agreed to a night out in George Town chaperoned by the delectable Lisa.

During the dark days he'd spent in prison, Hawk had never dared to dream of the luxury he was currently experiencing: a personal butler, unlimited alcoholic drinks, and an intimate massage scheduled for later in the evening. Perhaps it had seemed that visions of such surroundings and people were simply too far-fetched, improbable fantasies that could only propel his inner psyche toward insanity given the grim circumstances he'd faced previously.

But as the sun set over the Caribbean to the west, he was aware that he needed to keep a clear head. He'd used his own passport to travel to Grand Cayman, which was a minor risk, but one which he gauged to be acceptable. A second passport he'd carried with him, however, would provide the gateway to his future, and deliver the impetus for the revenge he'd craved so much. One or two final elements of the plan had still to be completed, the first one involving a touch of creativity, and the second concerning some necessary housekeeping. He had received two crucial texts, one earlier in the day, and one a few minutes previously, and both had confirmed that the plan was progressing smoothly. Tonight he could relax. First, he would enjoy the massage, and then, surely, any extras he could negotiate for later in the evening.

An intense blade of morning sunlight sliced into the room, urging an unwelcome consciousness upon Calum. His subsequent awareness of an acute headache was however tempered as he observed his surroundings, recalling the athletics of the previous evening. This was Lisa's hotel room, the scene of some extraordinary sexual gymnastics. He couldn't recall much about the journey back from George Town, but he did distinctly remember what had happened in bed. Lisa had even taken a line of cocaine on his navel, and Calum, against his better judgement had accepted a reciprocal offer. Drugs had always frightened him, but how could he refuse such a girl? He turned slowly in the super-king bed, observing that she was absent.

Nude, he wandered into the bathroom and viewed himself in the mirror. God, he looked like shit. Mixing drinks was more than enough for him, never mind things like the white stuff. He gulped down two glasses of water, and walked back into the bedroom.

'Hi, big boy.' The voice emanated from the balcony, so Calum grabbed a towel from the bathroom and ventured into the bright sunlight, sharp shards of pain jabbing behind his eyes. Lisa lay on a lounger, the perfect embodiment of the swimsuit model.

'Nice long lie?' she asked.

'Fabulous. Just like you.'

'Oh…do you Scottish guys study at charm school?'

Calum laughed. 'I'm a bit rough, actually. These cocktails take their toll.'

'You should have graduated onto something purer, complemented by Adam's ale,' she said, obviously versed in art of progressive mind enhancement. 'But I have the perfect cure for you. Delaney's in George Town does the most incredible brunch. Best on the island. I'm on a blow-out before I return to a sparrow diet next week, and I won't take 'no' for an answer.'

Calum scratched his head. 'Sure, sounds good.'

He popped back down to his room, took a pain killer, showered and shaved and put on a fresh pair of chinos and a light blue Oxford shirt. He'd had the obligatory European holiday romances when on trips with pals to places such as Corfu and Tenerife as a student, but this girl had genuine class. Sure, she'd encouraged him to indulge in cocaine the previous night, but any stereotypical conclusions concerning the intellect of models could be discounted. This girl was sharp, and funny, and although the circumstances of their evening were laced with the feel-good vacation factor, Lisa had proved to be genuinely stimulating company. He briefly pondered how fortunate he was to be asked out to lunch by a stunner who had only a few hours earlier shown him sexual tricks he'd never before envisaged.

Lisa ordered a cab, and they took the brief trip down the coast to George Town, which looked just as dazzling in the midday sun as it had during the sunset of the previous evening, the vivid colours of the harbour side roofs complementing the pastel parasols sprinkled around the water's edge. Tourists and traders jostled for space, a cruise liner having disembarked shortly before they'd arrived. As they walked amongst what Calum thought might be described as the casual bustle, Lisa linked her hand with his, smiling. She'd worn a short floral dress, and her auburn hair twisted gently in the breeze which only marginally succeeded in quelling the heat. Calum was aware of the attention that she drew from other men, some subtle and some less so. He didn't mind; content to enjoy the blank canvas that a new girlfriend provided.

Lisa pointed out Delaney's, which was situated near the commercial hub, obviously catering for business people as much as tourists. As they approached the restaurant, Lisa opened her hand bag, accessing her purse.

'Oh Calum, would you do me a favour? I've only got a five-hundred-dollar bill, US, and I need some smaller stuff. I hate using plastic everywhere. Would you mind going into the bank there and changing it, while I use that restroom? She pointed to a bank, Caribbean Chartered, a few yards away along the road. Calum looked over, before smiling at Lisa.

'No need, Lisa, let me pay. You can get change later.'

'Absolutely not! This is *my* treat. I need smaller notes, be a darling and pop in there? I'll see you back here in five.'

Calum shook his head, smiling. How unlikely was that? A beautiful chick, insisting that she pays for his brunch by breaking a high value bank note? He entered the bank, queuing briefly before asking the cashier for a set of mixed denominations in return for the note, before wandering back outside, where he momentarily stood at the front door.

Simultaneously, another man viewed events from across the street, sitting in an elevated position above the crowds. He'd practised with the zoom lens, ensuring that battery failure would not hinder progress. As Calum held open the door for an elderly man entering the building, he was perfectly framed against the distinctive red logo of the Caribbean Chartered Bank. The man across the road duly captured the moment, checking that the image had been properly saved, and digitally date stamped.

Around five minutes later Calum checked his watch, scanning the area for the public restrooms. Perhaps Lisa had known of one close by, or had nipped into an adjacent hotel. He was aware that most women who he'd dated took longer than expected when any sort of comfort stop presented itself. Reapplying make up alone could take two or three minutes, maybe longer for a model used to grooming a near-perfect appearance. Had Lisa permitted him to pay they could probably have ordered by now. The midday heat had accentuated his hangover, and he'd been looking forward to this famous brunch menu. But then models traditionally ate virtually nothing, didn't they? Lisa was probably in no hurry, despite her protestations about blowing her normal regime whilst on vacation. Fleetingly, he considered calling her, before realising that he'd not obtained her cell phone number. Usually it was one of the first pieces of information that newly acquainted singles traded, but then the speed of events had negated the need for such pleasantries.

After ten minutes he crossed the road and ventured into Delaney's, checking if Lisa had missed him outside for some reason and had acquired a table, awaiting his presence. The restaurant manager reported that they were fully booked and that there was a wait for tables. Calum then called the Caribbean Club at Seven Mile Beach, explaining that he was looking for Lisa White, who was checked into room 204. After a brief delay, the clerk explained that Ms White had already checked out earlier that morning, which made no sense to him. She hadn't produced any bags when he'd met her in the foyer after he'd showered in his own room, and she'd already told him the previous evening that she'd been booked in until Sunday, flying back on American Airways to New York in the afternoon. Then, hesitantly, he switched on his phone, pensive. He accessed Google and typed her name, adding 'Manhattan', and the model agency she'd mentioned when he'd asked the night before. Beautiful as the models listed were, none were named Lisa White, and none of the photos matched.

Did she model under a pseudonym?

While Calum contemplated the disappearance of the delectable Lisa, Hawk entered the Caribbean Chartered Bank across the road carrying a passport bearing the name 'Calum Mack' and a photo of Hawk. The type of account that he was due to access required not only a security code word and pin number to access funds in person, but also the passport. This had been arranged to create a tertiary level of security, but also to confirm the illusion that had been created. As he closed the account, withdrawing more than two million US dollars in high denomination notes, he smiled widely, knowing that there would not only be evidence of Calum Mack's current residency on the island, but proof of a passport being produced.

He'd paid the hooker; she'd been expensive at $5,000, but worth it. With high-class call girls you were paying for both articulacy and theatrical skills in addition to the obvious. But first there was still one other outstanding 'consultancy fee' to be paid.

Aurelia yawned as she stretched her arms, breathing in deeply to consume more air. She'd slept poorly the previous night, and had risen at 5:00 a.m. to make another early push for the office. You simply had to embrace Mondays, she'd always figured. Why waste a seventh of your life purely on chronological grounds? The sleeplessness might also have been precipitated by the text from Vinnie the day before, where he'd promised a call on Monday afternoon. He'd apparently employed his investigative charm but wanted to wait until Monday morning, Cayman time, to confirm what he suspected. Aurelia had decided to wait until she'd spoken to Vinnie before reporting anything further to Max, but she'd mentioned that something positive was in the offing to Jen, whom she trusted not to blurt to Adam.

At just after 5:30 p.m. in London, Vinnie called.

'I think you might owe me a pint of the black stuff right enough. It doesn't travel well across the Atlantic, so my thirst for the real thing is enormous. And I'm chomping my lunch here as you speak.'

'No problem…and I will owe you as much Guinness as you can drink.'

'Ah, music to my ears. Anyway, to the important stuff. Remember I told you that Black Isle's directors are two gents named A Smith and A Jones?'

'Yes.'

'Well, they don't exist, of course. But it appears that it's been set up simply to make a small number of transactions as you've identified. Nothing more, nothing less. What's interesting is that it's connected not to an account in Switzerland or a place like that, but to one right here in George Town. With all the instantaneous electronic routing possibilities,

I'm surprised, but there you go. The bank is less than half a mile from where I'm sitting right now.' Vinnie paused for a moment, enjoying telling the tale.

'Vinnie, do you know in what name the account is held?'

'I do indeed,' Vinnie said, chewing as he spoke.

'Vinnie! Stop *torturing* me. Tell me, is the account holder, by any chance, called Calum Mack?'

'He is indeed. You stole my thunder.'

'Vinnie, you're brilliant. What you have just done is confirm that this journalist's guilty of profiting directly from insider dealing.'

'Daft bastard. If he had inside information, why didn't he just trade on the quiet and forget the public endorsement?'

'That's what I thought too. What he's actually done, though, until the last two transactions, is sell the shares before the actual formal announcement about the reasons that the stock would subsequently move. I think he figured that he'd go under the radar if he sold beforehand. But then, I reckon he became greedy. Until now I've had no direct proof. Unless, by some bizarre coincidence someone of the same name is doing the dealing.'

'No chance, Aurelia, as I will explain.'

'Oh? There's more?' Aurelia grabbed a pad to take notes.

'Your man's been over here in George Town, Aurelia. If I'd known I could have gone for a beer with him myself, maybe to see what he was going to do with over two million dollars in cash.'

'Two million dollars? *Wow.* How do you know that?'

'Because less than an hour ago, he visited the bank and withdrew the money. Emptied the account. He even used his passport to verify his identity for closing the account, which means that there is irrefutable evidence of his personal involvement.'

'That corresponds almost exactly to the value of the transactions via Black Isle. Vinnie, how do you know all this? I mean, secrecy is the byword in the Caribbean.'

'Aurelia, I am owed some favours, and no offence, but this guy is small fry.'

'Not for us, Vinnie.'

'Well that's what I figured. But because this is a relatively small amount here I think that if you can put together a watertight investigation, then the bank here *might* co-operate. But you can't use what I've said directly, as the employee I know there might get fired. You need to try to use official channels, okay?'

'Vinnie, you're a gem.'

'No problem. Anything for a future Guinness. But just a word of warning, if the guy's closed the account…'

'He might just take off?'

'Exactly. Or maybe he'll just head back to London to blow his money.'

'Good point, Vinnie. But first I've one more hunch which I need to check out.'

Chapter 8

Aurelia's hunch proved to be prophetic. As with 'location, location, location' in the property game, 'research, research, research' repeatedly proved to be the essential ingredient in her profession. Calum Mack was indeed connected to staff working with, or for, each one of the companies in which Black Isle had invested prior to publication of the stock recommendations, and she was eager to confront him officially with her evidence. She was unsure if the Caribbean Chartered Bank would officially confirm the identity of the account holder responsible for the large withdrawal the previous Friday, however. Banks in tax havens were secretive principally as their very existence depended on being secretive, thus the strength of any favours owed to Vinnie would probably be insufficient for a prosecution.

The silver bullet in such cases—as Telford had often argued—was an immediate or early confession by the guilty party, which would reduce the necessity of compliance by a third party in a distant and uncertain jurisdiction. Therefore, Aurelia had agreed with Telford to meet both the police and Crown Prosecution Authority on Tuesday with a view to rumbling Mack on Wednesday, assuming he'd returned home. Unfortunately, Adam had predictably joined the case team at the behest of Telford, but would initially be involved only in further desk work.

'So let me get this right.' Ben scratched his chin. 'You screwed a beautiful, young American model in paradise, and then you failed to obtain her phone number? Are you losing it completely?'

Calum shook his head, essentially in agreement. Perhaps he *was* losing it. He'd waited until Wednesday to tell Ben most of the story, but glossed over the salient fact that he'd found no record of Lisa's existence at the modelling agency she'd mentioned. On the flight home he'd contemplated the bitter-sweet emotion of having connected in such an intimate way with Lisa, only for her to disappear into the ether. The remainder of the weekend in Grand Cayman had suddenly seemed flat in comparison, the stunning beaches having failed to compensate for the feeling of social failure. He'd then been jarred by Powell on his return, as the column he'd submitted from his own research the previous Thursday had ended up having to be rewritten late on Saturday as contradictory news had broken whilst he was on the trip. Calum had ignored the financial media when away, so the story had been a bit of a wakeup call on his return home.

'So, any more tips from this guy? Stuff the junkets mate, I'd like some of the dosh.' Ben spoke conspiratorially, sipping a Pepsi. They were standing in the corner of the staff room, which was unusually quiet.

'Keep your voice down,' Calum retorted, quickly scanning a couple of other colleagues to see if anyone had overheard. Journalism was the most inquisitive and least trustworthy profession, Calum had once opined to Ben.

'So that means no? The guy's gone silent?'

'Correct.'

'I was going to supply some capital and even offer to split the proceeds from your next dead cert. But I'll just have to spend it all on booze and chicks that *don't* disappear after I've impressed them in bed.'

'Just you do that.'

'Well, at least you've had a good run. Probably secured your job. You do wonder where this guy got his info, though. Can't be legal. Surprised that Powell hasn't insisted that you spill the beans.'

'I protect sources. Journalistic integrity,' Calum replied, dead pan, before they both laughed, drawing attention from some other staff in the room. Just then, Susie De Vere, the office manager, popped her head round the door.

'Call just came in for you, Calum. Someone called Aurelia Harley, from the Financial Conduct Authority? Says it's urgent.' Calum frowned as Susie passed him a note with a number written in red ink.

Ben grimaced at the note as if it were poisoned. 'Red ink, mate. That's a bad sign, like it's written in blood,' he said, before slapping Calum on the back and heading out of the room.

Aurelia had waited at her desk. She'd already agreed with Max Telford on Tuesday about how the liaison with the police and the Crown Prosecution Service would operate. The trilateral cooperation needed to proceed with a prosecution required subtle timing and concise coordination. Telford had undertaken the second briefing with Maxwell and Robson, the officers who'd been attached to the case, and formally requested that the police obtain a warrant to search Mack's apartment, the timing of which would be partially dependent on Mack's availability, and of course, his reaction.

Robson and Maxwell were a stereotypical CID duo—stoical, though clearly competent. She'd met their like before in a previous life. Indeed, her father had displayed some similar characteristics himself when in the Irish police. Her enthusiasm for the police involvement had been enhanced not only by Vinnie's call, but from the discovery of the link between Mack and some staff connected to the companies in which insider trading had occurred. Sometimes it was the simple, human failings that proved most damning. Just as murders were most likely to have been perpetrated by someone close to a victim, insider dealing invariably involved people who were, or had been, closely linked to one another. In effect, the level of trust involved usually necessitated a close relationship, a truism that those who perpetrated insider dealing often failed to consider when attempting to conceal such crimes. Initial checks made by DS Robson in the Police National Computer confirmed a clean record for Mack, though as DS Robson explained, every criminal had to be nailed a first time.

Aurelia had prepared her opening gambit carefully, having been cleared for take-off with an enthusiastic Max Telford, who could clearly smell blood. Adam had been in Max's office when she'd spoken to him in person about her approach to Calum Mack. Rather than returning after Adam had departed, she'd briefed Max in Adam's presence, feeling that expediency trumped interference. Adam had eyed her carefully, taking in every word, but Max had exuded a degree of confidence that had rubbed off on Aurelia. Max had agreed that she would make the initial approach. This type of strategy had been employed previously, where—in conjunction with police intervention and warrants—FCA executives could fire the initial investigative salvo.

Her phone rang.

'Aurelia Harley? Calum Mack, from the *Sentinel*. How can I help you?' Bingo. Aurelia smiled as she detected a note of caution, delivered with what she would have identified as a distinct northern Scottish accent, or perhaps a *Black Isle* one, should she have chosen to split hairs.

'Hi. I'm an investigator with the FCA,' she said, pausing briefly before continuing. 'I'm with the unit that deals with fighting financial crime.' She hesitated again, letting this salient fact sink in.

'Right…how can I help you?' At the other end of the line Calum's mind darted over several thoughts, transcending a number of angles almost instantaneously. What did she want? Why was she calling *him*?

'I'd like to speak to you in person,' she replied. 'Today, if possible? I think that it would be in your interest to cooperate.'

'Cooperate with what exactly? Can you tell me what this is about?'

'Well, I'd prefer to meet. It's always better to explain the details of an investigation face to face.' Aurelia had already seen Calum's photo, and pictured him with his dark locks, probably panicking at the other end of the line.

'I'm lost here. Look, I'm not a trader. I'm a financial journalist, so it would really help if you filled me in, as it's a busy day here at the *Sentinel*.'

'At the FCA every day is a busy day, though I'm sure that the same circumstances apply to you. Trust me, Mr Mack, I strongly recommend that you meet me today. We're at Canary Warf. North Colonnade. Are you free after lunch, say just after two o'clock?' Aurelia was aware that the police were now poised to search Mack's apartment, the minute that Telford gave them the nod.

Calum's mind raced. He could sense that something was wrong. But then he had done nothing illegal. Surely that clown Powell hadn't been buying shares in the firms he'd recently tipped? That actually wouldn't have surprised him. But personally, he'd nothing to hide. In fact it would appear suspicious, foolish even, if he refused to "cooperate" with whatever this Harley woman was investigating.

'Sure, I know where you are. I suppose it'll get me out of the office.'

Calum had visited the Financial Conduct Authority's offices on just one previous occasion, to interview an executive about a story, and his sentiments hadn't altered. It was a monstrosity of charcoal-tinted glass, originally home to the FCA's predecessor, the Financial Services Authority. He wondered what real difference the word 'conduct' made, and then briefly considered the tougher stance taken by the regulator in recent times. The place was packed with bureaucrats, the sort of operation of which Brussels or Strasbourg would be proud—a compendium of overpaid pedants whose only aim, apart from accumulating a secure pension, was to torpedo everyone else. And the irony was that they mainly appeared to nail the *little* guys. As he entered the building he reflected on the fact that there had been very few big hits recently, but they were sure to clobber some poor bastard that had benefitted from a one-off rogue stock tip. Who was that guy they got the last time—someone called Fleeting? Aptly named, as his gains before being arrested had indeed been ephemeral. The man had been jailed for a few thousand that he was going to split with his father-in-law. What a laugh. Meanwhile the multimillionaires continued to offshore their wealth and pay no tax.

A member of the secretarial staff showed Calum to a meeting room on the third floor where three members of staff were already present. Aurelia Harley stood firstly to introduce herself, instantly giving the impression of being the ambitious career type. She was attractive certainly, with striking blue eyes and dark hair complemented by silver earrings, though he detected a distinct aura of intellectual grit that accompanied her patterned platinum power suit. She introduced an older man in his fifties as Max Telford, her director. Calum had heard of Telford, though they had never met. He attempted to appear nonchalant, as Telford was a player. What did his presence mean? The third member of staff appeared to be some kind of assistant, though she was not introduced.

Telford spoke firstly. 'Mr Mack, if we can proceed? To set the record, these are preliminary enquiries. You are no under obligation to say anything, but if we are to make mutually beneficial progress on this matter, your input would be necessary.'

'Okay. I'm still stuck here. You'll need to fill me in.' Calum checked his watch, subconsciously willing the meeting to conclude before it had begun.

'Ms Harley?' Telford gestured to his direct report, who was sitting at his right hand side across the table from Calum.

'Mr Mack, we have reason to believe that you are directly involved in an insider trading scam, where you have used the publicity generated by your column at the *Sunday Sentinel* to personally benefit from the proceeds of such trading.'

'*What?*' Calum flinched visibly as the impact of the accusation struck. They must be bluffing. 'This is…ridiculous. I may not be the most able tipster in the city, but I'm no crook. In fact, I have a strong belief in straight dealing, ask the guys at the office. Honestly, this better be good.' He folded his arms in a defensive gesture as Telford and Harley glanced at each other.

'You made a trip to George Town in Grand Cayman last week.'

Calum momentarily looked up. 'I did. And?'

'What was the purpose of your visit?'

'This is about my holidays? Are you being serious? I haven't been away for ages, and I took a trip because I needed a break.' Instantly, Calum realised that this was a *lie*. He'd not decided to take a break at all. It had been offered to him by a third party and he'd accepted. Shit, he thought, swallowing.

'So you were on holiday?'

'Correct. And what shares are you talking about, exactly? I haven't bought a single stock since I took the job at the *Sentinel.* Check my bank account. It's in the red, by the way.'

'We *have* checked your bank account, actually,' Aurelia Harley said with a flat tone. 'But that's not of direct concern. Of concern, however, are the unusual trades in the following stocks.'

'What stocks?'

She briefly consulted her notes. 'Walltex, X4D4, Unreal Power, Simtrex, and Virtual Bank. All just prior to major announcements. And possibly related currency trading too. Do you recognise these companies?'

Calum nodded, swallowing again. 'Of course I do. I recommended these stocks. That's not a crime. It's my *job* to tips stocks, and yes, these companies did well after they were tipped in the column. So what? I can assure you that I did not buy shares in any of them. Why would I do that? How stupid would that actually be if I put my name to a tip I'd traded?'

Aurelia viewed Calum carefully for signs of evasion, before speaking. 'Perhaps you wouldn't interpret it as being stupid if you thought you'd covered your tracks. For example, if you sold the stock *before* the news formally broke in three of the cases.'

'What do you mean by that? I haven't got any tracks to cover!' Calum held out his hands, the frustration creeping in.

'You were brought up in the Black Isle, weren't you? Nice little scenic peninsula north of Inverness?' Aurelia asked, changing direction to assess Calum's reaction.

'Yes, but what has that got to do with these ridiculous accusations?' Calum stared at Aurelia and then glanced at Telford, who broke the silence.

'Don't you think it's a bit of a coincidence that shares in all of these companies were bought and sold through a company called Black Isle?' Telford looked over his glasses in a school masterly pose, his eyebrows raised at an acute angle.

'What? I've never heard of a firm called Black Isle. Is that what this is about? Some chance set of transactions, and you've gone on a fishing trip to snare me? Christ,' he said, his exasperation becoming evident as he mimicked quotation marks, '*Black Isle* must be a pretty generic title for any firm?'

'Not if it's registered in George Town, Grand Cayman.'

'What? I can assure you that if what you are saying is accurate, then I am *not* connected. This is madness.' Calum ran his hands through his dark hair, suddenly feeling beads of sweat on his forehead. He looked directly at Telford, who almost sneered back before Aurelia Harley spoke.

'Mr Mack, I would appreciate if you would give me a moment in private with Mr Telford.' Calum shrugged, expelling air as they left the room. Sure, he thought, why not devise more bullshit allegations? As these thoughts flooded his synapses, he considered the telephone tipster. Shit, what had this all been about? A free holiday in Grand Cayman, which was connected to share purchases for his tips?

Then another thought suddenly hit him.

Completely out of the blue.

When an overseas flight seat is booked, a passport number is needed, isn't it? How on earth did the phone tipster know his passport number?

Outside in the corridor Aurelia asked if she could pursue Mack just a little further. There was something else that she had uncovered based on the hunch she'd mentioned to Vinnie, an interesting twist that had bridged the gap in the case, and she wanted to test Mack to see if he would crack. So far he was in denial, but sometimes when faced with overwhelming evidence, an individual might opt for the simple escape route known as *admission*. Normally, preliminary enquiries were exactly that. Sometimes millions were at stake and if a suspect looked likely to flee, the FCA would simply engage the police for an arrest from the outset. However, in more regular cases they set up such meetings only if they felt the was a realistic prospect of acquiring further, damning information—ideally an admission in front of witnesses—that would strengthen any case before the police and prosecuting authorities formally interviewed and pressed charges. And due to the late deal Telford had struck with the police, at the current juncture officers were due to be in Mack's apartment, scanning for complementary evidence and removing any devices he possessed.

Telford frowned, and asked what 'twist' she had, expressing his concern that protocol would be best observed with direct police involvement. However, Aurelia was insistent. This was her opportunity to strike a real blow. Telford then smiled slowly. He could see the determination in Aurelia's features.

'Just watch for admissibility in court, Aurelia. Remember, he's entitled to representation, even if he looks guilty as hell.' He looked Aurelia in the eye, seeing the detective's daughter staring back rather that the economics graduate whom he'd originally hired.

'Don't worry, Max. This little gem is factual. It doesn't provide irrefutable proof of insider trading, but it might just push him into admission.' She briefly explained what she had in mind.

'Excellent,' Telford grinned. 'Go for it.'

When they re-entered the room, Calum sat grim-faced, his arms firmly folded. Aurelia and Telford sat opposite again.

'Mr Mack, could you confirm something for me?'

'I'll continue to tell you the truth.'

'Good. You were a student at Edinburgh University?'

'Some time back, yes. I was an undergraduate there. Is that a problem too?'

'Not in its own right.' Aurelia realised that she was occupying solid ground because she already knew the answer to the question she was about to pose. She'd seen the photo of a group of students on a weekend break, and had subsequently deduced some of the connections. Often during an investigation, nothing happened for a period, and a waiting game had to take place, and then three or four significant advances occurred in close succession.

This had been one of those occasions.

'When you were an undergraduate, did you study alongside the following individuals? Firstly, Nigel Tomlinson, CEO of Pan-Euro Investment Bank?'

Calum hesitated. 'Yes. I wouldn't say he was a close friend but yes, I know him.'

'And have you spoken to him recently?'

'I...yes, I did speak to him actually, but he would not disclose any information about...'

'About what?'

'About...X4D4.' Calum squinted. 'Look, he was very dismissive of me.'

'Really? That's difficult to believe,' Telford said. 'On what date did you call him?'

'I don't know. Just a few days before the column was published.'

'And what about Donald Wilson?'

'Donald Wilson? *Donnie* Wilson? Haven't spoken to him for long enough. Why is that relevant?'

'Donald Wilson is financial controller at Walltex.' Aurelia surveyed Calum carefully, his reaction one of apparent confusion.

'I didn't know that he'd moved there. I mean, you don't keep track of everyone you meet at university. And in any case I did not tip Walltex.'

Aurelia viewed one of the scanned columns. 'No, but you mentioned after the stock rocketed that you'd known in advance. One week afterwards. Or are you denying what's written in black and white before me?' Aurelia passed a paper copy of the column over to Max, who locked eyes with Calum.

'No, but there's a reason behind that,' Calum spoke shakily.

'Really? What about Anthony Rowland?' Once she'd considered the university connection, it had taken her less than twenty minutes to match the younger looking students to the professionals of today and their corporate careers. What was the chance of mere accidental connection to these share trades?

'Yes, I know Tony, but then so does half the city.'

'So his possible connection to the Unreal Power story is another coincidence?'

'Yes, it is. Again, I haven't spoken to him for some time either. And do you honestly think that a minister would risk his career to provide me with inside information?'

This time Telford replied. 'It wouldn't be the first time. And information can be passed very subtly, but then we don't need to tell you that fact, do we?'

'Look,' Calum said scratching his head. He'd been holding back, but this was clearly the time to explain his source of his predicament. 'I've had quite a bit of contact from what you might term an *anonymous* tipster. The information for these columns all came from the *same* source. A mystery caller. Normally, as a journalist, I wouldn't reveal a source, but you give me no alternative.'

'Okay, a mystery caller…so who is this source?' Aurelia asked, clearly unimpressed.

'I don't know.' As Calum spoke, Aurelia and Telford shared a knowing look.

'You don't know? That *is* a mystery,' Telford said.

'He refused to identify himself, but the tips were good. I'm under pressure at work to deliver, so why wouldn't I use a secret source? He paid for the trip to Grand Cayman, said it was a reward. You'd turn down a free trip, would you?' Calum placed his hands flat against the table, searching Aurelia's eyes, imploring her to accept the validity of the story, though he decided not to mention how his passport number could have been known to someone else.

Aurelia then asked a further question. 'So you *weren't* on a holiday as you said, but on a business trip paid by a mystery accomplice? If what you suggest was accurate, Mr Mack, you would presumably not have been known to Douglas Lyndon either. He was at Edinburgh University with you too.'

Calum looked upwards in frustration. 'Yes, I know Douglas Lyndon. But he doesn't work at any of these firms. I know that for a fact.'

'So where does he work, then?'

'I'm sure that Douglas is employed by Channing's Bank. He's an IT specialist.' Calum said, shaking his head.

'And Channing's just happens to advise Virtual Bank and Simtrex. Incredible coincidence, don't you think?' Aurelia peered directly at Calum, whose eyes were now darting from side to side.

'That's a complete…yes, coincidence.'

'And are you claiming that you haven't spoken to Lyndon recently either?' Telford asked.

'No, I have not.'

Aurelia shared another look with Telford, and he nodded in return. One more push before the cops arrived.

'Mr Mack, if your whole story held water, could you explain why last Friday you visited the Caribbean Chartered bank in George Town to withdraw over two million dollars from an account in your own name?'

'Two million dollars! This is *crazy*. I did go into a bank,' Calum blurted as he looked upwards, recalling the brief visit. 'But just to change money.'

'A lot of money, it seems.' Telford locked eyes with him.

'I need to speak to a lawyer.'

'I think you're right,' Telford said. 'The police will be looking to interview you here immediately after this meeting.'

Chapter 9

Calum agreed to stay on at the FCA to meet Detective Inspector Maxwell and Detective Sergeant Robson from the Met as the alternative involved an immediate trip to the Isle of Dogs police station. There was clearly some type of pincer movement being conducted, with Maxwell and Robson playing the part of the ugly sisters to complement Aurelia Harley's Cinderella. Calum suspected that he was being manipulated—forced almost— into some kind of confession. He was permitted to make a brief call, which he made to an incredulous Ben, imploring him to rush his brother Martin over to Canary Warf. Martin worked as a criminal lawyer in the City and they'd met socially on a number of occasions when Calum and Ben had hit the town. Martin had once pinched a girl from under his nose in a club, though this was no time to hold grudges. He desperately needed someone with chutzpah as the shock of the afternoon's events had crushed his confidence, and Martin had immediately sprung to mind.

Martin arrived within half an hour, and although Calum was relieved to see him, he feared that his appearance could only expedite the next grilling. He was allowed a fifteen-minute conference session in a briefing room with Martin before facing the police, on the proviso that he made no additional calls. Calum managed to provide a succinct version of events that contained all the salient facts. Martin remained impassive throughout. Undoubtedly he'd heard much worse from representatives of the criminal underworld, though this proved little consolation.

'If *you* did not withdraw the money from the bank in George Town, and there is no actual evidence of your presence there, then you might evade charges of improper gain, even if a third party has registered an account in your name.' Martin spoke candidly searching Calum's eyes for candour.

'Oh *shit.*' Calum suddenly held his head in his hands.

'What?'

'The girl. There was this model, Lisa…well, I don't know what she actually did or even if that was her real name, but she…she asked me to change money for her at a bank in George Town. I can't remember which one it was, but I can guess. *Damn it.*'

'So you think that you were set up to go into the same bank?'

'Shit, yes. This is awful.' Calum ran his fingers through his hair, feeling the sweat. 'I thought she'd just pissed off for some reason, but now it looks as if this was all orchestrated.'

Martin sat back in his chair. 'This doesn't look good, Calum, but it still doesn't prove that you spoke to the individuals that they claim you spoke to, however. Purely *knowing* someone does not prove criminal partnership, nor that you are a beneficiary of illegal actions. There needs to be more than that—greater connectivity.'

'I spoke to Tomlinson, that's all. But that was *after* the mystery caller spoke to me,' Calum replied, before there was a knock on the door and Robson appeared.

Martin pulled Calum aside for a moment and spoke in whispered tones before they left the briefing room. 'I hate to tell you, but if your story is correct—and I believe you that it is—someone out there has got it in for you. As far as the FCA and police are concerned, your story will probably look contrived, fabricated even. But remain resolute. It's the best defence, trust me. And say *nothing* unless I nod that it's okay? Got that?'

Aurelia and Max Telford attended the police interview, but did not speak apart from clarifying one or two specific points. Clearly they'd further briefed Robson and Maxwell while Calum had spoken to Martin, as although the questions repeated much of the same ground covered already, further probing occurred in terms of his relationship with the individuals with whom he'd been at Edinburgh University and the nature of the trades.

Despite their demeanour, the two cops were no plods, in fact, they seemed remarkably knowledgeable about financial crime, a concern that Martin twigged early on, and his interjections and signals to Calum became more accentuated as the interview progressed. After about an hour, Martin insisted that Calum answer no further questions.

At this juncture, Maxwell asked one final question. 'Can you confirm once more that *prior* to the dates we have indicated,' Maxwell showed Calum the dates on a piece of paper, repeating the specific times, 'you did not make any contact by telephone with Anthony Rowland, Douglas Lyndon or Donald Wilson?'

'For Christ's sake, *no*. I've answered that already,' Calum said, visibly exhibiting the tension that was tearing at his mind. 'I am innocent of any crime. I'd have to be a complete fool to undertake a scam like this. Can't you see that I have been set up?'

Both Maxwell and Robson remained expressionless, although Telford and Harley shared another look, before Maxwell broke the silence.

'We have obtained a search warrant for your apartment, and our officers are present there as we speak. We will be taking you to the station at the Isle of Dogs, where you will be interviewed further pending formal charges.'

Aurelia had seen the *Financial Times* online, noting that the story of Calum Mack's arrest had made the headlines. The FT had covered the story in some depth, schadenfreude flourishing in the media world. She noted that Mack's editor, Rod Powell, had been 'fully cooperative' with the investigation. Aurelia had sensed that Powell would happily sink Mack to save his own skin. Powell, as the *Sunday Sentinel's* Business Editor, had sanctioned all of the columns that were relevant to the investigation, and Telford had charged Adam with running checks on Powell and other colleagues at the publication in order to ascertain if the malaise had spread beyond Mack. The court, in conjunction with the FCA, had restrained Calum's assets on the application of the FCA, and both Aurelia and Telford had worked around the clock with the police and the CPS to substantiate a number of remaining elements of connective evidence. Rarely had Aurelia felt so overwhelmed, as the CPS required substantive proof not only of the money trail, but of any meetings, texts, emails or phone calls between Mack and the key players at the firms that had been involved. Evidence to secure further charges always required painstaking research.

The police had also questioned Nigel Tomlinson of Pan Euro, Douglas Lyndon of Channing's Investment Bank, and Donald Wilson of Walltex. They had postponed speaking to Anthony Rowland until, or if, further evidence emerged. In any case, Rowland had been abroad on official business and DI Maxwell had told Aurelia that he'd been asked by very senior officers at the Met to leave Rowland be for the time being. Rowland was the biggest fish, but also the one with loosest links with the shares that had been traded by Black Isle. Reading between the lines, however, Aurelia felt that Maxwell disapproved of what he appeared to consider the establishment closing ranks behind Rowland. She could see Maxwell's point of view, recalling her own father's similar frustration in the past with the two or three cases where he had been involved with investigating prominent public figures in Ireland.

DI Maxwell then called to request a meeting with Max Telford, Aurelia and Adam to brief them regarding the results of the interviews with Tomlinson, Lyndon and Wilson. Telford had ordered donuts, which was, in some respects, a metaphor for intent. Aurelia poured the coffee.

'They're definitely concealing something,' Maxwell said flatly, munching on a chocolate donut. 'All three are shifty as hell. Tomlinson, in particular, is a pain in the arse. Threatened us with all sorts, and he had *three* company solicitors at the meeting with him. Clearly used to getting his own way.' Maxwell rubbed crumbs from his finger tips and looked sideways toward Robson who smirked before speaking.

'I'd love to see him going down. He actually used that old cliché: *do you know who I am*? We explained that we knew all about him. But no confession or explanation.'

'And no admissions from any of them regarding discussions of any sort with Mack?' Telford asked.

'No. We've analysed Mack's work tablet and phone, and there's no record of any emails to the four amigos. Likewise, Mack's own phone has only the one call to Tomlinson, to which he admitted,' Maxwell said. 'And I don't know if we'll get a warrant to analyse their computers or phones without reasonable suspicion.'

'And so far, there's no evidence that any of them have actually traded in the same shares themselves,' Adam noted. He'd continued with the ancillary work checking out other potential illegal trades. 'But then again, Mack could have been about to pay them. Maybe you moved too quickly, Aurelia.'

Aurelia sighed. She'd been awaiting the first round of criticism from Adam, but decided to ignore the comment, before addressing Maxwell directly. 'So what was it that you think they're concealing, exactly?'

'I'm not sure,' Maxwell said. 'Tomlinson clearly dislikes Mack. That much is evident. Wilson was more non-committal, but he did ask who else we were interviewing. Of course, we said nothing, but the fact that the question was posed reveals something—he clearly knows that there's wider involvement here. We've released nothing to the media, so he was probably fishing to see how much we knew. Mack hasn't been able to contact him directly, as we have him in custody of course. Wilson could have been in contact with others, though we do not know for definite if they are all part of some type of syndicate, and Adam, you've no evidence of such, right?'

'No.' Adam's contribution had so far been insignificant.

Telford then spoke. 'Have you found anything else of interest at Mack's apartment? Could he have concealed something there?'

'Funny that you bring that up,' Maxwell scratched his head. 'We have a potential lead in that respect. We have three mobile phones that we found in Mack's apartment just this morning when we revisited. Quite often we operate a second sweep. They were hidden on a top shelf in a bedroom, inside an old towel, all recent models, two still with some charge. You usually find multiple phones when a guy is cheating on his wife or something like that, but Mack's currently single and lives on his own, so it's not that. Now, why would he have three extra phones hidden away?'

'That looks promising. I mean, if Mack was using secret phones,' Telford said.

'Exactly,' Maxwell replied. 'We should get the analysis of any calls made using these phones shortly. It might come to zilch, but if there is any connection to the other players in this case, that's another nail.'

Despite repeated efforts to use a positive mental programming technique he'd learned some years previously, Calum's mind danced in disturbing circles interrupted by intermittent noise. Only a few days previously he'd been living it up on Seven Mile Beach, and now his freedom consisted of a small cell and the company of an adjacent drug addict with apparent schizophrenia. Calum's heart beat raced, and he considered his mother, who suffered from angina and had broken into tears on the only other remaining call he'd been permitted to make. Remand—which usually permitted some restricted time outside of custody—had been rejected, since a judge had officially agreed with the CPS that he was a flight risk. What a laugh. He'd just flown *back* to London. How could they be so stupid?

His frustration had been aggravated by the isolation. Any attempts he'd made to piece together the elements that constituted his predicament were hampered by his own ignorance. He had no access to the world outside, and operating without the internet or even a phone, he felt, was tantamount to torture. Normally he inhabited a world of multifaceted communication, the buzz of the newsroom and the latest data fuelling the cognitive process. Information was available in an instant. In the limited moments of optimism that he'd experienced he considered that he would *prove* his innocence, most particularly as he *was* indeed innocent, and had made no financial gain.

Surely they'd have to prove that he'd benefitted? And *who was* the secret tipster? How the hell had he been so naive, incompetent enough to trust someone he'd never even met? Or *had* he met the guy?

Shit, what a mess.

Ben and Martin both came to visit that evening, with Ben showing a degree of solidarity, even saying that he felt guilty himself. When Calum asked why, Ben said something about wishing he had persuaded him to ignore the mystery tipster once he'd found out what was happening. He even offered money, which Calum refused. To make matters worse, Calum proved to have many more questions than Martin possessed answers. As with all lawyers tasked with defending the apparently indefensible actions of a client who insisted he was innocent, Martin's demeanour was based largely on tentative reassurances and process-driven explanation. Why couldn't Calum be released from the torture of this cell? Bail had been set at half a million and even if this was achieved his passport would be confiscated.

What?

'Yes, it's a high figure,' Martin accepted, 'but you are considered a potential absconder, even without your real passport.' Calum showered Martin with demands for detail, though many of the questions proved rhetorical, and Martin assured Calum that he would give his best. In the brief period available, Martin also quizzed Calum, noting the approximate times the tipster had called, and his relationship with those connected with the firms that Calum had recommended. All Calum could add was that they'd been student friends from the past who'd largely drifted their separate ways, as graduates often do, explaining that he'd only been in contact rarely. Martin then asked why Calum hadn't considered it odd that he knew people connected to the companies tipped. Again, Calum said he'd briefly pondered this, but that he knew hundreds of people in the City, including others he'd associated with while at Edinburgh University and with whom there were no current connections. Martin then asked again about the caller, and Calum remembered the phones he'd been given.

'Why would you use phones given by another party?'

'He insisted that I used his phones,' Calum said, arms folded tightly. 'It was part of the deal. I didn't see a problem as the phones were unconnected to me. Bear in mind that I was unaware how he came by the information. Sure, I considered that he might have inside knowledge, but that wasn't my business. We get calls from such people from time to time, and what I do is investigate to check for validity, and then publish if the tips look logical.

Some come good, others flop. That's the nature of the job. But I did not deal in stock as I never have since I took that job. Jesus, Ben, you were even asking for tips but I resolutely refused any takers at the office.' Ben just stared back, stone-faced.

Martin glanced at Ben before continuing. 'So you got rid of these phones afterwards, Calum?'

Calum scratched his chin. 'No, they're in my flat. In fact, he said I was to keep them at home in case he wanted to use them for future calls. But that obviously hasn't materialised.' Calum looked directly at Martin, who hesitated before replying.

'The police have searched your flat, Calum. So the chances are that they will now possess those phones.'

'Right…that could *help*. I mean, it could help prove my innocence! These phones should provide the proof that this guy called *me*, connecting to his number. The police could ascertain his identify from this, surely? I don't know why I didn't think of this before. My head's been such a mess.'

When Martin and Ben exited the visiting area, they discussed the fact that Calum's mood had lifted during the visit, but Martin felt that the case was a bummer. On the proviso that Calum was telling the truth—and Martin had met many polished liars in his time in criminal defence—it was still evident that the FCA would not have pursued the case had they not felt confident of a conviction. They'd restrained his assets, which implied that they believed he had the money secreted somewhere else. Telford and Harley did not look like gamblers. Martin was simply grateful that Ben's wish for inside information apparently hadn't been granted, or his brother would also be facing charges. The police and the Crown Prosecution Service, particularly when working with professional investigators such as those at the FCA, had the benefit of triangulation, a three-way perspective backed up by resources. Calum could apparently not afford to pay Martin to send an investigator to Grand Cayman, for instance, yet the FCA might pull in some favours over there to strengthen their own case.

To make matters worse, the police would often sit on evidence until legally obliged to share it, and this could leave the case for a poorly funded defence in tatters. Martin had listened to Calum explaining that he'd some limited extra resources available which his parents had retained for him when he'd moved south from Edinburgh, but this represented something of a quandary for Martin—if Calum *was* lying to him and also had over two million dollars stashed away somewhere in Grand Cayman, he ran the risk of being imprisoned through not resourcing the case properly. Alternatively, if he were indeed innocent and refused to admit guilt—yet was ultimately found guilty—the Crown would assume that he had secreted the money, and would increase the sentence accordingly. And Martin did not share Calum's optimism about these phones—if he really had been blind-sided by a conman, the phones would likely be an intricate part of the ruse, a decoy tactic employed to divert the target's attention away from the main illusion.

That night Calum awoke to the sound and odour of vomiting, as his fellow inmate's withdrawal symptoms kicked in again. Calum had been mid-nightmare, another recurrent theme of his earlier life this time magnified through the prism of current events.

The initial elation Aurelia had experienced as a consequence of Calum Mack's arrest had now subsided, and she pondered that the thrill of the chase perhaps offered her greater personal utility than the catch itself. Having interviewed Mack in person, his character had contrasted sharply with what she'd anticipated, in fact, she felt that he had appeared quite genuine despite the damning evidence presented. First impressions had always been important to her, another facet of her personality that had also been imprinted in her father's DNA. But then, some people were simply good liars. Maxwell and Robson were clearly arch cynics and had told her that Mack should go down. They were of course motivated by the collar, and given that she'd done most of the ground work they'd gained their own rewards from joining a band wagon. Unfortunately, Adam had too. He was now in almost constant dialogue with either the police or the CPS regarding the other participants. Clearly Adam had interpreted things correctly—if credit were to be allocated for the case he would demand his share.

Frustratingly—and Aurelia had debated this in a tangled way in her own mind—just as Adam became more involved, she began to experience minor doubts about the case. Initially she dismissed such thoughts as some kind of perverse, competitive desire to see Adam fail to secure success, even if the collapse of the case would ultimately reflect more badly on her. But then she looked at the evidence: Mack had a point. Why on earth would he have publically tipped the shares if he'd been buying privately? Why take the risk? Sure, his tips may have secured some initial, upward movement in the share prices, but these companies had underlying reasons for price movements that were to be revealed anyway. Had a smart, former investment banker such as Mack honestly believed that because the shares were, mainly, sold prior to actual company announcements, he'd be in the clear?

The Caribbean Chartered Bank had also not formally responded to requests for account information. This was par for the financial course in the Caribbean. Aurelia had discussed the problem with Max Telford, who said he'd already asked for some political pressure to be placed on the bank through the Foreign Office. Max had also said, however, that he'd been told informally that this was unlikely because the wider investigation involved the junior minister Anthony Rowland.

Then, just as Aurelia considered that the flaws in the case might create an impasse, two events occurred within one day. Firstly, DS Robson phoned with the details of calls made using the phones found in Calum Mack's flat. Aurelia could feel his enthusiasm inflate as he explained that calls had indeed been made to the work numbers all of the individuals concerned. So Mack had lied. What's more, the phones were all registered to Mack himself, demonstrating that he'd orchestrated the scam despite attempting to conceal the means. Further charges, there, Robson reported. Oddly, though, which Robson could not fully explain, calls had also been made from all these phones to Mack's number at the *Sentinel*. Robson surmised that this might have been another attempt to conceal events, with Mack having simply invented his mystery caller. Given this enthusiasm, Robson glossed over the need for a full account for the latter finding, content to provide a critique of how the bad guys usually end up making school boy errors, 'City' types or not. Robson then said they wanted to interview Tomlinson and company again now that further evidence had emerged, and that he would liaise regarding the strategy before the interviews took place.

The second break concerned a mysterious photograph sent by regular mail anonymously to the FCA, marked for Aurelia's attention. For an instant, Aurelia thought it was some kind of cryptic communication, perhaps from a friend on holiday. But then she recognised the individual in the picture, standing at the front door of Caribbean Chartered Bank. She noted the comments on the reverse of the photo, which read "Calum Mack, George Town, Grand Cayman". A digital date stamp was circled in red on the front of the picture. There was a London postmark on the envelope but no other clue as to who had sent it, because Mack clearly hadn't taken a selfie. Immediately, she spoke to Telford who called her in to his office. Given that the bank itself wasn't cooperating, this was a substantial help. Although curious as to how the photo could have been taken, Aurelia then called Maxwell, and asked about the validity of digital date stamps.

'The photo is interesting,' he said. 'Someone could probably forge a date stamp, but we know that Mack was on the Island anyway, so this might be a help. The only key thing we don't know is the whereabouts of the proceeds. And unless he comes clean, further denial is simply going to send him down for longer.'

Hawk had celebrated into the night when the news of Calum Mack's arrest had broken. Vengeance, he felt, was a commodity in short supply in life, and although his delight was tempered with caution in respect of what final outcome would prevail, he likened current circumstances to scoring a set play a team had practiced in football—the rewards for having worked out in advance how to win. He'd then cleared things up in London and headed west again, having acquired a taste for the Caribbean whilst in Grand Cayman.

He was watching news about the Middle East on CNN while sipping a beer in his hotel room in St Lawrence Gap, Barbados. He'd chosen Barbados as it offered fun, but it was probably still a stop-gap. He noted the unfolding events in Iraq, and he quietly reflected on his past. During his tenure as a student, he had learned about the concept of utility. Laymen called the same thing *satisfaction*, but Hawk preferred the economists' description. Surely there had to be tangible, practical, benefits to any form of satisfaction, and sufficient volume of such benefits, to lubricate the soul? He recalled the moustached Liverpudlian economics lecturer with the bottle green v-neck jumper he'd had in his first year, and his explanation of diminishing marginal utility. The first pint of beer, he'd said, staring at the graph on the old whiteboard, provided high levels of utility, euphoria, perhaps. The second was still hugely enjoyable, but didn't quite provide the edge, the buzz, of the first. The third? Well, you'd enjoy it, especially if paid for by that guy who never bought a round, but the utility was clearly diminished. The tenth pint, he'd rationalised, was likely to get you in debt, arrested, or pregnant. The class had sniggered. Hawk hadn't, but he'd known exactly what the man meant at the time, just as he did now. Basically, a person needed sufficient resources to keep acquiring *variety*, be it alcohol, drugs, women, cars, whatever. Variety in life allowed the law of diminishing marginal utility to be at least temporarily arrested, but variety required *money*.

When Hawk had made the final call from Grand Cayman to tidy up his little project, he'd underestimated the greed of his contact. The agreement had been for the return of the initial investment plus three hundred thousand. But when he called to confirm payment, a demand for a further five hundred thousand had been made. Five hundred grand, for very little indeed. He was seething, but he considered the possible problems of not paying, perhaps always looking over his shoulder, knowing the he himself might be the target for vengeance. He'd paid up, into a numbered account in Switzerland. His plans had been carefully constructed and the payment, however painful, offered some sort of insurance and final closure with this individual. However, two million dollars was the minimum sum he'd calculated was necessary to have a decent life, one that could at least partially compensate for the time he'd spent inside that shithole.

Now he was short.

What his selfish contact did not know, however, was that on Hawk's insistence, Douglas Lyndon had provided a third tip from his knowledge of the software programmes used by the top firms that Channing's advised. The value of this piece of inside information had however been conditional on very specific circumstances developing. Testament to the story on CNN, Hawk was now aware that these circumstances had now materialised, as the President of Iraq had died and was being replaced by a new, vibrant, younger man, one who had agreed specific tacit business deals in the event that he gained power. Douglas Lyndon had seen the minutes of the meetings and knew of a client company that specialised in developing power plants. It now stood to make hundreds of millions from Iraqi contracts.

Hawk faced a dilemma. He could use his clandestine knowledge once more, and potentially make a killing this last time, provided he acted quickly. On the other hand, such an act would break the rule he had set himself at the outset of his plan. *Calum Mack* was to have been the apparent beneficiary of all trades, and they would all take place via the Black Isle investment vehicle. Could he, Hawk, take the risk of using the tip provided by Lyndon now that Mack was out of the picture?

He reflected on his scam and the people involved; how incisively the fear of humiliation—being caught—affected people. Hawk had learned that fact quite early in life; how the anxiety of losing all you had could drive events. What he had done might be called blackmail, but Hawk viewed it as therapy, seasoned with a decent sprinkling of revenge. How he had enjoyed them all squirming about the photos, hearing their nervous voices on the phone, their pathetic and ultimately useless bluster, how they desperately hoped nothing would upset their cosy, pathetic lives. Manipulation was easy. Some hallucinogenic drugs, an underage girl supplied by a pimp he'd once met inside, and a resultant set of compromising photographs had secured the material he required, and engendered the compulsion for others to give him the information he desired to instigate his plan.

They wouldn't forget the consequences of moral virtue from their little reunion. And the beauty of it all was that they all believed that the individual who'd organised the whole shooting match was one Calum Mack, the very person who'd "invited" them yet had not appeared in person. Hawk had prevented Facebook and other social media being employed, and the voice modification technology he'd used was quite advanced. Mack would have been completely unaware that Hawk had called him anonymously a few weeks before to obtain a recording of Mack's voice in order to create the correct tone and enunciation during the sting itself. All that Mack had needed was greed—greed for information.

Now Hawk also had to contemplate his own potential avarice for more money, and as he poured another beer and surveyed some scantily clad women on the beach in front on his balcony, he considered his options.

Chapter 10

In the past Calum had styled himself as a 'short term pessimist, if long term optimist', believing that in the end things would always turn out right. Perhaps such faith reflected his formative quasi-Christian upbringing, even though his adulthood had witnessed the departure of belief in the afterlife itself. His continued custody in a new cell represented a curious paradox, as the minor improvement in escaping from the odours and verbal excess of the initial cell in which he had been incarcerated was replaced by a more thorough comprehension of the reality which he faced.

His parents had flown from Inverness to visit him. His mother had been very distraught. Calum had been the successful child of whom she had been justifiably proud, the one who'd starred academically, sailing through school and university, and embarking on a career in investment banking. He'd never let them down before, in fact the only thing he'd ever done wrong in her eyes was drift between different girlfriends instead of settling down. His brother worked offshore on the rigs and blew much of what he earned on booze when he came back onshore, but Calum had always been different, attitudinally. He'd always shown integrity, and he'd managed to reinvent himself as a financial journalist, the Calvinist work ethic cutting though the difficulties of uprooting from Scotland to London.

And now this.

They asked him lots of questions, and Calum knew instinctively that they believed him, and believed *in* him, even if they couldn't comprehend how this cruel sequence of events had occurred. He'd felt so lonely, his inner child suddenly overcome with the possibility of loss; loss of his family, loss of friends, loss of his soul. His father offered to mortgage their house to raise the punitive sum required for bail, but Calum had refused point blank as he felt that they shouldn't be penalised for the misdemeanours of others. Calum was touched, but he argued that their savings and home should remain secure. His father and mother then shared a quick look, which Calum queried.

'It's nothing, we're fine,' his mother said, brushing him off.

'What's nothing?' Calum asked as his father expelled air softly, and partly turned away.

'Look, son,' he said, turning back around, 'you've enough on your plate, so don't worry about our finances. We've both got pensions.'

'What is it? Please tell me! There's nothing worse than people hinting about something and then refusing to explain the issue.'

'Okay, I'll tell you. By the way, we're not blaming you as we know that you were sold a dummy, but unfortunately we were too.'

'Dad, you're speaking in riddles!'

'We invested most of our own savings—about twenty thousand—in that oil company, Dartmouth Petroleum. We read your column about the exploration in Canada and it looked so... so promising.'

'Oh, Christ, I'm sorry. I'd no idea. Why...why didn't you say before?'

'It was our risk.' His dad smiled sadly, as if the sins of the son had taken residence with the father. 'The shares have kind of bottomed out at about a fifth of their previous value, so we'll just sell and cut our losses.'

Calum shook his head, laughing, yet with no hint of humour. 'You know the irony? If you'd invested your money in any of the other shares I'm wrongly being charged with trading, you'd have made a fortune.'

When his parents left, he considered on a more pragmatic note that if convicted, he would likely lose everything, not only his only available savings after Martin's fee, but also the equity he held in his flat. Martin had delved into previous cases pursued by the FCA and its predecessor the FSA, and noted that where suspected proceeds of crime were not turned over to the authorities, confiscation orders were subsequently given by the court in addition to custodial sentences. Given that his assets had already been restrained by the court on the application of the CPA at the time of the arrest, a cruel irony had become transparent to him—those charged with financial crimes, and actually *guilty* of those crimes, were probably much better funded in terms of defending themselves. The innocent had much less opportunity to construct a war chest which they had never anticipated would be necessary. The Krugerrands he'd stashed in that safety deposit box in Edinburgh now seemed ridiculously insignificant, but he was determined to leave them be. Everyone needed something in future reserve, even when it was raining very heavily.

Ben had then come back to visit again, but he provided little comfort.

'This place is shit, man,' he reported, screwing up his face at the bare grey walls of the visiting room. 'If you'd given me all those stock tips when I asked, we could have made enough to pay the fuckers bail and could both have jetted off to the Caribbean.'

Calum smiled without any humour. 'You really wish you'd become complicit?'

'Na, just trying to cheer you up, buddy,' Ben replied, stretching out his arms.

'Well, if you think you owe me for keeping you out of the loop, please try to inspire your brother to do his utmost. I don't think he believes me.'

'He believes no one, Calum. Doesn't say so directly of course, but, for fuck's sake, you should see some of the…evil arseholes…he's represented.' Calum shot Ben a look, before they both saw the funny side. When the gallows humour subsided Ben became more serious. 'What do you think are your chances, mate?'

'Crap, by the look of it. I'm not sure if Martin said to you, but he thinks I might be better cutting a deal, admitting to something I didn't do. But even if I complied and lied—technically perjuring myself by pleading guilty—I'd still get a custodial sentence on two counts. Firstly, the serial nature of the trades and secondly, the fact that I wouldn't be able to cough up the two million bucks, even if the reason is that I never possessed it in the first place. They'd get the capital I own in my flat, as they can nab all my known assets. If I could magically identify the bastard who set me up, that would be a start. But he's hardly likely to be hanging around. They now say they've proof that I made calls to all of these people I knew from the past—people connected to the companies I tipped—and that the proof is that those phones are registered to me. I mean, why the hell would anyone register numbers and then keep phones in their own home that were incriminating?'

'Maybe they think that it was some form of insurance, or potential for blackmail,' Ben replied cautiously.

'You don't believe me either, do you?'

Ben bit his lower lip. 'Yes, I do, as a matter of fact. Remember, I was there when one of the calls was made to you. So you could call me up as a witness.'

'Yes, thanks. Your testimony would be a help, but I can just imagine some sharp prosecutor asking how you could actually hear what was said on the other end of the line. And I've asked Martin to ascertain from the cops where that call came from, and where the courier that delivered the phones got them from, but they're on holiday on that one, funnily enough. My only chance, Martin says, is the lack of proof that I benefitted but there's so much circumstantial evidence that I might get stuffed anyway, especially given the fact that I *did* know all these guys, albeit long ago. And I'm a bloody flight risk. Half a million in bail? Jesus, half the guys charged in the City for real insider trading have been fined less than that.' Calum sniffed, running his hands though his hair. 'What's Powell saying about it all?'

'I'm afraid there's no chance that Powell will support you.' Ben looked down.

'So he spoke to you?' Calum stood up abruptly, before being told immediately to sit down by a guard.

'No, he gave this big spiel to the whole office, raving about standards and integrity, and how someone like you would never be hired again. Sorry, buddy.'

'Bastard. I'm not surprised, though. He never liked me, not even when we first met. Would have been nice to be given the benefit of the doubt, though. You know, innocent until proven guilty and all that.'

The narrowest part of mainland Scotland lies between the firths of Forth and Clyde. Any international observer with little prior knowledge of the cities at either side of this modest divide might anticipate that such a short distance could only generate commonality of purpose and attitude. Douglas Lyndon however, like many before and after him, had found otherwise as a seventeen-year-old when he'd made the journey by bus from Glasgow to begin his studies through a place at Edinburgh University. Having been raised in the tough environs of Castlemilk in Glasgow, he'd been quietly bemused by the affectations of most of his more privileged classmates in Edinburgh, many of whom had benefitted from the best schooling and tutoring that parental income could acquire. Douglas had done things the hard way, attaining five 'A' grades in his Higher exams despite his circumstances, having learned to placate the gangs and forgo the drugs, comprehending that a good degree would provide the ultimate escape route to what others considered normality.

His standing as a student had been akin to being something of an intellectual punter, and those of equal cerebral acuity could clearly see beyond the stubble and hear beyond the vernacular which he typically employed. For any lecturers or tutors who might judge a book by its cover, the incisiveness of Douglas's written work and technical scores usually tempered their initial stereotypical judgements, and the first class honours degree and gold medal that he'd subsequently been awarded provided a small victory for Castlemilk as much as for Douglas himself.

Perhaps the primary reason that upon graduation he'd chosen to enter, and had subsequently excelled in, the technological side of banking, was that it proffered rationality. So much of his upbringing had been irrational, but a career based on the development of software for financial purposes made sense to him as it reduced risk, and risk had been a problem he'd faced so often in his formative years. When he'd learned in his first year microeconomics class about the Prisoner's Dilemma—a model based on rationality in the face of uncertainty—he'd got it straight away. He understood the concept of being arrested by the police, and being questioned in isolation from an accomplice who was also being interrogated. He understood that probabilities could be applied to the likelihood of specific outcomes, and that rewards or punishments would be administered by those seeking confessions or those casting blame. And he understood that these same rewards or punishments stood side by side, their odds being dependent not only on one's own actions but those of apparently trusted friends.

As he drove his car along the M1 at about 10:45 in the evening, he considered the meeting in which he was about to participate, and the various threats that had been made. When he'd initially faced the threat of blackmail, his innate reaction had been to track down the blackmailer and beat the shit out of him, but then his feelings were tempered by concerns for his wife and two young children, and the fact that the blackmailer might actually inflict real damage, damage that could result in him losing everything he'd worked for since he'd exited school. The blackmailer had expressly forbade contact with the others, which hadn't been a huge problem in its own right, as he'd less in common with them anyway these days. Calum Mack had now been arrested for suspicion of insider trading, and Douglas himself faced a second interview with the police, who were threatening charges of supplying Mack with information. They maintained they had proof that Mack had contacted him by phone prior to trading. He'd fobbed off his wife for the time being, insisting that the issue would be resolved, and that he'd done nothing wrong.

That, however, was untrue.

He *had* illegally supplied inside information on three companies, Simtrex, Virtual Bank and one further company, Electricon, which built power plants in the Middle East. The police hadn't mentioned the third firm, so he suspected that the tip had not been acted upon as it had been more speculative, until now, when news would probably break given the change of leadership in Iraq. The strange thing was that he'd never suspected Calum Mack of being a blackmailer—but he'd felt that the real blackmailer had been trying to give that impression. The whole thing was irrational. Why would Calum Mack, who he'd considered a genuine friend in the past, arrange a reunion, fail to turn up, and then blackmail his old university buddies in such a manner? Why, if he'd be disposed to act in such a duplicitous way, would Mack then draw attention to himself by tipping those companies publically in the media? Yet, the cops now apparently had proof that the guy who'd contacted him was indeed Mack. The voice he'd heard certainly sounded very like Mack's, though there had been something odd with the inflection, and he was aware that voices could be disguised quite effectively through electronic modification.

When he arrived at the Southern Edge services junction, he took a deep breath, wondering if the others would actually turn up this time. He parked his Audi Q7 at the rear of the car park as agreed, and waited. Five minutes later a silver Range Rover parked next to him, followed a minute or so later by a Porsche 911. Then a black Jaguar appeared, and Lyndon knew instantly that Anthony Rowland had arrived in what looked a ministerial car; Special Branch security rules apparently being synthesised with some extra-curricular activity.

The others exited their vehicles in an almost choreographed manner, and Lyndon followed suit, taking a deep breath, before Donnie Wilson pointed towards the back of the car park.

'What's over there, a couple of fourteen-year-old girls hiding in the bushes?' Tomlinson spoke first, his sarcasm cutting through the air.

'I meant, Nigel, that we should get away from any eavesdroppers, that's all,' Wilson replied.

'Look, chaps, best if there are no names used here, okay?' Anthony Rowland whispered. 'I've told my driver that this will take five minutes, so let's get on with it.'

'I agree,' Tomlinson said, eyes darting conspiratorially towards Rowland. 'Some of us have a lot to lose here.' They walked towards the edge of the car park, Rowland peering to see if there could conceivably be any spies in the rough ground to the rear.

'Personally, I'd shoot the bastard if I got the chance,' Tomlinson said abruptly.

'Who's that then, Nigel?' Lyndon asked, his Glasgow accent having scarcely altered during his years in Southern England.

'No names!' Rowland almost shouted the words in a whisper.

'I'd like to know who he means,' Lyndon enquired.

'You know *fine well*,' Tomlinson replied. 'The *audacity* of…the man. What sort of person sets you up for something so…awful…and then drugs you and blackmails you?'

'We don't know for certain who did it to us,' Lyndon said, looking at Tomlinson, 'as none of us presumably spoke to Mack himself after the event because of the threats made. It's a classic Catch-22 situation. And it's not the first time we've been in a shit position, as you all know.'

'No names! And we agreed never to speak about that other thing again!' Tomlinson croaked.

'Gentlemen, *gentlemen*, this is getting us nowhere.' Rowland spoke quietly. 'Look, the police have probably got the right man. Who else would have sent those letters and photos? I've done a little digging, and he might have been going to lose his job. He was the one who sent us the cloak and dagger invitation to the bloody reunion, and he was the one who said how good this would be for our careers, the publicity he was going to give us all—but then he didn't turn up. We all know what happened next. It was shocking what he did. None of us, I repeat *none of us* did anything, despite those photos. That bloody girl was clearly paid to do the poses. And unfortunately the pictures *look* real. Christ knows what hallucinogenic shit was in those drinks. But I, of all people, know how perceptions count, so we must agree a course of action tonight, once and for all.'

Lyndon then leaned forward, rubbing his prematurely grey curly hair. 'What are you going to do? Have him knocked off by MI5? I think you're barking up the wrong tree. Calum Mack's all right, and I think he's been set up too. Beats me who could have done it, but the whole thing doesn't make sense.'

'The police have proof he called us, for God's sake!' Tomlinson barked. 'And we stupidly gave him info—'

'Say nothing!' Rowland interjected. 'Look…this looks like the end of a less than beautiful friendship for us all. Sorry, but think it's best if we never see each other ever again.' He looked principally at Tomlinson, who nodded curtly.

'No argument there, but the point I'm trying to make is that they have proof *someone* called us,' Lyndon replied. 'But we do not know *who* that is. Voice synthesisers may change voice modulation, but not the pattern of how someone actually *speaks*. The man you are chastising might be just as much a victim as us. Have you all considered that?'

'You seem to know a lot about this.' Tomlinson stared at Lyndon, who simply shook his head before Rowland broke the silence.

'Here's what I propose. Hear me out, please.' Rowland spoke for about two minutes without interruption. After his suggestion sunk in with the others, he concluded by affirming his own special privileged position. 'I *know* more than you guys, if you're hearing me…and if you follow this plan, this thing should pretty much go away.'

Donnie Wilson then spoke. 'I agree. This thing has been a nightmare. I don't care if it's him or not, sorry.' He glanced at Lyndon. 'But I do care about my family and my career. So let's vote right now. Those in favour of what has been proposed raise a hand.'

Three hands were raised instantly—Wilson, Rowland and Tomlinson. They all glared at Lyndon, who shook his head, eyeing all three in turn.

'Well? Aren't you going to raise your hand?' Tomlinson asked. Lyndon then rotated, and began to walk back to his car.

'*Well?*'

Just before he unlocked the Audi, Lyndon turned, and raised an arm, though it was accompanied by a one-fingered salute.

DI Maxwell and DS Robson appeared out of Max Telford's office just as Aurelia arrived back from a policy meeting with the Bank of England. She smiled at Maxwell, though he simply nodded, remaining in character in keeping with the first occasion they'd met. Aurelia remembered her father's earthy sense of humour, and wondered if Maxwell had always been the stoical type, or whether any sense of mirth he'd possessed had simply evaporated during his tenure in the force. When the two policemen disappeared, Aurelia knocked on Telford's door, only to find him in dialogue with Adam. She folded her arms instinctively—Adam had clearly been included in a progress meeting of which she was unaware. Telford raised a hand defensively.

'Before you say anything, there has been some news. I didn't want to interrupt your meeting at the BoE, so we took the opportunity to learn of the latest developments with Maxwell and Robson, who have in turn been in conversation with the CPS. Have a seat.'

Aurelia glanced at Adam, before sitting down.

'Good news for two reasons, Aurelia. Firstly, the Caribbean Chartered Bank in George Town, Grand Cayman has caved into pressure from our people, and confirmed that one Calum Mack did indeed open an account connected to Black Isle Investments, and that he closed the account using his own passport for ID, withdrawing more than two million dollars in cash. They have given written documentation to that effect on the basis that we ask no further questions, or overtly publicise this information.'

Aurelia let Max Telford's words filter in, considering the juxtaposition she now faced. She'd been on the brink of challenging a couple of points of evidence in the case, but this development confirmed the validity of initial investigation. It was unusual for a foreign bank in an awkward jurisdiction to cooperate in such a way, but clearly someone in London had influence. What she couldn't figure, however, was why Mack had been so myopic.

'Fair enough,' she said flatly.

'You don't sound pleased. I thought you'd be delighted—you've worked hard on this investigation.' Telford laid his hands upon the table.

'It's just...oh, never mind. What's the other good news?'

Telford smiled as he played with a particularly bright orange floral tie. 'Mack's waived his right to extra time—in fact he's asked for a speedy trial. Normally it's the other way about, but what he didn't know when his solicitor made the request was that this bombshell was coming. Of course, he could now alter his request, in the light of this damning evidence but that's not going to look good in the eyes of the judge, who's been appointed.'

'What about the others? Adam—I presume you've got something more by now on those who supplied information? You've been liaising with Robson, Maxwell and the CPS about Tomlinson et al. A speedy trial won't allow enough time to make the investigation complete, unless you've a silver bullet there also?'

Adam and Telford shared a look, and Aurelia frowned instinctively, realising that there was more to the story, and that Adam was obviously party to further information to which she was not yet privileged.

'What is it?' she asked.

Adam cleared his throat. 'I've undertaken a…comprehensive…study of all of these individuals, and there is no substantive evidence of any direct impropriety or benefit. I'm very thorough with this sort of thing, as you know.' Adam nodded like a duck toward Telford, who nodded back.

'Adam is very thorough in his research, Aurelia.'

'Right, thorough. In no time flat?' Aurelia replied, looking anything but satisfied by this revelation. 'If we're pursuing Mack, surely we must pursue every avenue in relation to all those complicit in the case. What about relatives and friends of these executives? Have you ascertained whether other individuals connected to Tomlinson, Rowland, Lyndon and Wilson purchased these equities at the same time? I think it unlikely that they would all be as directly naive as Mack, but surely there must have been some *incentive* for them? Didn't Maxwell and Robson mention the motives of these individuals? That's bread and butter for the police.'

'Aurelia, you're hardly in a position to comprehend the nuances of police procedure.'

'Excuse me, Adam, but my father was a detective in the Irish police for thirty years, and I *do* happen to know something about police *procedure*. What they need, though, is financial leads from us—*you* in this case—to ascertain if there were any monetary links between those supplying the information and those who may have bought the same shares.'

Adam closed his eyes, apparently irritated. 'Aurelia, I haven't got the time to delve into every person any of these guys have met, it's ridiculous.'

'So the investigation stops here? That's it? These guys get away with it, because Adam can't be bothered looking at further irregular trading patterns and making the connections? Remember Daniel Fleeting—it was me who checked on his father-in-law.' Again, Adam and Max shared a look, and Aurelia frowned.

'We're not pursuing these individuals, Aurelia,' Max said flatly.

'Why? What do you two know that I clearly do not?'

Telford responded. 'Because it's not in this organisation's interest at the present time. We don't have the evidence, and we want to win matches we can win. Mack's cornered, and he wants a speedy trial, so we nail him because of his ego, or stupidity, or whatever.'

Aurelia bit her top lip. 'There's more to this, I can tell. It's Rowland, isn't it?' Both Max and Adam looked away this time before Aurelia continued. 'I've got it. You've decided not to pursue *any* of them because it would mean a more thorough investigation into *one* of them *in particular*. And he happens, just by sheer coincidence, to be a member of the Westminster Government. This is a cover up, isn't it? Is that how you got the information from Cayman—some kind of deal that Rowland was left alone, and by definition, the others too? A slap on the wrist for these guys and that's it?'

'You're being naive, Aurelia,' Adam said, 'if you think you can beat the people upstairs.'

Aurelia stared directly at her boss. 'Thanks, Max. Thanks for confiding in Adam here before me.' She stood up to leave.

'Aurelia, we'll get our collar, and yes, your name will be on it.' Max held his hands open.

'You know, Max, I'm not sure I even care.'

Chapter 11

After the preliminary hearing at the Magistrates' Court, the case, given its high profile and relative severity, had been elevated to Southwark Crown Court and Calum had subsequently been given an early trial date at his own request, despite advice to the contrary from Martin. Shortly before the trial was due, Martin ascertained that no charges were likely to be brought against Rowland, Tomlinson, Wilson or Lyndon. The Crown Prosecution Service had, according to Martin, dragged their collective heels over the charges relating to the others, and although such a strategy had direct implications for Calum's defence, the CPS was under no obligation to disclose decisions on forthcoming charges relating to other parties until the prosecutor in charge of the case saw fit.

'This is a bloody stitch up,' Calum responded to the news. '*I* didn't actually speak to three of these guys, yet apparently someone else did, and *they* shared information illegally, not me.'

Martin paced up and down in the windowless room. 'They've probably cut a deal of some kind, and Rowland is out of the loop completely now even as a witness. That means that the charges relating to your alleged trades in Unreal Power might well be dropped for lack of evidence. Let's face it, Rowland is in the Government and he hasn't even resigned, so you can bet that this has involved political pressure from the top so he can keep his job or resurface later after a break. It's happened before.'

'But if they all say nothing, surely it can't be proven that I based my columns on insider information?'

Martin placed his hand on Calum's arm. 'Look, we do not know what they'll say in testimony. We now know that the CPS has a statement from the bank in Grand Cayman, explaining that someone called Calum Mack—using a passport for ID, incidentally—closed his account and withdrew a shitload of cash on the very day you were there.'

'Can we not get that video footage from the bank? I know it's late, but they might keep the tapes and if we could have another go, it could prove that I did not withdraw money.'

'Calum, as you know we already requested the security tapes but I've heard nothing. I wouldn't hold my breath, frankly. We're in no position to demand security material from a business half way round the world. If you'd had more money...we could have hired a PI out there, but we're stuck for resources.'

Calum looked down, deflated. 'As they say in America, this is a crock of shit.'

'It sure is. I know that you've insisted that it was a set-up, but can you see how this looks to a jury? Another cheating, lying, "City boy"? This is all about *perception*. And Christ knows, Tomlinson and company could simply say that you forced them into it. There could be some kind of collective excuse. Trust me, Calum; I've seen it all before. There are lies, damned lies, and City boys' lies, and they'll do anything to protect themselves. But if you decide to cut a deal—and there's still time—you'd need to produce the money...which you don't possess.'

Calum sighed. 'Is there no way that I can speak to one of them? Douglas Lyndon is a decent guy, and I'm really disappointed if he's out to shaft me.'

'Three of them are listed as witnesses, irrespective of whether they choose to bring them in. But Calum, any attempt we make to influence them before the case opens could precipitate further charges against you.'

'Martin, you're supposed to be *helping* me here. You *know* I don't have the money, so I'm bloody snookered! What about this passport used to identify me at that bank, apparently?'

'They say it was your passport, I'm afraid. But they didn't photocopy it so we can't say if it was a fake using a different photo with your name. Has your passport been out of your sight?' Martin looked directly at Calum, who did not flinch.

'Martin, *I did not do it*. I can see that you still have doubts.'

'It doesn't matter if I have doubts. It's the judge and jury who need no doubts. All I can do is argue that you've been naive due to pressure at the *Sentinel*, and that someone has taken advantage of you. I can explain that the phones you'd been given and were manipulated into using render the charges unsound, as you'd have been incriminating yourself if they'd been your own. The courier that delivered them has given us a record of the deliveries, which is good, but these companies do not know what was inside the packages, of course, and they say they were delivered by hand to them by someone unknown, producing a scribbled address on the paperwork. I have listed Ben as a witness for the defence, and he can testify that you had a conversation with a third party in his presence. Rod Powell is also a witness for the prosecution, and I can hassle him in court, we but we won't hold out much there. I can also argue that there is no actual evidence of any current financial gain on your part, but I'm afraid that's about it.'

'That's about it?'

'I'm sorry, but I don't think that *snookered* is a strong enough expression.'

Southwark Crown Court proved to be an intimidating venue, particularly for the 'damned-accused', as Calum had begun to describe himself. The surroundings were as daunting as Calum had anticipated, the entire protocol gnawing at him not only psychologically, but physically. From the day he arrived at the court, a nauseating grip held his stomach for the first half hour or so, only to return in waves throughout the day. He'd already lost about a stone since his retention in custody, the synthesis of mediocre culinary offerings and acute stress providing a cruel platform for low energy levels and broken sleeping patterns, and now the trial itself confirmed his utter lack of control over events. Despite the fact that the charges relating to insider trading in Unreal Power shares had been dropped, as Martin had predicted, Calum felt more isolated than ever before.

He'd never visited a court previously. When in high school, his fifth year modern studies teacher had arranged a trip to Inverness Sheriff Court, but he'd been absent on the day in question. His class mates had apparently sniggered at the plight of one of the accused during the visit, and had reported back to him what "low life scum bags" were resident at the court. As he briefly reflected on that bygone occasion here in court he concluded that the law was actually a very capricious ass.

The judge, a silver-haired, ruddy-faced character in his sixties who reminded Calum of the politician Vince Cable, instructed that the case for the prosecution begin, and the prosecutor's opening statement painted a picture of a greedy and desperate individual, whose most obvious flaw was his inability to fully conceal his tracks. Martin's opening statement in response offered a depiction of an innocent man who had been framed, duped by an unknown but devious telephone tipster. He explained that there was no evidence of Calum having benefitted financially from the alleged crimes, and that had he actually been guilty, the easiest strategy to employ would have been to pay bail and disappear, yet Calum had remained determined to prove his innocence.

Martin initially exhibited an assertive courtroom demeanour, impressing Calum during the cross-examination of the first witness for the prosecution, Rod Powell. Powell had been unable to conceal what now amounted to loathing of Calum during his initial responses to the prosecutor, and Martin had decided to use that prejudice against him. Martin questioned the validity of what the prosecution was pursuing, and simultaneously criticised Powell's judgment in permitting Calum to use unknown sources, whilst flattering the jury when the opportunity arose. Powell, aware not only that his own personal reputation had been significantly damaged by permitting the columns to be published, was also present in a rear-guard action to reduce the likelihood of a heavy fine for the *Sentinel*. Martin had advised Calum that Powell would possibly lose his own job, perhaps just not yet.

The circumstances concerning the use of the phones that the 'mystery caller' had provided also created real conflict when Maxwell and Robson were called. According to the prosecution, the phones had been used to *avoid* detection, the hypothesis being that Calum had deliberately made calls on phones he'd secreted, rather than having used his own phone. The prosecutor read out a statement that Calum had made to the police and FCA officials on the first day they'd met, saying that he'd not made the calls to Wilson and Lyndon, yet phone records had now proved otherwise. Martin had countered during the cross-examination of DI Maxwell— who'd obtained the information about the phone usage—that this client would have to have been inordinately stupid to keep any such phones in his flat if this was the case. He also queried why he'd have 'called himself', so to speak, during the first apparent contact from the tipster, as this call had emanated from one of the phones found in Calum's flat. Unfortunately, it seemed that all counters were subject to further counters, as Maxwell then suggested that Calum could have done this deliberately, in some sort of attempt to construct the alibi of this mystery tipster's very existence should events have turned sour, which they of course had.

Then, on the second day of the trial, Martin's prophecy proved accurate. Calum's old mates from university appeared on the stand in quick succession. The prosecutor, when introducing the men, approached them almost with sympathy. He explained the gravity of the situation, and reminded them of the oaths they'd taken, exhibiting a form of deference normally afforded to victims rather than criminal accomplices. Calum had glanced at Martin, sensing that something was wrong.

Perhaps it was the manner in which Nigel Tomlinson replied to the initial background questions, but Calum could feel the mood of the trial changing during the prosecutor's questions. Wasn't breach of trust a terrible thing? What could have possibly motivated someone in Tomlinson's position to risk his career to offer inside information to a common hack such as Calum Mack, even if he had known him many years before?

Then Tomlinson replied. 'Attempted blackmail,' he intoned, as Calum gasped, audibly.

What a fucking lie.

Tomlinson stared pointedly at Calum as he spoke. 'I will not reveal what he attempted to do, for it is beyond discussion. But, foolishly, in some temporary fit of ill judgement, just to get rid of him, you understand, I deviated from my normal standards by giving one simple piece of information. I am not alone, as you will see. And I regret that I succumbed to such a devious trickster. I made no financial gain from this whatsoever as you will be aware, and as my records will prove, I deeply regret that I ever encountered the man.'

In order to introduce an obvious objection, the prosecutor then asked what the nature of the blackmail had been, but Tomlinson refused to divulge the details, clearly steering an agreed course. They'd done a deal, a dirty deal. Martin asked for a few minutes to confer with his client, during which he asked privately for absolute assurances that no such blackmail had occurred. Calum struggled to contain his fury, yet failed to offer a means of countering what could only be described as blatant perjury by Tomlinson. Calum demanded to know why Martin couldn't pursue the fact that Tomlinson should have been on trial instead of him, but Martin held his arm, stating flatly that this would only prove to be a diversion as the Crown itself apparently couldn't prove that Tomlinson, and probably the rest, had benefitted. Martin also warned Calum that they might decide to pursue blackmail charges if he pushed too hard. Infuriated, Calum gritted his teeth as proceedings restarted.

During the subsequent cross-examination, Martin, glancing back towards his client, said that he'd like to see evidence of the blackmail to provide categorical proof of Tomlinson's claims, but Tomlinson refused to budge.

To Calum's disbelief, Donnie Wilson then made the identical claim on the stand. Rather than the Crown requiring proof of the blackmail—which they clearly had no interest in pursuing as it wasn't listed as one of the charges—they were nonetheless going to use it in a corroborative pincer movement to explain how poor old Donnie and Nigel had been duped, allowing the two to get off with a slap on the wrist, but damning Calum with a compendium of accusations which he could not refute. And for good measure, just in case anyone had forgotten, the prosecutor reminded the judge and jury about those phone calls to Tomlinson and Lyndon, and the identity of the individual to whom those phones were registered.

Unfortunately, on cross-examination, Martin merely skirmished, further demands about the nature of the alleged blackmail resulting in a rebuff from the judge for bullying the witness. Douglas Lyndon then appeared on the stand, also claiming blackmail, though for some reason he refused to identify Calum Mack as the blackmailer, saying that he had been unaware of the identity of the caller. This curious aspect of the witness testimony led Martin to probe Lyndon further on cross-examination, but the damage had already been inflicted as the phone records confirmed that contact had taken place. The prosecutor then introduced as evidence a written statement from Adam Smart of the FCA, explaining that they could find no proof of any financial gain for any of the others.

When Aurelia Harley was introduced as a witness, she explained the procedures employed by the FCA during investigations, and then elucidated regarding the size and timing of all the trades, and dates of the articles Calum had written. She focused concisely on the nature of Black Isle Investments, including its incorporation in the Caribbean and the connection with Calum's place of birth. Copies of Calum's articles and printouts of the transactions made were accepted as evidence by the court. The transactions involving Unreal Power were, however, glossed over.

On cross-examination, Martin enquired subtly about trading in the shares of Unreal Power, though Aurelia quietly suggested that if he had information that further incriminated his client then he should advise the court. Calum drew Martin daggers at this turn of events, so Martin moved onto stronger ground, disputing the prosecution's assertion that Calum had any connection with Black Isle Investments, asking what proof the FCA possessed of Calum's involvement. Intuitively, Calum noticed Aurelia Harley's minor discomfort during this line of questioning. Her answers were curt, rather than passionate—she had no 'proof'—but she was simply explaining the lines of investigative inquiry that were pursued. Martin then put it to her that, in keeping with the mobile phone issue, his client would have had to be particularly stupid to name a criminal enterprise he'd dreamed up after a place he held dearly. She responded that in her experience, those pursuing financial crimes sometimes made peculiar errors, yet she stated this supposition without real conviction, avoiding eye contact with either Martin or Calum.

When she was then questioned about the accusations of financial benefit to the accused, Martin suggested that there was no evidence of him possessing the funds after the apparent withdrawal in George Town, nor any record of him having paid for the trip to Grand Cayman. He mentioned that Calum had been lured into the vicinity of the bank by a young woman and asked to cash in a US bank note. Hesitantly, she replied, however, that such circumstances might be consistent with the defendant having something to conceal. If he *were* guilty, *of course* he would have paid in cash for the trip, for he would have wanted to avoid advertising a trip for which he stood to benefit so handsomely, and illegally. Indeed, he would have needed his passport number to confirm the flights, wouldn't he?

The penultimate element of the prosecution case incorporated a specific piece of written evidence, and this time Max Telford was brought in as a witness to provide a complementary explanation. He initially outlined his many years of experience and knowledge. Then, when questioned, he surmised that the most common and rational thing for white-collar criminals to do was to attempt to conceal the proceeds of illegal financial gain overseas. Asked what he meant, specifically, Telford said that in many cases the FCA could not gain cooperation from foreign banks, and that in other scenarios the authorities could not locate the proceeds as they had been laundered or literally stashed in cash in a safe location or in a bank vault. He then explained numbered accounts and the "KYD" code, the IBAN prefix for a US dollar account in Grand Cayman. The prosecutor reminded the jury that there was documentary evidence of Calum Mack's appearance in Grand Cayman on the exact day of the withdrawal, before asking Telford to read out to the court from where the written evidence had been sent, and what it said.

Telford momentarily removed his glasses and wiped them on a handkerchief, before reading the letter. As Calum listened he closed his eyes, before then turning to observe the jury's reaction to apparent written verification that he had used his own passport as evidence of his identity in order to withdraw a fortune in cash in the Caribbean. Even though he had been briefed by Martin that this would occur, the pain of this fake incrimination felt like a hammer blow to the cranium. Eyebrows were raised across the jury and at least two members just shook their heads, clearly showing disgust.

The case for the defence proved to be much shorter than that for the prosecution. Martin had explained to Calum that this was partly as the lack of resources at their disposal meant that detailed investigative legwork could not be commissioned. They could not afford to send someone to the Caribbean to dig into the bank's business, or discover how the account had been set up, nor even commission exploratory research into precedents where lack of evidence of financial gain in unrelated criminal cases had hampered convictions. Martin also reminded Calum that he had advised him not to seek an early trial so that they could construct alternative theories, though Calum was in no mood to accept criticism. Both his parents had flown down to be present for the case as his defence opened, and he caught their undisguised anguish as the proceedings re-opened, his mother's hands held in a subconscious prayer position.

The first witness that Martin had elected to call was Firdu Debela, a trader who had worked with Calum in Edinburgh, and was now CEO of a small investment house based in London. Firdu, originally from Ethiopia, had agreed to testify on behalf of Calum, outlining two occasions where Calum had reported others for fraudulent behaviour during his stint in banking. Such character-based references, Martin argued, were useful in creating doubt for a jury. Martin asked the former trader what he thought about Calum, and he replied that in his opinion he was one of the straightest people he had ever met in business.

Martin had also arranged for a representative of the phone company with which the mobile phone contracts had been set up to appear in court. The tall thin woman in her fifties who'd been sent by the firm appeared petrified, as if on trial herself. She explained hesitantly under questioning that a passport had actually been used to verify the identity of the account holder. At this point Martin asked if the staff at the firm were authorities on fake passports, to which the prosecution objected, stating that the witness or her colleagues could not be expected to ascertain the validity of such documentation. Martin smiled, briefly, before re-phrasing the question. This little ruse had resonated a little with the jury as he noted one or two conferring at his revelation. He'd explained to Calum beforehand, that if he was innocent, clearly a fake passport must have been used, and therefore seeds of reservation had to be sown among those who would adjudicate in respect of his innocence.

Ben also provided a character reference, and stated that Calum had indeed undertaken a telephone conversation in the *Sentinel* offices about a share tip and forthcoming journey when he'd been present. Unfortunately, the prosecution had predicted this line of questioning and countered by enquiring how Ben could possibly know what had been said during a conversation in which one party could not be heard. Ben replied that he believed his former colleague implicitly, and even said that staff at the paper had sometimes jokingly attempted to quiz Calum for tips before publication, but that he had always shown complete probity in terms of journalistic ethics.

The concluding statement made by the prosecution was fairly predictable, the prosecutor emphasising that the FCA's role, and the jury's duty, was to punish financial greed. He outlined the key facts of the case and reminded the jury that Calum Mack had booked a flight to the Caribbean using his own passport number, visiting Grand Cayman on the day over two million dollars went missing, and that the bank in question had verified his presence. Mack had blatantly abused his position as a financial journalist at a respected publication to deceive the public, and by default, the state. The prosecutor cast doubt on the imaginary scamster that the defence had created. Who was this man, and where was he? Expert testimony, not figments of people's imagination, had proved Mack's guilt, and although wrongdoing had occurred in terms of the sources of insider information, Mack had forced the hand of these individuals, for whom there was no proof of financial gain. Mack had clearly acted alone, selfishly unconcerned about the fate of those he'd forced to reveal confidential information. In short, the man was liar and a cheat, and the jury should only consider a guilty verdict resulting in a punitive custodial sentence.

During the defence summation, Martin argued strongly that his client had been victim of an elaborate scam, yet one where obvious flaws had been uncovered. With greater resources, he argued, he could have chased the money and the girl who helped set Calum up in Grand Cayman, and sought to identify the real protagonist, but as his client was innocent and now bereft of funds his defence relied on the fairness of the jury in seeing his client's perspective.

He reminded the jury that the prosecutor himself had stated that staff at the phone company could not be expected to judge the validity of a fake passport. Logically, he continued, the staff at a bank six thousand miles away in the Caribbean would be even less able to identify a fake foreign passport if presented with the correct account details and passwords. He asked why Calum Mack, if indeed guilty of planning such a detailed scam, would have allowed his personal ID to be required as proof of identity with the possibility of incrimination at a later date? His client possessed an honours degree in economics from one of the best universities in the British Isles, yet according to the prosecution was so inept that he chose his birth place to name a clandestine investment vehicle in which he was going to trade. Worse, he had seemingly publicised his knowledge in a major publication in plain view of his editor and hundreds of thousands of readers, and made phone calls to old friends to allegedly blackmail them into submission despite the fact the court—and the jury—were not to allowed to enquire as to the nature of this duplicity.

Martin opined that had his client been guilty, he would surely have either absconded, or used the alleged proceeds to reduce a potential sentence by admitting guilt, or by funding a better defence. He explained that Calum, even if cleared as he fully expected, faced being ruined in both banking and journalism as mud sticks. He himself could testify that his client had exhausted his limited savings to seek justice.

Finally Martin asked the most salient question. 'Where is the money?' Convicting Calum Mack, he argued, would be akin to sending an accused murderer to purgatory in the absence of a body. The ease with which the FCA had obtained 'written evidence' of Calum's withdrawal was suspicious, he insisted, as such banks rarely gave up such details, yet the jury was expected to believe that this was gospel, and simultaneously trust that the money trail then disappeared.

After instruction from the judge, the jury's deliberations took barely half an hour, and then Calum was brought back into the court to await the verdict. As the verdict was read out loud an audible gasp could be heard from the public gallery, followed by more muted sound of tears of an older female breaking down.

Aurelia awaited the verdict at the FCA offices at Canary Warf. Telford had assumed that she'd have wanted to be part of the FCA media response, perhaps enjoying the reflected kudos if the verdict progressed as they hoped. His momentary displeasure at her reaction—that she'd prefer to explore other potential new investigative opportunities—was quickly replaced by a self-assured nod. He probably knew any void would be readily filled by Adam, who would gain great pleasure from any limelight in relation to a high profile case such as this one, particularly if he could at least in his own mind elevate himself beyond Aurelia. The case, however, had unexpectedly gotten under Aurelia's skin, unsettling her normal drive for justice. Then the text from Telford appeared.

Financial tipster found guilty of insider trading.

Tipster, indeed. She contemplated the term, wondering if Calum Mack's predictive powers could have foreseen such an outcome, or if he could have guessed the twin penalties of a custodial sentence and probable confiscation order that he would now face. Her own reaction was slightly muted, almost anticlimactic. Essentially, the verdict should be good for her career, but then Adam had muscled in again, and there would always be another case to begin all over again next week. She'd been encouraged by Max Telford to pursue high profile cases and this one had been a slam dunk, but something still nagged away at her.

As she sat back in her chair, she nibbled at a finger nail, a bad habit she'd developed as a child when deep in thought. When the FCA had been pursuing proof of Mack's withdrawal from the bank in George Town, a minor doubt had existed over the case. Mack had been on the island, but they could not prove he had been in George Town that day or had actually been at the bank, as the information Vinnie had given was only hearsay at that point. Then something had mysteriously arrived at the FCA. A photograph—a physical copy. This had not been introduced as evidence at the trial as the CPS, with agreement from the police and Max Telford, had stated that it was now redundant—irrelevant—because Telford had been able to testify in court in respect of the subsequent letter from the bank itself, including evidence of the use of Mack's ID. The validity of the bank's letter was not in question as it had come through official sources, but something still bugged Aurelia. The introduction of the photograph would *ostensibly* have strengthened the case against Mack, but in would also have generated other more subtle questions, doubts even. And as Aurelia considered this minor nuance, her mind framed the most salient two questions.

Who exactly had taken that picture, and why?

Another individual several thousand miles away in Barbados also celebrated the news of the verdict, though his pleasure was tempered by the realisation that only Mack would be formally punished for the affair. Hawk understood why the others, particularly Rowland, had escaped retribution. Such individuals operated in circles that he did not, and were protected to an extent by the system which had produced them. Hawk had known people in prison who'd been 'fitted up' or had even agreed to take a sentence for some powerful 'Mr Big' parked comfortably in a mansion elsewhere. The system was fatally flawed. Hawk was curious, though, about the CNN report he watched, which had taken a political view of events. 'Another damning indictment of the City of London,' the reporter stated. Had the authorities over there *ever* really embraced tougher regulation? How could investors trust the financial system, or indeed the media anywhere in Europe, when greed conquered fear so readily, and so transparently? Hawk laughed, acknowledging to himself that he had personally concocted this project and it was no more an indication of regulatory failure than flying to Mars. He noted that the *Sentinel* was also likely to be fined and censured in separate proceedings, given that the prosecution had alluded to the central conduit role the medium had played.

The irritation he felt that Rowland, Lyndon and Wilson—and that pompous prick, Tomlinson—would escape natural justice, also niggled. This would have to be addressed. He still had those pictures, and he momentarily considered employing deferred gratification—why not wait a while and *then* send the photos to their wives? He understood why Mack and his lawyer had evaded pushing for the evidence of blackmail—almost certainly they'd feared that additional charges might have been raised. They were operating in a vacuum, unsure of the actions of others, and probably under-resourced and frightened. And, partly due to the beauty of his plan, it seemed that at least three of the four musketeers had actually believed that Mack had set them up, so they thought they were home and dry now that he'd been found guilty. Well, fuck them. For their insouciance he'd turn up the heat at a later date.

While in Barbados he had dithered over whether to purchase shares in Electricon, the power plant company that would probably hit pay dirt in Iraq. When under pressure, Lyndon had assured him of the firm's prospects, depending on a change of leadership in Iraq. Hawk had held off for fear of a connection being created, but the odds against any trades he might make now, post trial, being traced to Lyndon and thus him, were tiny, and the prospect of perhaps doubling his money might help to compensate for his annoyance over the gang of four currently avoiding punishment. The newly-elected president in Iraq had now been sworn in, and he noted from the Al Jazeera news station that the president had appointed all his interior ministers, and that major policy decisions were imminent. So he accessed the website of a broker in Antigua to acquire a cool million in sterling of the London-based Electricon, and smiled to himself, knowing that he would soon enjoy hearing of the sentence to be imposed on one Calum Mack.

Chapter 12

Any notions Calum had harboured that white-collar criminals somehow enjoyed preferential treatment while serving at Her Majesty's pleasure had been cruelly misplaced. The alacrity with which the sentencing and custodial placement occurred had shocked him, perhaps because he had still been in a state of denial until the verdict had been read. He'd forlornly hoped that because he was in fact innocent justice would triumph, generating new strands of inquiry to aid the prosecution of the guilty. During the period awaiting trial he had acquired almost celestial hopes that he would receive a very public apology and some sort of compensation from his accusers.

But years in this hellhole?

Meaning, essentially *eight* years as a further two years would be added after a period of six months if the estimated proceeds of the trades, plus interest, were not repaid, which was impossible. He'd never so much as stolen a packet of crisps. Martin had warned, cautiously—given Calum's fragile state of mind—that any reduction for 'good behaviour' could not apply because of the non-payment issue. Even some killers and rapists could be freed in less than eight years, Calum argued. Calum's parents had offered once again to find some money in order to fund an appeal but he was so distraught that he didn't know what to do.

The only other thing of value he possessed that was unknown to the police was those Krugerrands he'd once bought with a cash bonus he'd received in his previous job. Now he was incarcerated he was in no position to visit the safety deposit box in Edinburgh in which they were held. His parents had the spare key for the box, but he wasn't going to burden them with a quasi-illegal act at this juncture.

When he arrived at Wandsworth, he entered the prison gates with his head bowed, barely able to face the institution he would now be forced to call home. Martin had advised him of the window dressing that had passed for modernisation—things such as the tiny in-cell screens to apparently offer privacy, and a pathetically inadequate programme of extracurricular activities. He also warned of overcrowding and the assorted unreconstructed inhabitants that Calum could expect to encounter. Inside, the municipal odour of the place almost made him heave, and it instantly felt every inch the Victorian chamber of punishment and incarceration which matched the intent of its original designers. His head sunken, he stared at his own wretched reflection on the industrial duty linoleum that coated the long entry corridor.

Art, his new cell mate, was perhaps the most nervous person Calum had ever met. Not 'pleasantly' nervous, however. Not an underdog wrongly incarcerated like Calum, but a stocky, prematurely wrinkled man of about fifty from Wolverhampton who functioned as a demented animal waiting to strike. After a brief introduction, Calum had enquired as to the basis for Art's imprisonment and the man suddenly leapt across the cell to grab Calum's shirt collar, forcing him against the wall.

'Did I *say* you could fuckin' ask me that?'

'Hang on! I'm only being polite,' Calum said, trying to release the man's fist from his throat without exacerbating the situation further.

Art shoved his back against the wall again. 'Polite my arse. You're a nosey bastard! *I'll* tell you why I'm inside when I'm *good and ready*. Got it?'

'Got it,' Calum said, backing off. This guy was a mad man.

'Right. As long as you understand who the boss is in this hotel room,' Art said, scratching his nose. 'I'm here because I decorate people's faces,' he stared menacingly, mimicking the use of an open razor across his face and throat. 'That's why they call me *Art*. Got it?'

'Got it.'

'Well if you don't do as you're told here you *will get it*. Got it?'

'Yes.' Calum replied in the affirmative, whilst not repeating what was clearly Art's trademark rhetorical question, in case this exchange lasted all night. Or perhaps not, if this psycho actually possessed the blade he professed to have creatively employed. Calum had vaguely hoped for someone like Morgan Freeman's character in *The Shawshank Redemption*. How naive. He closed his eyes, attempting to mentally summon the strength to deal with all this shit. This was day *one*. He had no idea if he could apply to have a different cell mate, but this was immediately one of his priorities, almost as pressing as his appeal, which according to Martin would take several months, perhaps more than a year.

Other than offering the predictable concoction of depression interspersed with periods of bitter anxiety, the following month passed by. Minor periods of light occurred when someone visited, but essentially, Calum kept his head down, placating Art and any other likely threat.

Then, one day during week five of his sentence he joined his fellow inmates in the prison food hall for lunch. The hall, no more than a model of basic municipality, seemed like an oasis to Calum compared to his cell, where he had learned that Art not only snored like a rhinoceros but swore threateningly at those individuals captured within his dreams. God only knew how the man had become so damaged, though Calum wasn't going to ask.

After he'd been served a gruel-like concoction of lamb and potatoes, one of the prison officers told him bluntly to 'sit on his arse'. However, when he attempted to select a space on the edge of a bench one inmate immediately shuffled up and said that the seat was taken. Calum averted eye contact and moved on, only for the same behaviour to be repeated, but with a greater degree of venom.

'That's *my fucking seat*,' the third prisoner spat. This had not happened on previous days. Calum tried to ignore the threat and shuffled further round again. On the fourth occasion that he was diverted from what appeared to be a free seat, the officer who had initially instructed him pointed to a bench at the far end of the hall where there was one available space, signalling angrily with his hands for Calum to reverse and walk quickly round the other way.

A foot appeared from nowhere.

As Calum fell, his shin caught the edge of one of the benches on the way down, the lamb dish distributing itself over the inmate at the end of the table. A collective ripple of laughter accompanied the incident and as Calum picked himself up the man who'd been sprayed by the food—a huge guy with a wild looking black beard—leapt out in front of him, shoving him back. Two supervising screws immediately moved in closer, but before they could reach black-beard, another man stood up and placed himself between Calum and the man, facing away from Calum.

Calum took a step back, momentarily confused by the sequence of events. His peripheral vision indicated that the officers had backed off slightly, and Calum noticed that the assembled audience was no longer focused upon on him, but rather on the two inmates in front of him. Then, in a sudden, almost conciliatory manner, black-beard nodded and took his place again at the table. As Calum then made to pick up his plate, the individual who had interjected on his behalf turned to face him.

The first thing Calum noticed were the eyes. Piercing, steely grey, Aryan in probable ancestry, they peered straight at him. He guessed that the man, who was about the same height as Calum, might be around about fifty-five, though he appeared to be in good shape.

The second thing Calum then observed was the voice.

'Like the man said, sit on your arse.' The words were measured, broadcast in a strangely pitched, threatening East End accent. The man, who was chewing gum vigorously, pointed to the spare seat at the far end that the officer had identified, and Calum mouthed the word 'thanks' before taking his anointed place. Calum then sat in silence. Nothing similar had happened during the initial weeks of his residence. No one spoke to him, those around him engaging in odd, almost menacing small talk you wouldn't wish to interrupt. Calum barely touched his food, his appetite tarnished by events. When the short lunch period elapsed and he rose with the other prisoners when instructed by the guards, he felt a tug at his arm, and turned round to see an older Oriental man facing him.

'Be careful who you accept help from,' the man said dryly, before walking off. Calum made to ask what that meant, but before he could obtain an explanation the screws had directed him in a different direction.

In his cell that night, Calum engaged in tortuous mental gymnastics as he contemplated whether he could possibly survive in a place so potentially volatile. Then, suddenly he became engulfed by emotion, the tensions of the past few weeks erupting with unstoppable force. Thankfully, Art was in full-throttle snoring mode as the tears flowed out. As he desperately attempted to muffle the noise, he remembered how, as a boy of about eight or nine in the Black Isle, his football team had been losing four-one at half time, and a feeling of inescapable doom had overwhelmed him. As the tears had flowed that day, his mother's father, Grandpa Cal, had witnessed his plight. He had wandered over from the sidelines, grabbing Calum and ruffling his hair, before gazing right into his eyes. He recalled the exact words Grandpa Cal had employed.

'*Son, you can turn this around.* I was in a prisoner of war camp for four years, and I turned it around. Go on, *turn it around.*'

Calum sniffed at the memory, warmth spreading from within as he wiped his face on the thin grey prison blanket. His Grandpa Cal wasn't here today, but his sentiments were. Calum swallowed, recalling the game.

His team had won five-four.

The reaction to the news that Max Telford had arranged an away day—and night—for his team had been relatively positive, insofar as the team were unaccustomed to such largess being thrust upon them. Aurelia's own response had been one of resignation, however, the uncomfortable aftermath of the Mack case having left her with an odd sense of alienation within the department. No one particularly seemed to share her concerns over Calum Mack's old university buddies' escape from justice, and no one had been remotely perturbed over the puzzling, central question surrounding the reasons for Mack having behaved in such an incriminatory manner. When she'd queried Max again about the photo of Mack outside the bank in George Town he'd simply laughed in response, suggesting that she should loosen up and enjoy the thrill of the conviction.

During the meal, Adam had toasted the conviction, and everyone had applauded. Telford had then acknowledged everyone who'd contributed, noting that influential people had noticed their recent successes and were impressed. Solid careers would be built on such results, he intoned. Aurelia had been on the brink of interjecting, to explain that those "influential people" had simply bought off the FCA and the police to protect their political cronies, and if that was what justice entailed, it was worthless. Yet, something held her back. Why disrupt her career unduly?

Perhaps it was courtesy of her third glass of Chilean Merlot, but a creative thought suddenly occurred to her. She would quietly continue the investigation into the Mack case, but do so in secrecy. That way, if she unearthed nothing, she would accept defeat—but if she uncovered something of greater substance then there would be grounds for re-opening the case.

She owed Calum Mack nothing, but the really odd thing was that when she'd been in his presence she'd actually liked the guy. He wasn't the typical, cocky, City suit, and nothing in his body language had suggested that he was being disingenuous. Aurelia had studied the literature on body language while at university and was aware how difficult it was to avoid the more subtle signs of dishonesty, particularly when under pressure. When following the trial she'd been surprised that Mack's lawyer—given Mack's insistence of his innocence—hadn't demanded a polygraph test, at least to muddy the waters. But then, might that indicate that his own lawyer hadn't believed him either? Based on the cheers that had erupted around the dinner table when Adam and Max spoke, she wondered if she was the only person who'd even partially doubted the verdict.

Later on that night as the alcohol had flowed more freely, she'd ventured into a corner in the lounge bar and enjoyed a bit of a bitch about Adam with her colleague Jen, who it transpired Adam had also hit on more than once.

'You too? Why don't you complain about sexual harassment to Max?' Aurelia asked.

'You didn't,' was the insightful reply, as Jen raised her eyebrows. '*Come on*, Aurelia, you know the story here. It's a male-dominated environment. The fourth course tonight was pure testosterone, don't you think, with all these stupid, blokey jokes? Let's not kid ourselves, if we started making what *they* considered to be spurious complaints it would lead to a dead end. We'd be given poorer cases, or more awkward ones, we'd be slowly excluded, and we'd end up leaving or being side tracked via maternity leave or something.'

Aurelia glanced down, which was noticed intuitively by Jen.

'Sorry…you're not…'

'No! No…I'm not,' Aurelia blurted, before suddenly laughing. 'No, it's just that it would be nice to be in that position *one* day. I'm a bit older than you, and time really flies. This job has consumed me so much that I don't even seem to have time to find a boyfriend. And the last thing I want is to deteriorate into a bitter old spinster.'

Jen nudged Aurelia, pointing to the bar. 'Well, there's always Adam. He'd make a *fabulous* father, don't you think?' They both burst into hysterics at this observation, and attracted the attention of Adam and another two guys at the bar. They shortly decided to retire to their rooms in case the entourage at the bar interpreted the noise as some kind of open invitation for sex.

Two days after the incident in the dinner hall Calum was passed a leaflet by another prisoner, telling him that he must read it. The leaflet denoted the prison chaplaincy services. However, on the back of the leaflet there was a handwritten note. *Attend the Anglican session on Tuesday morning. Make a request though the screws.* This threw Calum. He was not really religious, but someone had taken the trouble to offer him help; to show interest in him. Wondering if he should go, he then reflected that during his short tenure in prison he'd begun to see that any opportunity to escape his cell should be taken. Sharing with Art was something akin to perilous tedium—if such an oxymoron made sense—and he'd take any break offered.

He'd read about Nelson Mandela's incarceration on Robben Island, off Cape Town , and recalled how Mandela and his fellow inmates had been forced to undertake heartless manual labour designed to destroy their spirits. They'd broken rocks and then shifted them, before transporting them back to their original location. Pointless, backbreaking labour undertaken in bright sunlight with no caps or sunshades, supervised by racist guards. Mandela had spent 27 years in prison, yet had gone on to win the Nobel Peace Prize and lead a fledgling nation towards its new destiny. Calum only had to suffer eight years, and he remembered a relativity truism that his mother had often employed...*there's always someone 'worse off than yourself'*. Yes, he'd attend the session. He wasn't an Anglican, but that didn't matter.

At 10:00 a.m. on Tuesday, a group of prisoners sat quietly inside the plain room awaiting the Anglican chaplain. Calum already knew of two of the inmates—Little Dave and Skinny—so he sat beside them. These two were rough and ready, and appeared to spend most of their time competing with each other in the development of creative insults towards others, though underneath it seemed innocuous enough.

'Ah...it's the sweaty sock,' Skinny said, looking squarely at Calum. Calum simply nodded. This was London rhyming slang for 'Jock'. 'What are you doing at our service, Jock? You gone all religious?'

'Just giving my thanks,' Calum replied.

'Yeah, right. You mean just getting out of your cell for ten minutes like everyone else here.'

Then Little Dave craned his neck round to see who else was coming in the door.

'Oh Christ,' he said under his breath, prompting Calum and Skinny to look round. 'Don't tell me he's now a convert too.' Calum swallowed, seeing piercing steel grey eyes staring directly at him from the end of the room.

'Who is that guy?' Calum whispered.

'That's Reggie Benson.'

'And who is Reggie Benson?'

Skinny dragged an index finger across his throat. 'Do you know nothing? Well, for your information, he's probably the most evil bastard in this place.'

Benson approached the row in which Calum sat, and stared at the inmate beside Calum. The man immediately gave up his seat and moved. Calum simply nodded, suddenly realising where the leaflet had originated. When the chaplain arrived, he offered a brief prayer before the small congregation began to sing a hymn.

But Benson didn't sing, instead speaking directly into Calum's ear as the hymn progressed. 'You *owe me*. Understand?'

Calum nodded before replying 'Right…thanks for, eh, stepping in the other day. I appreciate—'

'Cut the shit. I don't want your appreciation.' He jabbed Calum in the ribs. 'Now, if you're smart, and play your cards right, you can have a better life.' Calum scratched his head, swallowing. What did this guy want—drugs, sex?

When the hymn ended and the chaplain spoke, Benson stared straight ahead, as if immersed in the words. Nothing more was said during the next hymn, and then the short service was concluded with another prayer.

Then, as the prisoners were shepherded out, Calum felt another jab in the ribs from behind. He turned, and Benson again spoke directly into his ear. 'We're going to have a proper conversation, so next time we're in the yard together for exercise I want *you* to come over to *me*. That's important. If I have to make any fucking sort of effort to *make* you come over to me I'm going to be raging, because I *am someone* in here, okay?'

Calum nodded, before continuing out of the room. Benson was led away by guards in another direction, leaving Calum with Little Dave and Skinny. 'What did he want?' Little Dave enquired.

'Haven't a clue,' Calum responded, avoiding eye contact. Little Dave then grabbed his arm, before whispering something Calum couldn't hear.

'What was that?'Calum asked him, prompting Skinny to turn around and smile.

'He said, "You're fucked".'

Chapter 13

Douglas Lyndon's letter of dismissal from Channing's Bank had come as no surprise. When the news had initially broken about theinquiry into Calum Mack's insider trading, Lyndon had a preliminary interview with two of Channing's directors and a representative from HR. The fact that potential charges were not subsequently brought against Lyndon had failed to save his job however, because at his second internal interview the bank had taken the view that as Mack had publically tipped one of its client's shares, and Lyndon had admitted at least indirect contact with Mack, then the bank's integrity had come into question. Clients needed absolute confidence in all staff at such a prestigious firm, and there could be no room for manoeuvre. Lyndon was now unworthy of the Channing's name.

Lyndon had been sanguine about his dismissal, and having formatively attended the school of hard knocks he considered that this simply represented another occasion when the establishment had attempted to crush a working class boy. He hadn't even bothered to fully elucidate regarding the blackmail, as that too would have resulted in the same decision—perhaps exacerbated it—but he insisted that he receive some financial compensation, explaining that if he came clean and said publically that the bank's IT systems were open to abuse, then the financial consequences for Channing's would be much greater. The bank had reluctantly acquiesced, insisting on a confidentiality agreement that prohibited any future discussion of the subject. Lyndon's wife was relieved. She was pregnant again and realised that without the financial safety net they could be facing a dismal future. She was also now aware of the blackmail attempt, but she trusted her husband, and was now relieved simply to progress with their lives.

Lyndon, however, now had time to consider events. Wide awake in bed, his mind meandered. His wife had taken the kids to a pre-school scheme early before going to her weekly volunteering day, and Lyndon considered the rare experience of being 'off'. Not on holiday, not sick, just off. As he stared at the ceiling identifying minor imperfections in the paintwork that he'd never previously noticed, he considered Calum Mack's case once again. The whole fiasco had frustrated him on two counts. Firstly, it had forestalled his career, and although he was confident that he could resurrect that aspect of his life, realignment would take time and effort. The second aspect was inextricably tied to the first. His major regret was not having talked to Calum Mack after the initial blackmail attempt. The blackmailer had forbidden contact between members of the group, and, acting out of character, Lyndon had followed those instructions. Given that Lyndon had been certain that the man he'd subsequently spoken to on the phone had employed some kind of voice distortion app, he was annoyed he hadn't spoken to Calum and killed the whole thing dead.

Now, in retrospect, it was patently obvious that the individual to whom Lyndon had spoken had been attempting to frame Calum. Did Calum know the man? One further complementary hypothesis was that Lyndon also knew this man. Possibly they all did. This thought had occurred to him previously, but had now come to the fore again as he wondered if the distortion app could have been used not solely to attempt to mimic Mack, but also to conceal the identity of the caller himself. Who was this guy?

He had liked Calum Mack. They'd not been really close, but they'd enjoyed the sort of mutual respect that emerges between individuals who have something subtle in common within a wider group of friends. Lyndon hailed from a fairly tough city suburb, which had sometimes generated ridicule at university, and Mack had often been ribbed on the grounds of occupying Teuchter/sheep-shagger status. Thus, the common bond had been that of partial outlier status amongst their peers. Now that Mack had been jailed by a justice system that searched for scapegoats rather than genuine protagonists, Lyndon felt a hint of transferable guilt, as he could have perhaps prevented the outcome, or at least mitigated against it if he'd been firmer with the caller. Why had he let the bastard away with it?

He made himself a strong tea and flipped on the television news. When the business section came on, he initially silenced the sound, but then saw the logo of a firm he knew well. He turned the sound back on to listen to a financial journalist reporting that Electricon had been awarded major contracts to build new power plants in Iraq. The journalist was gushing about the firm, suggesting that the news implied major growth prospects for Electricon throughout the entire Middle East, and possible elevation to the FTSE 100. The shares had jumped.

Lyndon smiled ironically. He'd rarely dabbled in the market personally, and certainly not to utilise inside information, yet against his moral principles he'd spilled his guts to a blackmailer. He'd lost his job, Mack had lost his freedom, but someone else had made a small fortune. Of course, Calum Mack hadn't tipped Electricon in his column, so had Mack been ignorant of the story, the blackmailer having chosen not to divulge this piece of information? Sure, Electricon's success had been a long shot at the time, but with the change of political leadership in Iraq events had altered.

Then another thought occurred to Lyndon. What if the blackmailer had by-passed Mack as the fall guy for this one, and quietly traded on his own behalf? When the story had broken a short while back regarding the Iraqi leadership position, the blackmailer would have been perfectly placed to benefit from the news. Mack had now been jailed, and Lyndon himself was the only one who knew what the blackmailer knew.

Lyndon raised himself from the comfort of his super-king bed and paced the room, energised by his own irritation. While at work he might have been able to access software to provide data on share trades, but to investigate the same thing here at home, he would probably have to engage in hacking. He pondered this possibility, considering whether embarking on a set of illegal acts at this juncture was a wise course of action. What if he was identified poking his nose into transactions regarding another of Channing's clients? This could lead to charges. It was also possible that investing time and effort on such a course of action might throw up nothing. Assuming that was he actually able to identify recent buyers of Electricon stock, how would he know if a particular speculative trade was undertaken by the blackmailer, especially if via another shell company? It would be akin to searching for a pin in a pile of needles, without fully being aware of the distinction.

Then something else occurred to him. That Irish girl who was the investigator on the case, Aurelia Harley, had very efficiently identified all the trades which had sent Calum Mack down. She'd actually seemed particularly straight as far as he could ascertain, and Lyndon prided himself on his judgement of character. He scratched his chin, considering if it would be worth incriminating himself further by letting Harley know that he'd also divulged confidential information about Electricon? Would she simply go for the jugular, or would she be willing to ignore the source in order to see if there had been a miscarriage of justice?

Given he'd evaded prosecution for his actions to date—and he had no doubt that had simply been due to his connections with the others, Rowland in particular—would he be taking an undue risk to assist an old friend, with no guarantee of anything concrete emerging? However, as he made himself a bacon sandwich, he contemplated what life in jail would be like for Calum Mack. Then, almost subconsciously, he fiddled with his phone, searching for Aurelia Harley's contact details at the FCA.

Calum's patience with Art had reached something of a nadir, as his cell mate's mood spectrum—drifting between paranoia and imminent violence—proved to be a constant frustration. Either he'd need to batter the man senseless and extend his sentence to life, or he'd have to escape from him. One of the guards had laughed almost uncontrollably when he'd subtly asked how he could request a change of cell mate.

'Never heard of the frying pan and the fire, Mack?'

'But the man's a *psycho*. I'm supposed to be a white-collar criminal, yet nightly I'm housed four feet from a nut case who could attack me in my sleep at any moment,' Calum responded. The screw, a man they nicknamed "Two-soups" on account of being called Campbell Baxter, suddenly became more serious.

'Look, you don't get to choose your company in here. Art may be a fruit cake, but the violent part is all bluster. He's a thief, and the best form of defence in here for people like him is to *look* tough. Ninety percent of the inmates in this place are probably shit-scared on a daily basis.'

'So who is it exactly they're all frightened of? They *all* look scary to me.' Two-soups smiled, almost sympathetically. Calum realised that the man could discern that he was a slightly different type of detainee from the run of the mill prisoner.

'Look, one guy I'd definitely keep clear of is the man who saved your bacon in the food hall. And I don't mean the cook that day.'

'What, Reggie Benson? He helped me out, though you're the second person who's said that to me. I've been wary of asking why he's in here.'

'You don't know? I mean, this would explain why you're better off shacking up with Art.'

Calum scratched his ear, latent fear and curiosity in competition with one another over why Benson had wanted to speak to him in private. 'What did he do?'

'He's done lots of horrible things, but only one where he's been convicted. He got someone to burn his home down and his wife and step-kids were there. His wife was bonking his pal. Technically he's here for inciting arson, but it was more serious.'

'You're joking?' Calum swallowed.

'I'd never kid about something like that. Surprised that you hadn't known about the case, because it was splashed all over the front pages of the tabloids at the time, around five years ago. They could only get an arson-related conviction due to various people who perjured themselves. That's why he's in with you guys. But then, you'd probably have been too busy to notice, buried in the *Financial Times* looking for your next scam.'

That afternoon Calum was due for an exercise session in the yard. Since his conversation with Two-soups he'd been preoccupied with the imminent problem of deciding how to deal with someone who had torched his closest family members. Suddenly Art seemed very decent. Grey skies provided a heavy wash over the yard. As Calum entered an open space which had provided the only fleeting freedom for so many notorious inmates since Victorian times, he spotted Benson standing with a small group at the perimeter wall at the far end.

Calum had always been the assertive type, a pragmatic individual apt to make occasional errors of judgement but unlikely to be subject to accusations of procrastination. In that sense, his relatively brief spell in journalism had suited him. Despite the rain he embarked on what seemed like one of the most awkward short walks of his life, briefly pondering how he had arrived in this position, a former professional from the City seeking the approval of a sociopath.

As he approached, the men around Benson clocked Calum and parted without command. Calum found the piercing eyes staring at him, with a slight upward movement of the lips indicating that Benson was getting what he expected—respect through suspicion. What had Charles Darwin said in The Descent of Man? *Suspicion, the offspring of fear, is eminently characteristic of most wild animals.* As before, this wild animal was chewing gum as if it was his last ever piece.

Benson snapped his fingers and pointed to the side, and the men around him immediately moved further away.

Calum swallowed, standing with his hands in his pockets.

'Know why I was convicted?' Benson asked, before Calum nodded. 'People think I got off lightly in court. Well, just so you know the truth, I'm no child killer. I didn't know her kids would be there. But if an adult crosses me I'd have no qualms about doing anything.'

Calum nodded again, initially uncertain as to how to respond. Nowhere at school or university had he learned how to navigate through such a conversation. If he were to agree with Benson too obviously it would appear disingenuous and he could be challenged, yet if he openly displayed signs of the disgust he actually felt internally then his chances of escaping unblemished would evaporate. Calum decided on taking a minor risk by employing a strategy he'd used on a number of occasions at the *Sentinel* whilst dealing with difficult or powerful interviewees: be straight, and tell no lies.

'I don't think I've ever been in your situation so I'm in absolutely no position to judge.'

Benson's raised his chin as he momentarily assessed Calum's response, looking at him squarely. 'That's a fucking good point. Too many idiots in here have tried to judge me.' Calum nodded again, looking down before talking the conversation further.

'So how can I help you? I appreciate that you did me a turn in the canteen.'

'You're a clever boy, aren't you? You're starting to ask the right questions. Half the clowns in here couldn't tell the difference between chocolate and shit. You want a passport out of here, mate?' As they stood side by side in the rain, Benson looked straight ahead, waiting for Calum to respond.

'I'm probably going to be stuck in here for eight years, so I'm not sure I follow you.'

'That's good to hear that you've got your personal custodial arithmetic right. An *eight-year* sentence. I'm pleased by that specific fact. If you'd said *six years*, I'd have been a little bit pissed off, especially as I stuck my neck out for you in the canteen.'

Calum frowned, trying to interpret Benson's words. Had he read up on Calum's case? This guy was a mindless thug, wasn't he? Why would he take an interest in white-collar crime or the length of sentence that the judge had imposed on Calum?

'I'm sorry, I don't follow. I was sentenced to six years by the court, but I will probably end up being here for—'

'*Eight years*. Yeah, I know. And why do you think that's important to me?'

Suddenly the proverbial penny dropped for Calum as he turned to look at Benson. 'Because you think I did it, and if I don't give up what they think I stole, I'll get an automatic two-year extension to my sentence with no parole, meaning eight years. So I'll be desperate to what? You mean escape, get out of here, somehow?'

'*Everyone* wants to escape, pal. You're different, however, because if, as you've admitted yourself, you're down for eight years, it means that you've a nice little nest egg of *at least* two million US dollars stashed away on the outside.'

Calum swallowed hard, avoiding eye contact. Shit, this guy assumed him *guilty*, and that he was a rich man on the outside, which implied that he could be financially useful or open to blackmail.

For crying out loud. A blackmailer on the outside created the circumstance surrounding his incarceration, and now he faced a similar threat on the inside.

'Look Mr Benson, I'm really sorry to disappoint you, but I was conned by a guy on the outside, someone who must have had a grudge. I don't have two million dollars. I've got absolutely nothing. I couldn't even afford to fund my defence properly.'

Benson suddenly spun round and grabbed Calum by the arm, staring at him nose to nose. Calum could smell the synthesis of stale breath and mint from the chewing gum, and could clearly see the red blood vessels within the whites of Benson's eyes. Water dropped from Benson's nostrils as he spoke, his cockney accent cutting deeply.

'*Wrong fucking answer.* I could have you *ripped apart* in this place. Do you know how many people like you get destroyed in prison? So don't tell me any fucking lies.'

Calum swallowed, before wiping rain water from his face. He had a split second to make a judgement, and he made it. Prevarication wasn't going to produce results in this conversation. He'd have to placate the man somehow.

'I...haven't told anyone...about the money. The money's...almost impossible to get hold of...' As the words emerged from Calum's lips, he barely believed that he'd uttered them; a crazy, false confession in front of a triple murderer.

Benson sniffed, holding his head back. 'Well, that had better be the final time that you tell me a lie,' he stated dryly, before grinning. 'You know, I wasn't sure if you were just some stupid, gullible fucker who actually had been framed, but fuck me, you actually did stash away two million bucks! Absolutely no one else knows?'

Calum stared, before shaking his head. Shit! Maybe he could have stuck to the truth, but now he'd be *forced* to consolidate the lie, or Benson might go mental.

'Right, first things first,' Benson said. 'You're going to keep your cake hole shut. Got it?'

Calum Nodded. 'Good. You keep up the denials to everyone else. Secondly, where's the loot?'

Calum swallowed again. 'It's…in the Caribbean, but…' More lies.

'No fucking buts. Where, specifically.'

Calum tried to ensure that the sigh he emitted was almost inaudible in the rain. 'In a numbered account.'

Benson momentarily stopped chewing, arms outstretched. 'Why didn't you do a runner? Did you really think you'd get off?'

'I suppose…'

'Stupid bastard. So the cash is in one of those famous numbered accounts. Who can access it?'

'Eh…just me, but…' Calum was inventing the story as he went along, desperate for the conversation to end. As the bell rang to end the exercise session, and the prison officers shouted for the inmates to return inside, Benson peered closely at him one last time.

'Correction, pal. A numbered account that only *we* can access. And as luck would have it, I've got a plan to get out of this place. That means *escape*.' As Benson whispered, Calum just stared. Escape? His head was swimming.

Benson continued, pressing a hand on to Calum's shoulder. 'You're one lucky bastard, do you know that? You've turned up here at a very opportune moment. But if you don't kiss my ass, you'll not finish your term because you'll be leaving in a box. So keep your trap shut, and I'll speak to you again within a week. Tell anyone at all and your folks get it. I know who your family are and where they live. Facebook is a great thing, and I know some horrible guys on the outside desperate to do me a favour.'

As a child growing up in Dundrum in Dublin, Aurelia's father had always advised her to transform negatives into positives. When her mother and father had quarrelled, for instance, her father had immediately gone out and bought flowers, or booked a table for a meal, arguing that such niceties could not have been precipitated but for the initial negative. This transformational advice could only work, though, if those who had gained from the outcome had done so on merit. In Aurelia's mother's case, this was so, but could this adage possibly hold for the undeserving?

When Adam had been selected to work with European counterparts on a major international banking fraud case, Aurelia had immediately felt a dull pain in the pit of her stomach. She knew how the system worked. International collaboration was one of the key benchmarks for advancement, and the fact that Adam had been picked by Max in front of her for this case meant only one thing. Suspecting that the promotion game was rigged differed from witnessing the evidence first hand, and now the engine for Adam's career development had been ignited. The pain in her abdomen reflected the realisation that all her years of commitment, all those late nights and the painstaking research she'd undertaken might count for nothing because the system favoured male sycophants. That the particular sycophant in question was none other than Adam Smart only exacerbated her personal emotions. What would her father have advised here—buying Adam a congratulatory drink to purge her frustration? Keeping Adam onside as a 'positive' in case he subsequently became her new boss? At this notion, she almost felt physically sick. In the past she'd have confronted Max immediately, arguing the injustice of the decision, but of recent weeks her capacity for a fight had waned.

As she took a five minute chill-out in the sanctity of the ladies' room, her phone buzzed. An unannounced visitor had appeared at reception. When she enquired as to the identity of the individual, the receptionist gave the name Douglas Lyndon, whom she recognised from the Mack case. Making full use of a handy pack of Kleenex, she went downstairs. The fact that Lyndon should technically have made an appointment was obscured by a tinge of curiosity as to the reason for his arrival at the FCA.

'Thanks for seeing me,' Lyndon said flatly, as they shook hands. Aurelia observed the prematurely grey—almost white—hair, wondering if he'd had an overly stressful life. She checked her watch to visually indicate that the unscheduled nature of the visit would have parameters, which Lyndon noticed.

'All I want is ten minutes of your time,' Lyndon said, holdings his hands outwardly in a non-threatening gesture. Aurelia nodded and led him upstairs towards the nearest vacant meeting room.

'What can I do for you, Mr Lyndon?'

'Look, I appreciate you seeing me, and I'd appreciate if this was off the record, at least for now.'

'That depends on what you have to say, of course,' Aurelia replied, suddenly aware of the clichéd nature of the conversation. 'Well, okay, I suppose that you could just walk out of the door if I don't agree, so why don't you test the water? The room's not under surveillance, and I just didn't have time to wear a wire.' She looked directly at Lyndon who suddenly realised that she was joking.

'A sense of humour at work, I see,' Lyndon said. 'Typically Irish.'

'Inability to be anything other than direct—typically Scottish.'

Lyndon cleared his throat, smiling. 'Good point. So I'll be direct. I think—in fact I'm certain—that Calum Mack is innocent.'

Aurelia sighed. 'Along with all the rest of you guys? Is this an old pals' act, some kind of retrospective rear-guard action designed to shape an appeal for the one who took the fall? Why didn't you speak up more forcefully at the trial if you had any doubts?' As she folded her own arms tightly, she watched his body language and facial expression carefully to check for signs of a forthcoming lie, but Lyndon didn't break eye contact, staring straight back as he replied.

'Because whoever set up Calum Mack also blackmailed me.'

'What was all this supposed blackmail in any case?'

'Fabricated photographs,' Lyndon said flatly, as Aurelia raised her eyebrows in an arch.

'Of what?'

'Never mind. Look, I'm not worried about my situation. I've lost my job now, which is my own fault, but that's nothing in comparison to being incarcerated for a crime you did not commit. And I like Calum Mack. I know that sounds corny, or biased, but I feel guilty that he took the fall, as you term it, and I want to do something about it if I can.'

Aurelia briefly considered Lyndon's words, recalling her gut reaction towards Mack when she'd initially interviewed him. Mack had appeared to her as an honest, likeable guy. Either that or he was indeed a very polished liar. She had seen no signs of the conceit that often appeared interspersed with the charm of a practiced fraudster. However, the evidence in support of Mack's conviction had been overwhelming. His appearance in Grand Cayman at the exact time of the withdrawal of the funds provided the keystone in the case, surely. That was what the prosecutor, Max Telford, and of course the jury, had believed.

'If you want me to take this at all seriously, you'll have to give me something more concrete. I'm a very busy person with lots of live cases. I'd just about forgotten about this one, and then you arrive feeling guilty.'

'Okay. I knew Calum quite well as a student, and that wasn't him on the phone. We may be from opposite ends of Scotland, but I can tell a fake Inverness accent, or one generated by some weird app. Anyway, I'll get to the point. Not all of the information I gave the guy on the phone appeared in Calum's column. There was another tip.'

'What was the name of the firm?' Aurelia now had her notebook out, curious as to where Lyndon was heading.

'Electricon.'

'The company that builds power plants? Just won big contracts in the Middle East?'

'Yes.'

'And you want me to do what, exactly?'

'Well, I thought that you could investigate if the company you claim Calum used—Black Isle—bought any shares in Electricon.'

'I don't think it did at the time, I'm pretty certain, but then you look as if you have already figured that out.'

Lyndon nodded, before continuing. 'I thought that, to be honest. When I gave the information over the phone about Electricon I explained that any rise in the share price would only occur if there was a change in leadership in Iraq, i.e. down the line. Ironically, that has now come to pass, and hey presto, the announcement about the Electricon deal happens right afterwards.'

Aurelia pursed her lips. 'So you want me to investigate if someone else made any major trades in Electricon shares immediately after the new Iraqi leadership decision?'

Lyndon smiled as Aurelia conceded the point. 'Yes. And as you clearly understand, if you could identify such a deal, or deals, and tie them in with the other trades…'

'You mean that it might, just might, demonstrate Mack's innocence, or at least cast serious doubt, because he's been in jail? Unless he's got an accomplice working with him on the outside? Have you considered that?'

'Who on earth would take the risk of being jailed if they really had two million stashed in a bank somewhere? And then try to orchestrate more crimes from prison? Come on.' Lyndon shook his head, before Aurelia raised her chin, thumb and forefinger supporting it.

'You're asking a lot here. This case is officially closed. Your friend can appeal, but I am not obliged to do anything unless instructed to by the CPS, should he actually make an appeal. I take it that you've talked to Mack, that he's still pleading his innocence?'

'I haven't spoken to him about this yet because I didn't want to be implicated. I admit to you that I've done something illegal, even though I didn't profit from it myself. On the contrary, I've actually been a victim as well as I've now been sacked. But if my hunch is correct, and this guy— whoever he is—couldn't resist one last trade, then some justice can be administered. Why would I come to you today and potentially incriminate myself if I wasn't telling the truth? There's a bigger fish to fry out there—aren't you interested in that? Or would an admission of incompetence be too much for the mighty FCA?' Lyndon sat back, arms folded.

Aurelia swivelled in her chair, recalling one specific fact from the array of evidence against Mack. A piece of evidence clearly designed to incriminate him, yet paradoxically spreading a shadow over the case. Perhaps it was a Celtic grittiness, or her concern about the photo that was rebutted by Max Telford once the case was in the bag, or even her revulsion at Adam's imminent advancement, but something inside her tipped at that moment.

'Okay, Mr Lyndon. This is *strictly* between you and me. If you talk to anyone about what I am about to say, I will deny it, because I think that if I raised this I wouldn't get permission to do it officially. I would be accused of going on a needless fishing trip at taxpayers' expense.' She looked at Lyndon squarely. 'I will look into trades in Electricon on the proviso that if I find nothing irregular, you accept it and move on. Agreed?'

'Agreed. And if you *do* find something?'

Aurelia sighed audibly. 'Then we open a whole new can of financial worms. And before you go, there is one startlingly obvious question.'

'What's that?'

'Have you absolutely no idea as to the identity of this mysterious guy?'

Lyndon bit his lip. 'I've given it some thought, but before I speak to you again, I need to see Calum Mack.'

Chapter 14

Nothing confirmed the reality of incarceration more than coming into contact with the emancipated world. When his parents had come to his first visiting session his father had asked if he could request a transfer to a Scottish prison to make visiting easier. Calum had hesitated, still believing that any forthcoming appeal might be more likely to succeed if he were based in London where the "crime" took place. He explained his uncertainty over the validity of any transfer in any case, with Scotland being a separate legal jurisdiction, and they agreed to hold fire before making any request. And so far Calum had spoken to no one about Benson's threat. When Calum was then informed of a forthcoming visit from Douglas Lyndon, his initial curiosity had been replaced by another bout of frustration.

The visiting room had strict rules of contact, so when Lyndon arrived there was no opportunity for handshakes or any other form of physical contact. Calum sat with his arms folded. Lyndon had been a disappointment during the trial, apparently collecting some form of joint "get out of jail free" card along with Tomlinson and company. Calum had expected more from a guy he'd liked while at university, but then, a surprising number of people had evaporated from his life the instant he'd been charged.

'Surprised to see you here, Douglas.'

Lyndon held his hands up. He'd known more than one person from his upbringing in Castlemilk who'd done time for serious crimes, but the difference was that they'd actually been guilty.

'If we could rewind events, I think that none of us would have been played for such idiots. I've been fired, but that's trivial, I accept. I'm sorry that you took the biggest fall.'

'So that's why your here? Belated sympathy? I'm looking at an eight-year sentence, Douglas. *Eight years.* It's the sort of thing that happens to someone else, such as some of the lunatics in here.'

'That bad?'

'Worse.'

Lyndon leaned in as close as he was permitted, checking his watch. 'Look,' he said, clearing his throat. 'I've been to see Aurelia Harley at the FCA.'

Calum sat back, wondering where this was leading. 'Why?'

'I admitted I passed information on to this guy—whoever he is—and the upshot is that one last tip I supplied has suddenly come into play. It's Electricon—the firm that specialises in building power plants.'

'Didn't know about that one. Keep going, we don't get Bloomberg in the cells.'

'Well, there's some good news.' Lyndon sneezed, temporarily halting his explanation. 'Excuse me. Aurelia Harley is prepared to investigate recent trades in this stock. You know, to see if this guy might have traded again? I know it's a long shot, but she's said she'd do it on the QT, which means that there could be a chance she believes that you're innocent.' Lyndon erred on the side of caution, fearful of overstating recent events.

'What? Bloody hell, that's rich, Douglas, don't you think? The FCA went for the jugular. What makes you think there's been a change of heart?' Calum's raised voice precipitated a stern finger wag from one of the prison officers so he reluctantly modulated his voice.

'Don't you think it's worth a go?' Lyndon asked, looking away, perhaps realising that Calum might simply flare up again.

'Douglas, I could use a fucking gun in here, not a hunch. Even if you're right, and the guy traded one last time, the bottom line is that we don't know who he is. How many people could have traded in the stock, corporations the lot?' He banged his hand on the table in front of him, his temples bright red in frustration.

An officer shot over immediately, forcefully aiming a hand at Calum's shoulder. 'Cut that out, Mack! Or your visitor leaves.'

Calum held his hands up to placate the guard, before scratching the back of his head, digesting Lyndon's argument. He'd been over this a thousand times in his mind, but most of the guys they might all know had nothing to gain by shafting them. Some were slick suits who were already millionaires. Why would they risk everything to set up such an elaborate scam?

Calum sighed deeply. 'The short answer is that I don't know who it was any more than you, Douglas. All our joint contacts have too much to lose by getting involved with something like this. I didn't think that I'd pissed anyone off quite enough to be set up for eight years inside, and in any case it could also be that it's just some crank, or someone who researched us through social networking and targeted me to make money. Or even someone who hated me because I gave them a bad tip in my column. But the bottom line is, however much I'd like to know who it was, it would drive me crazy if I thought there was a chance and *then* it proved to be a bummer. Know what I mean? It could finish me off, if some of the psychos in here don't first.'

As visiting time abruptly came to a close, Calum and Lyndon exchanged an odd look. Perhaps it was lack of trust, or some kind of huff on Calum's part, or even just the fear of consequences, but Lyndon chose not to disclose his hunch as to the identity of the mystery caller.

And Calum failed to mention Benson's mystery escape plan.

Saturdays at the FCA in Canary Warf helped facilitate the careers of the ambitious and the beleaguered, those who were either driven to work on weekends because they badly wished to scale the berry tree, or those who simply couldn't cope with the workload. Aurelia had invariably selected to work late during the week rather than give up what she considered her little oasis of Saturday, but on this occasion she opted to attend the office as she could enjoy relative solitude. Having grabbed a baguette from a kiosk adjacent to the subway station, she entered the building with a degree of investigative challenge. As with her father in a previous life in Dublin, her primary instinct was probably the ego drive, the need to gain results for their own sake rather than, say, for pecuniary gain, and after speaking to Douglas Lyndon she'd experienced a renewed feeling that the Mack case might indeed be inconclusive.

She made herself a strong coffee, partly to compensate for the bottle of Pinot Noir she'd shared with a friend the previous evening, but also to strengthen her mental acuity. Although technically operating on her own time, she had no official brief to follow a lead in a case where a guilty verdict had already been achieved with the full endorsement of her boss and departmental colleagues. Her relationship with Telford had suddenly deteriorated in inverse proportion to Adam's rising prominence, partly as she'd been unable to conceal her antipathy towards Adam.

As it transpired, there were only two colleagues present at the office, both of whom were leaving as she appeared. Each nodded in greeting, neither any the wiser that she was anything other than another workaholic. Once seated, Aurelia ran her fingers though her long dark hair.

Where would she start? As she viewed her home page and absentmindedly her email, she pondered how she might tackle the Electricon trading issue. Douglas Lyndon fleetingly crossed her mind again. He was an odd guy, strangely stoical. As she viewed the thirty or so messages that had appeared since seven the previous evening, one leapt out. It was from Lyndon, with whom she'd exchanged contact details.

AH

Re CM case—got a name. Tom Hawkins (or try Thomas). Nicknamed Hawk. Served fifteen years for murder in Saughton Prison, Edinburgh. Released fifteen months ago, but disappeared from sight. Knew all of us from Edinburgh University. Smart guy, but didn't complete his degree as he topped an old man in the street.

Long story. We were witnesses. Didn't really consider the significance at the trial as it was so long ago… but now…? I couldn't bring myself to mention it to CM…I didn't want to build his hopes up in case it's a bummer.

Can you have a look into it?

DL

Aurelia bit her top lip, intrigued not by Lyndon's too familiar use of initials, but by the nature of the communication. How curious. The recent famous five of insider trading had all been witnesses at a murder trial fifteen years previously? A quick Google search identified the archives of *The Evening News*, the Edinburgh-based tabloid that covered the story in most detail more than a decade and a half before.

Within the first article, which reported the verdict and sentencing for Hawkins, her eyes were drawn towards a colour photograph of a young man, the eyes green and serious. The nose was hooked. Scanning through the article she felt her distaste spreading, a sudden déjà vu engulfing her as she recalled 'borrowing' notes containing similar sorts of details from her father's police work cases as a teenager. The sort of gory minutiae that policemen and forensic experts collate, tabloid journalists openly glorify, and some of their readers more tacitly adore. Hawkins had used a nail gun to shoot a 67-year-old homeless man several times in the face. One nail had penetrated the old man's right eye. Expert testimony as to the cause of death was recounted, the pathologist's report explaining that although all the nails had been fired at point blank range the man had been killed by the shot to the right eye as the softer tissue had permitted entry to the brain.

She then scanned previous articles covering the case as it had progressed. Somewhat gruesomely, one was headed *Eye Witness*, and sure enough, each one of the individuals involved in the Calum Mack case was mentioned. They were all male acquaintances of Hawkins, who had a reputation of being something of an oddity and had threatened to 'shoot' more than one of them at a Halloween fancy dress party in the student union minutes before the incident. Tomlinson, Wilson and Rowland had produced virtually identical testimony, claiming to have witnessed Hawkins fire deliberately at the old man, and Lyndon had reported trying to save the victim's life as he lay on the street corner. However, Calum Mack had come in for particular criticism from the defence lawyer at the trial, being accused of goading the accused in the Underground night club at the union prior to the incident. Other witnesses had refuted this version of events, including a young female student who had not been present in the street, but had been inside the club. She claimed the opposite, that Hawkins had pestered her and others, having secreted the nail gun which had been part of a bizarre DIY-themed outfit.

As Aurelia read the next article from the archives, details of the defence case emerged. Hawkins had insisted on his innocence throughout, and Aurelia pondered the similarities to the Mack case itself. The defence, which had claimed that the incident had been a tragic accident, had therefore been drained of credibility due to the weight of evidence and the sheer volume of testimony from student witnesses. Hawkins had reportedly screamed out in court when the verdict had finally been reached. Aurelia swallowed when she read the words he'd been reported to have shouted: *I'll get all you bastards back.*

The fifteen-year sentence for murder in the first degree had been imposed primarily as Tomlinson, Wilson and Rowland had insisted that the gun had been aimed and fired deliberately from point-blank range. And thus, the student career and freedom of Tom Hawkins had been curtailed for a decade and a half. Subsequent appeals had all failed, and as Aurelia tracked the diminishing impact of the case in terms of newsworthiness over the period it became apparent that most people had forgotten about Tom Hawkins, who had not been released early on parole due to his lack of contrition. The old man he'd killed had had no known relatives, so there had been no familial pressure for such an outcome, but the Scottish legal system had still seen to it that Hawkins was retained at Her Majesty's pleasure.

Until recently.

Aurelia paced the area around her desk, before wandering towards the window, viewing the cityscape to the south of Canary Warf. Billions passed electronically though this locus every minute, she pondered. Money was an odd thing. Intangible, yet an eternal motivator that drove people to do strange things. Risky things. Had Calum Mack risked his career and freedom for money, or had someone like this Tom Hawkins guy actually resurfaced after fifteen years to exact revenge on Mack and his fellow former students, and make some dirty money?

His payback?

Lyndon had figured that Tom Hawkins had 'disappeared' since his release. That observation implied that Hawkins had either moved somewhere else, perhaps abroad, or had changed his identity in some way. She figured that the latter would be likely, aware from her father's work that such was not uncommon among those convicted of murder and seeking to retreat from their own murky past. She tried the archives of the *Evening News* again and typed his name plus an approximate release date. There was only a very short piece of two paragraphs in length, noting the outcome of the case fifteen years before, but no photo. There were no other recent web-based references to Thomas Hawkins that she felt matched the character who'd been freed from Saughton Prison. Hawkins had no longer been a prominent prisoner, thus had escaped the more recent clutches of the media, and given that his victim had no known relatives at the time of the incident, it stood to reason that there was little interest in the man upon release. Just another ex-con.

Aurelia was aware that she was straying well beyond her remit in pursuing the story, but her interest was tickled. If she could obtain a recent photo of Hawkins, it might be conceivable that she could ascertain if *he* had been in George Town that day, because the bank might have retained security tapes from the day in question, irrespective of any current pseudonym. She recalled Calum Mack's lawyer putting it on record in court that he'd requested the security tapes from the bank for the day of the withdrawal, but to no avail. Aurelia, in keeping with the prosecutor, the police and the remainder of the team at the FCA, had assumed that this was simply the sort of desperate smokescreen to which defence solicitors often resorted. She recalled how damning the auxiliary evidence had been, and the general feeling that Mack was going down anyway.

But what about that date-stamped photo that had mysteriously been sent to the FCA, showing Calum Mack standing outside the bank? Mack said he knew nothing about it. Who exactly had taken that photograph? Could it conceivably have been Hawkins? If she were to pursue hypothetical trades in Electricon stock by Hawkins then she would be occupying much stronger ground with Telford if she could demonstrate that the lead was valid because Hawkins was involved, even if she did not know if he now had any new alias.

Aurelia spun around in her chair again. For some odd reason, the revolutions appeared to stimulate her thought process. Where might she find a recent picture of Hawkins? How would her father have proceeded? She missed him very much since his death from cancer two years previously, but whenever sadness encroached on her memory, she often tried to replace the emotion with positivity by considering how he would have helped her tackle her problems. She recalled him saying that in the USA, inmates' photographs were common place on the internet, but not as common in other jurisdictions. Surely the prison service and the police would possess a recent image for security reasons, even if confidentiality prevented open dispersal. Using her official identity at the FCA would leave an imprint, which she currently wished to avoid. For related reasons, she also wished to avoid Maxwell and Robson at the Met.

Then, she recalled Ken Charleson. Ken, from Yorkshire, had worked with Aurelia's father on a major international drugs case where the English and Irish forces had collaborated, and they'd become close friends. Ken had promised at the funeral to offer her help if it were ever needed, not that Aurelia had ever anticipated such a circumstance. Feeling slightly guilty for having done nothing more that send an e-card at Christmas, she dialled the number she'd stored on her phone.

Ken's voice hadn't altered in years, the deep tone reminiscent of a kind of Yorkshire Johnny Cash.

'Aurelia…how lovely to hear from you.' She could feel the warmth from the man from Harrogate on the other end of the phone. 'Not inviting me to your wedding are you?'

'I'm still married to my job, unfortunately.'

'Like your dad before you,' Ken replied. There was a fleeting silence as both parties reflected on the past. 'Miss him still, you know. Probably the most principled guy I ever worked with, Aurelia, and I'd be happy to tell that to anyone.'

'Thanks Ken, I appreciate that. I've a favour to ask.'

Aurelia produced a potted history of the case, explaining how she intended to operate below the official radar until she could provide evidence of a more substantive nature. Ken listened attentively, merely enquiring as to the occasional point of fact or procedure. When Aurelia finished, he spoke more candidly.

'I remember this case. I thought here's another greedy ex-banker—he can't make the ridiculous bonuses any more so he resorts to insider trading and blackmail. It sounded so believable. One of the tabloids kind of annihilated him. But you really think Mack's just taken the fall?'

Aurelia affirmed her doubts, though she firstly explained how her boss and colleagues had been increasingly eager for the conviction and faced no obvious barriers from either the police officers on the case or the CPS. Ken then enquired further about the evidence presented in the case, and Aurelia was forced to admit that there were testimonials from those who had supplied insider information, and even more damning, Mack's trip to Grand Cayman to access an account in his name. She then mentioned Douglas Lyndon's involvement and her own thoughts, especially about the issue of the mobile phones used, and the odd photograph that had turned up at the FCA offices. He repeated the question about her opinion of Mack's innocence.

'He may well be innocent, Ken. I had a hunch that something was amiss, but by the time I began asking more searching questions the whole bandwagon was motoring towards a conviction. The fact that a photograph had been taken implies that someone else was present in George Town that day—someone who knew why Mack was there, and the importance of his visit to that bank. Mack's lawyer had what seemed like a far-fetched story concerning a girl who'd lured him to the bank, but that might actually be accurate. He wouldn't have been the first person in financial history to have been successfully framed. These doubts have remained in my mind, and now Lyndon shows up, asking similar questions.'

'Your old man operated on hunches, you'll recall.'

'He did Ken, and I was contemplating what he would have done in the circumstances. It would have bugged him if he thought he'd put away a completely innocent man. I guess I can't help it either, and I figured you'd be in the same camp.'

'I am. Look, I can't promise anything huge, but I'm sure I can get a picture and make some unofficial enquiries as to where this Tom Hawkins bloke might have gone, or if he has a known alias. Some people owe me favours.'

'And I will be one of them.'

'No, Aurelia,' he stated flatly in his inimitable, rich voice. 'Your father helped me out in more ways than you can imagine. I'm teetotal now, thanks to him, but you probably didn't know that.'

'I didn't.'

'That was the kind of man he was—he'd never belittle someone or break a confidence. He helped saved my career, and probably my marriage as a consequence, so it would be a privilege to help pay him back though his daughter. I've contacts in both the Scottish force and Scottish Prison Service as lots of cases cover multiple jurisdictions. Leave it with me.'

When Aurelia said goodbye, a tinge of pride competed with a feeling of sadness for the father who was in some senses helping her from beyond the grave. He'd always been there and then he wasn't. Despite her religious upbringing in Ireland, she'd always been inwardly agnostic at best, but she did believe that humans could remain alive in spirit as long as others whom they knew cared sufficiently to retain and celebrate that memory.

Given that Ken sounded optimistic that he could obtain a picture of Hawkins surreptitiously, it would be worth delving into trades in Electricon stock as part of a simultaneous action. After, all, that was why she was spending Saturday at the office.

Electricon was the type of stock that ultimately benefitted from derived demand, with a strategic emphasis. When international economies performed well, businesses and consumers demanded more power. Enhanced power generation required new power plants to be constructed, but only when long term demand looked secure, and regulatory authorities permitted construction. Not knowing the firm well, Aurelia suspected therefore that Electricon was probably slightly cyclical in terms of its performance—the stock rising or falling in front of or behind economic growth or decline, if still subject to shocks in key markets. That meant that the stock had probably been seen as a recovery stock, but was some way off its previous peak, and a quick check of recent charts confirmed this hunch. Given that the story Lyndon had provided suggested that the change of leadership in Iraq was a pivotal development for the business, and therefore may have precipitated the recent share price rise, she checked the specific date when the new leader had entered office.

Using a specific algorithm she traced the typical pattern of trades in the firm prior to the announcement in Iraq, and compared this to the pattern over the previous six months. Various institutional investors appeared to have been strengthening their positions in the firm over this short period, and one or two sovereign wealth funds had also increased holdings. One well known entrepreneur had also traded in the firm's stock on several occasions, though Aurelia looked back and found that he'd a history of such trades in the firm over a period of years, so she could eliminate him from the equation. She briefly pondered what level of investment she should consider as a minimum amount to analyse in more detail, as there were numerous trades of less than one hundred thousand pounds around the time of the announcement.

Then one particular trade jumped out at her.

An online broker registered in Antigua had purchased four hundred and thirty two thousand shares for a total of $1.593 million, or, perhaps interestingly, almost exactly one million in sterling at the exchange rate on that day, based on a quick calculation. Aurelia stood, and once again peered out of the window. Might someone—perhaps Thomas Hawkins—have invested an exact round number in sterling as a final gamble, secure in the knowledge that Mack had already been safely convicted and his supposed affiliates such as Lyndon were now tarnished by association?

She noted the broker's name, considering that the Caribbean was once again the conduit for a stock intrinsically connected to this case. Of course, an online trade could have originated anywhere, as there were few stipulations in respect of ownership nationality for firms quoted on the London Stock Exchange, but the connection was interesting. Then Aurelia's phone buzzed: Ken.

'Aurelia, I've got a picture of Hawkins, or whatever he might be known as now. Want to see? Hold on a minute and I'll send it.'

She waited for the photo, before calling back. 'Bloody hell, you were quick there. Odd looking guy. Did you get this from the prison service itself?'

'Sort of. Someone I know works at Saughton itself and happened to be on shift when I called. Just a bit of luck. The guy used to be a cop in Edinburgh. Usual story, burnt out at fifty so took a sideways move into an allied area. Didn't want to say earlier in case he couldn't help, but there you go. Anyway, this Hawkins guy is one strange looking bugger.'

Aurelia peered at the diagonal red line running straight across his left cheek. 'That's a scar, I take it. Do you think he acquired it inside?'

Ken laughed without humour. 'Absolutely. This guy was on the receiving end of a bit of random violence. Often happens to those seen as weak, or guilty of a crime against someone weak. He killed an old man in cold blood, so that sort of thing is a green light for some of the prison hard nuts. But there is more. The contact I have there has filled me in on a couple of details. Got a pen?'

Aurelia listened as Ken explained what he'd learned. Initially Hawkins had been classed as dangerous and had served in solitary confinement for various periods. When he'd been re-assessed, he'd shared a cell with one or two interesting characters. Ken explained that the police often took cognisance of co-habitants of prison cells once inmates were released, as it often provided leads in relation to recidivism.

'So who did he share with?' Aurelia was intrigued.

'Well, he was in with one guy who'd also gone down for a violent crime. He ran over his girlfriend and left her in a wheel chair. However, that's not all the story, because he'd been a stock broker. Hawkins spent three years in the same cell as a stock market expert.'

Aurelia considered the profession of the cell mate, who had been released before Hawkins. 'Hawkins spent, what, more than 1000 days in close proximity with a guy who traded shares for a living?'

'Exactly. Fits your theory, doesn't it? You've said that Hawkins had been a student at Edinburgh University, which means that he was bright. Then he ends up sharing a cell with another bright guy—in fact they probably put them in together for that reason. What do they talk about?'

'Their skills and their crimes, I suppose?' she asked.

'Yes and no, Aurelia. Skills, yes, but I bet inmates with a white-collar profile want to forget about the reasons then entered prison, and dream about the day they regain their freedom. These guys make plans, clever plans.'

'And perhaps part of those plans incorporate retribution if they think they've been stitched up?'

'Wouldn't be the first time, Aurelia. I knew one man who served seventeen years for murdering one of his rivals, and on the day he was released he proceeded to hack the guy's brother to death with a machete. Sentenced to thirty years on the second occasion.'

'Wow. But a *smart* con would wish to deliver revenge but not be caught. And even better if he made money in the process.'

Ken sniffed. 'Indeed, and creating a new identity might be one of the first things such a person would do. So wait 'til you hear this. What my contact also told me is that Hawkins was thick with another con, used to eat lunch with the guy all the time. And guess what he did for a living?'

'Oh, surprise me.'

'Counterfeiter.'

Aurelia processed this information, pausing briefly. 'This is all highly circumstantial, and I usually deal with numbers at the FCA. Certainties. But I did inherit Dad's inquisitiveness, and everything you've said to me supports the idea that this guy Hawkins could be our man. But where is he? The parole period will be over, and where would we start?'

'I quickly checked, and Hawkins is out of his parole period. But there is a glimmer of hope that we might ascertain any new identity Hawkins has assumed, if he has one.'

'The counterfeiter?'

'I know he's in London.'

'How on earth do you know that?'

'Another quick call.'

'You're incredible, Ken. The counterfeiter might have changed his *own* identity.'

'Counterfeiters tend not to, ironically. They'd lose too much business if they themselves suddenly disappeared. His name is—believe it or not—John Smith. As generic as they come, eh? We'd need to track him down in the capital.'

'I'm not sure I could get the two cops who covered the Mack case to make enquiries now that Mack has been sent down. They'd say it was spurious. Maybe I could try to find the man myself.'

'Certainly not, but I can try. I'm retired now, so I can take the train down and make a visit.'

'Ken, that's ridiculous. There's no way—'

'It's the only way, Aurelia. I said I owed your father and I meant it.'

Chapter 15

The fledgling emotions of hope that Calum felt after Douglas Lyndon's visit had been tempered by the knowledge that an imminent conundrum also awaited him. He'd been dreading his next meeting with Benson. In the outside world, Benson would clearly have been categorised 'avoid', but the only method of attaining evasion in prison would be to request special confinement by claiming vulnerability. A transfer to another prison was out of the question at this juncture.

He'd learned that those considered 'vulnerable' included not only inmates who had attempted suicide and others who'd simply cracked up, but also those seeking to escape a specific threat, which needed to be identified. Calum didn't fancy grassing up Benson. His volatile and opinionated cellmate, Art, had mentioned that anyone who appealed for special protection due to a threat could either spend his entire sentence in the relative exclusion of a protected wing with little freedom, or emerge again at some point to face that threat. Calum had enquired as to the resultant safety of such individuals, and Art, with an eidetic recall of violence, described some of the vivid acts of vengeance that had been orchestrated. One inmate Art knew had been so badly disfigured in such an attack that he'd later committed suicide.

Not that Calum had been about to explain his specific predicament to Art. In an attempt to placate the man, Calum had foolishly used the term 'hypothetical', which had only created confusion and suspicion. Confusion, because Art had failed to comprehend such complex syntax, and suspicion, because the use of any such incomprehensible term implied that Calum had something to conceal. When Calum then suggested a very loose synonym, 'kidding', Art had gone ape-shit, threatening all sorts for Calum having dared to wind him up. Information appeared to be a valuable currency in this institution, and Calum once again pledged to himself to consider more cautiously the consequences of any jail bird conversation prior to its inception.

The following day in the yard, Calum was summoned to meet Benson. This time Benson motioned towards another con, a tall unshaven blond man with bad teeth Calum had seen once or twice previously. Benson then ushered Calum and the other man to the side, other convicts parting as they made space in order to create privacy. Benson chewed gum at a rate of knots, and offered Calum a piece, which he accepted.

'This is Chisel. He's part of the plan.'

Calum glanced at Chisel, before replying to Benson. 'Look. I'm not sure if this will work. I've read the prison blurb. It reinforces the view that we cannot escape, as the place has maximum security. All measures possible are used to ensure that no one escapes. Almost every attempt over the years has failed.' Calum, although afraid of Benson, continued to peer at him directly. The eyes peered back.

'You don't have a choice. I thought you understood that? If you speak to any screws or any of these fucking social worker types they employ in here about this, you know what will happen?'

Calum stared back blankly. 'You'd kill me.'

Benson looked at Chisel, laughing. 'That's a good idea, Mack, but you know what? We might just grass you up, and explain to the governor how you confessed. Got it on my phone here.' Benson pulled a mobile phone out of his pocket and played a recording of Calum making the false confession. Calum swallowed hard feeling the tension rise. 'And that's going to set you back more time right away. And *then* we might kick your head in. Before we kill you.'

Calum meekly attempted one further counter. 'I thought that it was against the rules to possess a mobile phone in prison.'

'Do you think I give a fuck about rules? I have special privileges. And this isn't my phone. Fuck all to do with me, so don't think that I will be incriminated by it. You should be very grateful that we are *permitting* you to exit this shit hole with us, as this has taken a long time to prepare. Now, given that Chisel and I have been decent enough to *allow* you to have the opportunity, you will be giving us a third each from your little stash out west, after all my expenses. Let's get that sorted for starters. It's the very least you can do given what we're about to do for you. Understand?'

It began to rain again, and Calum simply nodded. They would get two thirds of nothing, plus zero expenses.

'Right, listen carefully. A week on Friday our lunch shifts coincide. Don't fucking bother asking how I know that, but I do. You're going to select the chicken tikka that day, and a special sauce that just us three will have. You, me and Chisel. But before you eat anything the following morning I will be giving you a little pill.' Benson smiled, as Calum began to see where this was going.

Calum scratched his ear. 'You're going to feign illness in some way? And get sent to a hospital on the outside. Is that the plan? They'll spot it a mile away, and we won't get out, because there's an infirmary *here*.'

'Not for what they'll think we've contracted.'

'What?'

'Botulism.'

'Botulism?'

'You heard me. It takes up to eighteen hours from eating contaminated food for botulism to be detected. The little pill I have can help mirror a couple of the symptoms and we feign the rest. You'll look totally fucking feverish and be screaming your head off as best you can, but you'll actually be pretty okay. They'll need to take us to a proper hospital on the outside because botulism can kill you if it's not treated immediately. And to make sure, the doctor here is,' Benson grinned at Chisel, 'shall we say, compromised.'

'You've got something over the prison doctor?'

'A little insurance.'

'This is unbelievable.' Calum swallowed. 'How can you guarantee this?' Benson and Chisel shared another moment before Calum interpreted their postural echo, raising an eyebrow. 'You'll know he's on shift? How did you manage that?'

'Keep your voice down, for fuck's sake.' Benson gritted his teeth. 'He's a quack…with some problems…and his brother is a con in Pentonville.'

Chisel then interjected, speaking for the first time. 'And if he doesn't do as he's told, one of my pals in Pentonville will finish off his brother. Simple as that.'

'But—'

'No fucking buts,' Benson said flatly. 'You've too many questions, you know that? Accept that this is a gold-plated opportunity.'

Calum glanced down towards the tarmac below, hands in pockets. His gut instinct told him to shut up, to roll with the punches until he had time to consider his options further. Benson and Chisel now possessed evidence of a stupid momentary relapse, his fake admission. Shit, he wished he'd simply told the truth and insisted he'd no money. The court hadn't believed him, but maybe he could explain to Benson that he was genuinely incarcerated by an act of misfortune, that there was no buck-free two million, but rather a tragic, horrible miscarriage of justice. Maybe if he'd told the truth he'd simply have been beaten up and left alone, a useless white-collar convict who was of no value to thugs like these guys.

Or perhaps he could try once again make these clowns reconsider.

'So, assuming that we're transferred, you want to escape from a secure hospital—on the outside? When we're feigning illness, throwing up?'

Chisel interrupted. 'Don't be thick. You will only be slightly sick, okay? The symptoms will look much worse than they actually are.'

'But isn't there an actual blood test for botulism, Chisel? They could confirm we're not actually sick.'

Benson replied flatly. 'Takes a bit of time to confirm, by which time we will be off-ski.'

'So how do we escape from a secure hospital? We could be placed in different units. How would we coordinate that? They will be armed, and we could be handcuffed to a steel rail in a bed within a secure unit, guarded round the clock.'

'We will not be visiting any secure units,' said Benson impatiently, as if to a child.

'Why not?'

'We will be escaping before that,' Chisel replied, nodding towards Benson, as if the whole plan had been perfected and refined over many years.

Calum folded his arms. 'But we could be transferred in different ambulances. How would that work?'

Chisel stepped towards Calum, pushing him up against the red brick wall to the rear. They were suddenly nose to nose. 'You're an awkward bastard, do you know that?' Calum could feel the hot breath of another psycho. 'We *know* what we're fucking doing here, all right? We will be moved in one these armoured transporters. It always happens, but we can get sorted before we go anywhere.' He spat on the ground beside Calum.

Then Benson interjected, leaning in. 'There will be a diversion right at the same time.'

'Diversion?'

'Yes, a *diversion*,' Chisel spat. 'Do we have to explain what a fucking diversion is too? How the hell could you have worked in the stock market but understand fuck all? Did you actually go to school?' He shook his head as he spoke, bad teeth gritted.

Calum held out two hands, showing his palms. 'I'm only trying to figure how this will work, guys. I take it that you don't want me to fuck it all up because I'm short on detail, do you? I appreciate that you must have invested a lot of time and, well…ingenuity…in this…plan. But as it's all new to me I'm just trying to look at it, say, objectively. It's better for me to appear like a stupid prick but also spot a potential pitfall, than to shut up and say nothing. That's all I'm doing. Being a stupid prick.'

Both nodded, accepting that Calum was a stupid prick.

Benson checked his watch. 'Heard of Radical Jihad? It's the Islamic terrorist group that bombed a police HQ in Paris last year. Tried something in Manchester recently but the cops kept that quiet, because they're shit-scared of them. Well, I met one of these guys when he was here on a short sentence. They got him on something daft like reset because they couldn't convict him on terrorist charges. I saved him from being finished off by one of the gangs.' Benson smiled, as if such actions were everyday occurrences in life. Calum hesitated, obviously intrigued yet cautious about enquiring as to the connection with the current subject matter.

'Don't look at me like that. I'm not a bloody radical Muslim, okay? But you never know the value of having someone *owe you*. You might even recognise that yourself, eh? Well, it turned out that this guy thought I was sent by Allah. Can you believe that?' Benson sniggered, clearly amused by his own recollection.

'So what did he offer you?' Calum, still confused as to where this avenue of conversation was heading, asked the obvious question.

Benson moved in close to Calum, and whispered. 'He offered me a codeword.'

'A codeword?'

'Yes, a Bona fide fucking codeword from an organisation that blows people up. A codeword which has only been used once before, in a real incident and is only known to the security forces. A useful device if you're ever robbing a bank, he said, and a gift from God for me to use at a later date. Sends the cops crazy, this sort of thing, apparently. But seeing I was sent by the big man himself to save this piece of shit, I said that I needed to continue my *good work*. And I needed one more piece of help on the outside.' Benson and Chisel grinned at the absurdity of it all. Even Calum struggled to contain a smile.

'So what else did you ask him to do?'

Chisel glanced around again, before replying. 'To threaten to blow somewhere close by to fucking high heaven exactly when our transfer out to the hospital happens. They'll have no option but to let us out, because there will be chaos.'

Calum swallowed hard, contemplating how ludicrous this idea was, cognitively processing the risks and dangers, and concluding that only career criminals with years of spare time spent dreaming of escape could possibly conceive of a scheme so fraught with potential for disaster and with such limited hope of success.

'Brilliant plan, guys. Count me in.'

Ken Charleson met Aurelia at a small Italian restaurant on Euston Road not far from Kings Cross station, having explained on the phone that he'd come to the city the previous day and made some interesting progress on the case. He wanted to speak to her in person rather than talk on the phone. Aurelia received a warm embrace and she recalled poignantly the aftershave he wore from the occasions they'd met before. He wore a camel coat and matching felt hat, reminiscent of some kind of TV detective from a retro detective series, which only triggered Aurelia's sense of nostalgia.

As they perused the menu, Aurelia received a text from Douglas Lyndon, enquiring as to how her investigations were proceeding. Ken frowned, advising her to be, at best, non-committal, or preferably, to fob him off. Aurelia recognised the advice for what it was—rational guidance from a former cop with a lifetime of experience which had sculpted caution. As it turned out, Aurelia agreed. People could leak like porous tiles on old homes. While Lyndon had precipitated her actions without any obvious personal advantage and partially incriminated himself to assist Mack, it was also true that she did not know the man, and if he blabbed to Mack about miscarriages of justice being seriously investigated by the FCA, Mack could pressurise his lawyer to camp at Max Telford's desk. Ken, as a man equally suspicious of both criminals and superiors, agreed that she shouldn't risk her career, even if he admitted that both he and Aurelia's father had bucked the rules during the big drugs case where they'd first worked together. Aurelia texted Lyndon insisting on his patience, and when the drinks arrived at the table Ken began to explain what he'd discovered.

'I spent an hour or so with John Smith, today.'

'Fantastic! You actually found him? You didn't say on the phone.' Aurelia bit her lower lip in surprise.

Ken nodded, sipping his pint of bitter. 'Yeah, got a tip off from a guy I know in the Met who has just arrested a gangster whose identity mysteriously changed recently. Turns out to be the handiwork of Mr Smith. The officer I know has bigger fish to fry at the moment so he said he'd give me a bit of slack to have a word with Smith before he moves in.'

Aurelia eagerly awaited the outcome, but managed simply to say, 'keep going.'

'Well, Smith could be viewed like a regular, skilled artisan. Cynical guy in his fifties, little wire-rimmed glasses. I've met that type of criminal before—not dangerous personally, but casually instrumental in other crimes, if you follow me. But he's actually a seasoned con because people who get caught don't fear him, and to reduce their sentences in any way, he's been fingered five times and served sentences every time. But the thing is, he's sick of it and doesn't want to go back in.'

'But he will, won't he?'

'He will,' Ken said directly. 'Not that I told him that today. The Met will be down on him within a week or two, but that's his fault, not mine.'

'You're actually enjoying this, aren't you? Being back on a case?'

Ken smiled, and they briefly halted the conversation while the waiter delivered their antipasti. Then Ken cleared his throat 'Yes, I am enjoying it, Aurelia. Old habits die hard. I feel like a former smoker being offered a Cuban cigar. Can't resist.'

'Well, you're driving me mad here! What did Smith say? Has he seen Hawkins?'

Ken frowned. 'That's the strange news.'

Aurelia mirrored his image, suddenly deflated. 'Strange news?'

'When I pressurised him he admitted he'd seen Hawkins within the past year, and produced fake ID for him.'

Aurelia brightened. 'That's good news, because it gives us a lead in terms of following Hawkins. What was name on the ID?'

'Two names, I'm afraid, on two passports.' Ken looked at Aurelia squarely.

'That's okay. I can follow multiple leads in terms of searching for trades or bank accounts.'

'I know, but that's not the problem. The first name is interesting, and provides you with extremely strong circumstantial evidence.'

Aurelia stopped chewing, realising where Ken was heading. 'The name is Calum Mack, isn't it?'

'Bingo.'

'*Wow*. That's explosive!' Aurelia got up from her seat and gave Ken a kiss. 'This is amazing, Ken. But what's the problem? What's the other name?'

'The other name is Sam Adams.'

'Like the Boston beer?'

Ken smiled. 'Yes, but the interesting thing is that our forger friend kept a copy of the photograph used for this passport.'

'What—it's not Hawkins picture?' Aurelia enquired.

'No.' Ken opened his wallet, pulling out a scanned picture and placing it before Aurelia on the table. Recognise this guy?'

'That's…my colleague, Adam Smart.'

Around half a minute prior to when Ken dropped the bombshell, Aurelia had fleetingly considered halting him in mid-flow and calling Telford to explain that there had been a serious miscarriage of justice in the Mack case. If Hawkins possessed a forged passport in Calum Mack's name, and could be credibly described as possessing a strong motive—vengeance, presumably—then there existed substantial circumstantial evidence to question Mack's conviction.

Her initial gut instinct that Mack had been telling the truth under questioning from the police now seemed vindicated. Her father had consistently believed in trusting his own judgement, even in the face of apparently contradictory evidence, though Aurelia knew that was not how a rule-driven society operated. Ken had warned her of making any snap decisions; indeed, he'd admitted that he'd consciously concealed the second identity until he met her in person because he wanted to ensure that she proceeded cautiously with this information. She'd already mentioned Adam Smart's name to him previously over the phone so he'd been aware of the connection when the forger Smith had divulged the name. As with many law enforcement officers, Ken had acquired a strong audio-graphic memory, rarely forgetting a name or an identity. Before meeting Aurelia he'd double checked on the web to confirm that Smart was indeed a colleague at the FCA in the same department as Aurelia.

This revelation about a second fake identity—incriminating one of her colleagues at the FCA—had twisted the character of the case by incubating more questions than solutions. Ken had reminded her of the inadmissibility of the evidence he'd acquired during his visit to Smith, and the awkward position of Smith's imminent threat of arrest by the police on unrelated charges. If Smith was charged and held, there existed the possibility that re-opening the Mack case would enjoy second stage to other more pressing charges. Worse still, if Smith simply disappeared prior to any arrest, confirming that he had provided fake ID incriminating Tom Hawkins and Adam Smart might prove impossible.

Aurelia asked if Ken could ask that the Met speed up their arrest plans, but he outlined how the officer he knew had explained that a premature raid on Smith might blow a more critical operation. That was the reason Ken had been forced to visit Smith on a completely different pretext, and had still ended up reassuring the man—falsely—that he faced no immediate action. That was the debt Ken felt he owed Aurelia's father, and thus Aurelia.

Ken, naturally, enquired about Adam Smart.

He listened intently to Aurelia's passionate description of her colleague, nodding and shaking his head as she evaluated the personality of the ambitious egotist with whom she'd clashed on numerous occasions.

'So, basically, he's an arsehole?'

'Complete and utter.'

'But how was he implicated in the scam to set up Mack?' Ken spoke quietly, as Aurelia hesitated to respond, throwing her hands up in frustration. Ken then bit his bottom lip, weighing up how the criminal mind operated. 'How keen would you say Adam Smart was to convict Mack?'

'*Very keen.*'

'That would provide a clue. Maybe he got a kickback once Mack was convicted? Has Adam Smart just bought a Ferrari or something?'

Aurelia slapped the table gently. 'No, he hasn't but that means nothing. He consistently kept muscling in on the case despite my request to Max Telford to keep him distant but it seemed a fait accompli that he became involved. Come to think about it, I even spotted him standing over my computer once I'd began working on the case. I challenged him straight away. That was after my initial research, when Max had asked me to start exploratory research regarding new insider trading cases. Adam could have been in it from the start, but Hawkins may also have recruited him. Shit, he might even have been in Grand Cayman taking that photograph for all I know. I can't believe this. Though it doesn't explain specifically why a fake passport was produced for Adam, does it?'

Ken peered at Aurelia directly. 'I think I know why.'

'Insurance?'

'Correct. In the event that things go pear-shaped, crooks often leave a false trail, and it is possible that Adam Smart is *none the wiser* that a fake passport was produced by an accomplice and what that might be used for next. Alternatively, it's his personal getaway opportunity. Remember, it's easier to get *out* of this country with a false passport than get *back in*. If he needed to take off, this would help.'

'Makes sense. Dishonour among thieves.'

Then Ken scratched his chin. 'How's the culture regarding whistle blowing at the FCA? What would Telford do if you approached him about Smart?' He sat back raising his eyebrows.

The expulsion of air from Aurelia's lips was audible to the young couple at the nearest table, who glanced upwards, noting tension beside them. 'Well, given that Adam Smart is so far up Telford's backside,' Aurelia spoke more softly, her Dublin brogue suddenly more accentuated, 'if I blew a whistle I guess it would reverberate through his mouth.'

They both laughed, partially relieving the anxiety, before Aurelia ran her fingers though her dark hair, rubbing her temples.

'It's a pain in the butt, right?' Ken said rhetorically. 'I guess you're thinking it would have been much simpler if Mack had just been guilty?' Ken's fingers interlocked on the table, watching Aurelia as she nodded before he continued. 'I had cases like this that eventually haunted me. I think that you should take a little time before you say anything officially, however difficult that might seem. Try to locate Hawkins—he may even have another identity by now, but you'd be amazed by the criminals who become complacent once they figure the law has put away another party. For certain, keep Mack and his pal out of it for the moment, or you could be subject to an internal investigation if his lawyer goes to the media. On the other hand, if you wait too long and someone else spots this, the FCA runs the risk of being accused of presiding over a miscarriage of justice and a whitewash.'

After affirming his commitment to the most insane scheme in which he'd ever been involved, apart perhaps from one pot-induced and almost instantly abandoned plan to rob the Scottish Crown jewels from Edinburgh Castle when he'd been a student, Calum had acquired the proverbial chilly feet. What the hell had he been thinking? Time spent in the company of other weirdoes in the vulnerable prisoners' wing might now be interpreted as a refreshing holiday, even if additional time was forcibly added to his sentence on the basis of the recording that Benson had made on his illicit phone.

His problem however, was that psychos like Benson and his sidekick Chisel weren't kidding. Calum hadn't even enquired what Chisel was in for, assuming instantly that his crime or crimes would naturally have involved extreme violence. Even if he were to apply for an internal transfer, he'd need to request an interview and provide evidence of the threat, thereby incriminating himself anyway. During any intervening period, he'd have to play along with Benson, and Benson might get to him anyway in this establishment, as it was clear that the man had some influence.

Perhaps Douglas Lyndon had a point, and his visit had been motivated by more than belated guilt over complicity in Calum's sentence. So, in retrospect, he sent a letter to Lyndon, thanking him for his intervention and urging him to keep hassling Aurelia Harley at the FCA, even if it was a long shot. But then, on the day he posted the letter, he also received one. Martin, his lawyer, had written a note to Calum, explaining that his girlfriend wanted to move back to Australia and that he was probably going off with her.

Terrific.

Despondency had visited Calum once again: just when one door opened, another appeared to slam in his face. One of the players in this game could look forward to a new life in the sunny Antipodes, while another faced either being kicked to pieces by mindless thugs or potential death whilst attempting a ludicrous escape bid.

Chapter 16

Torrential rain battered the bay window of the lounge in Aurelia's flat, momentarily prompting her to witness the spectacle first hand. As she drew back the curtain, she shivered at the thought of what it might be like being homeless on a night like this. In fact, what must it be like to sleep rough in London, full stop? The wealth of the capital was far from being evenly distributed. Somewhere out there were people who had nothing, except perhaps their freedom.

And then her thoughts drifted to Calum Mack. He didn't even possess his freedom. After her discussion with Ken Charleson, she'd been further conflicted. Ken had returned to Yorkshire, albeit with a promise of future assistance if required. She was also aware that if she forged ahead on her own and accused Adam of complicity, she'd need hard facts, and also a full explanation why she'd pursued the case on her own with no remit from Max Telford, the police, or the CPS. Any case could be blown due to procedural errors. And the forger himself could simply disappear—who would be better placed to do so? And the fact that a forger who knew Tom Hawkins in prison had produced a second fake passport for one Adam Smart at the FCA did not in itself *prove* that either Mack was innocent or that Adam was indeed guilty.

But it smelled awfully bad.

What she did possess, however, were copies of two recent photographs, one of Tom Hawkins, and one of Adam Smart. What a laugh. She'd studiously avoided close contact with Adam on any occasion when pictures were taken at office events, and now she'd acquired an individual photo of her colleague though a totally fortuitous route. What amused her, however, was that Adam was unaware that she possessed such a picture and this knowledge offered her the upper hand.

One option was to attempt to place Hawkins or Adam at the Caribbean Chartered Bank in George Town on the day Calum Mack had been present and the withdrawal made. It was just conceivable that Adam had done a flier to the island that weekend, but she checked the dates and he'd been in attendance at the FCA on both the Monday and the Friday of that weekend, making travel to Grand Cayman almost impossible.

Damn.

During the investigation, the CPS had failed to convince the bank to release security tapes of the day in question, but at a later date the bank had mysteriously provided confirmation that Mack's passport had been used to provide identification for the withdrawal. Aurelia then recalled the conversation she'd had with Max Telford and Adam, where Max had alluded to intervention at a higher level to secure information from the notoriously secretive islanders.

Who exactly had pressurised the bank?

Aurelia made herself a coffee, attempting to stimulate her mental acuity as the rain continued its aggressive attack on the lounge window. The only character in the frame who had real influence was Anthony Rowland, the junior government minister, who had evaded any scrutiny in the affair. It had irked her that attainment of power had permitted evasion of responsibility. But then, could this be his weakness, something she could harness to help identify who had been in George Town that day?

She checked the website for the Energy Ministry, looking for an email contact for Rowland's private secretary. She was aware that a phone call would probably be rebuffed unless pursued officially through the FCA, which she could not do yet. The name noted was Alan Mersey, whom she emailed.

Hi Alan

It's crucial, politically, that Anthony speaks to me privately about a matter of some importance. Please speak to Anthony ASAP, mentioning Calum Mack and Unreal Power. This is simply a request for assistance in order to clear up a potential miscarriage of justice. Failure to respond could result in official channels being re-opened.

Ahrumand raisin@hotmail.com

Aurelia used an old private email account, recalling the fact she'd used her favourite ice cream to differentiate herself many years before. The man should at least speak to her, and she'd then explain what she wanted from him.

When Benson and Chisel pulled up next to Calum at the lunch queue, the only noticeable communication was Benson's raised eyebrows. Calum then faced straight ahead, aware that this was decision day in relation to the Great Escape mark II. The attempt had been arranged for the following day. He'd still not decided for sure to what to do, partly as he'd been unable to consult a single soul regarding his dilemma. And how could he have passed a warning to his mother and father without scaring them to pieces? Their health wasn't so good these days, and he feared that even if Benson's threat proved hollow, the possibility of danger would create problems for them in its own right. And if he blurted to the prison authorities, he'd be placed on the secure wing for the next seven to eight years, meaning even greater confinement, and his life could still be in jeopardy at a later date.

Fear trumping hope. That's what prison did to a person—it provided vast periods of time for negative contemplation, yet no facility to take action in your life. Logic instructed that he speak to the governor; fear demanded that he join the plan, or at least play along. Then, as he looked ahead in the queue, Calum felt a thumb digging into his ribs. As he turned around, Benson's piercing eyes were partnered with a scrunched up piece of paper being forced into his palm.

As Benson whispered into his ear, Calum could feel his hot breath. 'Remember, take the chicken tikka, and eat it all. *And that sauce.* Read these instructions in your cell, and then swallow them. Don't show anyone. Eat the blue tablet *first thing* tomorrow in morning, about seven o'clock, and make sure it goes down. It's going to make you sweat and feel a bit sick, that's all. But you need to feign the other symptoms, okay? If you don't, you know what will happen. Remember, I know where your folks live, and I can get a message outside here at a moment's notice. Have you got that?'

Calum nodded. When they reached the servers, three portions of chicken tikka appeared, just as planned. There was a special sauce, which appeared magically for the three of them.

'Yes, chicken tikka my favourite!' Benson said from behind Calum, loudly enough to be detected by the two guards standing to their right. As Calum was being served, Benson piped up again. 'Hey, that sauce looks good.'

'Quiet in the queue,' one of the screws then said to Benson.

'What? I'm not allowed to say that chicken tikka is my favourite dish?'

'And mine,' Chisel spoke for the first time. 'And obviously his too,' he said, pointing directly at Calum.

'Just shut it, right. Go and eat your lunch.'

Calum sat separately from Benson and Chisel, just as he normally would, though he spotted Chisel's eyes boring into him from a distance at another table as he chewed the rubbery chicken. Strangely, it had been one of his favourite dishes in the past yet his appetite had all but disappeared. One of the other prisoners said he would eat the chicken if Calum didn't, prompting Calum to force himself to eat the food, aware that it was actually not poisoned. If the dish was genuinely infected with botulism, they couldn't even begin to pull off the stunt, so there was no actual danger in physical digestion.

Once back in his cell, he waited for his cellmate to begin reading the Sport newspaper, a ritual that Calum had learned not to interrupt. The paper would no doubt bamboozle Art for some time, though probably he just looked at the pictures. As Calum unfolded the note, he read the small printout on botulism that Benson had given him before inhaling deeply.

Initial symptoms include blurred or double vision and difficulty swallowing and speaking. Possible gastrointestinal problems include nausea, constipation and vomiting. As botulism progresses, the victim experiences weakness or paralysis, starting with the head muscles and progressing down the body. Breathing becomes increasingly difficult. Without medical care, respiratory failure and death are very likely.

How had it come to this? When he eventually fell asleep, a disturbance ensued, evidenced by the repeated screaming of other inmates. Unfortunately this was not an infrequent occurrence on this wing. Despite the efforts of the screws, silence often proved to be a scarce commodity in prison. He turned his pillow over for what must have been the tenth time, thrusting against the loose mattress in frustration.

'Shut the fuck up or I'll choke you in your sleep, *you dick*!' Art's voice synthesised badly with the cacophony of other convicts' abuse, though the threat was directed at Calum, who'd merely shuffled some bed clothes. At that point, Calum decided enough was enough—tomorrow he'd request a meeting with prison management and demand a move to the secure wing. Things there couldn't be any worse than this waking nightmare.

Initially, Calum perceived the voices approaching his cell as part of a dream, having eventually fallen into a deep slumber an hour or two after the disturbance the previous evening had subsided. However, as the volume of the footsteps and animated discussion increased and then terminated at his cell door, he knew that something was wrong.

The familiar clunk of the heavy steel cell door was partnered by a bright torch ray being directed onto his face.

'Right, Mack, up you get!' Although Calum couldn't see the face, he recognised the voice of one of the senior officers named Wilson.

'What's the time? Why are you waking me up?' Art suddenly burst into life, assuming that he was the centre of attention for the nocturnal visit.

'Not you. Go back to sleep.' As Calum squinted towards the light, he recognised the prison medic, Dr Strang, staring directly at him. 'It's Mack we need to see. Put your clothes on immediately.'

'But why? What's the matter?' Calum's words tailed off as he realised what was happening. Benson and Chisel must have pulled the plan forward without telling him. It was around 2:50 a.m. in the morning. Shit, what was he to do now?

Wilson and Strang ushered him out of the door before he had an opportunity to protest, but as they marched him along the landing towards the metal stairs Calum spoke clearly.

'What's this all about?'

Dr Strang cleared his throat, speaking in a low voice as they passed the other cells. His pupils were dilated, making Calum consider if he himself had taken something. 'You took the chicken tikka yesterday, at lunch, with a special sauce?'

Calum hesitated. This was his best chance to blow the plan apart, but before he could respond Strang answered for him. 'Sorry, that wasn't a question, more of a confirmation. We already know that you'd selected the chicken…and this special sauce.' Strang's voice betrayed the tension he evidently felt; here was a bona fide professional aiding and abetting a group of felons, even if he himself was driven by fear for his brother and something else.

'Yes, but I feel…okay.' Calum felt tempted to tell it like it was, but something in Strang's eyes almost pleaded with him to comply.

'You need to be tested for botulism immediately. It could be a deadly strain. Two of your fellow inmates have fairly severe symptoms and you ate the same dish at lunchtime yesterday. It is imperative that you are tested.' Strang glared at Calum, and as they began to proceed downstairs, he mouthed something behind the guard's back.

Take the tablet.

Calum motioned back, hands thrust outwardly, indicating that he didn't have the tablet. Instantly, a blue tablet was thrust into his hand. The Strang whispered into his ear. *Please do as I say now. These guys aren't playing around. Please!*

Calum looked into the man's eyes, sighing as Wilson momentarily turned round and spoke. '*Move it* Mack. Didn't you hear what the doc said?'

When they reached the infirmary Calum spotted Benson and Chisel, and he was taken over to be seated beside them. They were both sweating and shaking in two adjacent beds, and a nurse appeared to take a blood sample from Chisel. Two extra prison guards stood to one side, displaying no signs of compassion whatsoever. They probably wished that the pair would simply keel over and perish—and do the world a favour. Calum didn't disagree.

Then Chisel leaned over and whispered in his ear. 'West Croft, Cromarty.'

Calum looked up cursing under his breath. This was his parents' address. He stared at the sweating Chisel, and then Benson, trying to evaluate if there really was a threat.

'Take the fucking tablet or they go up in flames.' As Benson spoke Calum looked at the little tablet in his palm. Benson glanced at the guards, who were ogling the young nurse through the internal window, and then, without warning, Chisel grabbed Calum's head and forced it back, thrusting the tablet into his mouth.

Calum yelped, coughing.

One of the officers immediately turned round. 'What's happening here?' 'I'm—'

'He's bloody ill too! Can't you see that?' Benson interjected. 'He needs a glass of water right now!' The nurse then produced a glass of water. The tablet had actually gone down his throat. He coughed, but it did not resurface. As the nurse looked on Calum took a sip of water, suddenly aware that symptoms would begin in earnest.

Within a few minutes, he was shown to a bed, and the nurse asked him to roll up his sleeve. Then, as he attempted to undo the button at the lower end of his left sleeve using his right hand he realised he too had begun a slight tremor, the effects of the little tablet kicking in surprisingly quickly. The nurse noticed and nodded towards the doctor, who walked towards Calum, checking his temperature.

At that point Benson screamed, and everyone turned round. 'Doctor, for fuck's sake! We need to get to a proper hospital! We have *human rights*. I don't want to die in this place and it's the bloody cooking that's caused this!' Benson was sweating profusely, and apparently beginning to convulse.

'Right, Mr Wilson. I need to speak with you in private.' Dr Strang and Wilson moved into an adjacent treatment room, and although Calum could only detect part of the ensuing conversation, he was able to monitor an animated conversation through the glass window that separated the rooms. The gist of the discussion appeared to centre on the fact that due to a staff shortage some senior staff members were not present in the prison to sign off the transfer of these prisoners to a state hospital. Wilson and Strang debated protocol and Wilson wanted to wait for four hours until the next shift brought in the deputy governor. Wilson was refusing to make a call to wake up the deputy governor, as he had apparently been at a night out, and on the previous occasion something like this had occurred, he'd carpeted the officer who had made the call: Wilson.

Dr Strang could then be heard arguing that his job was to save lives, and if they made a strategic error to wait, there could be three dead prisoners on their books, and could Wilson please imagine all the attendant scrutiny that would bring? Wilson appeared to shrug with indifference at such an outcome.

Medical expertise took precedence, though, and Strang suddenly returned to the room to announce that the three amigos would be transferred to a state hospital with immediate effect. That was when Calum interrupted.

'Dr Strang,' he whispered, just out of earshot of Benson and Chisel, who were still trying hard to look as ill as possible. 'Look, I'm feeling, eh, fairly okay. Maybe you can take the other guys…they seem worse than me.' Then, just as he finished the sentence, Calum felt an odd surge within his stomach, and he suddenly lurched forward, involuntarily spewing onto the floor. The nurse got a mop, and then gave him a glass of water.

Dr Strang stared intensely at Calum, gripping him on the shoulder as he whispered back. '*Just go*. Play along. They've said if you *all* don't go then my brother dies. *Please.*' He looked toward Benson and Chisel, who had noted the green light. Despite Calum's reaction to the tablet, he noticed Benson pressing something on his watch.

A signal?

Calum sat on the edge of the bed, closing his eyes. He trembled as the effects of the tablet worsened. He couldn't think clearly, unable to concentrate for more than a few seconds, growing waves of nausea infiltrating his system.

As they were moved towards the side door of the infirmary, heavy rain pelted at the door. One of the guards checked the security of their handcuffs, and the dark armoured transport vehicle drew up towards the door. The three were able to walk slowly through the cool rain, though Benson was doubled over, complaining about having no feeling in one leg. They were accompanied by two guards to the rear of the vehicle, where Wilson explained that there was to be no funny business during the transfer. The guards were professionals and Wilson said they would not hesitate to use force if there was any trouble, illness or not.

Despite the symptoms on display, Wilson eyed the three prisoners suspiciously as they sat down, glancing sideways at Strang as he spoke. 'You know, it's odd how just you three took the chicken tikka with this special sauce? Strange, that. Not normal.' No one responded, and Wilson just shook his head.

Then, as the door of the transporter clunked shut, Benson—out of view of the guards for the first time—clocked Calum directly, a slow, malevolent smile spreading across his face.

The transporter jerked forwards towards the main perimeter gate, and Calum spotted Benson checking his watch yet again, despite the cuffs.

Clearly he was waiting for something. Despite his nausea a number of questions darted through Calum's muddled mind. How ironic, that this pair didn't trust *him*. Because of the altered timing, how could they expect him to react the way they wanted if he hadn't been fully briefed? Or did they perceive that if their plan had been made fully transparent to him he'd simply have grassed? And a more prominent question arose: how on earth could Benson and Chisel actually expect some Islamic terrorist to facilitate their escape?

Then the van stopped abruptly, complemented by a muffled, though animated discussion heard from the front compartment as a radio message of some kind came through. Suddenly, two guards came running from the main block, and approached the driver's side of the transporter. The driver lowered the front window.

'There's been some kind of terrorist bomb threat to those tower blocks next to the park area down there!' The guard shouted, pointing along the road.

'Terrorist threat? In the middle of the night?' The guard in the front passenger seat shook his head.

'They're taking it seriously. The Met think it might be genuine because they've used a real codeword. We heard it on the police radio inside. Armoured cops from the Met will be there within minutes, so you'll need to go the other way.'

The occupants in the rear had heard every word, prompting a reaction from Benson. 'You need to get us out of here now! I have no feeling in my legs.' He shouted, before being told to be quiet.

'Maybe we should wait, I don't want to get caught up in this thing,' the driver yelled through to the guards in the rear holding the three prisoners.

As the man's words trailed off, Calum sat with his eyes closed, cursing his predicament. Then Chisel interjected, screaming. 'We could be dying! I can hardly feel my legs either. You need to get us to hospital now!'

'Shut it until we say otherwise,' the guard who sat across from him replied. Chisel held his stomach, moaning.

At that point Dr Strang emerged from darkness, the rain pounding down as he knocked on the front passenger seat window, hollering over the noise of the alarm. Then guard lowered the window.

'These men are extremely ill, and must be transported to the hospital immediately. Do you understand? Go that way,' he said, pointing in the opposite direction from the park.

'The road outside might need to be checked.'

'No!' Strang shouted in reply, banging the door. '*You need to go.* If there's a hold up now, these three could die. Do you understand?' Strang walked toward the main exit gate, gesticulating to the guard.

At that moment, the main exit gate was leveraged open, and the transporter juddered forward. It was now exactly 3:15 a.m., the dead of night, and despite the prison's exterior lighting, the heavy rain had made visibility in the dark very poor, and the vehicle slowly moved forward, taking a right onto Heathfield Road. Despite the conditions, a cacophony of sirens and emergency service vehicle lights could be witnessed to the north on Trinity Road.

Then, when they took a left onto Magdalen Road three hundred yards further along, a white Ford van appeared behind the vehicle. The two vehicles travelled for around four hundred yards and then the van veered abruptly out from behind them, overtook, and then cut in. The transporter was forced to swerve, veering off to the side of the road into an empty car park. As it juddered to a halt, the driver cursed, cranking his head round to look for the white van through the downpour.

Three hooded men leapt from the back of the white van and ran straight towards the transporter. One man banged on the window, holding a black holdall in one hand and pointing what appeared to be a revolver at the driver.

'*For fuck's sake!*' the driver bawled. 'He's got a gun.'

'Christ, don't open the window!' the guard in the passenger seat screamed.

The two guards in the rear then reacted, one roaring through the grill to the front. 'What the hell's happening?'

'Don't get out! This is an ambush,' the front seat guard bellowed, thumping the dashboard and grabbing the driver's arm. 'Drive!'

But as the driver engaged first gear, the unmistakable hiss of air escaping under pressure was clearly audible: One! Two! Three! Four!

'They've punctured the tyres! *Radio for help.*' the driver barked at the guard before yelling outside at the hooded man who'd jumped back up and was pointing at them to get out. 'These windows are bullet proof! You're wasting your time. This place will be flooded with armed cops in no time!'

But the hooded man ignored the driver, instead pulling a small black contraption out of the holdall he carried with him. In clear view he lit it using a cigarette lighter, before placing it underneath. 'Burn in hell!' The man screamed.

Smoke immediately filled the air, engulfing the vehicle. Within seconds, everyone in the transporter could smell the acrid odour as it permeated the vehicle. And no one could see outside.

'Shit, we're the target,' the driver yelled. 'They're going to blow *us* up! Out! Out!'

The guards in the back complied without thought—momentarily unable to process from where the greatest threat arose—thrusting the rear door open the second the driver released the door security mechanism. But as they exited the transporter, they were instantly engulfed in smoke, unable to judge their immediate surroundings.

But their adversaries knew exactly where they were all coming from.

The driver was floored first, a baseball bat making crushing contact with his left shoulder blade the moment he jumped onto the road. He screamed in agony, but the others couldn't see him as they'd come out of the other side.

Before he could locate the threat, the first of the two guards who exited at the rear was jumped from behind, and shoved to the ground. He squealed as his assailants kicked viciously, before he was whacked with another blunt instrument of some kind. The passenger-seat guard, aware of the cries to the rear, shouted his colleagues' names before feeling his way round the back. The pungent smoke was now complemented not only by the dark, but by sirens in the distance, those emergency personnel unaware of the need to divert to the scene due to the impending threat to civilians less than a mile away.

Then the guard panicked as he heard the voices from behind, kicking out. Unfortunately for him, and his advancing colleague from the rear of the transporter his boot connected directly, eliciting a dull scream as his colleague collapsed.

'Shit, Bill? Did I hit you?' he yelled. Then, as he scrambled towards his stricken co-worker he stood on an outstretched leg, stumbling.

'Aaagh! My leg!' A cry was heard from below as he stood directly on his colleague.

'Bill…is that you?' As the guard lowered himself to attend to Bill, the baseball bat connected with his rear legs, sending him right over Bill onto the tarmac, screaming. As he then kneeled, trying to regain his balance, he was kicked in the face and knocked unconscious.

Only then did Benson and Chisel leap from the transporter. This had been the agreement. 'Stop! Allahu Akbar! Allahu Akbar.' This was their code. *God is great.*

'Allahu Akbar!' the reply came from one of the masked men. 'Four down! They even kicked themselves! God is definitely on our side. Quick! Get the keys from that one there for the handcuffs!'

'Yes, Ahmed,' Benson said flatly, coughing. 'And let's get out of here before anyone comes!'

Once the cuffs were loosened Chisel jumped into the back of the van, but Benson turned round, peering through the smoke. There was something missing.

Calum.

He cursed under his breath.

'Wait!'

Initially he thought that Calum must have done a runner during the confusion, but then something drew him back to the transporter, so he stepped back inside, the rear lights conflicting with the smoke which was still pumping inside.

Calum sat crouched in at the front of the compartment, staring ahead. Benson grabbed him by the arm, hauling him out towards the van. '*Move it, Mack.* Don't you hear the sirens? Stay here and you're dead. You're up to your eyeballs in this.'

For the third time that morning, Calum made a decision against his better judgement, and got into the white van. As they took the first left along the road three armed police vehicles sped by in the other direction. Ahmed spoke from the front. 'That was close, Reggie. God spared the traffic until we were safe.'

Benson simply stared at Calum. 'And God spared this prick by the skin of his teeth. If you pull any more stunts, Mack, we'll see just what God instructs me to do with you.'

Calum was about to protest, to insist that he'd actually *gone along* with their insane plan. Now, they were all probably screwed, because any extension of their sentences for escaping would be augmented with charges in relation to beating the shit out of prison staff, if indeed any of these guys hadn't actually died back there on the road.

What a mess.

If he'd any idea of the level of violence that would have ensued, he'd have found a way to back out, but the second they'd forced him to take that bloody tablet he'd felt so weak, unable to think clearly. Now that he could think more clearly, Benson had begun to threaten him again.

Calum decided there and then to demand to get out. 'Let me out of here right now!' As he spoke, Benson glared.

'Right, Chisel, plan B.' Chisel suddenly grabbed Calum's arms from behind and before he could react, one of the Asian guys stuffed a sock or something similar in his mouth, and a dark hood was placed over his head. Calum attempted to scream but all that he heard himself utter was a muffled moan. Then, a dull thud was followed by searing pain. Everything went blank.

Chapter 17

First thing in the morning, Aurelia took the tube to Kings Cross. Unusually, she'd avoided the morning news because she wanted to retain a clear and uncluttered head for her forthcoming meeting at 7:45 a.m. Normally she was something of a news buff, aware that there were often financial leads appearing that might merit a new investigation. She'd even switched off her phone, something she would never normally contemplate as her phone felt almost like an essential bodily appendage. However, today, had she chosen to access any mainstream media platform, she'd have learned about the events at Wandsworth Prison, which may well have dissuaded her from attending her meeting.

Exiting the tube, she chose to walk along Whitehall before taking a left into Whitehall Place, home of the Department of Energy and Climate Change. In common with the FCA, this government department had been rebranded to reflect the nuances of politics and apparent priorities. As she stepped out of the cold breeze into the foyer, though, she reflected on how so much of this nomenclature was simply bullshit. It mattered not what something was named when so many of the mandarins and executives who worked within these organisations were perpetual liars and cheats. As she gave her details to the reception staff, she considered how this meeting might destroy a couple of careers.

Anthony Rowland's private secretary had acted in the character of a real politician when she'd emailed him. He'd replied within minutes, initially obfuscating. Then, over the course of several electronic exchanges, he'd repeatedly asked for further clarification, clearly attempting to evaluate the degree of risk in respect of any threat she might pose to either Rowland, or by association, himself. Who was she? Why was she involved? What was the substantive nature of the enquiry? The man was transparent—superficially displaying 'loyalty' to his boss while simultaneously attempting personal damage limitation should this new unexpected challenge explode.

When Aurelia had threatened to go to the media, the private secretary had kicked the hot potato upstairs and Rowland had granted her a short private meeting. When she'd lied to Telford that she was undertaking some research interviews in the City, she'd experienced a momentary tinge of guilt, aware of how her relationship with her employer had taken a dive in recent times. She comforted herself knowing that what she was undertaking was for the greater good, and a quick call to Ken Charleson had assured her of such—he'd even offered to accompany her, though this time she'd refused his help, uncertain as to the risk associated with the meeting.

An assistant showed her to an oak-panelled meeting room that exhibited a faint, musty odour. Anthony Rowland's tall frame appeared before her as the assistant left them alone. No witnesses, then, she thought.

'Desperately busy, Ms…Hartley,' he said, offering a hand. No smile.

'Harley,' Aurelia corrected.

'Yes. A bit cloak and dagger, all this, don't you think? I'm able to see you for five minutes merely out of curiosity, you see.' He checked his watch very obviously.

'Mr Rowland, I do not wish to waste your time, so I'll speak plainly.'

'Good.'

'I was one of the investigative team at the FCA that secured the conviction of Calum Mack. But then, you will already know that.'

'Did I? I barely knew Mack, and even that was donkey's years ago. I was aware he was on trial, of course—and he has been convicted by a court of law—so I don't see how I can help.'

Aurelia sighed, frustrated at the bluster. 'Mr Rowland, please hear me out. I believe that you escaped lightly in the Mack case, having provided inside information to a third party about Unreal Power. Because of your position, your involvement was swept under the carpet.'

'Absolute nonsense,' Rowland replied, momentarily looking downwards. 'It's more than my job's worth to divulge confidential information. Do you know how many classified titbits I see every day? I'd be very, very stupid to do something like that. I'm not sure where you've obtained your information.' Rowland tailed off, clearly fishing.

'Douglas Lyndon, for starters,' Aurelia suggested, pursing her lips. Rowland attempted to appear impassive as she spoke, but his dark eyes were clearly computing this information. She cleared her throat before continuing. 'Look, I'm not actually asking to have you investigated. But I believe that there's been a miscarriage of justice, and that another party, not Mack, was guilty of the crime.'

'So who is this mystery third party? Isn't that what the guilty person always says? Someone else did it? The butler, perhaps, except I doubt that Mack would have had a butler.' Rowland's smooth tones oozed sarcasm, and he smiled without mirth.

'I cannot divulge the identity of the third party until I obtain further proof, with which you, I believe, can assist. Would you be willing to help me if all I was requesting was a bit of pressure to be placed on a bank in Grand Cayman to provide us with a copy of their security film? It's all I ask, and if I can obtain the footage I need, then I would be off your back.'

'Off my back? Is that a threat? What official remit do you have here?'

Aurelia swallowed involuntarily, the question throwing her, even though she'd considered such a query before the appointment had been made.

'As I said, Mr Rowland, I was one of the investigating team in the Mack case. In fact I was the officer who indentified the pattern of trades in the first instance,' she said flatly, deflecting.

'That's not what I asked. What authority do you have to pursue this case post-conviction? There is an appeals procedure for any such convictions, and I suspect that you have no remit whatsoever to be here. If there had been an official re-opening of an investigation—and that would have absolutely nothing to do with me—then, if by some bizarre twist I was needed simply because I knew Mack years ago, then I presume someone more senior than *you* would have contacted me directly. And you also used a private email address.' Rowland held his hands in front of him, fingers interlocking.

'I'm simply trying to prevent a miscarriage of justice. We are charged with meeting the objectives of the FCA, and I am permitted to pursue leads where they are deemed applicable,' Aurelia held his gaze, determined not to capitulate.

'You are making a very serious error of judgement if you're attempting to threaten me or encourage me to place pressure on a bank overseas or anyone else. I believe that this case is closed. Mack has been convicted, and I will ask my assistant to see you out.'

Aurelia stood up, deflated. As she turned to leave the room, Rowland spoke once more. 'Oh, and Ms...Harley, for such a motivated investigator, one would have thought that you would have done your homework before wasting a minister's time. Clearly you are unaware that Calum Mack and two other violent felons escaped from prison in the middle of the night. Hardly the behaviour an innocent man, eh? Now, I hope I make myself clear—I don't expect to hear from you again.'

Max Telford removed his glasses and rubbed his eyes, attempting to alleviate the headache that had begun in earnest this morning since he had heard the breaking news first thing. He checked his watch again, and dialled Aurelia's mobile number for the third or fourth time. No reply, yet he'd left two voicemail messages. Where the hell was she? To reach his position in life he'd often been forced to simultaneously juggle diverse splinters of complex financial information, but today he had only two frustrations, and these had irked much more than normal.

The first was that Calum Mack, the man they had not long ago convicted on major insider trading charges, had actually managed to escape prison in a daring night time ruse. The prison officers who had been assaulted in what amounted to an ingenious, if bizarre, breakout involving some kind of terrorist alert, were said to have avoided serious injury. That fact might just aid Mack in avoiding life imprisonment if or when he was ultimately recaptured. But Telford liked to see neat conclusions—closure, in effect. Mack was on the loose, which made a mockery of the whole system and the huge effort that had been invested in securing the conviction. He could not recall in his thirty years in this business a single financial criminal who'd managed to abscond from confinement.

However, this issue was matched by a secondary problem. No sooner had he absorbed the breaking news concerning the jailbreak than he'd received a cutting telephone rebuff from Anthony Rowland at the Department of Energy and Climate Change. His direct report, Aurelia Harley, who had previously offered such promise, had of her own volition deviated to pursue new evidence in the Mack case. Telford demanded loyalty from his staff, but he also demanded the elimination of loose ends, and now Aurelia Harley was tacitly loosening previously tight knots. Bizarrely, she had chosen the very day Mack had escaped from prison to harass Rowland, apparently oblivious to the events across the city. The sheer incompetence of her actions infuriated him, and her attempts to deliberately thwart his instructions were now proving to be a departmental embarrassment.

What also bugged Telford was that the FCA had been complicit in steering the Mack investigation away from any involvement with Rowland, courtesy of the bank of favours and a little help gaining crucial, incriminating evidence from a certain bank in Grand Cayman. Now Rowland was pulling rank on *him*, threatening him with all sorts if he didn't deal with Aurelia Harley.

He thumped his desk in anger, before buzzing his secretary. 'Let me know when Aurelia Harley gets in, will you?'

'She's here, I saw her about ten minutes ago,' came the reply. This enraged Telford further, as he realised that Aurelia must have been deliberately avoiding him.

'Well, please locate her, and send her into me. *Immediately.*'

About two minutes later, Aurelia appeared in Telford's office. He was on a call when she came in, but he beckoned her in, glaring at her. Aurelia sensed the hostile atmosphere instantly, scarcely having time to prepare her argument before Telford excused himself and banged the phone down.

'I expressly instructed you to let the Mack case lie, and now we have a public relations disaster on our hands. I've had Anthony Rowland on the blower threatening my job. Do you hear that? You have been out harassing a government minister, specifically concealing that fact from me. You have lied to me, making up some bullshit story about a meeting in the City. Whitehall is not the City, in case you are unaware of that fact.'

'I—'

'*Let me finish.*' Telford held up a hand in a traffic policeman gesture. 'Apart from the lies, you were presumably also unaware that Mack actually broke out of prison this morning, which makes us look even more inept. Does a prison breakout look like the hallmark of an innocent man?'

'I only heard that at the end of the meeting.'

'Well, that's pathetic. You must have been the last person in this office to clock the story. Everyone else in here knew, I can tell you that.' Telford's voice dripped of sarcasm. 'Mack is guilty, and you, for some unknown reason, seem to be intent on conducting a personal crusade to alter one of the hallmark convictions we've made in this department in recent times. Rowland has been cleared, and you'd better accept that, too. There was overwhelming evidence to convict Mack. You know that. You were on the bloody team that secured the conviction! Now, if you have one shred, even one tiny sliver of *concrete* evidence to cast doubt on this conviction, I would like to hear it.'

Aurelia suddenly clammed up, tears threatening. The man sitting before her had actually been something of a mentor figure until recently, yet that relationship had become twisted, damaged. How could she possibly justify herself? She did not possess 'concrete' evidence. What she possessed was a theory about an old enemy of Mack's from university who appeared to have borne a grudge. Circumstantial. What she also possessed was further circumstantial evidence, secured second hand from an unreliable ex-con who might abscond at any time. She did not have *proof*, and although the report about the passports in the names Calum Mack and Adam Smart seemed like a killer piece of information Aurelia could not bring herself to share that finding with Telford for fear of ridicule. She needed more time to acquire evidence, and her one decent opportunity—the meeting with Rowland—had backfired. Telford stared, waiting a further few seconds before speaking.

'Nothing?'

'Nothing you'd probably want to hear.'

Telford searched her eyes before replying. 'Well, in that case I have no option but to suspend you from your duties, immediately. You will receive full pay pending investigation, but let me warn you, what you have done this morning amounts to a gross breach of conduct in my opinion. The only reason I'm not firing you right now is so that I can follow due process, and consult HR. Now please leave the premises immediately.'

Once Aurelia had exited, Telford called Adam Smart into his office to explain the events that had occurred and to request his assistance in dealing with Aurelia's workload and any potential fallout from the Mack case.

Adam agreed immediately.

When Calum awoke, not only did his head throb more acutely than any hangover he'd ever experienced, but his arms and legs felt completely numb. He'd opened his eyes to a synthesis of darkness and dampness, lying on a cold, hard stone floor of some sort, the limited light leaving assessment of his new environment almost impossible. There was a mouldy smell akin to rotting vegetation. When he attempted to move his joints, he discovered that his arms were not only still handcuffed, but also tethered to something fixed, but he couldn't see behind him to ascertain what. Benson and company must have stowed him somewhere out of the way, because all he could hear was the sound of silence interrupted only by the occasional gust of wind. The experience of the tight space afforded by his prison cell had been horrendous, but this was worse. This was freedom? He cried out once, and then again, but there was no reply.

As he shuffled further in an attempt to loosen the ties and handcuffs, he then smelled the unpleasant aroma of stale vomit. His own? Fuzzily, he considered that he might have nearly choked on his own sick, no doubt aggravated by the effects of that blue tablet they'd forced him to take.

Then, a further revelation turned his stomach once again, as he recounted the violence perpetrated against those prison officers. They could have been seriously injured or even killed.

He swallowed hard, recriminating. Boy, did his head hurt. The previous day he'd made up his mind to avoid Benson's escape plan, and yet here he was, once again an accessory to a crime he had not committed, this time with more malignant consequences. Why hadn't he spoken to Wilson, the prison officer who'd been suspicious? That fractional delay in making a decision had been a measure of sheer stupidity, akin to his folly in publishing the mystery tipster's advice at the *Sentinel*. By the time he'd been forced to swallow that tablet it had been too late, just as the decision to publish the first tip had set in motion a stream of negative events.

More than anything, he felt ashamed of himself, the ineptitude that had dominated his existence in the past few months. He gritted his teeth. Surely it was time to fight back. To take control. To *kick back*. He pressed his eyes together tightly wondering if a higher being could possibly interject on his behalf.

Please, God.

But no such higher power appeared to intervene directly, so he breathed deeply again. Then, a minute or so later he became aware of the sound of approaching voices which appeared to take a circuitous route before finally coming to a halt outside. Hushed voices permeated the air, before Calum heard footsteps followed by the heavy clunk of a metal door being opened behind him.

'Let's see if Prince Charming has woken up.' Chisel.

As the hood was removed Calum reacted to the light that shone through the skylight of what looked like an old barn, before resting his eyes on an automatic pistol. Both Chisel and Benson stared at him directly, waiting for Calum to open the dialogue. Calum peered back, before taking a further deep breath and deciding to swear as much as possible.

'Thank fuck you're here!' Calum said forcefully. 'And what the fuck's that gun for? I'm itching to get our plan going. Why the fuck did you hit me, and leave me here, tied up and still cuffed? I'm on *your side* in case you hadn't noticed. Do you fucking mind?' He pushed his arms out towards them as much as was feasible.

'We don't trust you, how about that?' Chisel spat.

'You don't trust *me*?' Calum shouted, pushing the indignation as much as he could. 'I've followed every instruction you gave me. You didn't tell me I was going to get dragged up in the middle of the fucking night. How the fuck was I supposed to know that? And I was all set to take the tablet. Don't fucking talk to me about trust.' Calum shook his head, feigning anger.

Chisel spoke again. 'You're soft as shit, Mack. We could finish you off in a minute flat.'

'*Fuck you*, Chisel. I might have worked in finance, but I'm no fucking soft mark. You know nothing about me. I'm every bit as much a fucking criminal as you, and you'd better understand that right now. How the fuck are we—and I mean *we*—going to get fucking rich if I'm tied up? We're supposed to be partners. And where the fuck am I going to run to on my own with no cash, wearing these prison clothes? Unless we *stick together* and sort a plan out, we're *all* fucked. I need you, but you both need *me*. Now untie me, right fucking now!'

Chisel stood stationary, his eyes darting between Benson and Calum. Benson, chewing gum as per usual, slowly nodded towards the rope.

'Untie him.'

'But I thought...'

'City boy has a point. If he gets out of here on his tod, he's fucked.'

Chisel shook his head, but pulled out a sharp knife and cut the rope that tethered his arms. Chisel then used a rock to smash his way through the cuffs which eventually came loose after several attempts. Once Calum's arms were free, he immediately massaged where the cuffs had cut into the skin. Silently, Chisel then repeated the same exercise with the rope restraining Calum's legs, permitting him to stand up.

Benson then stood less than six inches from Calum's face, eyeballing him as he spoke. 'Now listen carefully, partner. You've passed the test for now. But cross me and you'll wish you'd never been born.'

Calum eyed him straight back. 'Fair enough, you've made your point. But right now I've got a bloody sore head. Now can you please get me drink of water so we can figure out where we go from here?'

Hawk's final inside trade in Electricon shares had netted another $760,000 in profits when he'd sold the stock after the announcement about the company's new deals in Iraq. The stock market adored firms that acquired guaranteed future income streams from governments, especially those rich in oil. He was aware that three days was probably sufficient for strategic purchases to be made by the international investment funds, and sure enough, patience proved fortuitous as two of the key Middle Eastern sovereign wealth funds had subsequently bought Electricon stock, pushing up the premium even further before Hawk sold.

Something still frustrated him, however. The proceeds of the sale had replenished his overall wealth, more than replacing what amounted to blackmail by his contact, but that was not the point. His contact had experienced less risk than he, yet had demanded additional money, which Hawk had paid. His contact may have provided the initial investment but his return to date had also been handsome. Should the same demand have been made now, he'd have refused. Now it rankled that he'd been manipulated into parting with the money.

On the day he'd sold the Electricon shares he'd spotted a snazzy new rental, a bright three bedroom deluxe villa with a forty-foot pool on the edge of Sandy Lane, and had decided impulsively to move up the coast from St Lawrence Gap to a more luxurious part of the island. No one here gave a shit. No one asked questions and the rum was cheaper than fresh milk. Why leave paradise? He'd plenty of cash to get by, and no debts. Calum Mack was safely ensconced in prison, and no one would trace his trades in the power company for the very rational reason that no one was looking. He smiled inwardly and mixed himself a rum punch which he sipped at the poolside. He'd never been much of a nature lover, but he'd suddenly begun to appreciate the bright tonal contrast of the palm trees and honeysuckle that surrounded the pool here, and the seclusion they afforded.

Then he went inside and switched on the satellite TV.

Bored with the usual day time crap, he ventured to Bloomberg, nosiness leading him to the channel just to see if any of the stocks through which he'd made his small fortune had shifted. Now and again curiosity had tempted him.

As he accessed the channel, his jaw slumped.

He kneeled down right in front of the screen, raising the volume. It wasn't share prices that had seized his attention, but something much more personal. An American newscaster with a synthetic smile uttered the words 'Calum', 'Mack' and 'escape' in the same sentence. Despite the 35 degree heat he'd noted on the temperature gauge earlier that morning, Hawk froze.

Mack had escaped during a transfer from prison to hospital? He'd been complicit in a daring breakout together with other 'highly dangerous' criminals, and unconfirmed rumours were circulating that he'd helped set up a diversion with Muslim terrorists, prompting immediate calls by politicians for a review of prison security?

This was absurd.

Mack wasn't 'dangerous'—the man was an inept fool who he'd run rings around. Yet now Bloomberg—*yes,* Bloomberg—had him pegged as the financial Ronnie fucking Biggs. Hawk shook his head, the ramifications of this twist of fortune sparking a chain of cognition.

What did this mean? A massive man-hunt and quick arrest followed by a longer conviction, surely. Or did it leave the possibility of Mack escaping to a foreign land? Mack had no resources, he was sure of that, because had he been wealthy he'd have funded a more robust defence. But Mack on the loose? This was not the plan. He cursed out loud. The bastard had obviously become involved with some more serious criminals during his short tenure inside, and Hawk knew how the system worked. Shit, he'd suffered for years in the system. He downed his punch before pouring himself a stronger one, and as he began to sweat, anger oozed from his pores. How *dare* Mack escape! The bastard *deserved* to serve his sentence in hell just as Hawk had done.

He flung the remote at the TV, the batteries spilling out across the floor. He'd foolishly assumed that his ploy had reached a final satisfying conclusion when the proceeds from the Electricon sale were transferred to his off-shore account. But a number of people had been very, very lucky. For some inexplicable reason, Tomlinson, Wilson and Lyndon had escaped justice. Yet, because he still held dirt that he could distribute to their wives at a later date, he'd subconsciously accepted their custodial reprieve safe in the knowledge that he could enjoy striking later when they least expected it.

But Mack did not deserve his liberty. He'd robbed Hawk of his early adult life, and he would have to pay for it. His contact had also profited handsomely, but now he also stood potentially exposed, because there was a small risk that Mack had escaped incarceration to seek his revenge on those who had convicted him. Mack might have been a naive fool earlier on, but Hawk of all people was aware that vengeance could prove to be a powerful motivator, and anyone who could succeed in a jail break from a major prison was showing substantial tenacity.

Still fuming, and with the effects of a strong rum spurring him on, he decided to take a minor risk, if only to assuage his temper.

From memory he dialled the number, and the familiar voice responded within ten seconds, immediately suggesting that he would call back later. Some time ago they'd agreed that no names would be used during any calls.

'You will not fucking call me back,' Hawk barked.

'So you've obviously heard the news.'

'What do you think? I'm not happy about this at all. This was supposed to be wrapped up.'

'I can hardly be held responsible,' the reply reported tersely, followed by a brief pause.

'You know as well as I do that's not the issue. *You*, for starters could be very exposed if he starts to dig, do you know that? It may not be the primary reason he's on the loose, but it doesn't take a genius to work that out. And if you're exposed you had better fucking well keep quiet about *me*. Have you got that? You've done very well out of this, remember.'

'So you're calling to threaten me, is that it?'

'Call it whatever you like. But I seem to remember that you pocketed a tidy sum the last time we spoke. Well, fucking earn it. Use everything in your brain to get this man captured. You must be able to do something. And I hate loose ends almost as much as I hate Calum Mack.'

'It's that personal, isn't it?'

'That's none of your business.'

'Is it not?' The voice betrayed a degree of curiosity, which elicited immediate regret from Hawk that he'd shared such an intimate emotion. 'If I get caught and go down, you're going down with me,' the man said flatly, ending the call before Hawk could reply.

The man on the phone in London swallowed, contemplating his options. He'd just made an explicit threat, which he instantly regretted. Then surely he'd nothing to fear? Almost certainly, Mack would be re-arrested, wouldn't he? He was on the loose with no personal resources and all the strength of the Met pitted against him. There were probably more surveillance cameras here than in any other place in the free world, and sooner or later Mack would be caught. There would be watchers at every major point of exit and the phone conversation had been so short he'd not even had time to reinforce these points.

Yet in a villa in Sandy Lane some four thousand miles distant Hawk was unable to return the call as he'd smashed his phone off the tiled floor where it joined the remnants of the television remote. He'd attempted to quell his violent eruptions over the years, not least in jail, but he exploded periodically when simmering might have proved a more effective form of behaviour. He detested being out of control, so he made a decision: he would return to London one more time to guarantee that any personal threat to him was eliminated.

Chapter 18

The outbuildings where Calum, Benson and Chisel were holed up were part of an abandoned pig farm in a wooded area located south east of Tonbridge in Kent. The place was far enough from neighbouring properties to provide some seclusion, though the scent of damp and decay complemented the lack of running water. They were living off a case of basic food and drinks that the terrorist group had provided after they'd dropped them off. Apart from the pistol, they'd also been bequeathed some blankets and other basics—toiletries and a change of clothes each, but they enjoyed no further means of transport, nor, apparently, any additional money. The debt deemed to be owed to Benson had now been repaid, and they were on their own. Calum had changed into trainers which were a good fit, a pair of jeans that were slightly too tight, and a checked shirt and fleece that were too large. He was third in the queue for the use of an electric razor, though this was the least of his concerns.

He had persuaded the others to stay put for a day at least, to permit him to formulate a plan. He blustered that if they could secure some cash, they could obtain fake passports and leave the country via an unusual route. Chisel boasted that he had contacts who could obtain fake passports, though Benson insisted that all he need do was borrow his half-brother's who was apparently his double, and only two years older. Calum let this go. He had no intention of travelling anywhere with them, but he had to protect the illusion.

Chisel's frequent mood swings and eagerness to secure the non-existent millions had persuaded Calum that the man was psychotic, perhaps damaged by a difficult childhood and cruelly fashioned by a hazardous life of criminal endeavour, and at one point Calum had contemplated just taking off. However, he was dissuaded as Chisel had also acted like a trigger happy petulant child, and Calum didn't fancy a bullet in the back. He also suspected that there was friction between Benson and Chisel in addition to the common animosity they clearly felt towards him, so he decided to await an opportunity to exploit this discord.

Calum then concealed his relief when Benson, initially obsessed with preserving battery power, had briefly accessed the news on his phone—the only means of contact they had with the world outside—and discovered that none of the prison guards had sustained life-threatening injuries during the breakout. Benson and Chisel, however, were disappointed, employing several colourful expletives in their competitive descriptions of what they would do to these guys if they had a second opportunity. This made Calum slightly sick, but he remained quiet, instead choosing to divert them with future fortune.

Krugerrands.

For once, Benson shut up as Calum took the opportunity to employ some journalistic licence. Once Benson had listened to Calum's plan for funding their trip to the Caribbean, Benson willingly agreed to part with his phone, permitting Calum to ascertain the current price of gold. Calum smiled without humour when he discovered that there had been a significant recovery in the value of the yellow metal during his period of incarceration. How ironic. Gold now stood at $1305 an ounce, meaning that each Krugerrand was worth around $1360. Wow. He'd fifteen of them sitting in that bank safe deposit box in Edinburgh. Even if these were sold on the black market, at, say a 25 percent discount, he calculated that they could fetch around £9,000, *technically* sufficient for three tickets to Grand Cayman and enough spare cash to create the illusion of potential escape overseas for his fellow convicts.

Both Benson and Chisel immediately claimed they were acquainted with people who would buy the coins for cash. Initially, this suited Calum perfectly as his plan required them to believe they were genuinely resourcing a trip to George Town to pick up their share of the non-existent two million dollars.

When Benson ventured outside to scout the surroundings, Chisel closed his eyes for a moment and Calum contemplated his options. The next part of his strategy was more problematic, so Calum initially kept his thoughts to himself. Clearly, he couldn't appear in a bank branch in Edinburgh in person as he would run a substantial risk of being recognised and captured in highly incriminating circumstances. The only reason that the safety deposit box had been overlooked by the authorities when they sequestered his assets is that this box was registered to his parents' address in the Black Isle, not his address in London. This had been fortuitous and purely coincidental when he'd hired the box, which still had six months of rental paid in advance, yet it now presented an opportunity partially owing to an anachronistic naming convention still sometimes used in the Highlands.

Calum's father was also named Calum, even though Calum had actually been named in the traditional manner after his maternal grandfather, not his father. Calum's dad was known to everyone as Fergie, so the Calum angle hadn't occurred to him before. This was now potentially convenient as Calum's father could, technically, provide genuine ID and proof of address to access the box—if he was able to travel to the bank. Unfortunately, even if his father agreed, he'd need another accomplice with a car at a later stage, as he was pretty certain that his parents should not risk long distance travel to meet dangerous escapees.

In essence, Calum knew that his parents might well disapprove of the bizarre escape, particularly as violence had occurred, yet they were unaware of the contributing events that had transpired. However, if he could speak to them and explain the circumstances and his intent to prove his innocence, then perhaps his dad would agree to help. His parents also possessed the key for the box. What Calum did not want was for Benson or Chisel to come into contact with his family as they'd already threatened them, and God only knew what they might do. So what he needed was someone else, someone he could trust.

Ben.

At least his former colleague at the *Sentinel* had bothered to visit him during his period inside and had remained loyal. No one else from the *Sentinel* had bothered to come—in fact, the only other communications had been two anonymous letters of denigration blaming him for bringing the publication into disrepute and undermining former colleagues' jobs.

Reggie Benson had assured Calum that his phone was unknown to the authorities as it had been secreted into the prison by a third party as part of another favour owed and was thus untraceable. Calum's plan would require Ben to contact Calum's parents, though he was fairly certain that his folks' phones and emails might be under observation.

Then he had a brainwave. If he could communicate via a third party it might just help him evade police surveillance. Calum knew Ben's sister's number from when Ben had shared a flat with her. Although Calum had never dated Shirley, Ben had joked that his sister had lobbied him a number of times to persuade Calum to date her. Could Calum exploit this old crush? The girl had been a bit of a rebel, having been cautioned by the police for minor drug offences, so she might sympathise. If Shirley was willing to meet Ben and persuade him to get in contact with Calum's parents through another party, then Calum's father might be willing to help. And he knew the ideal person for Ben to contact in the Black Isle— his aunt, Jessie. She was a neighbour of his parents who was eighty, coming on eighteen.

But how was he going to sell this convoluted scheme to Chisel and Benson? When Benson returned to the partially ruined building, the man glared at the snoozing Chisel, giving him a kick on the leg. Chisel bolted upright, just managing not to shoot Calum in the process. Benson cursed at Chisel, but Calum quickly interrupted, explaining his plan.

'That's fucking stupid!' Chisel spat.

'Yeah, why should we trust your people?' Benson asked, before Calum looked at them both in turn, aiming to appear as forthright as possible.

'The reason, guys, is that you are both *bigger league convicts* than me— major bad guys—in the eyes of the law. And that means that you need a

greater degree of protection than me in the early stages of this operation.'
He held his hands out, appealing to their egos.

'That sounds like bullshit to me,' Chisel said.

'And it sound like bullshit to me,' Benson repeated.

'It's not bullshit—it's for your own protection. Think about it. Your contacts are mainly criminals. The cops will have tabs on them all. I can't do this without you guys. Remember, we're in this *together*. That's what you told me, right? If we dare contact your people just now we would get nabbed right away. What's the point of that, after all the planning you've put into the escape? My contacts are ordinary folk. If you don't think I can be trusted, let me ask you just one question.'

'What?' Benson glowered.

'Why would I have told you about the gold in the first place? And I might have taken off when you were outside and Chisel here was sound asleep, Reggie.'

Benson glared at Chisel again before turning to Calum. 'Okay, brains. You make your calls, but this is what you're going to say. You're going to tell your father that *he's* going to cash in the gold and get the cash directly to *us*, pronto. He's going to a bank, for fuck's sake. You do that maths— this is going to get us a couple of grand more, and save time, so we can just arrange the flights to paradise.'

Calum stared at Benson. He inwardly cursed because he'd already considered the possibility of this specific demand, but not really generated a counter argument.

'Do you know what age my father is? If he gets done it would kill him.'

'I don't give a toss,' Benson replied. 'Do you Chisel?' Chisel shook his head.

'What if he needs paperwork to transact officially?'

'Figure it out. You were a banker. And remember, we've got the gun,' Chisel said, pointing the pistol directly at Calum. 'Now, make your calls, *Goldfinger.*'

The first call Calum made was to Aunt Jessie, who answered after about ten rings. Calum explained succinctly his urgent need for help though he could not labour his innocence, because Benson and Chisel were listening to every word. Naturally, she was shocked, but she quickly adapted to the surreal circumstances in which she could aid and abet a man on the run, albeit one who had been unjustly convicted.

'This is *so* exciting,' she said. 'In fact, nothing as mad has happened to me since your Uncle Arthur died.' Despite the awkward circumstances, Calum couldn't help but smile, even if he was also grateful that Benson and Chisel couldn't actually hear what Jessie had said, because they just wouldn't get it. When Uncle Arthur had died, Calum happened to be at home and had been asked to help lift the body downstairs with his father, unaware that Arthur was actually dead. At the bottom of the stairs Calum had asked Jessie what was wrong with Arthur anyway? He had then dropped the body when the truth was revealed. For some reason Jessie had burst into hysterics, opining that Arthur would have 'killed himself laughing at that one', which had simply precipitated further mirth. Black humour, on the Black Isle.

'I can't thank you enough, Jessie. Now, I want you to listen carefully while I outline what I need you to do, and what my dad needs to do.' Calum briefly explained the plan, and exacted a promise that Jessie would tell no one else.

Aware that there was little remaining charge on the phone, Calum let Benson quickly check online what place to choose as a future meeting point. Better to let Benson and Chisel pick, that way they'd be more likely to acquiesce. They chose the Thomson Motel which was near an industrial estate on the outskirts of Tonbridge. He had to quickly explain to them that this was a different place from Royal Tunbridge Wells which was also nearby. This confused Chisel. Calum then made his second call, to Ben's sister, Shirley, who he guessed might be at the salon in which she'd worked for the past three or four years. The number rang out.

Then, a minute later, a text appeared. *Who's that calling?*

Calum rang back immediately. 'Shirley? Remember me, your favourite convict?'

Silence.

Calum was acutely aware that he was taking a chance here, and both Benson and Chisel stared intently, awaiting some indication of a double cross or a dead end. Then came a bold reply.

'You're shittin' me? Calum Mack? Or should I say Clyde Barrow himself?'

'One and the same. You at work, Shirley?'

'On a break. Outside havin' a fag.'

'Great. Now, can you keep a secret and are you willing to aid and abet a convicted man?'

'Does the Pope shit in the woods?'

Calum explained as quickly as possible what he needed, and to his amazement Shirley repeated it back, seemingly energised by absurdity of the plan. Yes, she'd sort calls out, and kick Ben's arse into gear. Yes, she'd try to book this Thomson Motel place as a meeting point. Where was it? He waited as she went online and checked. What date? Two days, hence, at 3:00 p.m. He could leave it with her: she reminded Calum that she had watched *Thelma and Louise* at least five times.

Aurelia's initial reaction towards being suspended had been self pity, which had prompted an evening of tears and recrimination complemented by a take-away curry and two old movies—weepies. The only time she'd felt more isolated had been after her father died, as although her mother's death whilst she'd been a teenager had been awful, at least her dad had been there for her at that juncture, and vice versa. This time her career—arguably her other 'family'—had been struck a fatal blow. She'd no boyfriend, no brothers or sisters, and no husband or children from whom she could receive the necessary injection of unconditional love.

Unwilling to call any friends, she'd cried herself to sleep.

She decided to bury herself away, so she switched off all modes of communication in her flat. Then the following morning, after some time had elapsed, a different emotion had awoken her early: *anger*. Adam Smart's face may have appeared in convoluted guises during her confused dreams, but the reality was that she was now officially estranged from these colleagues. Kicked out by the FCA, humiliated.

How dare they?

Aurelia was aware that although anger typically manifested itself in a malignant pose, it might also be positively harnessed if the energy it created could produce both magnitude and direction. She made herself a strong coffee, and paced the floor of her lounge, contemplating what action she might take. Plonking herself down squarely on the sofa, she accidentally bumped her phone off the arm rest. Picking it up, she noticed two texts that had been sent the evening before when she'd been blocking out the world.

The first was from Ken, who'd given a few brief, frustrating words on Calum Mack's escape: *maybe he was involved after all*. This was harsh love. He advised her to pause in her investigations, if for no other reason than the fact that Mack would be going down on other charges now anyway. She couldn't face calling him to explain that she was now off the case as her career had entered meltdown. Aurelia had contemplated the same thing as Ken had, even if she'd been reluctant to admit it to herself. This case had driven her mad at times. Why would an innocent man actually break out of prison with hardened criminals, in a plan organised by terrorists? It seemed ridiculous, and did nothing to explain the fake passports or the involvement of the mysterious Tom Hawkins, or indeed that bastard Adam Smart.

The second text had come from Douglas Lyndon, who'd initially prompted her to dig into the Tom Hawkins angle. All it said was *please call me.*

'It is 5:45 in the morning,' Lyndon said hoarsely, when she called.

'You asked *me* to call *you*,' Aurelia replied.

'Okay, okay, let me move into another room.' Aurelia heard a female voice enquiring as to the identity of the caller disturbing them at this early hour, and then the sound of a door clunking shut.

'Do you know where Calum Mack is?' She decided just to blurt out the obvious question.

'No, I do not.' The immediate, direct negative appeared to demonstrate honesty, but if was followed by a brief silence before Lyndon replied.

'Do *you* know here he is?'

'If I did, I wouldn't be asking you, would I? It's a hell of a story though, your pal Mack busting out of a secure prison accompanied by hardened criminals, all washed down with a bucketful of Al Qaeda or some other group of lunatics. Look, I've had a bad week. No, let me rephrase that. I've had a really *shit* week. I've been suspended at the FCA because I dug further into the case, so if you're calling me wanting me to do more, you're wasting your time.'

'Oh. I'm sorry to hear that. But that puts us both in a similar position then.'

'Really? Except I've done nothing but pursue the truth.'

'That's what I'm trying to help you with now, Aurelia. I didn't ask for any of this either. Look, I'm sorry about your job—what happened?'

Aurelia sighed, realising that Lyndon was the first person she'd actually confided in since Telford had run her out. So, slowly, she explained how she'd been suspended for seeking to push a government minister into helping, having followed Lyndon's lead regarding Tom Hawkins, and that an old friend of her father's had helped her find the extraordinary connection between Hawkins and the counterfeiter, and, startlingly, the names on the fake passports.

'But you've hit pay-dirt! How could they suspend you for that?' Lyndon sounded incredulous.

'I haven't told my boss this yet,' she said, suddenly aware as she spoke how ludicrous her words might seem.

'*Excuse me*? You've found direct evidence that could exonerate Calum, and simultaneously incriminate Hawkins and one of your colleagues at the FCA, and you've not reported it? Am I missing something here?'

'We didn't have hard evidence, something that would stand up in court. I don't have the passports.'

'But this links together pieces of a jigsaw! The forger could be put on the stand, and the longer you wait, the more likely it is that he takes off, for fuck's sake.'

'Swear at me once more and it will be the last time you will ever speak to me. Understand?' A brief silence ensued, broken only by air being expelled from Lyndon's nostrils.

'Okay, okay, I'm *sorry*. It's just…well…it's so bloody frustrating…sorry…you know what I mean?'

'Frustration isn't a strong enough description. Now, why did you text me?'

'Because I've been doing some digging of my own, and now that Calum's on the loose, I figured I'd better fill you in. I think I have complementary information.'

'Oh Christ, I don't know if I can stand being dragged into this further.'

'What are you doing for breakfast?'

They met at the Getti cafe on Jermyn Street, just off Piccadilly, which was handy for Aurelia. She could have offered to host Lyndon in her flat, but she barely knew the man so the cafe option prevailed. They sat at a quiet corner table and both ordered coffee and traditional breakfasts, Lyndon insisting that he pay given he'd instigated the meeting, before praising Aurelia for her fortitude.

'So what's *your* big story? Someone's stormed the FCA headquarters and taken my boss hostage on the roof?' Aurelia smiled without mirth, though Lyndon returned the gesture with greater warmth.

'See, you've retained a sense of humour despite your circumstances. And what I have might just bring more of a smile.'

'Go.'

'I've been doing some hacking,' he intoned, briefly checking around to see if they were being observed. 'And found out that a broker in Antigua traded exactly one million worth of Electricon stock just before the news came out.'

'I got that far myself. Is that it?'

Lyndon took a large swig of coffee. 'Nope, there's more. I have followed the money trail. Granted, there were a few twists and turns, as it was routed back and forth, and then finally credited to an account in Barbados, of all places. Just an island hop away from Antigua.' He toyed with a piece of bacon, tempting Aurelia to ask the obvious question.

'Oh, spit it out!'

'The bacon? It's perfectly okay,' he grinned.

'No! The name of the final account holder in Barbados.'

'Oh…Tom Hawkins.' Lyndon managed to chew almost pompously, with that smugness techy people sometimes display when they've demonstrated trouble-shooting skills.

'That's bizarre. So he actually used his *own* name after all the re-routing?'

'It seems complacent given what you've said about fake passports, though he was a cocky bastard years ago in university, and he's probably still one now. But I think I know why he's done it.'

Aurelia scratched her chin. 'He thinks he's in the clear with his perfect scam and he might want to return here. And only a genuine passport would guarantee entry?'

'That's right. You're not a bad detective.'

'I learned from an expert as a child. And Ken talked about this very issue.'

'The fake passport thing might just have been a ruse, something to throw a potential investigator off the scent. But now he's in the clear—or so he thinks—he can use his own name, as no one knows about his crime.'

'Apart from Adam Smart, though he might not know Hawkins' real identity.'

'But we do.'

'And potentially a very angry Calum Mack back out on the loose,' Aurelia suggested.

'Exactly. And I have something else from my little hacking exercise—an address in Barbados for Hawkins.'

'How did you do that? I should pretend I haven't heard any of this in case I get my job back. So he's at the Hilton or something?'

'Better that that, the bastard's making up for his time inside. He's in a snazzy villa at Sandy Lane.'

'The place the footballers and movie stars go?'

'One and the same. And, on a roll, I tracked down his neighbour, explaining that I was a relative having difficulty getting in touch with nice Mr Hawkins next door—that his granny had died over here, and would he mind awfully checking if Mr Hawkins was currently next door?'

Aurelia smiled, simultaneously shaking her head. 'And?'

'And if you buy me another coffee I'll tell you.'

'You're infuriating! If you don't tell me right now, I'll pour my coffee over your head.'

Lyndon grinned. 'You're a hard taskmaster. Okay, the irony is you're right about the passport thing. It appears that Hawk, Mr Tom Hawkins, criminal at large, actually asked his next door neighbour at Sandy Lane to keep an eye on his house while he took a short break back here in London. He left last night. So assuming he told his neighbour the truth, he could be landing in the city any time now. There are two flights due this morning— BA and Virgin.'

'That's incredible,' Aurelia said, scratching the top of her head. 'Why do you think he's back here? Surely not Calum's escape? Hawkins and Calum can't actually be in league, surely.' Aurelia held her head in her hands, the thought of some further twist sending a shiver down her back.

'No chance at all. Hawkins hated Calum because of what happened in court all those years ago. His crime may have been partly motivated by greed, but it was also clearly inspired by vengeance. He didn't just want to make money, he wanted to send Calum Mack down—the rest of us got lucky, though I have my theories about that too.' A waitress passed by and took away some of their used plates. Neither spoke until she had departed.

'So you think that blackmail threat might still come back to haunt you?'

'It won't haunt me, because I've explained to my wife what happened. But the others? He set us up with an underage hooker. I didn't do anything, by the way, but that's not the way the pictures may appear. It's a smoke and fire argument, enough to threaten someone with a big career to lose.'

'Why didn't you just come clean in court?'

'Why do you think?'

'Fair enough, I suppose, from your position at the time. You didn't answer my question about why Hawkins is coming back here.'

'I don't know. But given that you and I have some time on our hands…do you fancy trying to figure this out?'

Chapter 19

Benson had been strangely subdued, but Chisel's fragile patience had almost expired when a single call back from Ben's sister Shirley confirmed that Ben was willing to call in sick at work, and drive to the Black Isle in order pick up Calum's father and facilitate a journey to Edinburgh. Ben was then due to drive south and deliver the proceeds to them, and they would take over from that point. Only Shirley was to call Benson's phone. Shirley remarked on the quirky nature of Jessie, how she seemed energised by the prospect of the criminal underworld coming into her life, but Calum said nothing, lacking any trust in his fellow escapees.

Calum had requested a single text to confirm when the safety deposit box had been accessed successfully and some sort of transaction made, and, allowing sufficient time for the journey back south, a time to meet at the Thomson Motel, where a room was now booked.

Calum couldn't tell Shirley the whole story on the phone because Benson and Chisel were monitoring every word. He couldn't warn her that his accomplices were psychos, or explain the next part of his plan. However dank and unpleasant the place was, they'd heard no sirens at the abandoned piggery yet and he'd managed to convince Benson to stay put until now as Calum had concluded that the authorities were still blithely unaware of their whereabouts. Chisel kept ranting about fake passports for travel to Grand Cayman, though Calum knew that this would be an illusory obstacle given the salient fact that they wouldn't actually be going anywhere.

Ultimately, he wanted to speak to Aurelia Harley at the FCA, because she was the only person within the system who might doubt his guilt, but he was unable to make such a call on Benson's phone, and the charge on the phone was now running so low that they could make no further calls in order to conserve the remaining charge for the all important incoming text. Benson then mentioned a contact *he* had that might be able to obtain fake passports.

This is when Chisel erupted.

'Are we fuck using your contact!' He kicked out at an old corrugated iron sheet, his boot breaking though the rusted metal, jamming in the process. He then struggled to free his foot, which precipitated a further round of expletives. *'Fuck you and fuck this fucking place!'* He spat out the words as he turned to face Benson, who had been sitting idly by. Benson now suddenly stood to square up to Chisel.

'Calm down, mate.'

'Fucking calm down yourself. I didn't spend seven years in fucking prison to sit around in a place full of old pig shit, waiting for instructions from people with no fucking clue. How the hell do we know if smart boy here hasn't used a code to set us up, eh?'

'Because we're too smart to let that happen. We listened to very word he said. He needs *us* too. My contact can get passports no problem.' Benson stood a matter of inches from Chisel, staring him out, as Calum marvelled at how the man was actually taking his side.

'How the hell do you know that? You haven't called anyone. Give me that phone and I'll call my brother Phil right fucking now.' Chisel held out his hand, but Benson remained static.

'Right, fuck you, that's decided—we're using *my* guy. We're finding the nearest empty house, and making the call from there. And you're both coming with me. I don't trust anyone else because I don't know shit about them.'

Calum then interjected. 'What house are you going to? You're just going to break in, and do what? Hold people at gunpoint until you make a call? Our photos will be all over the media.' Calum's voice was raised as he feared that the whole thing would unravel courtesy of this impatient and volatile nutcase.

Chisel then leapt forward, pinning Calum against the wall of the main outbuilding. He grabbed the hand gun from his jacket pocket and thrust the end of the barrel against Calum's temple. 'No, arsehole. I could blow your brains out and drag your fucking corpse to the nearest house and then let *you* make the call as a fucking dead man.'

Benson then stepped sideways, momentarily looking at Calum when he turned. 'Back off, Chisel. You've got a point. Stay here long enough and someone's going to find us. Could be kids mucking about, or a farmer, or anything. So far we've been lucky, so, sure, we'll use your contact.'

'What, three of us just walk into a house? It's crazy,' Calum said.

'With two million bucks sitting unclaimed in the bank? Staying *here* is dumb,' Chisel said flatly. 'For your information, Mack, I've broken into more locked houses than you've spent nights inside, so don't have me pegged as some fucking clown. Got me?'

Benson then spoke once more. 'We wait here for one more day, and then we move. If we go too early into civilisation the chances are that we'll be caught hanging about. Chisel, you've been patient for seven years, don't blow it for the sake of one more day.'

And for some unexplained reason, the volatile Chisel sat down and closed his eyes.

Douglas Lyndon tried to persuade Aurelia to leave the police out of matters for as long as feasible, intimating that he could be charged with computer hacking unless he could firstly cover his tracks. They'd gone to Aurelia's flat. Previously she'd never have countenanced having someone involved with a case invade her personal space, but circumstances had changed. Lyndon enquired how she felt about her colleague Adam probably profiting from the whole scam as she enjoyed suspension and likely sacking, to which Aurelia reacted badly.

'How do you think?'

'Sorry. It's just that you seem to be holding this in reserve as some sort of trump card. But if the forger guy disappears, so might your proof.'

With that prompt, Aurelia called Ken Charleson, who offered to check the situation regarding the forger. Around ten minutes later Ken called back.

'Bad news, Aurelia,' Ken said flatly. 'The cops swooped at dawn this morning as part of a bust for the other case I mentioned to you. Looks like John Smith flew the nest. He's probably somewhere in Europe by now.'

'Damn, *damn*. If only I'd pushed Telford to pursue this instead of going higher up. I feel so... so foolish now.' She'd filled Ken in on what had transpired.

'Hindsight's a great thing, Aurelia.'

'It's probably a stupid question, but did they say if Smith left anything behind?'

'No they didn't, but unfortunately this type of criminal is equipped to disappear. If you need me to call the police back at some time, let me know. I'll also happily testify in court as to what Smith told me. It's not hard evidence—hearsay in effect—but I can still do it if it helps.' Ken signed off, leaving Aurelia downcast.

'I've got an idea,' Lyndon then suggested. 'Why don't we rumble Adam Smart directly? What have we got to lose?'

'My job, actually. Are you suggesting that I just have a go at him, without physical evidence?"

'No, I'm suggesting that *I* have a go at him. This is a financial crime. We don't *need physical* evidence—I thought you'd know that in your job.'

Aurelia picked up a magazine that lay on the coffee table and threw it at Lyndon. 'You're insufferable. How did your colleagues put up with you?'

'I'm in IT, we tend to hide away. Anyway, what if I have a go at Smart? *I've* certainly got nothing to lose.' Lyndon held out his hands, pursing his lips.

'You know, Douglas, maybe you have a point.' She checked her watch. 'It's ten past eleven. I do have friends at the FCA—if he's in the office I could probably find out when he's due to take lunch today. He normally goes to the same place to pick up a sandwich. The bastard even attempted to get me to go with him several times. Hang on.'

Aurelia left the room to make a call to the office. After a couple minutes, she returned and explained to Lyndon that Adam Smart was due to finish a meeting at 12:30 p.m. 'If we take the tube then a train, we've just enough time to make it over there to see if he exits his lair.'

A strong wind welcomed them after they left their train to make their way along the walkway towards the FCA headquarters at Canary Warf. Aurelia wondered if Adam Smart would recognise Lyndon, but then he pointed out that given Adam's guilt, recognition might prove beneficial, perhaps inducing fear or forcing some type of admission. Who knew how he'd react? They'd hoped to record any subsequent conversation on Lyndon's phone, with Aurelia listening out of view, though any success depended partially on whether the power of the wind would hinder potential audibility. They stationed themselves about forty yards from the main entrance and waited in silence. After around ten minutes, Adam appeared, boasting a camel overcoat and a long bottle-green scarf.

'What a twat,' Lyndon reflected as he viewed the man from a distance.

'Douglas, you have excellent powers of observation. I'll call you when you give the signal.'

They faced in the other direction until Adam had passed, and then began to follow. Aurelia had explained where his likely route might take them, and at the first major juncture where no one else was in the immediate vicinity Lyndon made his move, leaping out in front of Adam.

'What the hell?' Adam gasped, recoiling backwards.

'Yeah, hell's where *you're* going pal,' Lyndon replied in his broad Glasgow accent. A trace of recognition crossed Adam's face, creating a momentary hesitation.

'What exactly are you playing at? Hang on. You're...Lyndon? Yes, Douglas Lyndon. Is this some kind of joke? Because I can tell you the FCA charter forbids—'

'*Shut it,*' Lyndon said forcefully enough for other passers-by to recognise the emerging conflict. Two young women immediately gave them a wide berth as Lyndon moved towards Adam, forcing him backwards again towards a high wall to the rear.

'Now just listen to me, Mr Smart…arse. I happen to know—yes *know*—what your game is. You're a corrupt bastard. At. It. I know all about your secret activities and how you've abused your position at the FCA.' Lyndon glanced around to capture the small audience that had gathered close by, raising his voice. 'He's a crook, folks! Yes, an arrogant, slimy crook, and he works for the *FCA*. Now, does everyone here want to hear his name and what he's been up to? His name is—'

'Stop it! Stop it!' Adam yelled.

'Why?' Lyndon asked. 'I was beginning to enjoy myself. You're on the take, mate. Simple as that.' The fear emanating from Adam's eyes created further hesitation as he swallowed, wildly eyeing Lyndon.

'I've no idea what you're talking about! This is a slur on my name.' He then raised his own voice. 'I've a good mind to call the police.' Just as the word 'police' exited Adam's lips, two policemen appeared from nowhere.

'Problem here, gents?'

Adam, clearly uncomfortable with the turn of events, glanced quickly from side to side before addressing the constabulary. 'Not at all, officers,' he attempted a smile. 'I was just joking with an old…eh, acquaintance here…how we could really do with more officers on the beat. Delighted to see you here. Difficult job, and all that.'

The taller officer the addressed Lyndon directly. 'That correct, sir?'

'In a manner of words, officer. We could certainly do with arresting more criminals. With a bit of luck there will be a few high profile cases coming up,' Lyndon replied, as he glared at Adam, and Adam smiled at Lyndon through gritted teeth before the officer suggested that they be on their way.

Adam walked off at a rapid pace, continuing away from the FCA offices, and then Aurelia emerged from behind the small crowd that had now built up in a ring at a safe distance. She grinned broadly.

'Did you capture that?'

'Yes. Took a while for him to deny anything,' said Aurelia, checking her phone.

'I think he's guilty. No doubt about it. What do you think he'll do now?'

'Not sure, Douglas. Probably try to kiss Telford's ass further. Build up some kind of defence. Or maybe he'll take off.'

As fate would have it, the remaining charge left on Benson's phone had dissipated, precipitating the need to find another phone. Calum began to dread the potential consequences of their arrival at the quaint hamlet that suddenly appeared through a gap in the oak woods to the north of the abandoned pig farm. They'd walked for just ten minutes. The houses had been obscured from view when Calum had argued that the best chance of concealment was staying put at the pig farm, and the irony now was that they could very easily have been rumbled should a local resident have chosen to take a short walk south. There were four large Tudor-style properties and another smaller cottage on a lane to the rear of the last larger house. The three fell silent as they contemplated their next move: they needed access to a phone, or at least a re-charge, but entry to the wrong property could prove ruinous.

All four of the large houses had at least one car present in the gardens. Only the cottage at the back had no vehicle evident, though there was a garage which might well have housed a car. Either way, absence or indeed presence of a vehicle did not equate to absence or presence of a resident.

Chisel checked his watch. 'Half past ten. At work, I bet, or he's at work and she's out for a tennis lesson. Bet they're posh bastards.'

'Thing is, which one is likely to be empty and has an alarm you can deactivate?' Benson asked.

'The one at the back,' Chisel said robustly.

'Look guys…I think that this might be a bad move. Any noise in a quiet place like this would stand out like a sore thumb. We'd be better off finding a house on its own.'

'I'm not waiting any fucking longer,' Chisel said shortly, waving the pistol about as he spoke, the implication being that he was increasingly itching to use the weapon.

'Okay,' Benson replied. 'Let's get on with it. Right Mack, I'll keep a look out, you go knock at the door. Easiest way to find out if there's anyone inside.'

'What am I supposed to say if someone answers the door?'

'Fucking improvise. Tell them you're hoping to clear the gutters, I don't give a shit. We can move on elsewhere.'

Calum swallowed. 'What if I'm recognised?'

'Get on with it,' Benson spat.

'Okay, but strictly on the basis that if there's someone in we go elsewhere.' He glanced at the pistol in Chisel's hand. 'The last thing we want is any casualties.'

'Just do it,' Chisel said before he and Benson moved behind some rhododendrons to the side of the cottage.

Calum briefly closed his eyes, before checking that no neighbours were observing his movements as he ventured up the driveway. At the front door, he cleared his throat before ringing the bell. The sound of the bell inside the cottage was clearly discernible. He took a step back, before peering in the front window. There was no sound or movement from within, so he rang the bell once more.

Nothing.

As Calum glanced towards the bushes again, Benson and Chisel shuffled out and began walking to the rear of the property. Calum followed as they opened an old wrought iron gate and brushed overgrown bushes aside to approach the back door. Chisel looked up at an ancient looking alarm box housed above the door. Searching around, he found a rusty spade that was leaning against the side fence.

'What are you going to do, hit it?' Calum asked.

'That alarm is an old piece of shit. I can fix this in a minute.' He then lifted the spade above him and placed the metal edge behind the lower screws on the box, prising them away to reveal the electrics behind. He moved an old garden seat and stood on it, reaching up, before suddenly yanking wires away from an electric circuit board.

Nothing happened. 'See? A piece of shit.' Chisel then smiled, and laid his hand on the back door handle, slowly turning it. The door simply opened, creaking eerily as it slowly swung inwards into a utility room.

Chisel grinned. 'These country bastards don't even lock their doors. How stupid is that?'

Calum then spoke more quietly. 'But what if there's someone in?'

'Well they'd need to be totally fucking deaf, wouldn't they? You rang the bell twice and I could hear it from the bushes.'

'I need a leak,' Chisel then said. 'I've a good mind to piss on the floor right here and now.'

Benson grabbed his arm. 'Don't be daft, Chisel. No trail. No DNA. Take a piss in the bloody toilet. And shoes off!' Chisel thrust Benson's hand away, but then reluctantly removed his shoes. Calum and Benson followed suit, before they walked into the kitchen. Benson looked under the kitchen sink and found a packet of rubber gloves, telling the other two to put them on right away.

Moving from the kitchen, Benson said 'That'll probably be the bog there.' He pointed to a door adjacent to the front door. 'You take a piss while we find a phone.' Then, just as Calum and Benson turned into the lounge, a loud scream emanated from behind them.

'You bastard! Get out of my home!'

Benson and Calum leapt backwards to see the open toilet door reveal an old man in his late eighties sitting on the toilet and waving his fist at Chisel.

'Well, stuff you, you old shitter!' Chisel said, before sticking the gun to the man's face. The man suddenly evacuated his bowel, holding his hands to his face in shock, prompting Chisel to laugh cruelly.

'Uuugh! What a stink. You've probably been there for a week, old man, so I've done you a favour.'

'I can't hear what you're saying!' The man shouted, covering himself. 'My hearing aid is in the kitchen. What are you doing here? Leave me alone! *Please*. I've nothing of value.'

Calum then spoke. 'Let him get his trousers on. This is a mess.'

'What say I blow him away right now? He can't hear a thing, so he won't even know what I'm suggesting right now,' Chisel said, an evil smile on his face.

'No,' Benson replied. 'If you go back inside prison, you'll never get out.'

'I'm not going back inside prison, Reggie.'

'Then we'll need to tie him up rather than shoot him. And see if he has a car in the garage. And you,' Benson looked directly at Calum. 'Don't think about doing a runner now that there's a bit of action.'

Calum blinked at Benson, knowing that he'd tracked his exact thoughts. This scenario was combustive and Calum was once more out of his depth. These guys were hardened criminals who cared little for the sanctity of life, and Calum was intrinsically aware how volatile the situation might become. The poor old guy could suffer if they tied him up, but if Calum ran? He stared directly back at Benson.

'Sure, Reggie. We're in this together. I'll look in the garage for a rope. Chisel, can you cover this guy while I search outside? Give me a couple of minutes. Reggie, why don't you look upstairs?'

'No, *you* look upstairs, Mack. *I'll* check the garage for ropes and a car, eh?' This was what Calum actually wanted. The second Benson turned the corner, Calum raced upstairs, scanning the contents of the main bedroom. Then he saw the phone.

Aware he had at best a minute or two, he dialled Shirley's number, waiting six or seven rings before she answered. He spoke as quietly as was feasible. They'd sold the gold? *Fantastic*. Ben was within striking distance of London. What a hero. Breathing deeply, Calum rushed what he had to say, asking her to agree a change of plan. Yes, Ben still to leave the money at the Thomson Motel near Tonbridge. Room booked as Mr Smith, number 15, key to be left at reception? Money to go under the bed as agreed. But could she quickly access her phone to check the specific vicinity of the motel again? Any waste ground, car parks not used, say within half a mile of the motel? Calum waited, hearing noises downstairs. He'd call her back.

'What are you doing up there, Mack?' Chisel shouted from below.

'I'm in the bathroom up here. Give me a break.'

'Well, move it!'

Just as Calum dialled Shirley back, he noticed a car key on the dresser. That almost certainly meant a car in the garage. Shirley answered immediately, breathing heavily. She explained that she'd quickly checked online and there was a large open car park to the rear of a golf range on the north side of Tonbridge, bordering trees. He then suggested that they needed to meet at the trees at the back around 2:30 p.m. He said that if he could use the old man's car, it could provide a focus for his plan. However, when he speedily outlined the plan details, her nerves suddenly became more audible over the phone.

He then asked her to call Aurelia Harley at the FCA, telling her that he'd be in touch…and that he was innocent. Harley seemed his best bet, especially as Douglas Lyndon had mentioned her during his prison visit. Whispering, he then raced though the remaining details of what he needed her to do, emphasising that if he used a specific codeword in a subsequent call it meant that Chisel and Benson were listening and to stick with this current plan despite what he might say in company.

He thrust the phone down just as he heard footsteps thumping up the stairs, grabbing the car key on the dresser the second before the door opened.

'What the hell are you doing in here?' Benson screeched. He glared suspiciously at Calum, before his gaze fell toward Calum's left hand. Calum held up the car key.

'Found this—we're going to need it to go anywhere in the old man's car, aren't we?'

Benson stood nose to nose with Calum, echoing the threatening mannerisms he'd employed in jail. 'I'll be watching you all the way until I get my money.' They locked eyes. 'We tie the old guy up and gag him, and find a phone because we need to make some calls before we leave. We need to check if that gold's been sold and the money's on its way. There had better not be any problems.' Benson then noticed the phone by the bed, holding Calum's gaze suspiciously for a few seconds.

Downstairs, despite Chisel's brute strength, Calum tried his best to ameliorate the effects of the knots used to tie their victim, aware that given the man's age this exercise might actually kill him. He gestured towards the old man while Benson and Chisel were looking elsewhere, signalling apologetically with his arms. The man stared, before nodding; perhaps he understood that Calum was also being coerced. Calum had taken a mental note of the phone number so that he could call the police and have the man freed as soon as practicable. The address of the property was unclear, and the last thing he wanted was an avoidable death on his conscience because of the sheer stupidity of two thugs. After a bizarre and threatening phone call from Benson to his half-brother, Chisel called some other ex-con to enquire about fake passports.

Benson and Chisel then made Calum call Shirley, and he utilised the codeword that they'd agreed to accompany the plan as Benson and Chisel were to understand it. Benson and Chisel heard the name of the Thomson Motel in Tonbridge, together with the room number and the fact the gold had been cashed. Both cheered like football supporters, but Calum knew instinctively that every point of contact with the outside world would surely precipitate the tightening of the net, and he desperately needed the next part of his plan to take shape before official police intervention.

Chapter 20

Aurelia's spirits dipped after she'd parted from Lyndon; almost as if the progress they'd made had evaporated the second Adam had gone. Like a worm, Adam had one special skill: the ability to wriggle out of shit. He might go straight to Telford and claim harassment, which could place the final nail in the coffin of her career. Lyndon promised to assist further, but right then he needed to pick his kids up from school. When he'd mentioned his children, Aurelia had momentarily avoided eye contact. Lyndon might have parted from his own career as a consequence of this whole fiasco, but at least he had a partner and children. Right now, Aurelia felt desperately alone.

As she rode the escalator up from the underground her phone buzzed. Her heart sank; surely this wasn't Telford already? But the caller introduced herself as a friend of Calum Mack, and awaited a response from Aurelia, who was briefly side-footed by the statement, questioning how she'd obtained her personal number.

'Look,' the woman said in a broad East End accent, 'I called the FCA. It took some lies to get your personal number…and for them to tell me that you are off work, what, pending investigation?' This woman had a nerve.

'Who are you exactly? I've had so much trouble lately that I don't know who to trust and an unknown caller is pretty low on the list. Give me one good reason why I shouldn't put the phone down right now.'

'Because Calum was set up, both for the insider trading case, and for the prison break, and he thinks you are aware of this situation. A friend of his is involved…' The woman paused as if checking detail. 'Douglas Lyndon?

Well, he visited Calum in prison and told him he was going to see you. Does that help?'

Aurelia stopped in the street, sheltering in a doorway to avoid the crowds. 'So why doesn't Calum Mack call me himself? He's on the run isn't he? And technically a free man right now.'

'He's under the control of the gangsters who broke him out of prison. They think he has money stashed away in the Caribbean, and they have a gun. He can't call you until he gives them the slip, which I'm about to help him with. I'm going to dress up in a car park in Kent this afternoon—'

'What? This is crazy. Look, all I can say is that I did meet Douglas Lyndon and we uncovered something interesting, though I can hardly tell a stranger on the phone.'

'Calum told me he thought you were straight up and that you'd genuinely look into a miscarriage of justice, but he could only speak to me for a couple of minutes undetected because these guys he broke out with are serious trouble. Watch the news later, would you? If things go to plan, he needs to speak to you. Will you hear out an innocent man later today?'

Aurelia sighed heavily. 'Of course I will.'

Adam Smart wiped his brow, running his fingers through his hair. This was an involuntary, nervous reaction, a cold sweat evident on both his forehead and his hands. He'd called Telford, only for his secretary to answer the call informing him that he'd have to wait until the afternoon to speak to the boss. Adam had often employed the mantra of attack offering the optimum means of defence, yet he'd been thrown by the oblique offensive by Douglas Lyndon, in the street of all places. How could Lyndon know of his indiscretions?

Telford's secretary said he'd briefly be available after 2:00 p.m. and Adam waited at his desk, blocking out his diary until Telford was available. He desperately needed to remain focused in order to inspire confidence and trust, especially if Telford began to ask probing questions. Just after two o'clock Telford's secretary called and Adam made his way into Telford's office.

Sporting a particularly bright floral tie, Max Telford waved Adam into the office as he finished a call. 'What's up?' He checked his watch. 'I can give you five minutes.'

Adam involuntarily cleared his throat, instantly regretting this less than subtle sign of discomfort. 'I was accosted between here and the train station by someone connected to a previous case. I thought I should report it.' Adam had decided to report the problem directly.

Telford viewed Adam carefully through his bifocals, raising his eyebrows inquisitively. 'Who accosted you?'

'Douglas Lyndon. Remember, from the Mack case? The guy from Glasgow.'

'I remember Lyndon. Lucky to get off. What did he say?' Telford viewed Adam squarely, but Adam held his gaze.

'Well, he began to shout at me, and some folk were watching. Said he knew what,' he held up his fingers in inverted comma mode, 'we were up to.' Adam subtly relayed the conversation using the first person plural.

Telford sat back, pursing his lips. 'And what exactly are we up to, Adam?'

'Nothing!' Adam blurted, bumping Telford's desk a little too strongly. 'I mean, Max, this has *really* annoyed me. We work our socks off in here as you know. That case is *closed*. Mack was categorically convicted by the court and is now on the run with a bunch of thugs! We're the *good guys*, and some idiot with misplaced loyalty to a convict has a go at *us*? You couldn't make it up.'

Telford drummed his fingers on the table. 'What else did he say?'

'Nothing really, just some incoherent rant. Bullshit, if you will excuse my language. The man's clearly got a grudge, or is deranged—or both. I just wanted to put you in the picture in case he starts making calls to you or anyone else.'

'Nothing more? Any specific details?'

'Oh, I think he said I'd go to hell, if I remember correctly. Maybe he's a religious freak.'

'And what did you say?'

'Not much at all, I was so taken aback. And then the police arrived.'

'Police?' Telford frowned again.

'Coincidentally.'

'Coincidentally?'

'I mean by accident. There were just, sort of, on their rounds,' Adam said, before Telford suddenly laughed.

'Police? They're never there when you need them, eh? Then they turn up when there's no crime.'

'How true, Max.'

'It sounds as if Lyndon has cracked up. I think he lost his job after Mack's conviction, but we then we happen to know he could have been jailed for supplying sensitive information. You did the right thing, Adam,' Telford said, rolling a fountain pen between his right index finger and thumb. 'We've got to be careful, though. Let me know if he makes contact again—and I mean immediately. If there's another incident we need to nip it in the bud and press charges—remind him that he could be jailed for harassing public officials. Aurelia hasn't done us any favours either, so we need to be squeaky clean, which I take it you are?'

'Of course!'

As Adam departed Telford's office, he swallowed, relieved to have withstood any real scrutiny. Telford had accepted his augmented version of events at face value, even reinforcing the assertion that Lyndon must simply have cracked up, bitter about having lost his job. Right there and then Adam promised himself if he overcame this obstacle he'd never again get involved with a financial criminal, and he knew he'd have to speak to the man one final time to bury the issue for good.

Despite the anger he'd experienced in relation to Calum Mack's escape, and the frustration that had accompanied his compunction to return across the Atlantic, Hawk had slept well on the night flight. After the years in prison any form of voluntary nocturnal accommodation was still a luxury, and he'd imbibed four vodkas before reclining to the maximum in his business class scat. Once his flight landed in the predictable rain, though, the irritation returned as he considered the problem at hand.

While grabbing his luggage, he checked the status of the prison escapees on his phone. Unbelievable. Neither Mack nor his accomplices had been captured, despite police statements about significant resources being invested in a man-hunt. While attempting to compute how the authorities in London could be so inept, he stepped into the heavy downpour to hail a cab to the Hilton on Park Lane. The inside of the cab's windows were steamed up, the condensation synthesised with city grime. As the meter clocked up, the cab driver said nothing but did manage to blast his horn twice and curse other drivers. Welcome to London, Hawk observed, the "lived in city". In Barbados he'd noticed that cars habitually stopped just to let pedestrians cross the road.

After he'd checked into his room on the upper level of the Hilton, Hawk began some research. He'd a couple of items to purchase. After all, he was now a regular traveller using his own passport to go about his personal business and he did not wish to take meaningless risks when subject to the paranoia of modern immigration authorities. There had been no point in risking arrest by using false documentation when a genuine passport would suffice, and apart from the man he was going to see first, no one knew of his involvement with Calum Mack. No one had blinked an eye at customs when he'd arrived, and once he'd finished his business in the country, he expected no one to particularly notice when he left.

But first he had one greedy bastard to visit. And another one to eliminate.

Ben arrived at Watford, exhausted. He'd stopped not far up the M1 at a services area near Luton, afraid to leave the cash Calum's father had received for the gold coins in the car, yet also apprehensive about talking it with him into the cafe. He was officially off sick from the *Sentinel*, something quite rare in the media sector due to the short-term contracts on offer and resultant competition over jobs. However, latent sympathy for Calum and the possibility of a future knockout exclusive story had driven him to assist, and a lie to his employer appeared small beer in comparison to meeting murdering jail breakers. But now he feared this imminent encounter because he'd checked out the crimes of Reggie Benson and Chisel Dekkers on Google.

Whilst munching on a bacon roll at the motorway services he'd received a call from Shirley about a slight change of plan, which he'd queried. Weren't they going to leave the cash in a motel room in Kent as agreed, and just leave them to it? These guys were top of the wanted list. Then she explained the key element of the modified, crazy plan. They were to dress as police officers in an attempt to separate Calum from the other hoods; to detain Calum alone yet somehow not get killed, because, yes, one of the hoods had a gun. So far no one had mentioned actually getting killed, and momentarily Ben refused.

Then Shirley lost her temper, as little sisters sometimes do, intimating that if he was unable to help, she'd do it on her own. How could he contemplate leaving Calum stranded? Fearful of his sibling's wrath, Ben eventually acquiesced, and reluctantly agreed to meet her at Watford, where she would bring the outfits she'd acquired at a fancy dress shop that morning. She'd even instructed him to shave at the motorway services to fit the bill, which he'd done.

When they then met in a Tesco car park in Watford, Shirley insisted on a hug, before explaining that they needed to drive to Tonbridge in advance of Calum and company, ready to intervene at the agreed car park after they'd placed the money in the hotel room. They checked the money in the rucksack Ben had with him, Shirley noting that she'd never seen that much cash before.

Ben, still concerned about the validity of the plan, asked what was to happen to this money—were they simply going to gift it to these hoodlums once they'd accessed the hotel room?

'No, we'll be calling the police.'

'What? This is madness—why would we do that? Why can't he just do that right now? We'll get cornered too, and Calum will be back in jail.'

'No, stupid. We'll be at the golf place, sufficiently far out of the way. It's too early to call the cops now, but we need to do it once we leave the cash. Don't you see? It's a kind of decoy.'

'Yes, it's brilliant,' Ben replied, dripping with sarcasm. 'I've worked with Calum for two or three years and this is as fantastic as his share tips. Christ knows how we'll get through this without being caught. Can we not make the initial rendezvous further away from the hotel room?'

'No, it's all been agreed.' Shirley slapped the dashboard. 'Calum's going to make up an excuse to stop, but he can only do that once they're nearly there, in case they smell a rat.'

Ben looked at her directly. 'You still fancy him, don't you?' When Shirley reddened before looking downwards, he knew the answer to his question. 'Well, I'm sure glad it's common sense and not just lust that's driving this deranged plan.' They then briefly headed north again before joining the M25 east towards Tonbridge. Shirley had abandoned her jeep at the supermarket, though that was the least of her worries. And just for good measure they decided to postpone trying on the fancy dress outfits until after they'd left a five-figure sum in cash at the Thomson Motel.

The old guy moaned, pleading visually with the convicts once more as they left the house. The man clearly feared asphyxiation due to the gag that Benson had secured. Chisel swore at the pensioner and pushed the gun to his head, which quickly silenced him. Benson then gave him the steely eye treatment, explaining in a loud voice that they would return later, and if there was any sign of movement Chisel would cut off the man's balls. Calum winced at the thought, but still managed, almost imperceptibly to signal to the man by shaking his head.

The garage contained a black Jaguar XF, which smelled a little damp inside, perhaps suggesting that it had been resident inside for a while. Chisel immediately said he would drive, but Calum stood back, once again mining the depths of his persuasive powers to influence events.

'No,' he stated firmly, folding his arms. '*I'll* drive.'

'Don't start Mack. You probably drive like a pussy. Give me the keys, I could let this baby rip.'

'Give me the keys.' Calum held out a hand towards Chisel, who then stood staring, the threat of violence once again imminent. Calum held his stare. 'There are three good reasons for me to drive. Number one, if you're in the back seat you're less likely to be recognised by other drivers, cameras or the cops, because you can hide your head from view with your hands. If a driver does that it sticks out like a sore thumb. Surely you don't want to be recognised? As we've already established you're both bigger criminals than me, and thus wanted more by the cops. Number two, I drove not that long ago but you haven't driven for how many years? No offence, but that's an accident waiting to happen, especially if you can't help "letting it rip". And number three: I think I know roughly where I'm going, but if I muck it up it will be *my* fault, not yours, so you two can relax in the back while I take the blame. And yes, I drive like a pussy, so then no one will stop us, okay?' Silently, Benson nodded sideways to Chisel, who grudgingly handed the keys over to Calum.

Calum turned on the ignition, which initially coughed uncomfortably a couple of times before firing up properly. He then turned to the others.

'*Shit*. What about the finger prints?'

'We put on rubber bloody gloves!' Chisel barked.

'But we only put on the rubber gloves once we were *inside*. The old guy probably can't see well, and he's deaf as a post so he didn't hear what we said, so why risk leaving another trail? The cops will start looking for his car at some point, but we could change the plates. But if we left prints on the door handles—'

'Okay!' Benson growled. 'Go and wipe down all the back area. But move it!' Calum ran into the property, but wiped no prints. He already knew that the phone calls they'd made would identify them anyway. Rather, he grabbed a sheet of paper in the kitchen and scribbled a note in large capital letters, and then raced into the toilet, where the man looked petrified. He held an index finger to his lips, before showing the old man the note. The old man frowned, before pleading with his eyes for the gag to be removed. Calum removed the gag, and amazingly, the man remained silent. Calum patted the old guy's shoulder before bolting back out of the house. On the note he'd written: *I'll get you freed as soon as I can. Sorry. I was forced into this.*

When they left the garden, analysing the surrounding houses for signs of observation, it appeared that everyone else in the vicinity was absent. Calum turned on to a B-road of some sort, initially checking the direction of the sun. They were heading generally north, so the sun needed to be roughly to their rear. He subtly checked his watch: 2:15 p.m. Earlier, he'd managed to persuade Benson and the volatile Chisel to wait just a little longer at the house to ensure sufficient time for the money to be delivered, whereas he in reality he feared arriving at the agreed car park too early in case Shirley and Ben weren't ready. That assumed of course that Shirley had been able to convince her brother to engage, which was an 'if'. Initially aware only that they were driving from the south east somewhere, they'd then found an old local map in the house which had helped Calum locate the golf range but not the motel. He needed to find the A21 north, and then follow the A26 round to the north side of the town, which would facilitate a quicker route to the golf range.

They joined the A21 surprisingly quickly, but then encountered a traffic jam at the junction with the A26. Chisel in particular, cursed and gesticulated at every hold up, despite being warned by Benson to take it easy and avoid drawing attention to the occupants of the Jaguar. God only knew what had wired the man the way it had, but whatever combination of nature and nurture responsible for engineering his personality had created a very short fuse indeed.

Then Calum spotted a sign for the golf range ahead, and swallowed involuntarily. The prison break had been traumatic enough, but now, two feet to his rear, Chisel held a loaded gun, and he, Calum, was trying to pull a ridiculous stunt. He'd scarcely had the time or opportunity to figure a suitable ruse to pull in, so he thought: *just go for it.*

'Bastard! I don't believe it!'

'What?' Benson asked.

'Cops! For God's sake, *don't* turn round and look! They're in an unmarked car, two or three back, but I could see them, in uniform.'

As Calum checked in the rear view mirror, Chisel's eyes were darting around from side to side, belying his desperation to look to the rear. Then Benson spoke. 'Mack's right. Don't panic Chisel, and don't look. What else is between us and them?'

'A van and a motor bike. That's why everyone's doing thirty miles an hour. Where can we pull in?' As Calum asked the question, the entrance to the golf place became visible about fifty yards ahead.

'There! Go in *there*. That green sign, *golf range*,' Chisel shouted, pointing ahead. 'Get them off our tail now or I swear I'll use this thing.' The gun nudged Calum's left arm as he changed down gears.

'Okay, okay, Chisel, no problem,' Calum said, hardly able to believe that Chisel had made the suggestion himself. He slowly edged the Jaguar into the car park heading toward the trees at the back where they came to a standstill, engine still running. Calum expelled air. 'Shit, that was close. They've gone, but my nerves are shot through. I need to see that map to check the directions.'

'Give me the map,' Benson instructed. But just as Calum passed the map into the back seat, he spotted two figures in black approaching slowly from behind the trees.

'I don't believe it,' Calum whispered. '*More* cops. Straight ahead. Sit tight.' Calum was only just able to discern Ben's features in the distance under the police hat. Benson then cursed, helping launch Chisel into another incomprehensible ramble of expletives and threats.

'They're coming right towards us!' Chisel spat, slapping Calum on the back of his head. Why the hell did you come in here?' Calum rubbed his head, trying not to lose his cool.

'*You* told me to turn in here, Chisel. Remember?'

'You were driving the fucking car! Look, one of them is pointing right at us…right, the safety catch is off, I mean it…'

Calum turned round to the two thugs in the rear, stone-faced. 'Let me deal with this, *please*. They clearly don't know who we are or they'd be moving more quickly, or calling backup but maybe they've spotted *something*. If I go out and speak to them, maybe I can keep them away from you guys. I'll ask directions or something. There's a chance they won't recognise me, but if they see three wanted convicts together, well…' He pursed his lips, reading Chisel's eyes and then, more particularly, Benson's.

Benson held his gaze. 'Leave the keys in the ignition, Mack, and keep these pigs away from us. One false move and we take them out and maybe you too. And just in case, give me that address again.' Calum passed over the piece of paper with the motel details, and Benson read aloud. 'Thomson Motel, room Number 15. Mr Smith, okay, got it. And Mack, your acting skills had better be fucking perfect.'

Calum left the Jaguar, slowly approaching Ben and Shirley with his back to the car. Despite the gravity of the situation both Ben and Shirley looked like they were actually trying to stifle grins, so Calum attempted, as best he could, to block the view between the Jaguar and the Keystone Cops.

'Hi Calum!' Shirley said enthusiastically.

Ben then grinned, turning slightly away from the Jaguar. 'Calum, you smell like shit. And these jeans are way too tight.' Calum smiled in response before replying.

'Well thank you, Ben. I too love your brilliant disguise. Now please don't go any closer to the car and *please* try not to laugh. They've got a gun and are threatening to use it. Is the money at the motel?'

'Yes,' Ben said sadly. 'After hundreds of miles it broke my heart to leave it, but what are friends for? I'm so knackered from the drive I was tempted to go and blow it on a suite at the Savoy.' Ben then grinned, taking out a note pad. 'Now, given you've probably prepared bugger all here Calum, I'm going to act all cop-like and point all over the place while we quickly decide what will convince them to leave without you.'

Shirley leaned closer to Calum. 'We could tell them that we just heard on the police radio that a drunk driver was just spotted driving away from the scene of an accident on the road out there? You're a potential witness or something. No one got the car number, but we're going to take you to a mobile unit a street away to take a statement. Tell them that you have no choice in the matter without arousing suspicion.'

Calum looked at Ben who in turn clocked Shirley's now quizzical expression. 'You know, that might just work, Shirley. These guys want away from cops. They're both nutters and Chisel—probably chief nutter of the nut tribe—might just go mental if you as much as approach the car, so why not? I say I'll join them after I get rid of you guys. Okay, I'll wave my arms about a little more to make this look authentic, and then I'll give it a go. If they grab me and we take off, well, *don't* call the real cops. If not, though, we call the Met the second they leave. I want these guys locked up.'

Calum pointed to both the road and the trees, before holding his arms in the air as if in exasperation. Ben responded by pointing all over the place. As Shirley and Ben then engaged in postural echo, both standing rigid with arms folded, Calum walked slowly back to the Jaguar.

'Stupid fucking plods! Why didn't they just take a statement over there?' Chisel erupted in character to the ruse, before being calmed by Benson, who was nonetheless viewing Calum cautiously.

Benson then said flatly. 'And that's all they said?'

'Yes.'

'What if they demand your details at the station?'

'Well...I'll give them my brother's details; I'll say I don't have my licence or driver details with me.'

'What if they ask who else is in the car?'

Calum maintained eye contact as he responded. 'My father's old pals? I don't know. Look, this lets you two off the hook. You guys go to the motel and lay low, and I'll walk over there later because it's only a couple of miles away. There's a stack of cash at the motel, and remember, stick with me and there's a ton more in Grand Cayman. Remember, we can use that for the flights. Just stay cool here, okay?' Benson glanced at Chisel, who initially shook his head, but then looked away.

'Chisel, let him go.'

Calum, Shirley and Ben stood motionless as the two thugs drove out of the car park. Then, when they were out of view, Calum spoke rapidly.

'Shirley, this needs to be quick. Can I use your phone? I realise it makes you a more overt accomplice, but I've no choice.' Shirley smiled as if resigned to anything now, and handed Calum the phone, and Ben and Shirley then listened to one half of a conversation. Calum obtained the direct number of one DI Maxwell, and once he'd made contact with the policeman he then spoke quickly, almost without interruption. Maxwell was so stunned to hear from Calum that he accepted his request simply to listen. Calum explained what vehicle Benson and Chisel were driving and where they were headed, and that they were armed and very volatile but motivated to go the motel because of the cash that was hidden there. He briefly reiterated his innocence and frustration at the circumstances that had ruined his life, but then awkwardly explained that an even more innocent man, a vulnerable pensioner—the owner of the Jaguar—was tied up in his home south east of Tonbridge. Calum gave the house phone number and details of the clothes worn by Benson and Chisel. Only when Calum finished did Maxwell try to demand he hand himself in. When this was refused he began to interrogate, but at that point Calum cut the call, conscious that the longer he remained on the line the sooner they'd be surrounded by marksmen.

'Ben, can you take me back to London? I need to get out of here quickly or there might be a roadblock.'

'Why not, Calum? I've just avoided being executed by two murderers so I'm on a high. As long as we pick you up a change of clothes, some deodorant and maybe a wig or something to improve your stinky looks as we drive about the public highway, we might just be able to share a vehicle. Where would sir like to go?'

'To visit Aurelia Harley of the FCA if at all possible. Shirley—did you manage to get hold of her?'

'Yes,' Shirley replied as they drove off.

'What did she say?'

'She's been suspended because of your case—didn't say how—but she actually agreed to help. I think she's also pissed off at the system and she's been talking to your old pal Douglas. She's got some interesting information but didn't trust me enough to speak openly on the phone.'

'That's *brilliant* work Shirley,' Calum said, giving her a hug in the back seat. 'I'm afraid they'll trace this number to you but I can say I stole it from you.' Shirley just laughed, before showing Calum a hairdresser's kit.

'Mr thief, if you don't fancy a wig,' she said, holding up some scissors, 'I can give you a skin-head on the journey back to the city, because right now you must be number one on the most wanted list.' Within seconds, four police cars raced past on the way back into town.

'I owe you guys.'

'I kind of owe you too,' Ben replied. Before Calum could ask why, Ben then quipped: 'I hope no one's trying to have a quiet afternoon kip at the Thomson Motel.'

Chapter 21

Hawk's visit to B&Q had been a bit of a revelation. Not only had these stores changed dramatically during his time inside, but the quality of the nail guns had also improved. He'd selected a top of the range model, with a five year guarantee, not that he'd need to return the product if defective— he simply wanted a 'weapon' that would work, and one which was subject to little in the way of regulatory control. He was just another DIY enthusiast, so to speak. How ironic that although all those years ago at the Teviot student union in Edinburgh his use of such a weapon had been involuntary, he now had no qualms about such direct action.

It was much easier than obtaining a gun.

His contact had initially refused to meet at all, and then, when Hawk had threatened to show up at the man's office or home, only a brief meeting in a non-confined space was offered. So, akin to a spy movie, they'd settled on Hyde Park. How corny, he considered. But although Hawk felt he occupied the driving seat he nonetheless needed just a little more assistance to locate Calum Mack. The meeting was set for 4:00 p.m. He'd one final job to do before the meeting—to post some long overdue photos to a Mrs Tomlinson, a Mrs Wilson, a Mrs Lyndon and a Mrs Rowland.

At around three o'clock he'd stopped at the *Dog and Bell* pub about a mile north of the park simply to enjoy a pint of real ale, something unavailable in the Caribbean and which had been absent from his life whilst in prison. However, he involuntarily spat out his second mouthful as he witnessed the breaking news on the pub's large screen.

The reporter, a young blonde woman clearly eager to dramatise events to the limit, was interviewing eyewitnesses who'd seen police shoot dead two of the most wanted men in the country. One bystander spoke of his incredulity at how events had unfolded, barely able to contain himself as he explained that during the event a suitcase containing thousands of pounds had opened, and notes had blow all over the surrounding area as a shootout with police ensued.

Hawk stood transfixed, awaiting the identities of the two men. *Please let one of them be Calum Mack.* The reporter then asked a female eyewitness to describe the men, clearly fishing for confirmation of the identities which the police had not released. Although officials were clearly relieved that no officers had been injured, protocol nonetheless had to be respected, and full details were being guarded. The witness was however able to describe two men in their *fifties*. No, she hadn't been close during the shootout, but she worked in the Thomson Motel and had seen them check into room 15 earlier on. Yes, that was the very room from which the men had appeared just as the shooting began and she remembered that the room had been booked and paid in advance. A uniformed officer then ushered the woman away from cameras and the reporter continued, speculating with the anchorman in the studio that the two men matched the descriptions of Reggie Benson and "Chisel" Dekkers.

Not Mack.

Inevitably, the reporter then began to speculate regarding the whereabouts of Calum Mack, the City fraudster, who had recently escaped from prison with Benson and Dekkers. An unnamed source had confirmed that the police received a tip-off about the location of those involved, but that there was no sign of Mack. Had he gone his separate way, or was he too at large near the small town of Tonbridge? And where had the two felons killed in this very American-style shootout acquired the thousands of pounds that witnesses had seen being dispersed in the windy conditions at the motel? Had this been received from the same terrorist group that was complicit with the prison escape or had they secured financial assistance from someone else on the outside, or from Mack himself who had been convicted of secreting a seven figure sum? She then explained that another witness had seen local residents picking up bank notes after the shooting had subsided but before police could fully secure the wider area, so it might be unlikely that a specific estimate of the value of the cash would be possible. The anchorman produced an almost imperceptible wry smile in response to this point before reiterating the gravity of the situation.

Hawk cursed again, because although he was aware that the reporter was skirting around sub-judicial matters, the gist of the reportage was probably accurate. A further piece of breaking news then ensued. Police had announced that an elderly man had been found at his rural home near Tonbridge. The pensioner had been bound, but was uninjured. *Three* men matching the description of the escaped cons had apparently captured the man in his own home a matter of hours earlier. So, Mack had been in the vicinity, and had escaped again? Simmering, Hawk headed straight out of the door and then directly towards Hyde Park.

A short, bald man of around sixty who sported bifocal glasses and an unusually bright orange floral tie sat alone on a wooden bench near the north east part of Hyde Park. Despite his seniority and impressive tenure in the financial services sector, where he'd witnessed the effects of Black Mondays and Wednesdays, the dotcom and banking crashes, Euro crises, unregulated greed and the tedious pandering to governments of diametrically opposed ideologies, he was currently experiencing the greatest level of anxiety he could recall during his time in the City.

He checked his Tag Heuer watch for the fifth or sixth time, swivelling his head around for signs of the man's arrival. Witnessing no one, he briefly smiled, albeit with a sardonic pursing of the lips. How could he have been so stupid? He possessed a gold-plated final salary pension in the waiting, and a charming Victorian villa near St Albans. He'd simply wanted more, particularly that tacit offshore account which all the big guns possessed. Perhaps he could blame his predicament on his constant immersion in the greed of those they actually prosecuted at the FCA. Maybe he could blame some horribly unlucky investments of his own. Perhaps he could excuse himself because he knew for a fact that only a tiny percentage of financial crime was actually detected. Certainly his ex-wife, the bitch, was at fault for milking him silly ten years before, or perhaps, at a real push, he could even attribute his actions to latent sympathy for Tom Hawkins' youthful incarceration and the old family connection.

But none of these excuses mattered now, and if he were truthful to himself he'd never actually liked Hawkins or his family, but like many friendships, they'd become entwined years before which had fortuitously engendered a course of action which he now regretted. It was hard to believe that when Hawkins had grown up he used to see him playing in a sand pit over the garden fence.

He then heard a shuffling in the bushes to the rear, and as he turned he witnessed a heavily tanned Tom Hawkins walking towards him and then sitting down, staring straight ahead. He had brought a sports bag with him.

'I've come a long way, so I'm going to get to the point, and you'd better have some answers,' Hawk said flatly. 'I take it that you've heard the news?'

'What news?' Telford asked, looking round.

'Don't look at me, okay? I don't know what planet you inhabit but the bad news, yes the *fucking bad news* is that Mack's pals have been shot by the cops but *he* hasn't. They kidnapped some old guy in Kent but Mack's taken off.'

'What? When did this happen?' Telford pulled out his phone, but Hawk placed his hand over the phone. 'What, you're stopping me having a look?'

'Just *listen*. What matters is that Mack has eluded detection. You were supposed to deal with this problem. Haven't you spoken to the cops about the importance of nailing this guy? Can you not say you're worried he'll come after you for revenge or something?'

'Of course I spoke to the police, but there's only so much I can do.'

'You promised me *no loose ends*, and I stupidly paid you extra money!'

'I provided the initial investment.'

'That returned a packet! What if Mack starts to investigate? If you hadn't been so bloody greedy in asking for extra money, I might just have stayed away, but now this combination of your avarice and incompetence is pissing me off. Can you not get that chick Harley onto this? She looked like she knew what she was doing during the case so maybe she could dig a bit into Mack's life and whereabouts given the cops are so stupid?'

Telford swallowed and then paused momentarily, just sufficient for Hawk to notice. 'What?'

'I can't use her...' Telford stalled again, his nervousness pouring from every pore. Hawk turned to face him directly. 'Why not?'

'She's...suspended. Look, the police will do the job.'

'Why's she suspended? You're hiding something.'

Telford scratched his nose. 'She was digging into...eh, the case. Now look, this isn't really the point.'

'What do you mean by digging into the case? What did she do exactly?'

Telford expelled some air. 'She went to see Rowland at the Energy Department.'

'*What?* And you didn't inform me? This is unbelievable! What did Rowland say? *Nothing*, I presume?' Hawk thumped the handrail on the bench

Telford sighed. 'Rowland called me, threatening all sorts. Not that he knows of our connection, of course. But Harley's off the job, I assure you, and I intend to fire her as soon as her case is heard.'

'Bit bloody late if you ask me! What about the other guy, Adam Smart? The one you were going to use as insurance if something went wrong? Remember, you were the one who insisted I get an extra fake passport with his photo on it so you could implicate him if things went belly up. It sounded like a useless idea at the time but now I'm beginning to wonder if you were simply more aware of your *own ineptitude* than I was.'

As Hawk asked the question, Telford looked down as if contemplating his shoes. 'What is it now?' Hawk asked, anger scorching his voice again.

'Adam, well...he might actually be a problem too.'

'Why?'

'He told me this week that Douglas Lyndon approached him in the street near the office and harassed him about FCA fraud.'

'What?' Hawk leapt up, thrusting a finger directly at Telford. 'What kind of fucking show are you running in there?' An old lady with a terrier on a lead stopped as she approached, suddenly aware of the foul language being deployed.

'Fuck off, dear,' Hawk spat.

'*Keep your voice down,*' Telford said in a loud whisper, but Hawk glared at both the lady, and then Telford, who abruptly turned away. 'Look, you've hardly been perfect yourself. You sent that bloody photo of Mack in Grand Cayman to Harley at our office for starters. That nearly caused problems, but luckily it was overlooked.'

'I needed to push the case forward for the cops in case you guys at the FCA fucked up.'

Telford ignored the point. 'Look, the heat's on for a number of reasons. I can't help it if Mack escaped. How on earth could I know he'd gotten in league with killers and a terrorist organisation? He'll get apprehended, and before you know it he'll be arrested and go down again, and they'll throw away the key this time. You need to calm down, and think rationally. There's no proof of our involvement. Mack may have been initially innocent of any crime, but now he's been involved in terrorism and kidnapping. It'll be an open and shut case. Trust me.'

Hawk then leaned over Telford. 'Trust *you*? You've made a total fuck up of all this. I don't care if we were neighbours when I was a kid, I think you're a buffoon, incapable of being trusted. I shouldn't have bothered contacting you again after all these years. And Mack destroyed years of *my* life, remember? He wasn't bloody "innocent". I want him and the loose ends to disappear.'

'And how are you going to achieve that?' Telford enquired. Hawk gestured towards the sports bag, prompting Telford to raise his eyebrows.

'You've got a *gun*?'

'You could say that,' Hawk said, grabbing Telford's shoulder, their faces now less than six inches apart. 'Obviously I'm going to have to find Mack on my own. And I'm pretty tempted to use what I have here on you right fucking now.'

'People like you are a menace to society!' Both Hawk and Telford jerked their heads to the left as the little old lady who'd passed earlier with the terrier pointed a smart phone directly at the pair. 'I may be old, but I know how to use these things when I see a criminal act.'

Hawk leapt up. 'Give me that phone right now, you old cow.' Hawk's words echoed.

'I certainly will not!' she replied loudly, the volume of the response suddenly acquiring attention from others in the wider vicinity. The woman stared firstly at Hawk, but then at Telford, almost with a hint of recognition, prompting Telford to look in the other direction.

'Everything all right over there?' A man shouted from another park bench, causing Hawk to raise a hand in mock conciliation.

'No problem here!' Hawk said, glaring at the old woman, who had partially lowered her phone and now appeared uncertain as to what to do, backing off a few yards. Teeth gritted, Hawk stood up then locked eyes with Telford, who sat transfixed on the bench. 'I should never have agreed to meet in a public place.' As he began to walk away, he turned and pointed. 'And this isn't the last you've heard from me.'

By the time they'd reached central London, Calum could have qualified as a life model for a Peter Howson painting, the skin-head administered by Shirley—with his head anchored between her legs in the back seat— perfectly complementing the stubble he'd acquired at the abandoned piggery. Calum was now wearing the new clothes they'd bought, complemented by a black cap and a pair of shades. Emotions had been running high, with Ben and Shirley competing for airspace to glean the juicy details of the daring escape from prison and his brief tenure on the run with two serious heavies. Engrossed with the story, they'd temporarily forgotten to check the media for anything that might have occurred at the Thomson Motel.

Then, when they did, the shock struck home.

'*Both of them are dead?* Just like that?' Calum expelled air. 'It's scarcely an hour and a half ago when we left them. Bloody hell…I caused their deaths.' He suddenly held his head in his hands, and Shirley reacted by placing an arm round him.

'It's not your fault, Calum—these guys were scum. You'd no choice. They could have turned their gun on you, would you rather that?'

'I don't know…it's just, well so sudden.'

'Shirley's right, Calum,' Ben then said, before slapping the dashboard. 'Shit, man, that was close, but you're okay—that's the most important thing. But look, buddy, it's going to be no time before the Shirley connection is made if they analyse the phone calls. I'm not trying to get rid of you, but you need to find somewhere to hide. Sorry mate.' Calum nodded at Ben in the rear view mirror, acknowledging the validity of his remarks. He was a dangerous commodity to be in company with, one that could only threaten the lives and freedom of those around him.

'Good point, Ben. Look, you guys have helped save my ass and I owe you big style, but I need to contact Aurelia Harley.' Shirley responded by offering Calum her phone once more, but he shook his head. 'You've already called her once using that phone, which might just be passed off as research on your part. But if I call her on the phone and Maxwell and company start looking at call linkages right now, it's not going to help, particularly as she'd suspended. I can only hope that she's really on my side, though, and if she's seen Douglas Lyndon that's promising. I think she's my only hope. Did she say where she lived?'

'Sure, and I got her date of birth and national insurance number too. Calum, I didn't get that far. Remember, you were holed up at the time.' Shirley smiled comically, before they all erupted with guffaws, the tension mildly erased.

Despite the heavy traffic they agreed to let him off near Blackfriars tube station, Ben lending him £300 in cash. Calum gave them both brief hugs before cutting loose.

As Calum observed them disappear into the traffic he considered that despite returning to a city of over eight million people, he'd never felt quite so alone.

Keeping his head low, he walked up Blackfriars Road before turning right down Southwark Street. Within seconds he passed an electrical store displaying televisions, his attention suddenly pinched by the mug shots of Benson and Chisel displayed on Sky News. From the street he couldn't hear the commentary, but guessed at the general content. Just as he considered whether his own name was being broadcast, his own photograph appeared on screen. Instinctively, he lowered the dark cap, turning away. Three or four hundred yards down the street he then spotted what he was looking for—a bespoke mobile phone store. Inside, he spoke to a sales assistant in a fake Yorkshire accent, one which he could pull off as he'd once rehearsed such for weeks for a comedy skit at university. The young man chatted briefly about alternative products before Calum selected one model and asked if he could make a test call outside on the street, as he wanted to test the audibility with a high level of ambient noise. The assistant explained that they did not normally permit phones to leave the store, so Calum stuffed a twenty pound note into the man's hand, explaining that he would remain in view outside the store. The assistant hesitated before being distracted by another customer, so Calum grabbed the opportunity to step into the street and dial the number Shirley had given him for Aurelia Harley.

After three or four rings Aurelia answered, and Calum identified himself. 'I must be insane talking to you,' Aurelia responded curtly. 'Do you know how much this thing has escalated? It's all over the media.'

'I'm desperate, Aurelia, and I've nowhere else to turn.'

'You could just turn yourself in.'

'I'd be hammered if I did that right now.' Aurelia didn't reply, so Calum continued. 'The friend of mine who you spoke with earlier told me you'd promised to help.'

'That was before two men were shot dead and a pensioner was kidnapped.' A brief silence ensued and the sales assistant inside the store beckoned Calum back inside through the shop window. He frowned, using a wavering hand as if assessing the validity of the signal. He then turned away from pedestrians, aware of the potential for eavesdropping.

'Look Aurelia, I was the one who called the cops. These thugs forced me to escape prison with them and *they* kidnapped the old guy, not me. I think he's free now anyway because I called the cops and told them where he was. I hear that you're suspended.'

The responding sigh was actually audible despite the ambient street noise. 'Yes, on your account. Where are you exactly?'

'Southwark Street. I'm sorry, but are you at home? I've nowhere else to go.' There was another gap in the conversation and then, when he pleaded once more, Aurelia gave him her address just as the sales assistant appeared from the shop. Calum then handed the phone back, saying, 'No, pal, I don't think that phone would work well on the Dales, what with the wind and all that. But keep the twenty as a tip.'

Despite the hour, Calum sought to find a cab to take him over the river to Broadwick Street in order to reduce the possibility of recognition that might prevail on the tube. His face would potentially be appearing on several thousand phones alone round the centre of the city and one eager beaver might scupper his chances of survival. Once he hailed a taxi, he kept his cap down low to avoid eye contact, grunting to the driver in his recently practised Yorkshire accent. The driver even managed to bring up the shootings in Kent, opining that the cops were quite right to 'blow these guys away'. Then, when Calum agreed, he was confronted with a further opinion: 'that other guy should have been strung up too—these City crooks are what brought the economy down, mate. Cost me thousands in lost fares, the bastards.'

At Broadwick Street he buzzed Aurelia on the security entry system whilst clocking that she lived in a pricey part of a notoriously expensive city. Perhaps she shared a flat with a boyfriend, though she'd not mentioned anyone when he'd called and then, subconsciously, he recalled seeing no wedding band on her hand at their first meeting.

'Up you come.'

As she opened her apartment door upstairs, he immediately took in the azure eyes, recalling how even though they'd been adversaries something subtle had passed between them when they'd locked eyes on their first encounter at Canary Warf. There was also some warmth, her generous lips displaying a slight upward curl at the sides. She wore light blue jeans and a white wool sweater, complemented by a subtle fragrance—was that *Knowing*? After three days without a shower it smelled fantastic. Once inside the apartment, Aurelia took his jacket and led him into the lounge, which appeared luxurious to Calum after Wandsworth and the old piggery building.

'Would you like to shower?' Aurelia enquired, having noted his stubble.

'You're an angel. Yes, that would be fantastic.'

When he emerged from the bathroom ten minutes later, Calum complimented the flat, noting three Vettriano prints above the fireplace. 'Nice pad. Hey, the FCA must be paying well these days.' As he spoke, she glared at him before he apologised. 'Sorry, it's none of my business and I, eh, appreciate that your job has been difficult if you've been suspended.' He coughed. 'How did that happen?'

'I went see your old university buddy Rowland in Whitehall. Tried to rumble him, and he called my boss to complain.'

'So you were only trying to get to the truth?' She nodded sadly, and he then eagerly accepted the offer of a coffee and a sandwich.

'This is *so good*,' Calum mumbled, his mouth half-full. 'I really appreciate what you're doing here, because this whole thing's been a total nightmare. These thugs have just been shot dead by the police...it still hasn't sunk in. And you actually helped convict me and yet I've never really had the chance to fully explain my innocence face to face since we first met at the FCA. Do you believe me now?'

Aurelia swallowed, slowly contemplating the arrival of her new guest. 'Yes, I do actually. And I'm sorry for your ordeal. You've obviously been through a pile of crap.' She tucked her calves under her thighs on the armchair. 'I guess that I've just be so absorbed in my own predicament that I've overlooked how hellish this must have been for you. I had some doubts about your case previously, but ultimately the evidence looked so overwhelming that I went with the tide. There are all these targets at the

FCA and they're obsessed with convictions. Who were the friends who helped rescue you?'

'Ben—my former colleague at the *Sentinel*—and his sister, who tracked you down. Their brother Martin was actually my lawyer at the trial so they've really been great as a family, and they've taken a huge risk by association. But then so have you by having me here right now.' Calum spoke softly, simultaneously slurping his coffee. 'Sorry, but this coffee's so welcome. So, what made you change your mind? Shirley said you'd been speaking to Douglas Lyndon and had something to tell me that was important.'

Aurelia held his gaze for three or four seconds before speaking. 'Do you remember a guy called Tom Hawkins from when you were at Edinburgh University?'

Calum frowned before putting down his mug and leaning forward in his chair. 'Tom Hawkins? *Hawk*? Well, that's what we called him. Douglas told you about him?' Aurelia nodded before Calum spoke again. 'Yes, of course I remember him, though I've tried to erase him from my memory over the years. What about him?'

'I searched the archives from the Edinburgh press.'

'Then you'll know he's serving life for murder.'

'He's been out for a while, and Douglas pointed me in his direction. In fact, Douglas said he almost mentioned him to you when he saw you in Wandsworth.'

'He never said a thing. But Hawkins is out of prison?' Calum scratched his cheek, considering the news, though Aurelia waited until Calum stopped chewing.

'Oh, hang on a minute.' Calum looked towards the ceiling and ran his fingers though his hair, suddenly accessing a kaleidoscope of memories and consequences. 'Douglas thinks that Hawk—*Hawkins*—was my mystery share tipster?'

'Pretty much.'

'*Bloody hell*. This isn't easy to digest. I mean the man was still in jail as far as I was aware, a distant memory—history. I've deliberately blocked him out over the years. He killed an old man with a nail gun at point blank range…' Calum tailed off, memories of the event flooding back.

'I read about it. Pretty gruesome.'

Calum nodded. 'The voice of the guy who made the calls to me was unrecognisable, nothing like Hawkins. Are you sure? Why did Douglas consider him after all this time?'

'Revenge and opportunity. He was probably using some kind of voice modification app. Douglas said that Hawkins detested the whole group, but you in particular. So there's a definite motive. But all of your group were open to blackmail—he apparently set up some sort of fake underage sex sting and took pictures, and you provided the perfect fall guy because of your role at the *Sentinel*.'

Calum sat back, arms behind his head, the consequences filtering in. 'This was the blackmail thing they mentioned in court. I take it that you have some sort of proof?'

'Pieces of a jigsaw more like. But there's a lot more to it.'

'Jesus, can I have more coffee? Or do you have anything stronger?'

'Whisky?' Aurelia asked, and when Calum nodded she went into the kitchen and brought out a bottle of Bowmore 15 year-old malt, pouring two generous measures.

'You drink whisky?'

'Yes. My mother's father was Scottish, originally from Islay. He was a blender at Bowmore distillery before he moved over the water to work for Jameson in Dublin. He bought me a bottle of Bowmore malt on my 18th birthday, believe it or not.'

Impressed, Calum sniffed the contents of the glass. 'This is a tonic. Nice stuff, peaty. You'll like this because you've some West Highland blood, then.'

'You could say that. But look, there's much more you need to know. Ken, a retired policeman who was an old friend of my father's, helped track Hawkins down. He's been holed up in Barbados—in Sandy Lane, the place the top footballers go.'

'So Hawk's been living it up?'

'Yes. How could a recently released prisoner afford that? You see, the Caribbean provides three connections. First, the whole Black Isle scam in Grand Cayman that helped convict you, because Hawkins *knew* where you were originally from. Second, because my father's old friend found a forger that Hawkins had known in jail who produced fake passports for him after he was released…one of which bore the name Calum Mack.'

Calum leapt of from his chair. 'That's dynamite for me! If you have details of a fake passport, it could prove…that *I didn't make* that withdrawal in George Town.'

'We don't have the details, I'm afraid, and the forger's now taken off.'

'Taken off where?'

'We don't know.'

'That's unbelievable. Just when there's a break…'

'But look, there's a third Caribbean connection that helps leave a trail. There was one further trade made via a broker out there based on inside information that was acquired beforehand from Douglas Lyndon—a company that builds power plants. The initial share deal was worth a million in sterling, but it occurred *after* you were jailed, and can ultimately be traced to him as Hawkins is actually using his own identity over there. That was what really confirmed your innocence.'

Calum slouched back into the arm chair. 'So it wasn't enough for the greedy bastard to set me up and make a pile, he actually came back for more assuming that the trail was cold after I was jailed?'

'Sums it up.' Aurelia sipped the malt, swirling its contents in the crystal glass. 'And you're not going to believe this. Hawkins—Hawk as you call him—has just come back here. He flew into London within the last 24 hours. Why exactly, we don't know, but it's very possibly connected to your escape.'

Calum swallowed, absorbing this new accumulated data. 'You know, I've had recurring nightmares over the years about Tom Hawkins and the nail gun he used that night. That's why I've tried to block him out—therapy, you might say. We all agreed never to talk about it again after the trial. Fresh start, and all that. He was a menace, a loner. We testified against him, dressing it up a bit but only because he deserved it. I never considered him during this disaster, because all that happened more than fifteen years ago and I thought he was still in prison. And the other guys, well, afterwards we mainly drifted apart. But if you're right about Hawkins and the police can reopen the case, there's still a couple of missing pieces in your jigsaw.'

Aurelia looked directly at Calum. 'My father was a cop in Dublin, so I know there are antecedents to all parts of a crime. Are you wondering how I began to investigate the case in the *first* instance? How was the FCA given the scent?'

'Exactly.'

'Adam Smart, my colleague, is almost certainly the weak link. Excuse my language, but he's a total arsehole. I hadn't even mentioned that I went to the FCA with Douglas Lyndon, and we kind of ambushed Adam outside. And when challenged, he was rumbled. We didn't get an admission, but we noised him up.'

'Sounds like the Douglas I knew. But why this guy Smart? Being an arsehole isn't enough because I'm sure there are lots of them at the FCA.'

Aurelia bit her lower lip before eventually smiling. 'There was a time in the past that I'd have been annoyed by that comment.'

'Sorry...'

'It's okay. I guess from your perspective you have a point. Why Smart? He was hovering over my computer one day when I was digging into the case and I immediately reported this to the director, Max Telford, but to no avail. And get ready for this—the forger who produced a fake Calum Mack passport *also* produced a fake passport with Adam Smart's photo on it.'

Calum shook his head. 'That's compelling. So Smart alerted you in the first instance, you know, to dig into this case? There had to be a lead, a push from somewhere.'

Aurelia looked upwards, searching for her earliest recollections of the case. 'I can't actually remember Adam being involved really early on. I tried to keep him at a distance because he's stolen cases in the past. No, if I remember correctly, I first looked at a new website I'd been recommended which details big City deals.'

'Who suggested the website, Smart?''

Aurelia looked down, frowning. 'Max Telford, actually. Yes, Telford. He told me specifically to look at this new site, and the lead story of the day was about Walltex, which kicked off my investigation.'

'So why would Telford recommend that site on that particular day?' Calum stared at Aurelia.

'I see where you're going. Telford may have suspended me, but he's straight as an arrow. Adam Smart is the man. He must have alerted Telford.'

Just then, the security entry system buzzed, Calum's eyes darting to the door. 'Are you expecting someone? Your boyfriend?'

Aurelia shook her head. 'Probably for someone else in the block, happens all the time.' She went into the hall and buzzed back. 'Who is it?'

'Ms Harley, DI Maxwell from the Met, with DS Robson.' Aurelia froze, momentarily unable to respond. Maxwell continued. 'You may remember that we partnered on the Mack case a few months ago? I wonder if we could have a quick chat?'

Chapter 22

With the theatricality of pantomime farce, Calum was thrust into a walk-in wardrobe in Aurelia's bedroom. In the minute or so they possessed before the cops arrived at her door, Aurelia rapidly outlined typical police procedure to Calum, having absorbed quite a bit during her youth. What if the police had a warrant? Technically, as Maxwell had requested entry at the *bottom* without mentioning a warrant, then they could be denied subsequent entry at the apartment door.

When the duo arrived at the door, no such warrant was mentioned and Aurelia played dumb and permitted the cops to enter her home. Calum attempted anxiously to listen to the ensuing conversation in the lounge, but fearful of standing on a creaky floorboard, he failed to move far from the wardrobe itself so he could only ascertain snippets. Then he heard some salient words. *Shirley's call to Aurelia.* Of course. And other calls to and from Shirley from a phone which had apparently belonged to either Benson or Chisel.

Shit, Calum thought. Everyone who helped him was going to be charged while he sat in a wardrobe on top of a pile of knickers.

Aurelia's voice remained quiet and steady, but then she became more forceful. Yes, she had been suspended, and yes, she happened to have received a call from some unknown female. No, she would not divulge what was said. Wise girl, Calum thought, because Aurelia did not know what Shirley might say if questioned separately. And *yes*, Aurelia did believe there had been a miscarriage of justice and that Calum Mack was innocent.

Unfortunately, one of the policemen guffawed loudly at this point, precipitating the movement of conversation towards the hallway.

'There's no need to be hostile, Ms Harley. We're on the same side, you know,' Maxwell stated in that flat police tone in which officers take classes.

'Look, my father was a detective in the Irish police. I'm not being hostile and you know it. But I will stand up for what is right, and I predict that you'll be apologising to me when the whole story comes to light.'

'Well…if you receive any more calls, let us know,' Robson offered.

'Somehow I think you'll know what calls I receive at the same time I get them. Good evening officers.'

Both Robson and Maxwell remained silent until they exited the door entry system onto the street. 'She's hiding something,' Robson said as they crossed the street towards the unmarked car. 'When we asked if she'd had contact with Mack, she deliberately looked me in the eye, unblinkingly. *Too* directly. That's an attempt at concealment.'

The two then sat in the car. 'Today has been a whirlwind. What do we know, so far?' Maxwell asked.

Robson began to count using his fingers. 'We have two dead scumbags. That's the good news. We know for a fact that the phone found at Tonbridge today had been used to call Mack's pal's sister, Shirley. She's been grilled and is gumming up, but we can keep her in for a bit before we officially charge her. We know that the same phone was also used to contact Mack's aunt in the north of Scotland. The force up there is going to speak to her. We also know that Shirley called her brother Ben more than once—and that he took time off work unexpectedly, but thankfully we've just got hold of him so he's being questioned as we speak. But Mack also called us to tip us off about the motel in Kent. That counts in Mack's favour, but we'll park that for the moment. Shirley also called Aurelia Harley, who's also clamming up. She's suspended, and for good measure no one at the FCA had a clue earlier on where Max Telford was. That sum it up?'

Maxwell nodded. 'It would really help if we had the full details of why Aurelia Harley was suspended. Telford might just have sneaked an afternoon off, but it does seem a little odd that this has happened today, especially as he's so connected to this case. His secretary seemed very clear when I called her, and she said he'd cancelled his appointments, and unusually, not given any explanation of where he was going. I'd asked them earlier at the station to try Telford again. Let's see if they've had any joy.' Maxwell called in and made the relevant enquiry, before listening to the response, Robson observing his colleague's facial expression.

Maxwell shook his head. 'That was Brooks. He says they still can't trace Telford. However, get this. Some old lady called at the Hyde Park station and reported that she'd seen Max Telford being attacked at the park earlier on this afternoon. They called us as there's an alert out regarding a number of leads in the case, and his name is now flagged too. This old dear said she recognised Telford as she used to work in the City and follows the market as a hobby. Bit strange, but we'd better follow it up.'

Aurelia watched from above as Maxwell and Robson drove off. 'They've gone, but they'll be back. I don't think Robson believed me when I said I'd had no contact with you. Next time they'll have a warrant.'

'I'll go, Aurelia.'

'We'll go.'

'We? Look, I've gotten enough people in trouble in these past few days. I'll think of something.'

Aurelia held his gaze. 'Calum, right now I'm on no charges but as I'm suspended I'm free to go wherever I want. And if I can help solve your problem, then maybe I can solve my own. If I stay here they could turn up and arrest me. What use is that to any of us?' She smiled, and held out her hands, and he returned the gesture.

'Have you a car?' Calum enquired.

'I have access to a car. I don't own it, which is even better because no one knows that except the owner and me. My neighbour across the hall left just days ago to go home to New Zealand for three months and she asked me to take her car for a spin now and again while she's away. I'm insured and it's in an underground car park just three streets away.' Calum gave her the thumbs up, before explaining that it might be worth packing an overnight bag just in case. And did she have any cash, per chance? She raised her eyes upwards, asking if there was anything else he wanted, and at this point he replied, suggesting a phone, but not one belonging to Aurelia.

Aurelia bit her tongue. 'My neighbour has a second mobile in her flat. I saw it when I checked the place last week. But taking it would be stealing—she asked me to drive her car, which is different.'

'I'd take the rap. I was squeaky clean before I went inside, oddly enough, but after what I've been through this would be trivial.' Aurelia gave in, and quickly accessed her neighbour's flat and took the phone, which they agreed to charge up in the car.

They proceeded cautiously from the building, checking for any potential observers. Calum once more donned his cap and coat, keeping his head lowered as they walked. When they reached the underground car park, and located the black Golf, Aurelia asked the obvious question. 'Where exactly are we going?'

'Where does Max Telford live?'

'Telford? I don't know if that's a good idea. I'm suspended, and our last conversation was far from pleasant. What if he just calls the police?'

'I think he's our best bet, Aurelia. He's got clout with the cops and he's going to look stupid if we subsequently prove my innocence. You and I both need his support.' He suggested that they get into the car rather than discuss the issue in the open.

Aurelia sighed as she drove up the ramp on to street. 'Telford lives in St Albans. Well, a small village outside actually.'

Calum tapped her on the arm. 'Could you stop the car for a minute?' Aurelia frowned but pulled over to a free space beside a convenience store. 'St Albans, Hertfordshire?'

'Is there another one?'

'No, I don't think so.'

'Well?'

'Hear me out. This is a long shot. He doesn't, per chance, happen to live in Bricket Wood, the naturist place? It has nudist conventions and stuff like that.'

Aurelia bit her lower lip, nodding. 'Yes, that's exactly where he lives. How did you know that? Are you a secret nudist?'

'No, but I might know a limerick about Bricket Wood. Want to hear it?'

'What? This is a bit off the wall, Calum. We're being chased by the Met who you tipped off about two convicts. They've now been shot dead, and you want to recite poetry?' He nodded. 'Oh, what the hell,' Aurelia said, watching as Calum looked up, searching for the correct words.

There once was…was…a dick from Bricket,
Whose arse, you'd just want to kick it.
But these guys from the Wood,
They're all in the nude,
So forget him, he's just a thicket.

Aurelia stared. 'That's a load of crap. Did you just make it up?'

'No, that was a limerick someone made up at Edinburgh University.'

'So who is the dick?'

'Tom Hawkins. *He* was from Bricket Wood.'

'What?'

'What, indeed. How long's Telford lived there?'

Aurelia held out her hands. 'I think he's originally from there, family goes back.'

'He was there twenty years ago, then?'

She stared at him. 'Yes…I think so. I've been to his home a couple of times for Christmas parties. The village is quite small, three thousand, maybe four. He lives in Ross Street, the first house on the street if I remember correctly.'

'That's unbelievable. *Hawkins* came from Ross Street.'

She screwed up her face. 'This is a wind up, surely? How can you recall a detail like that? I thought you'd didn't get on with this Hawk guy.'

'I can picture the address on a blue course folder he had all those years back. I've a partial photographic memory, and "Ross-Shire" is where I'm from. Black Isle, remember? It may be the best part of twenty years ago, but I remember talking about it specifically at the time.'

Aurelia held her head in her hands. 'I can't believe this...Telford and Hawkins lived in the same *street*? They were *neighbours*?'

Then they shared a look before Calum spoke. 'Telford's in on this. The odds against anything else are massive. And think about it—when he recommended that website to you I bet he knew you were an assiduous investigator who would spot a lead a mile away. Am I right?' Calum shook his head.

Aurelia took a deep breath, biting her index finger. 'Something else has just come back to me. I met Max Telford for lunch the day I first told him what I'd discovered about Black Isle. He gave me an odd look...which I interpreted as an almost imperceptible glint of pride in *my* work. But now I know what that look meant. It was an almost imperceptible look of pride in *his* work. No wonder he wants to fire me—I'm the only one who wants to re-open the case. Shit, what a set up. You, and me too. Look Calum, why not just turn yourself in? Surely they'd listen now?'

'No one listened to me before. No one listened to you either, and you were *in* the system, Aurelia. I heard that cop laughing at you in your flat. Our best bet is to confront those involved directly. *Then* we can call in the cops. It might be rush hour, but we need to find the best route up to the M1 and see if we can visit Telford. If we get no joy there then I think we should head north where there's less chance of me being spotted. Can I use that phone to contact my aunt?'

Calum dialled his aunt's number for the second time since the prison escape, aware that there was now a greater risk of Jessie's detection should Benson's phone have been found. Jessie answered and explained that the police had visited but that she'd simply told them that Calum had passed on a message through someone else to say he was all right. Calum smiled at his aunt's acuity, particularly for a pensioner, and explained that he was likely heading home—possibly the following day—and could she subtly inform his parents? Jessie said she'd witnessed no current physical police surveillance and promised to pop along the road and break the news to the Macks. Aurelia followed the gist of the conversation and by the time Calum had hung up she'd programmed the Sat-Nav for Ross Street, Bricket Wood.

Hawk had taken quite some time to cool off after his meeting with Telford. Aware that he'd been filmed on someone's phone engaging in a pubic altercation with the man, he'd marched off in the opposite direction to that of Telford. Hawk had wanted to punch the old lady and stamp on her phone, though such a course of action might have courted disaster if the other bystanders had been drawn in. As he'd exited Hyde Park, he cursed his decision to go there. Briefly, he had downed another two pints of real ale in the first pub he encountered, considering his options. Should he simply board the first flight back to Barbados, or was he man enough to finish the job? News feeds continued to show details of the shootings at Tonbridge, intercut with photos of that bastard Mack, though at this point he disliked Telford nearly as much as Mack. The man was greedy, and demonstrably incompetent. And worse, he was beginning to crumble, Hawk could tell. Hawk had witnessed substantially tougher individuals in prison squealing to the screws the minute something went wrong, and if the heat was turned up, Telford could simply squeal.

But Telford was not the primary reason he'd come back. He needed to find a man that even the police could not locate. And within five minutes he'd found a means of potentially achieving what he wanted by searching online. Calum Mack's parents, it turned out, were alive and well and still housed nicely in the Black Isle.

Hawk's call to the Macks proved more enlightening than he'd expected. He'd told them that he was a special investigator with the FCA and was interested in re-opening Calum's case. Hawk could tell instantly that Calum's father had had some kind of contact with his son since his escape because the tone of this voice wavered noticeably when Hawk asked the question. He could almost touch the hope and expectation in the man's response to the ruse, so he told him he'd like to visit them, but that they mustn't discuss this topic with anyone, not even their son if he called, because it might jeopardise the case. Hawk grinned when he ended the call. How gullible were these people? Within a further three minutes he'd booked the last fight of the day to Inverness.

Several thoughts raced through Max Telford's mind as he stuffed clothing and other essentials into a large suitcase. Number one was panic. His home suddenly seemed a transitory place as he packed, a lifetime of memories interspersed with practical fear. Not least in his thoughts was how irrational he'd become during his latter tenure at the FCA. He mainly blamed his ex-wife, that cynical cow who'd virtually cleaned him out. She'd barely worked a day in her life yet she'd left him with only half a future pension and a house that had originally belonged to his parents. He still paid her bills monthly. One or two unlucky investments a couple of years before had left him with no savings and a depleted income until he retired. If rationality had played a more prominent role in shaping his current actions, though, he'd have almost certainly been better off retaining the reduced pension and house rather than being lured by the prospect of easy gains through Tom Hawkins' plan. At least he had the money from that, stashed away overseas.

But fear of being caught was now over-riding greed.

Hawkins' plan had nearly worked, but for the nagging persistence of Aurelia Harley. How ironic that his former protégé had provided the investigative nous to pick away at a closed lock. Pick, pick, pick. He'd originally liked Aurelia, but now she was simply reminiscent of his ex-wife—a meddler. All it would take was for the police to interview her—and she now owed him no loyalty—and parts of the puzzle would be plugged. Calum Mack was now also on the loose, and Adam Smart had warned him that one of Mack's old pals implicated in the case, Douglas Lyndon, had harassed him in public. What exactly did Lyndon know, and might he speak to the police?

If Hawkins appeared on the police radar due to his imbalanced actions, the connection between himself and Mack would be made, and then his relationship with Hawkins would be identified. And in any case, now that Hawkins was back in the country, he sensed that he would come after him again, which was too great a risk. Hawkins was unstable and had threatened nothing less, and this was a man who'd tasted blood before. Hawkins, by definition, also knew exactly where he lived. How foolish he'd been to venture into a pact with such an individual. It had just seemed like very easy money.

Telford checked his watch, nervous about how long he could safely remain at home. While he packed, paranoia took centre stage. He'd even switched off his phone for the afternoon so as to avoid distractions from the office as he planned his exit. He'd concluded that the safest thing was to cut his losses and disappear before either Hawkins turned up with vengeance in mind or the shit hit the financial fan. Geneva at least held some promise, the numbered account opened with Hawkins' payments offering an escape route of sorts. Unfortunately, all remaining flights between London and Geneva had been full for the evening, so he'd booked a flight with Swiss International the following day, and, for peace of mind, a room at Heathrow.

Then, as he placed an old photograph of his parents in the case alongside one of his favourite floral ties, he distinctly heard a car pulling into the driveway. Momentarily, he froze. Then, in a delayed reaction he sprang up. Who the hell was at his home at seven o'clock on a Friday night? He moved towards the front window, subtly looking down to see a dark VW Golf backing up towards the front door. He'd never seen the vehicle before.

Then, as he backed away from the upstairs window, a car door clunked shut, and a few seconds later the front of the house door shuddered with a repeated, heavy knock. He then listened as the door handle was turned. Thankfully it was locked.

Telford felt panic sweeping through his body. Could it be Hawkins, the persistent bastard—or even the police in an unmarked car? Grabbing the suitcase, his car key, passport and wallet, he ran down the back staircase of the Edwardian villa—the same one he and his brother had used to fool pals when they'd played hide and seek as children. This staircase took him to the conservatory which offered an alternative route from the building towards his car. He'd parked his six-series BMW about a hundred yards down the road, just in case of this sort of eventuality.

As quietly as he was able, Telford unlocked the conservatory door and ventured outside towards the side garden. There, he could hear voices emanating from the front of the house, but had difficulty discerning much detail because of other ambient noise. Then he heard what sounded like a male, Scottish accent. He pushed the conservatory door shut, before realising that the key was lodged on the inside. Instantly, he realised that opening the door again from the outside would probably precipitate enough noise to alert those at the front of his presence.

He cursed inwardly, realising that he'd have to leave the side door open. Oh, what the hell, maybe he'd never be back.

Telford then exited his back garden through the gate that connected to an old pathway running between Ross Street and the street to the rear. As he laboured with his full suitcase along the pathway, he missed the footsteps and accompanying voices approaching the side conservatory door. Telford was on a mission, and only when he reached his BMW did he look back to check that no one had followed. He'd known too many financial criminals who should have cut and run before they were nailed. It had proved to be an inglorious departure from his home, but at least he was possession of an airline reservation and some resources for a new life far away.

'Place looks empty, but he might show up at any point. What car does he drive? Something expensive to go with the house?' Calum spoke quietly as they ventured round the side of Telford's home.

'He's got a top of the range BMW.'

'Figures. Maybe we could offer him a welcome party if we can get inside. This could be the second time I've broken into a house today. Bloody hell.'

'It's hardly as if he's going to leave the doors open. And there will be an alarm too, don't you think?'

Calum shrugged at the logic, before trying the handle of the conservatory door to the side of the house. Unexpectedly, the door opened without argument. Calum smiled before whispering. 'What, this guy chases millions in fraud every year, but he leaves doors unlocked? And the front door was locked, and nobody answered when we knocked.' This time Aurelia shrugged in response, and they both entered the house cautiously, listening for any signs of human presence.

Nothing.

'Hello!' Calum shouted.

'*Calum!*' Aurelia barked in a loud whisper, but silence prevailed.

'Well, we've confirmed that Telford is just an absent minded householder. Alarm off, door open.'

Cautiously, they checked the lounge before heading upstairs. Then, on the top landing Aurelia pointed towards an open bedroom door. 'Look at that,' she whispered. Clothing and some toiletries were strewn all over the carpet.

'I think that you can stop whispering now,' Calum suggested, before Aurelia pointed out the coat hangers lying around the room, and drawers left open. Two or three floral ties lay loose on the bed.

Aurelia then made an observation. 'He's gone somewhere in a hurry. Having worked with the man for several years I can tell you he's the ordered, meticulous type. If he's left stuff discarded all over the place then it's out of character. Let's look downstairs.'

They ventured into the kitchen, and Aurelia noticed water spilled on the surface beside the kettle. She then touched the kettle, reacting to the heat.

'Hot?'

'Not long boiled. He must have just left. But where?'

'Look at this.' A pad lay on the kitchen table, with scribbled notes. That his handwriting?'

'Yes.' She pointed to number and digits. 'LX359...and does that say 1200? A flight number and time?' Aurelia grabbed her phone and quickly accessed a flight app she sometimes used. 'It's the code for Swiss Airlines. What do you reckon, midday? Tomorrow? I mean, if the kettle's not long boiled it can't have been today.'

'Doesn't look good. Bastard's taken off right enough. It's too much of a coincidence, going to the home of dirty money at our expense.'

'I'm going to call a colleague at the office. Give me a second.' Aurelia walked into the hall and phoned Jen Hoffman at the FCA. Rather than listening in, Calum wandered around a bit, still taking in the unexpected circumstances of his newfound liberty—the escape, Benson and Chisel's demise, and his own complicity in a kidnapping. After a couple of minutes Aurelia appeared.

'That was Jen in the office. She's one of the good guys. It turns out that Max Telford's secretary had a bit of a problem this afternoon. The police called at the office later on this afternoon, but Telford's been missing since late morning. His secretary is very straight so she wouldn't have lied to the police. I think you're right and he's taken off. We can't go to Heathrow ourselves. You can't risk that, unless you now want to hand yourself in?' Calum shook his head in response. 'Then we'll need to find a way of contacting the police about Max Telford without using my neighbour's phone again.'

'We could call from here…but then…'

'But then they'd be hot on our trail,' replied Aurelia.

'And my jailbird finger prints are all over the joint. And I was just thinking while you were on the phone how odd it feels escaping incarceration. Prison is torment and I don't know if I could stand another night inside. But it could be worse. If the cops turn up here who can say I wouldn't be gunned down like Benson and Chisel? Right now they've got me flagged as being in league with murderers and a terrorist gang, and as of this morning, I'm a kidnapper to boot. Let's head north. Jessie will have passed on the message to my folks by now, I'm sure.'

Aurelia shrugged. 'If we can get time to create a dossier, we could make a case, but if I go home to London right now the police could bring *me* in. We don't have the resources to chase Hawkins, but we can inform the cops somewhere on our way where we think Telford's heading.' Once again, she held Calum's gaze for just a little longer than might be expected.

Calum smiled and gave her a partial hug, and perhaps oddly, neither of them felt awkward. 'You know, Aurelia, despite the circumstance when we first met at the FCA headquarters, I liked you immediately. Call it gut instinct or whatever, but I thought you were straight, honest. Of course, there are other reasons to like…'

Aurelia bit her bottom lip, contemplating his words, knowing that something previously unspoken had now been said. She replied simply by smiling. And as they left the driveway Calum contemplated his return home to Scotland after almost a year's exile.

Ben and Shirley had been held in separate interview rooms, Shirley for almost three hours and Ben for over an hour once they'd finally caught up with him at his flat. Both had been quizzed about their relationship with Calum Mack, their movements over the past forty-eight hours, and telephone calls they had allegedly made and received. Despite being unable to confer, both realised in isolation that roadside cameras and phone records would probably be able to refute any lies that they told at this juncture, so both had been very guarded, failing to respond to a number of questions. Perhaps unsurprisingly, each sibling had inwardly cursed Martin's departure for Australia, their obvious source of counsel now being unavailable.

Robson and Maxwell had arrived back at the same station, the reality of the competing demands of this organic case sinking in. Due to the shootings in Kent, officers from different jurisdictions were now combining their efforts to speed up progress, with senior staff from the Met demanding reports by the hour. As with all detectives, they knew that schedules meant nothing when things blew up, and already an array of politicians had entered the fray ranting about both gun laws and police reactions as a consequence of events at Tonbridge. Mack's capture had become the number one priority. After checking on the limited progress made with Ben and Shirley, they grabbed some strong coffee and looked through the other updates in the incident room.

'Right, let's see what we've got. We're clear that Telford is the man in the old lady's picture?'

'Yes.'

'Have we got an ID yet on the man who accosted Telford in Hyde Park?' Maxwell asked.

Robson checked through the notes. 'Nothing here yet. The picture's not that clear but the digital guys are trying to enhance it further before they run it through the image matching software again. Obviously it's not Mack as he couldn't have got there by that time, and why would Telford have met him anyway? '

'Correct.'

Maxwell was due to report to the chief in a matter of minutes, so he called in some of the staff involved to the incident room.

'Any word on Max Telford yet?'

'It seems not, sir,' said Evans, one of the other detective sergeants. A squad car visited his home earlier but no one was present. Gone AWOL, it seems.'

'The brother and sister act next door is less than forthcoming,' another detective then offered. 'Should we place more pressure on them? Potential charges?'

'Won't do any harm, particularly with the girl. We've got her receiving the calls from the phone we recovered in Kent, and also calling her brother and Aurelia Harley. And in Ben's case we have the camera footage of him making an unplanned visit to Edinburgh whilst apparently off work ill. DS Robson and I believe that Harley is not telling us everything she knows, so another visit there will be required. Not sure if it would merit a warrant, though we're currently seeking advice on that one. This case has more loose ends than a brothel.'

There were a few muffled laughs before another officer asked about the Scottish angle.

'Different jurisdiction of course,' Maxwell said flatly. 'And no doubt there's no word as fast as 'tomorrow' up there but the detective I spoke to said they'd report back tonight. The fact that contact was made with one of Mack's close relatives near Inverness means that there's a chance he'll head back there. Criminals do it sooner or later—I don't mean returning to the scene of the crime, but rather, returning home.'

'That's assuming he's completely guilty, sir,' one of the other detective sergeants suggested, before drawing daggers from Maxwell.

'That's a career-limiting remark if ever I heard one.'

'Sorry, sir. I just mean…there appears to be further, eh, confusing evidence entering the case by the hour.'

'Not evidence. *Supposition*, more like. But yes, for the record, we are honour-bound to investigate all angles with an open mind despite the list of new charges Mack would now face when we nail his arse.'

A young female uniformed officer then knocked and entered the room. She approached Maxwell and spoke quietly in his ear. 'A call just came in, sir. A message was left by an unidentified male who insisted that we write down the message verbatim and pass it onto you. He said that someone had given him money to make the call.'

Maxwell read the note, raising an eyebrow. 'This is bizarre.'

'What does it say?' Robson asked.

Maxwell cleared his throat, before speaking quietly. 'Probably bullshit, but here we go. I quote. "DI Maxwell: you should be looking for Max Telford at Heathrow, bound for Geneva at 1200 tomorrow on Swiss. Where's he off to, and why? Also, in respect of Calum Mack's innocence, consider a man called Tom Hawkins, who served a life sentence for murder in Edinburgh and had a grudge/motive to frame Calum Mack."' Maxwell looked up, as if considering for the first occasion that there might be some miniscule crack in the Mack conviction.

'Is there more?' Robson asked eagerly.

Maxwell glared at Robson. 'Yes, there's more. "Hawkins grew up as a next door neighbour of guess who? Yes, Max Telford. Hawkins has just flown into London after a luxury holiday in the Caribbean. How could an ex-con afford that?" Then it says they'll be in touch in due course.' Maxwell bit his top lip, looking downwards this time.

Robson cleared his throat, suspecting a potential game changer. 'Do we share this now?'

Maxwell sighed. 'There's probably no option. Right, listen up folks.' He paraphrased the details for the wider group before beginning instructions.

'Okay Evans, you can get onto this one—check out if Max Telford is indeed booked to travel to Switzerland tomorrow, and while you're at it, some of you guys could run a check on city and airport hotels.' A collective groan emitted from the room. 'No complaints—this is potentially a lead, just like the rest. I know…there are hundreds of hotels. DS Robson and I will follow up on this message for the bullshit factor to see if we're being spun a yarn. And Sergeant Renton, get me the number of that caller, please.'

When the number was passed to Maxwell, Robson took Maxwell with him into another room and dialled right away, and after three or four rings a young male answered. Robson waited as Maxwell read the riot act to the man about wasting police time. However, there were clear gaps in the conversation as the caller provided some sort of explanation. Maxwell demanded his name and details and then asked where he had been when approached by this young, apparently attractive woman. 'Describe her to me.'

When he ended the call, Maxwell sighed again, this time deeply. He explained to Robson that the man—a trucker—had been given twenty quid to make the call. He'd thought it was a wind-up, so it was easy money. He'd also described someone strikingly similar to Aurelia Harley, and all this had happened on a north-bound service station forty miles up the M1, less than half an hour previously. And no, the man had not seen the vehicle the young woman he'd spoken to had been driving.

'This could be problematic,' Robson observed.

'The possibility that Mack's actually innocent? Well, he's up to his neck in it for the breakout, kidnapping, and conspiracy, but of the original crime…who knows what this all means.' Robson nodded in response before

Maxwell continued. 'It could look bad for us, but if we solve the continuing case, things might be different.'

'Damage limitation?'

'Mmm. Do you think Aurelia Harley's joined forces with Mack? And if he's really innocent why hasn't he given himself up? We'll need to see any security tapes from this services place, and let's get some uniforms to identify if she drives or has hired a car. 'And,' Maxwell checked the note he'd been given. 'This Tom Hawkins guy, that's new. Can you see if he exists, and if he has a record? Access the PNC again—see what you can dig up. When Telford was accosted in Hyde Park, could it have been by the same guy? Right now that doesn't make Mack one iota more innocent, but it would give us something to tell the brass, who I'm supposed to report to in approximately,' he checked his watch again, 'four minutes.' He rubbed his eyes, suddenly weighed down by the plethora of new facts and angles that had arisen in such a short space of time.

Robson scratched his nose. 'If Harley and Mack are potentially travelling north, your hunch could be accurate—he's heading back home?'

'It's an outside possibility. I think we should get this fully briefed round the team and get a few hours kip. We can tackle the Telford angle first thing tomorrow, and decide if instead we fly north or not. You'll need to let the wife know her weekend's buggered again.'

Chapter 23

Early in the morning Hawk paid cash for a white Vauxhall Vectra, acquiring the five-year-old car at a dealership on Longman Road in Inverness. The car was a cost he'd been forced to factor into the trip, though in terms of remaining incognito he was aware that the flight north—where he'd been forced to use his real identity—might entail a minor risk, but only if Telford squealed, which should not be in Telford's interest. After his flight had landed he'd stayed the night in a cheap hotel on the banks of the Ness before planning his attack the following morning. Without haggling at the car dealership he'd given fake details to the garage owner, and the man had been conveniently distracted by another customer who'd arrived to complain about having been sold a lemon the previous day. Hawk was aware he'd probably been sold a lemon too, but when he left the premises uninsured and still fairly rusty behind the wheel, his only concern was to avoid detection until he picked up a couple of replacement items—duct tape, two knives and another nail gun in a small DIY store, as he'd been forced to jettison the one he'd bought in London in order to transit. In London he'd already acquired a navy suit and overcoat.

When he called ahead and spoke to Calum Mack's father for the second time he could hear Mrs Mack's excitement in the background. He explained that there had been yet another breakthrough in terms of re-opening the case, and that he would be arriving to interview them in three quarters of an hour. And bingo, they *had* heard from their son! They would be at home and would tell no one else of his arrival.

Hawk checked his watch: 8:30 a.m. It would take a little over thirty minutes to cross the Kessock Bridge onto the Black Isle and head further north to the little village where Calum Mack had been raised. He used his phone to access some details about Cromarty, the local website claiming it was the best preserved historic town in the Highlands, resplendent with little whitewashed streets complementing old churches by the seaside. Tourist bullshit, Hawk thought. The Black Isle wasn't even an island, and how could you ever believe the locals' assessment of their own place? He identified where the Macks lived—a red sandstone villa situated on its own about a mile outside the village. How quaint. One advantage however, was that it should be easy to contain them without interference from neighbours.

Road works on the bridge added another few minutes to the journey meaning that Hawk arrived on time. He parked in a gravelled area within the rear garden—the Vauxhall car obscured from the road to the front— and as he approached the main door he was pleased that one obvious sign of human weakness had prevailed: that Calum Mack had found a means of making contact with his parents since his escape from prison. When he'd checked the Macks online he'd initially been uncertain of Mack's father's first name. It seemed as if he was nicknamed Fergie, but formally named Calum. How stupid was that?

A man looking strikingly like an older, greyer version of Calum Mack answered the door, unadulterated hope appearing in the man's immediate facial expression as he welcomed the duplicitous visitor. Hawk used the pseudonym he'd employed on the phone, and marched into the lounge, where he was introduced to Calum's mother, Annie Mack.

Annie Mack enthusiastically enquired if Hawk had been liaising with the local police, explaining that they'd called but hadn't mentioned any breakthrough as such about Calum's case. Hawk took this in his stride, outlining that this was a slightly different matter and that the local constabulary needn't know about this development. He adopted a positive demeanour and accepted coffee, and when the coffee arrived—with fresh scones, could you believe—he asked if they'd remained quiet about the visit to anyone else locally. The Macks eagerly affirmed their secrecy in anticipation of the promised revelatory news.

'Now, Mrs Mack, if you would sit beside me on the sofa here I'll show you something that will surprise you,' Hawk requested, prompting Annie Mack to locate next to him. As he adjusted the case with his left hand, Hawk lowered his right hand into his inside coat pocket. Annie looked at the case, and then, suddenly, in one sweeping motion, Hawk grabbed her neck towards him with his left hand and drew a gleaming nine-inch blade towards her throat.

Annie screamed, and Fergie Mack leapt to his feet.

'What the hell do you think—'

'Shut up! Just *shut up!*' Hawk shouted, seizing her hair. 'I'll slit her throat right this second!! Now *back off.*' Annie Mack began to sob, complemented by a steely glare from Fergie, who hovered uncertainly a few feet away. 'Now, *sit down.*'

Fergie sat down as requested, before suddenly speaking. 'Is it money you want?'

'What did I tell you? Do you know how sharp this knife is?' Hawk held Annie tightly, telling her to remove the duct tape from his bag. She obliged, despite shaking visibly.

'Now, peel back the edge and wrap it tightly round your mouth.'

'She'll choke!'

'She'll fucking well die if she doesn't, okay?'

'Fergie, it's okay.' Annie shook as she spoke. 'Please. I'll do as he says.'

'If you do as you are told, you will live, okay?' Hawk spoke curtly, bringing out the nail gun with his free hand. He pointed the nail gun towards Fergie Mack's head, but then, glancing to the side, he noticed shotgun cartridges on a table by the back window. 'You own a shotgun?'

Fergie Mack nodded, still stunned by the course of events, and when Hawk suddenly drew a small amount of blood by nicking Annie Mack's neck, Hawk knew he would obtain further cooperation. Within two minutes the locked cabinet in the utility room where the shotgun had been secured was successfully accessed. Both barrels were now loaded and the gun pointed directly at Fergie Mack.

'This is much better ordinance,' Hawk said, smiling. 'Now we can get down to the business of your son.'

Max Telford had experienced a frustrating night, nervousness and minor paranoia injecting irrational fears into his broken sleep. He'd given a false name when he'd booked into the hotel, but the flight itself had been reserved in his own name because he himself had never anticipated requiring a false passport. He'd fleetingly been tempted to head for Dover and the relative anonymity a ferry would provide in comparison to a flight, but then he'd been reassured that no one was looking for him. Yet. All he'd done was take a few hours off work without explanation. So what? He was the boss. Sure, he could have phoned in sick, but that was unnecessary. It was now Saturday morning, he was the director of the section and no one would really miss him until Monday morning. At least he'd avoided any further time with Tom Hawkins, because clearly the man had become unhinged and when that happened it would lead in only one direction.

He'd checked in online and had decided to leave the minimum duration necessary to drop his bag, clear security and arrive at the gate. As he entered the terminal he used his phone to check the location of the bag drop, then suddenly smiled, relieved that his irrational fears had been unfounded. The armed police guards he'd just passed had barely glanced at him as he entered the doors. And as far as anyone of any importance would be concerned, he was a respected figure serving the public, *fighting* crime. One of the good guys.

He dropped off the bag with no problems, and made his way immediately through security, which proceeded more quickly than normal. However, when he arrived at the gate, he knew instantly that something was wrong, noticing that two men with dark suits and distinctly not allied to Swiss Airlines were standing at the gate.

Telford knew them both.

These were the police officers from the Mack case.

Shit, shit, shit. He bit his upper lip to the point of almost drawing blood, and decided to turn around. He'd exit the building, claiming a health problem, an emergency. No one was actually obliged to fly on a plane they hadn't yet boarded, were they?

However, when he traced his steps backwards to security, it appeared that two more officers were standing there. Of course, now they knew where he was…cornered. How they knew, and why they knew, eluded him. Telford winced, deciding to convert defence into attack, so he turned and marched back to the gate.

'DI Maxwell? What a coincidence…but thank goodness you're here.' Telford momentarily cleared his throat as Maxwell met his eyes impassively with that expressionless stare which policemen learn to perfect. Telford then continued, briefly looking downwards before speaking. 'I'd actually been going to give you a call but decided to wait until Monday…I'm just taking a short break.'

Maxwell and Robson briefly glanced at one another before Maxwell spoke. 'Ah, we didn't realise that you'd booked a return ticket, Mr Telford.'

'I…wasn't sure of when…an old girlfriend of mine…was going home…so I hadn't done so yet…' Telford swallowed, noticeably. 'So, as I said, I was going to tell you something important. I think that the man we both put away—Calum Mack—came to my home. Today! I'm certain it was him, but luckily…I think I managed to get out in time. I think he may have been trying to exact revenge of some sort against the system…and therefore me.'

'Calum Mack came to visit you? So you decided to take a flight to Switzerland instead of calling us immediately? Well, it's lucky we caught you in time,' Robson intervened, raising his eyebrows. One or two other passengers in the vicinity were now taking in parts of the conversation, aware that something slightly out of the ordinary was going down. 'You see, Mr Telford, we need to speak to you at the station about a number of things.'

Telford's eyes darted from side to side. 'Couldn't this wait until Monday? I am the director of my section at the FCA, and I should be afforded some notification for any police interview,' he said, checking his watch. 'My flight's about to board, gentlemen, if you could let me past.'

Maxwell and Robson both stood stationary before Maxwell spoke. 'Mr Telford, do you know a man called Tom Hawkins?' Maxwell stared at Telford, who then closed his eyes, holding the bridge of his nose with his thumb and index finger. When he opened his eyes, Telford turned and noticed that three other officers had created a semi-circular formation to his rear.

Maxwell followed his eyes. 'Surely you're not thinking of making a scene or a run for it, Mr Telford?'

'I…this is not…what you may think. I've been under pressure, subject to threats, I can assure you. But right now…I think I need to speak…to my lawyer.'

Exhaustion had eventually triggered a break in the journey north. Calum and Aurelia made it over the border before stopping at the Days Inn near Abingdon, just off the M74. They called in on spec and paid cash for the room. Despite the signs of mutual attraction that had emerged at Bricket Wood, fatigue dictated an immediate crash-out, particularly for Calum who'd hardly slept over the previous four days.

When they awoke at around 8:00 am to the cry of a nearby car alarm, they quickly showered before Aurelia suggested she acquire some take-away breakfast at the nearby services cafe. When she returned, she told Calum she felt part of some modern day Bonnie and Clyde act, minus the guns.

'You've got me marked as a young Warren Beatty type then, Faye?'

She smiled, running her tongue over her upper teeth. 'Why, of course.'

'You'll need to work on that accent.'

'I'm just working on staying out of jail.'

Calum scratched his head, sighing heavily. 'Yes, reality beckons. I'm just wondering if we could warn them when we might arrive. For all we know the place could be under surveillance.'

'And their phone tapped. What about using your aunt again. You could speak in semi-code in case?'

'That's probably the only option.'

When they called Jessie, they spoke guardedly. In a round-about way, she outlined how she had visited Calum's parents the night before and that they were brimming with anticipation. She explained that they'd said they couldn't say much, but that the FCA might be interested in re-opening the case, and that she'd go round again and pass on the message that they expected to arrive around one o'clock, traffic permitting. When the call ended, Aurelia briefly queried this with Calum, unsure if the FCA could have acted so quickly. Jen Hoffman had said nothing about this when Aurelia had called the previous day. They momentarily discussed whether to surrender themselves to the police, but caution prevailed and instead they continued north.

For once DS Robson was grateful for his subordinate ranking, as DI Maxwell had borne the brunt of the tongue-lashing by Superintendent Lang, predicated on the emergence of evidence that could leave the Mack verdict seriously compromised and the Met's reputation tarnished. During his rant, Lang had chastised Maxwell for a number of previous actions and outcomes in the case, all for the first time. This had occurred just after they'd reported the results of their first interview with Telford, where the man had broken down and desperately attempted to gain a deal by exposing Tom Hawkins. That Max Telford himself had now admitted complicity in the emerging fiasco had particularly ignited Lang, not only because Maxwell and Robson had made a number of assumptions about Mack's case on the word of Telford, but because Lang had appeared all over the media with Telford the day the original verdict had been reached at Southwark Crown Court. The fact that Lang had signed off the case without question was seemingly beside the point, and Maxwell, silently seething, was now retrospectively being accused of incompetence.

What had also emerged was the absolute requirement to investigate Tom Hawkins. This was apparent not only as a consequence of Telford's confession, but because background checks substantiated Hawkins' movements in the Caribbean. And even with his potential use of a fake passport to impersonate Calum Mack, it had been confirmed that Hawkins had used his own identity to return to London, apparently confident in his ability to remain undetected.

An alert to apprehend Hawkins was posted just after 12:30 p.m. Then, Robson called Calum Mack's father. When there was no answer, Robson suggested that they fly north on the presumption that Mack's parents were probably as good a lead as any other. Maxwell sucked on a pen, suddenly uncertain whether the hunch about Calum travelling home to the Black Isle would prove their salvation, or alternatively, their damnation. Things might ignite if Superintendant Lang interpreted that the wrong course of action had been pursued. Fearful of Lang's wrath, Maxwell rejected the idea, suggesting that they should concentrate enquiries on London given this was where Hawkins was last spotted. Bizarrely, during the various discussions no one had suggested checking if anyone named Hawkins had travelled to Inverness by air the previous evening.

Jessie Mack's home was a ten-minute walk from her brother's house. She was savvy enough to know that the semi-coded phone message about Calum's imminent arrival back in Cromarty could have been picked up by the authorities if they were also now monitoring her calls. She had no idea what resources might have been invested in the case in which her nephew had become embroiled, so she decided the best course of action was simply to do as asked. Only God knew what her brother and sister-in-law had been through in the past few months so at least she was the bearer of some better news.

The first thing that she noticed was the car parked out the back of the house. Like many people in rural areas, Fergie and Annie used the back door as a more informal point of entry, but the car meant that a visitor was present and she did not recognise the vehicle. She rang the front door bell just in case the visitor was the formal type.

There was no response.

Jessie then knocked on the back door, and when silence ensued, she tried the door, which was locked. Unperturbed, she popped into the back shed where a spare key was hidden in an old paint can. However, when she tried inserting the key in the back door it became apparent that a key was already lodged on the inside of the door. This puzzled Jessie because it suggested that they were in residence, yet the upstairs curtains were open and there were no lights switched on that she could see.

Tom Hawkins nudged the shotgun against Fergie Mack's back as he observed through a gap in the side of the curtains the old lady's third attempt to gain entry. Why didn't she just piss off?

Then, the old lady made off round the front again, and for about a minute Hawk assumed she'd left.

Clunk. 'Hi! It's only me.' The voice echoed through the house. 'I forgot I had a spare front door key in my hand bag. Fergie, Annie, are you home?'

In the lounge, Hawk held his index finger to his lips, silently instructing Fergie Mack to remain quiet. Annie Mack also remained soundless because she was tied and gagged, seated in a spare room to the left of the hallway, out of sight.

'Are you asleep, Fergie? I've good news. You're getting a visit from a young man you'd love to see—'

'Is that right?!' Hawk threw the lounge door open, revealing the shotgun, now being thrust against Fergie's head.

Jessie screamed and dropped her handbag, hands suddenly frozen by her sides. Hawk spoke menacingly. 'One move and he's dead.'

He then pushed Jessie towards the lounge. 'Who the fuck are you?'

Mouth open, moisture dribbled from her lips. 'I'm…I'm…'

'She's my sister,' Fergie interrupted. 'Please leave her alone. This has got nothing to do with her.'

'Did I ask you?'

'What young man's coming to visit? Calum?' Hawk's eyes seared into Jessie's.

'No, no. Not him…he's—'

'You're lying, old dear. And if by the time I count to three you've not told me when he's coming, I'll kill your brother. One, two…'

She glanced at the porcelain clock above the mantelpiece, her panic betraying any ability she possessed to conceal the truth. Hawk then followed her eyes towards the clock before whispering. 'What, imminently?' He then shoved Fergie onto the floor, grabbing his hair. 'Do you know how painful this would be? You'd have to pick out pieces of shot from his brain.'

'He'll be here by one o'clock,' she said flatly.

'One o'clock? Excellent! Now come here. I've something to show you.' And then, as Jessie moved towards him he lashed out with his left elbow, causing her to fall back onto the sofa. She whimpered and coughed before lying motionless.

'For God's sake, man!'

'Shut you face, *Fergie*.' Hawk checked Jessie's pulse.

'She's only stunned,' Hawk said, pointing the gun at Fergie once more. 'But drag her to the spare room, *now*. And put a smile on your face— Calum boy is coming home.'

Rain passed briefly before a sliver of sunshine speared through the platinum cloud high above the Kessock Bridge, prompting Calum to smile. Nearly home. This was the kind of capricious weather he recalled from his formative years. Aurelia had eventually drifted asleep on the A9, and although Calum harboured cumulative fatigue, adrenalin had powered him north. He'd contemplated all kinds of outcomes, aware that he was still a wanted man who had committed crimes, if only as a consequence of incarceration for crimes he had not committed. How paradoxical life could be. When they halted at temporary traffic lights at the northern end of the bridge, Aurelia stirred, asking where they were.

'God's country,' Calum replied, prompting Aurelia to enquire if he were the religious type. He smiled and shook his head, realising that despite their intense entanglement they actually knew virtually nothing about each other.

Twenty-five minutes later they pulled up in the back garden of Calum's parents' home, outside of Cromarty. He immediately noticed the white

Vectra parked to the rear, and mentioned to Aurelia that he didn't know to whom it belonged. Both of them stretched as they stood up outside the car. There was silence.

Suddenly Calum felt a little perturbed. No welcome party.

'Do you think your aunt's been round?'

'I'd be aghast if she hadn't bothered. And I'm curious about the Vectra.'

'I doubt that it's police.'

'No. If the cops were here they'd surely be onto us right now. Could be a local I don't know. Look, this might sound a bit daft, but do you mind going in first just in case it's a nosy neighbour that shouldn't know I'm here? I can keep a lookout. Use the back door, and if they're on their own give me a shout. I can't wait to get a cup of tea and some of my mum's home-made rock buns.'

As Aurelia approached the back door something odd happened. A woman screamed inside. Not a theatrical scream, but one communicating fear or pain. Initially uncertain, Aurelia turned and held her hands out in Calum's direction, but before rotating back towards the door, further raised voices emanated from inside.

The words 'You fucking bitch!' cut through the air.

'Calum!' Aurelia shouted, prompting him to sprint over towards the door. The door was locked. Desperately looking for something with which he could smash the glass, Calum glanced through the back window, where he could see shadows reflecting swift movements, accompanied by muffled voices and another scream.

'Mum? Dad?! It's Calum! What's happening?' The only heavy item he could find was a curling stone that had sat outside the back porch for many years. He clattered it against the glass window of the porch, shattering fragments all over the porch and the back step. 'Aurelia, *stay here.*'

He leapt through the space the window had occupied, bursting into the kitchen. 'What the hell…'

His father lay on the floor, bleeding, his hands thrust against his stomach. Another man about his own age stood at the rear of the kitchen with one foot on top of his Aunt Jessie's head, pointing a shotgun directly at Calum. He was around ten feet away.

Calum squinted, taking the man in.

The hooked nose.

The eyes.

Yes, the green eyes. Bloody hell, he knew those eyes.

It was *him*.

It was Hawk.

Calum stood back, breathless and dumbstruck.

'Well, well, Calum Mack. You were supposed to be tucked up in prison, *just like you did to me*. But you escaped.'

'Tom? This is…ridiculous.'

'Stealing years of someone's life is *ridiculous*. You have no idea what I went through.'

'I spent—'

'Enough! A few weeks in a social worker's haven? You're comparing that to the sentence I got? *And served*. More than fifteen years! It was no fucking scout camp, and *your* testimony put me away.' Hawkins held the gun steady, his gaze not deviating. 'How about an apology?'

Calum stood transfixed. 'I'm sorry.'

'Not enough. I just wanted you to say it, though. One thing that prison taught me was this, Mack. I feel sympathy for no one. Not a single soul consoled me when I was inside and I learned that absolutely everyone is selfish. It's not survival of the fittest in this world, it's survival of the most selfish. You're a very selfish bastard. You couldn't wait to get inside information when I called you. I could hear it in your sorry voice. Yes sir, no sir, three bags full sir. I had you eating out of my hand! Yes, I'll take your phones, sir, and your free holiday!' Hawkins laughed. 'Enjoy the call girl, did you? Bet you didn't figure what was coming next, eh? What a prick you are. Never changed a bit, you always thought you were something, didn't you? And I knew you'd take the bait for the share tips and the hooker because I remembered from years back that you had no imagination. Unfortunately, people in that student union remembered me because I was different, I stood out. But I have learned not to stand out any more, to *blend in*.' Hawkins spat on the floor, prompting Jessie to whimper under his shoe.

'Shut it, old dear!'

'Please leave them alone,' Calum implored. 'They have no part in this.'

'I heard a similar cliché from your old pops here less than an hour ago. Has this whole family no originality at all? You're all pathetic.'

Calum held out his arms. 'Have my family and I to pay for all your demons? What about Tomlinson and the others?'

'Don't worry about them. Some nice pictures are on the way to their wives.'

Calum barely computed this information before desperately trying to stall for time. He stepped forward, pleading. 'Look, I'm sorry. I realise that you're bitter. But what happened in Edinburgh was years ago. Surely hurting us further doesn't benefit you now? I'm ruined and on the run. You've made a stash out of all this, so why come after me again? Why jeopardise yourself further with charges for…whatever. I'm stuffed as it is, as I have escaped and will have new charges. The police will catch me, and probably Telford.'

Hawkins frowned, his jaw dropping. 'How do you know about Telford?'

'I just…figured things out.' Calum realised his error immediately and Hawkins shook his head, watching Calum's response.

Hawkins then said, 'I doubt that very much. Well, this little piece of news simply confirms that I made the correct decision coming here today. You, like Telford, are a complete liability.'

'Look, if you leave now you're in the clear. You have the money from your scam.'

'This was never only about the money. Don't you know that by now? Sure, that was a bonus, but this was about *retribution*. Plain and simple.'

Calum took a further step forward. 'So what are you going to do, kill us all?'

'Stand there, loser. If you move I might well blow your head off, and once that's done torch the rest of these clowns and destroy any record of my appearance here. This house is far enough away from neighbours. I just wanted to let you know first. *To see the look you have on your sorry face right now.* Yes, the look on your gullible face. That was the only thing that I missed when we talked on the phone, when you were kissing my ass for inside information.' Hawkins chuckled before levelling the shotgun at Calum's face from about six feet away, steadying his aim.

'Put the shotgun down, Hawkins.' The Irish accent severed the air, causing Hawkins to thrust his head round. A young woman with dark hair and bare feet was pointing the nail gun against the back of his head. She'd appeared from the hallway to the rear.

'Where the fuck did you come from?' Then, in a sudden sweeping motion Hawkins propelled the shotgun around in a horizontal arc, battering Aurelia to the floor and causing the gun to discharge into the ceiling. Plaster collapsed on the floor, and Aurelia shrieked, as did Jessie, who had stirred and rolled over, away from under Hawkins' foot.

Calum dived forwards towards Hawkins' legs, grabbing him in a rugby tackle, propelling both of them towards the oven.

But Calum slipped on the tiles, clattering his head off the oven door, momentarily stunned. Hawkins snatched the advantage and hauled the shotgun towards him by the barrel, swivelling it round towards Calum's head.

'I've one shot left, asshole!'

But the one thing he could not see from the angle at which he lay was the wrinkled hand that extended towards his along the wet tiles. Jessie Mack silently lifted something quite heavy for a woman of her age and pressed it firmly against the back of Hawkins' head.

A nail gun.

No warnings, just a pneumatic *thunk*, followed by an elongated scream.

Then, as the scream subsided, a deep crimson spread across the floor tiles.

And as distress and awe of what had just occurred permeated the household, the muffled sound of sobbing merged with the wail of an emergency vehicle becoming audible in the distance. Was that an ambulance siren they could now hear? Or was it a police car?

In an emergency you can never tell the difference.

Epilogue

Several days elapsed before the media cavalcade subsided. Initially, many reporters couldn't decide whether to camp out at Raigmore Hospital in Inverness or at the Mack residence in Cromarty. Tom Hawkins had survived the entry of a four-inch nail to the base of his skull, but internal bleeding had caused substantial brain damage. That's if anyone could call the best case prognosis of a persistent vegetative state 'survival' in any meaningful sense of the word. Aurelia suffered a dislocated shoulder and a broken arm, coupled with heavy bruising to her neck and head. Fergie Mack and his sister Jessie were also housed in adjacent wards in Raigmore Hospital, one block away from Tom Hawkins. Fergie's two cracked ribs and concussion were mirrored by Jessie's head and arm injuries. They did not complain—they were of old Highland stock and were both seen cracking jokes with other people on the ward. Only Calum and his mother had avoided injury, though the trauma of having been tied and gagged had knocked Annie Mack's confidence. Everyone had been interviewed by Highland police officers and also by Maxwell and Robson, and other senior staff from the Met who had flown from England later on Saturday in an attempt to unpick the knotted ball of string into which this case had morphed.

Calum had apologised profusely for his role in bringing such hardship to Aurelia and his own family, though none of them seemed to blame him. He'd also discussed the small matter of Aurelia having helped save his life and those of his family. The Mack clan were acutely aware of the debt they now owed, yet Aurelia again appeared nonchalant, perhaps simply relieved that the ordeal was over. No one had said they wished Hawkins had died, the penury the man now faced being sufficient justice in the eyes of those still shocked by his reappearance and role in the affair.

Financial journalists were enjoying a field day, raking over the debris at the FCA. Corporate governance and moral leadership were the talk of the day, and the FT had labelled the organisation the 'Financial Misconduct Authority'. Max Telford's initial attempts on arrest to bargain at the expense of Tom Hawkins were destroyed almost immediately due to events in the Black Isle. With Hawkins out of the picture, a fall guy was essential. The CEO of the FCA had promised a 'root and branch' review of procedures and accountability, with the temporary suspension of the department which Telford had overseen heralding the first casualty of forensic scrutiny.

Adam Smart, upon fear of discovery, admitted supplying insider information about an entirely different case, and when Douglas Lyndon flew to Inverness to see Calum and Aurelia they shared a wry joke at the irony of Adam's innocence regarding Calum's case, yet guilt over something unrelated. Then, the nursing staff attempted to insist upon "two to a bed" because Ben and Shirley turned up at the same visiting session as Lyndon. When Douglas Lyndon mentioned that he'd heard on the grapevine that Nigel Tomlinson's wife had walked out on him, Calum told his assembled visitors of the photos Hawkins had sent out by mail. Lyndon smiled inwardly, knowing that his integrity and marriage were secure.

Calum then sat open-mouthed as Ben admitted having bribed a sub-editor to see his copy regarding the last tip that Hawkins had given him.

'Wow, you kept that quiet,' Calum said, shaking his head. 'Is that what you meant in the car when you said you owed me one?'

Ben nodded. 'Sorry, mate. I thought I'd been rumbled, but I escaped. I made about five thou, but I'm going to give it to Shirley to help set up her own salon. Hopefully that will make amends. But, hey—there's also some other good news. Powell's been fired at the *Sentinel*. Nothing to do with your case. He made a sexist remark to a young woman in the elevator and it turns out that it's the Chairman's daughter. What goes around, eh?'

Once it had become apparent the extent of the serious strategic and procedural errors that had occurred in the case against Calum Mack, and that the conviction was clearly unsafe, the combined force of the CPS and the Metropolitan Police contrived to negotiate the trading of concessions. The CPS wanted to eliminate "irregularities" that were not in the public interest, and the police and the FCA wanted to limit the damaging publicity that had engulfed the media and questioned their investigative competence. Calum's emotions were tempered by an odd, bitter-sweet feeling. He experienced latent frustration at his wrongful conviction, yet he had become aware that virtually no one believed that he'd not been fully complicit in the escape from prison. Officers had been injured in the breakout, and damage had been done to public property. Terrorists had apparently been involved, though no direct evidence had actually emerged about the identities of the men who had assisted in the breakout, principally as Benson was dead. Calum could of course shed no light. Dr Strang, the prison medic who'd been blackmailed by Benson, had been charged with drug offences and had previously run into all kinds of financial problems, which at least partly explained his behaviour in aiding the escape. The prison officers who had transported the three convicts were non-committal about Calum's story, now aware that he had been set up, yet still bitter about what had happened to them.

The old man that they'd tied up near Tonbridge had however expressed support for Calum, and once the dust had settled Calum made the effort to visit him in order to apologise for the actions in which he had become complicit. Charges by the Met against Ben, Aurelia and Shirley were also dropped as part of a wider arrangement and Calum had been forced to sign an agreement that he would drop counter charges in return for immunity from further prosecution.

The procurator fiscal in Inverness had acquiesced on any residual charges in relation to the Cromarty incident, given that the incapacitated Hawkins was unable to contradict five other witnesses who had substantial injuries inflicted by someone with motive and who had entered the house uninvited. Ben's brother Martin had flown from Sydney to represent him in the negotiation and Calum, though grateful, was aware that the publicity was probably more beneficial to Martin's career than his own.

Numerous offers from the Scottish, London-based, and some international media channels had been made to him for his full story, but due to the agreement he'd reached with the CPS and FCA, he was not permitted to discuss things in any detail. Ironically, Bloomberg was one of the media outlets that Calum had declined.

Just as Calum had accepted that he'd remain a net loser from his role in the whole escapade, Aurelia's future appeared a little brighter. She'd managed to treat both Ken and Vinnie to dinner as a 'thank you' for their help during the case. In terms of her career, the fact that she'd been suspended by Max Telford for privately investigating something in which Telford himself had been complicit actually seemed to impress the FCA management. Email trails and other case records also confirmed that Aurelia had asked a number of pertinent questions about Calum Mack's guilt during the investigation but had been rebuffed. As soon as she was sufficiently well, she was released from Raigmore to fly back to London in order to attend an official debriefing at the FCA. At the end of the meeting, the Chief Executive asked to see her privately.

When the door was closed, he suggested bluntly that Aurelia would be the ideal replacement for Max Telford.

'I don't think I would be, actually.' As she relayed the words, she surprised herself.

He frowned in response. 'You'd be making a mistake to turn down an offer like that. You've demonstrated tenacity and a forensic ability to investigate, and you'd have support internally. You could be a new, better Telford.'

'I think that's just the problem. He was so consumed by his work, that I think it rotted him from the inside. Thanks, but I think I need a break from the City.'

He told her to let him know if she experienced a change of heart. Then, as she exited the building for what would be the last occasion, tears suddenly surfaced. He'd used the word *heart*. The 'City', as it was known, had *no* heart; it was a monstrosity of greed and fear, nothing less. Heart was about human emotion, about love. Something she hadn't experienced for some time.

Or had she?

On the flight north, Aurelia suddenly found herself laughing out loud, prompting the elderly man sitting beside her to smile in response. He'd probably assumed that she'd responded to something she'd read or heard on her headphones, yet this was incorrect. What had elicited the mirth had been the fact that this trip to Cromarty was uninvited, and that she'd *assumed* her welcome. On a whim, she'd booked the first available flight to Inverness. She'd been unable to get through when she'd called. And she knew only four people there, three of whom were old fogies, though the other one was a little younger and kind of special.

What if he told her to bugger off? She may have helped save his life, as he'd insisted, though he might have held some latent frustration that she'd also helped convict him in the first instance. And that girl Shirley seemed to have the hots for him too.

Yet, underneath, she knew. She also knew that *he* knew, and each knew the other knew. One of those ones. Oddly, nothing had been said explicitly, perhaps due to the injuries sustained and the pressure of the media frenzy, but there was an imperceptible feeling of attachment. Something special. What had she felt when she first met him at the FCA? A Celtic bond? Surprise that he'd been genuine, even when under investigation. She felt her gut instinct had been accurate, as her father would surely have advised. And as she viewed the emerald coastline bordering the Moray Firth on the approach to the landing, she felt in a strange manner as if she were coming home. Sure, it rained a bit here, but she had some ancestry in the Scottish Highlands. Roots. And the whisky, even if they couldn't spell it properly, was fabulous.

She called Calum on landing, and this time he picked up. 'Aurelia! You're here?' There was anticipation in his voice. He explained that he'd been out dolphin watching earlier on and had switched off his phone. 'I went because when I was imprisoned it was something I never thought I'd do again. Now my attitude's changed. Carpe diem, and all that. Give me half an hour and I'll pick you up.'

When their eyes met just outside the terminal building both rushed forwards, and this time neither one held back. He kissed her fully on the lips, before standing back to take in the azure eyes before him. 'Carpe diem,' she reiterated, softly, knowing she'd made the right decision to come. He bundled her bag in the back of his father's jeep and they made their way to the Black Isle.

An impromptu welcome party greeted them on arrival, with a few neighbours and long lost relatives turning up to engage in something of a ceilidh. Aurelia pondered how they could all have arrived so quickly given the short notice, but she guessed that Cromarty might just operate like that. She'd seen *Local Hero* as a child, and recalled the type of village camaraderie that had been portrayed. One cousin of Calum's had even brought along an accordion.

Once the initial buzz had settled, Aurelia and Calum enjoyed a quiet moment in the back living room. They kissed again, suddenly less shy. As he once more drank up Aurelia's eyes, something distracted him, making him briefly disengage. The television had been left on with the sound down in the room, and he could see the reflection of the screen in her eyes.

Bloomberg.

'I think I'll just turn that off. My dad must have been watching it after I left for the airport.' He lifted the remote but accidentally turned off the mute. Then, as the sound acquired their attention, both of them stared at the screen as the American presenter spoke.

...Breaking news in from Canada. The oil company, Dartmouth Petroleum, has just released a report that it has discovered...and I quote...a massive oil field in Northern Alberta. The firm said that geological reports confirm that the field could be the largest yet discovered in Canada. For the

company, which has recently been successful in defending accusations of corruption, this marks a dramatic u-turn in its fortunes, and as we speak, the share price has rocketed to more than $28 dollars, some twenty times the value of the stock before the corruption allegations were defended. And the stock looks to race higher as the market fully absorbs the news...

Calum and Aurelia traded looks, Calum open-mouthed.

'Isn't that one you tipped, just before this all kicked off?' Aurelia asked.

Calum nodded. 'I can't believe that. If this had happened then I'd probably never have been tempted to take those stupid tips. What's worse is that my mother and father lost all their savings on this punt. They believed in my column so much they invested themselves, but they sold at a low when I was in prison. And before you ask,' Calum smiled sadly, 'yes, they bought on the Monday after my story was published, but it doesn't matter a damn now. This is difficult to take.' Calum held the door open, shouting through the house. 'Dad! Come in here. Wait 'til you see this!'

Fergie ambled into the room, still limping from the ordeal with Hawkins. 'What is it son? Young Maggie from down the road has just asked me to dance! At my age? This better be good.'

'Sorry, Dad,' Calum touched his father's arm. 'Afraid it's bad news.' He pointed at the TV.

'Not that bloody Bloomberg station again. Your mother insists on watching it just in case something miraculous happens. Sorry, Calum, but you weren't much of a tipster in my opinion. Your mother believed in you, though. That's why I can't have a new 4X4, by the way—because all of our money is stuck in that blasted Canadian oil company you tipped.'

Calum gasped. 'Dartmouth? I thought you sold?'

'I was desperate to sell and cut our losses, but your mother actually bought *more* shares when the price went down. She used a stash she had for our funerals. How mad is that! But you know your mother, she insisted we hang on, but we daren't have told you—'

'Stop, Dad! You've still got the shares?'

'Yes, waste of time, but you know your mother—'

'Sorry to interrupt, how much did you actually invest?'

'What?' Fergie scratched his head, eyes darting between Aurelia and Calum. 'What's happened?'

'How much, Dad?'

'I think we put in the lot—about twenty thousand originally, and then another seven, I think. Why? Has something happened?'

'Yahoo!' Calum grabbed his father and Aurelia in one giant hug. 'Jesus, Dad, if you bought when I think you did, you've just made about...*four hundred grand.*'

Fergie Mack recoiled back, slumping on a chair. 'Four hundred thousand? Is this for real?'

'Well, you would have to pay capital gains tax,' Aurelia said, bemused. 'It might only be about three hundred thousand.'

And as father and son shouted 'three hundred thousand!' simultaneously, a newsfeed at the bottom of the Bloomberg screen stated that Dartmouth was now trading in excess of $30 per share. Calum and Aurelia cheered again, ending up on the floor, kissing. The commotion prompted Annie and Jessie to come through.

'What is it, Fergie?' Annie stood with her hands on her hips, confused.

'Annie, I'm going to get that 4X4 after all! And open that 25 year-old bottle of Chivas Regal for all the folks next door. But that's not all...judging by these two love birds on the floor we may even have to pay for...a reception down the line.' Fergie said this out of the blue, grinning inanely. Annie appeared very confused, and Aurelia blushed as Calum helped her stand up.

An unspoken, subtle look then passed between them, and perhaps oddly, neither bothered to contradict the controversial presumption.

Acknowledgements

I am indebted to all of my family members for their patience, and Jean Campbell for a considered edit. Any errors within are mine alone. Many thanks also to you, the reader.

Printed in Great Britain
by Amazon